FATE BE DAMNED

John R. Dann

Revised and Ilustrated by Janet M. Dann

DannWorks

Friday Harbor, WA

Fate Be Damned

Revised and
Illustrated by Janet M. Dann

Fate Be Damned

Published by DannWorks, Friday Harbor,
WA Publishing services by W. Bruce Conway

ORIGINAL PRINTING HISTORY (*The Good Neighbors*)
First Printing 1995
Second Printing 2008
Third Printing 2012
Fourth Printing 2017

Edited in 2012 by Janet Dann
Fully revised and illustrated by Janet M. Dann
Cover embroidery by Janet M. Dann
from *Designs of Saxon Transylvania*

ISBN: 978-1-7334951-0-3

Printed in the United States of America
by Kindle Direct Publishing

Dedicated to my father and mother, who, through their courage, faith, and sense of humor, brought our family through the time of the Dust Bowl and The Great Depression. Also to my wife Barbara and our children, John, Janet, and Catherine, for their unfailing love and encouragement.

—J. R. Dann

Characters

JOSIF and IZABELLA DACIA – Romanians who immigrated to America in 1920 via Ellis Island and settled on a rented farm in Oklahoma

ALEXANDER, MARIE, ROSE, CAROLINE and MICHAEL-JOSEPH – Children of the DACIAS
UNCLE JON and AUNT MAGDA – JON is JOSIF'S uncle on his father's side

ALAN JOHNSON – Centerford banker

ELLEN OLSON – ALAN'S assistant at the bank

VERNE LAMB – Neighbor of the DACIAS

BELLE and JULIUS LAMB – VERNE'S wife and son, respectively

FRANK ARIOSTO – BELLE LAMB'S brother and sheriff in Centerford

VINCE LAMB – VERNE'S brother; a Chicago mob associate
CLARENCE LAMB, aka C.D. – also an associate of the Italian mob and uncle of VERNE and VINCE

ANGELO MORETTI and LOU FALLUCCA – South-Side mobsters who accompanied C.D. to the LAMB farm. ANGELO is brother to mob boss, PRIMO MORETTI, currently in Leavenworth Penitentiary

FRITZ and AUGUST WAGNER – Brothers and neighbors of the DACIAS

GERHARD and GERTRUDE WAGNER – Grandparents of FRITZ and AUGUST

MRS. HORSEFALL – School teacher at the Mt. Faith School

MR. and MRS. BOWMAN – Neighbors who provide housing for MRS. HORSEFALL

Table of Contents

Prologue

When ye be come to the land which the Lord will give you.
—*Exodus 12:25*

* * *

The hardest situation for the immigrant comes when the future seems in doubt and when America seems about to default on its promise.

—Henry Grunwald, *Time*, July 8, 1985.
with permission.

* * *

On June 18, 1928, three simultaneous events occurred which ultimately caused Josif Dacia to steal across his fields under cover of night toward his neighbor's farm, with his grandfather's curved Turkish knife in his fist, and vengeance in his heart.

* * *

The first was on Wells Street in the Irish-controlled North Side of Chicago. Two couriers were on their way to deliver money they had collected from gambling and bootlegging operations to their boss, Bugs Moran.

They were only three blocks from their destination when a befuddled elderly gentleman approached them with a humble look on his face and his hat in his hands.

Before suspicion took hold, C.D. Lamb shot each of them in the chest with his silencer-equipped .38, which was hidden behind his hat.

Vince Lamb, C.D.'s nephew, jumped out of a nearby parked car. He kicked each of the men and yelled at them with contempt. "Why don't you go back where you came from, you fuckin' clown-faced Micks!"

Then he shot each of them in the head to make sure they were dead, and took their guns and all of the money they were carrying.

Vince and C.D. were working for the Italian Outfit of the Chicago South Side and this hit and theft would demand retribution. Clarence decided it was time to develop a profitable plan and disappear. His other nephew, Verne, had a farm in South Dakota which would suit his needs perfectly.

* * *

The second event occurred near Centerford, South Dakota. Verne Lamb returned from the District Court of Appeals in Sioux Falls to his farm where he ran a small bootlegging operation. Verne went to the bedroom where his wife, Belle, lay ill. "They decided against us," he raged. "That damn bank gets to keep your folks' farm just because those bastards snapped it up for back taxes. I'll kill anybody tries to rent that farm!"

* * *

The third happened in the seared and suffering state of Oklahoma where the soil had turned to fine red dust and held no water, no life. Hector Thompson went into a real estate office in Tyson. "I wanna put both farms up fer sale," he said sadly. "I cain't hold on no longer."

One of Mr. Thompson's farms was sharecropped by Josif Dacia, and Josif would take his family to South Dakota looking for a farm to rent.

Chapter One
Important Decisions

Josif, Uncle Jon and the boys watched from the barn as the car came through the shimmering heat toward the farm. Even when Josif recognized Mr. Thompson's old Essex, his premonition of bad things to come remained.

The Essex turned into the Dacia's barnyard with a cloud of thick dust swirling behind it. The chickens ran listlessly for cover into the dead lilac bushes south of the house, where they settled down in the powdery red earth, panting in the heat and peering out with their yellow eyes at Mr. Thompson as he stopped the car and worked himself out. Mr. Thompson wore a dirty white shirt, a pair of wrinkled brown canvas trousers, and a sweat-stained straw hat. He mopped at his round red face with a bandana handkerchief as he looked around the barnyard.

Josif and Uncle Jon came out of the barn with Alexander and Michael-Joseph tagging behind. Mr. Thompson walked toward them; he shook hands with Josif and Uncle Jon, his hand moist and sticky from the steering wheel. He ran the handkerchief across the beads of sweat forming on his forehead. "It's a hunderd an' ten in the shade in Tyson. Feels like a hunderd an' fifty out here!"

Josif nodded. "Is hot. Thermometer on porch say hundred fifteen."

Mr. Thompson led the way back into the barn. It seemed cooler there, out of the sun, but still the heat came through the walls and roof as if they were in an oven.

Mr. Thompson took off his straw hat and dried his bald head with the handkerchief. "I'm afraid I got bad news fer you folks." He mopped his face again. "I cain't say it any different. I'm sellin' out." He fanned himself with the straw hat. "There ain't no other way."

They stared at him. "You sell farms?" Josif asked. "You sell this farm?"

Mr. Thompson wiped under his chin with the bandana. The creases in the fat were wet and red. "This farm, the home farm. I sure tried, but I cain't hold on no longer. Me an' Emmie an' Darlene are headin' fer California. Get a new start out there. Maybe have us a little orange grove."

Josif looked through the barn door at the weather-beaten house. Far back in the kitchen so that Mr. Thompson couldn't see them, Izabella, Aunt Magda, and the girls would be looking out the window, watching and wondering why Mr. Thompson had come out. He felt Alexander and Michael-Joseph looking at him, and he saw that Uncle Jon was chewing at his mustache. "We have to go?"

Mr. Thompson put his straw hat back on. "There ain't no other way. I'm sorry. We ain't had a decent cotton crop or price fer three years. It ain't you folks' fault. It's just the way it is. I cain't hang on no more."

Josif looked down the aisle of the barn where Peter and Paul stood in their stall with their harnesses still on, waiting to go out into the field again. "How soon we have to go?" he asked.

"They're bringin' the 'dozers out next week. All these buildin's is comin' down. Same with the home farm. They're gonna make it one big farm. Run it scientific-like."

"Maybe they let us work for them," Josif said hopefully. "Then we stay here."

Mr. Thompson shook his head. "I asked 'em that. They said they was sorry, but they don't need no more help. We all hafta go." He kicked at the dry chaff and manure on the barn floor. "Why don't you folks git yourselves some old car and head west, too? Lotsa jobs out there – pickin' oranges, strawberries."

"Can buy land in California?" Josif asked.

"Well, I hope so! That's why me an' Emmie an' Darlene are goin' out. Take the money we git from the farms, buy us a little orange grove. Git one near the water where them ocean breezes come in nice an' cool. Just set there drinkin' orange juice an' lookin' at the palm trees." Mr. Thompson's eyes went soft for a moment.

Josif felt the boys' excitement. He put his hand in the pocket of his overalls and touched his wallet where he knew only seventeen dollars and thirty-five cents lay. "How much farm cost in California?"

Mr. Thompson looked up at the roof of the barn where shafts of sunlight blazed down through holes in the shingles. "Prob'ly thirty-four dollars an acre. Depends on the land. I s'pose you could git somethin' out in the desert with them Mexicans cheaper, but somethin' nice, near the ocean, is gonna be higher."

Uncle Jon spoke in Romanian to Josif. "How much did he say? Forty dollars an acre?"

Josif nodded. "That's what he said, forty dollars." He spoke in English to Mr. Thompson."We thank you coming tell us. We not blame you. You been honest to us."

"Well, I was hopin' you'd see it that way. Like I said, I'm real sorry." Mr. Thompson fanned himself with his hat, then put it back on. "I ain't tryin' to tell y'all how ta run yer affairs, but if I was you, I'd sure head fer California." He stuck a thumb out toward the dry fields. "Things has just gone from bad to worse around here, and there ain't no use in stayin'."

"How far to California?" Josif asked.

Mr. Thompson looked off to the west, squinting his eyes against the glare of the afternoon sun. "Oh, 'bout fifteen hunderd miles prob'ly, maybe a little more, say fifteen fifty to be safe. There's good highway all the way, Route 66.

Once you git on that, it's clear sailin'. Takes you right down into them orange groves by the ocean." He mopped at his face again. "Well, I hafta be gettin' back ta the farm. Emmie and Darlene are startin' packin'. We plan to leave day after tomorrow." He looked at Josif, "Could you and me have just a quick little talk afore I go? There's somethin' I wanna mention to ya."

Josif motioned to the boys. "Alexander, you and Michael-Joseph help Uncle Jon take Peter and Paul out to tank for drink. You better say goodbye to Mr. Thompson now."

Mr. Thompson shook hands with Uncle Jon and the boys. "You folks been real good workers an' tenants. I don't have no complaints about you folks. No sir, y'all been good tenants."

Mr. Thompson and Josif stepped out of the barn into the heat of the sun and walked slowly to the Essex. Mr. Thompson opened the door and felt the seat. "You could fry an egg on this." He spread his bandana on the seat and squirmed his way under the steering wheel. "What I wanted to talk to you 'bout, Mr. Dacia, was somethin' that prob'ly ain't none a my business, but I thought I better just mention it. I hope you ain't gonna take it the wrong way an' get mad."

"You tell me. I not get mad."

Mr. Thompson fanned at the air in the car with his hat. "Well, it's about how you and that fam'ly a yours are gonna git out ta California if you decide to head out that way."

Josif looked out toward the barn. "I think just hitch horses to wagon and go to west. Must get there someday."

"Well that's just it. There's 'bout a thousan' miles a desert 'tween Oklahoma an' California, and there ain't no water to speak of. Your horses ain't gonna last. You're gonna hafta have a car." Mr. Thompson nodded out toward the barn where Uncle Jon and the boys were leading the horses toward the stock tank. "I know how those boys a yours likes them horses, that's why I didn't wanna say nothin' 'bout it with them listenin',' but I figure money must be kinda short

in your fam'ly, what with not gettin' any crops ta speak of, and nine mouths ta feed."

Josif felt a second premonition of bad things. "I not understand what you mean about horses and money."

"Well, that's just it. If you folks wanna git outta here without thirstin' or starvin' ta death, you're gonna hafta sell them horses an' buy a car. Now I know that's gonna hit all your fam'ly pretty hard, 'cause they all treat them horses like members a the family."

Josif shook his head. "We not sell horses. They been good friends."

"I know how ya feel. I hated ta let mine go, too, but sometimes you just hafta go ahead an' do things you don't wanna if you're gonna survive." Mr. Thompson started the Essex. "There's a fella in Tyson buyin' up horses. His name is Montgomery. You ask at the depot for him. He's rigged up a corral just outside a town where he's holdin' 'em till he gits enough ta ship out. You could git enough for that team ta prob'ly buy some sorta car that would git you out west. Shorty's garage has got a pretty good lookin' '21 Dodge that he wants about seventy five dollars fer."

Mr. Thompson reached over on the front seat and sorted through a pile of papers. He handed Josif a worn and battered road map. "This here's a map a the whole United States. It might come in handy for ya." He opened the map. "This here's Oklahoma." He pointed. "Here's where we are. This here's all desert between us an' California." He put the car in gear. "I sure wish you folks good luck. You tell that wife a yours what I said 'bout y'all bein' real good tenants."

Mr. Thompson drove the Essex in a big slow circle around through the barnyard and headed out into the road. The dust rose up behind the car again, swirling like a small red tornado in the brassy heat of the afternoon sun.

Josif went back to Uncle Jon and the boys with the road map in his hand. "Come in the house. We have to talk to the women."

They scraped the manure off their shoes and went through the red dust of the barnyard to the house, two dark, wiry, mustachioed men and two thin boys, walking slowly in their despondency. They left their shoes on the porch and entered the house.

The women and girls were in the kitchen. Izabella and Aunt Magda had come forward from where they had watched Mr. Thompson. Marie, Rose, and Caroline peeped out from behind Izabella's skirt like frightened little chickens. They were all barefooted, the Romanian custom in a house in farmland.

Josif felt how vulnerable they were with nothing between them and the bad thing he had to tell them, just as there was nothing between their bare feet and the rough wood floor.

He spoke in Romanian as they always did among themselves, and also so there would be no misunderstanding of what he said. "Mr. Thompson came to tell us that he has sold this farm and his home farm. We will have to leave this place."

Izabella's shoulders slumped. She said nothing, but waited for him to speak again.

"We have to leave before next week. They are coming with machines to push these buildings down."

"Mr. Thompson is going to California," Uncle Jon said. "They are going to buy an orange grove by the ocean where it is cool. He said that we should come out there too."

Izabella's eyes brightened. "Is California a good place?"

Josif shrugged his shoulders. "Mr. Thompson has lived in America a long time. He thinks it's a good place."

Three-year-old Michael-Joseph said, "Oranges. Good."

"It might be a good place," Josif said to Izabella. Then looking at Michael-Joseph added, "It's not good to interrupt when adults are speaking." Michael-Joseph clapped both hands over his mouth and looked at Josif with wide eyes.

Izabella's eyes held a look of hope. "How far is it to this place?"

Josif thought, *Now I am going to have to tell her, and the dark look will come again.* He said to her, "It's a long way from here, maybe 1,500 miles. There is desert and little water between here and there. We cannot take the horses. We will have to sell them and buy a car."

Silence filled the old kitchen.

Josif could not look at any of them. He felt them all crying, but there was no sound from any of them. The crying was inside where it could not be seen or heard. He placed the road map on the table and flattened out the wrinkles and creases.

"This is a map of the United States." He put his hand on the state of Oklahoma. "Here is where we are." He slowly drew his finger across the map of the U.S. westward until it came to the edge of the continent. "Here is California. That is all desert between. The horses would die if we tried to take them across there."

Uncle Jon pulled at his mustache. "Josif, without the horses we are people with nothing. You saw it in our homeland. People without horses can only be peasants, always working for someone else, without pride or hope."

Josif did not look up from the map. "What you say is true. But now the time for pride is past. We must survive. That comes first, then pride." He looked up at them. "Tomorrow I will take the horses into Tyson."

Aunt Magda spoke for the first time since the men had come into the house. "I have the old necklace from my mother. Sell the necklace, Josif, but keep the horses."

Uncle Jon added, "Sell my old gold watch, too, Josif."

Josif shook his head. "I thank you, but even if we find someone to buy the necklace and the watch, giving us enough money to buy a car, we still cannot keep the horses. There is no way to take them to California with us." He looked at Izabella, seeing the sadness in her eyes. He said to her, "This must be. There is no other way."

She stared at him, holding the girls close to her. Finally, she said, "If it must be, then it must. We will all say goodbye to Peter and Paul before you take them away."

He saw that she would not cry. He looked around at the others. Alexander and Michael-Joseph were biting their lips, and the girls had their faces buried in Izabella's skirt.

"We will get more horses someday," he said. "Peter and Paul will not blame us for this. They will go to someone who will take good care of them."

"May I say something, Papa?" Alexander asked.

Josif nodded and looked at his son.

"Why do we have to go to California?" he asked quietly looking at Josif. "Why can't we stay here in Oklahoma? Maybe we can find another farm where we can live. Then Peter and Paul can stay with us."

Michael-Joseph and the girls looked up at Josif in silent hope.

Josif saw the hope come back into Izabella's eyes, and even Uncle Jon and Aunt Magda seemed about to smile. He put his hand on the map, over Oklahoma. "This land is dry and blowing with dust. You have seen our crops shrivel and burn up in the heat of the sun. Soon many farmers will give up, just as Mr. Thompson has, and they will go to California. If we go out there now, maybe we can find some land, and work on it and buy it. If we stay here, we will become poorer and poorer, and when we do finally go to California, everyone else will be out there and there will be no land, no work." He looked up at them.

"We have not come to America to be peasants or slaves. We have come because America is where there is opportunity and freedom. We will not stay here and die in the dust! We will find land of our own!" He struck the table. "There will be no more talk about staying here! Tomorrow I take the horses to Tyson and get money for a car. We are going to California. I will not have my family starve to death and die in shame wearing only these rags."

Izabella drew back from him.

Aunt Magda put her arm around Izabella. She looked at Josif, her eyes fierce as a mother hen's. "Shame on you, Josif," she said. "It's bad enough that you will sell the horses, but that you should shame your wife before her children is not worthy of you. She has mended these clothes as well as any seamstress and made fine dresses out of flour sack cloth. There is no shame in these clothes."

Josif clenched his fists. "It is not my wife that should be ashamed. It is I, who cannot buy clothes for my family, who cannot buy a nice dress for my wife. I am the one who is shamed, not her. Now you see why we will go to California. Why we will sell the horses. There is nothing here for us in this country. We should have stayed in Romania, bad as it was. We were born there, it was our fate to live there; we have tried to change our fate, but we haven't." Josif looked dejected.

Uncle Jon put his hand on Josif's shoulder. "Josif, do not blame yourself. It is I who am to blame for letting you help us come to America. It is my fault, not yours, that you have little money. But have you forgotten the Iron Guard, the police, the prisons? America does not have these things. We are all lucky to be here."

Josif shook off the hand. "Lucky! How can you say lucky when we have tried to farm in dust and now are forced to leave here with nothing to show for all our work?" Josif scowled at the family. "Say goodbye to the horses. Tomorrow I will sell them. Nothing can change my mind."

* * *

About ten bushels of shelled corn and twenty-five bushels of oats remained in the granary, the last of the previous year's stunted crops. Josif brought the wagon around into the granary with Peter and Paul, and scooped the corn and oats into gunnysacks which he and Uncle Jon loaded into the wagon.

After the horses were back in the barn for the night, all the family came and petted them, stroking their soft noses, rubbing their necks, talking to them. Peter whickered softly at them, and Paul nuzzled them gently, as if saying that nothing had changed between themselves and the family; that they still loved them.

That night none of the family slept well, and in the morning Josif got up at first light and went out past Izabella in the kitchen making bread, to do the chores. He curried and brushed each of the horses carefully, talking gently to them, explaining why he had to sell them.

Uncle Jon came into the barn as Josif was talking to them, and he went quietly outside again. When Josif came out of the barn, Uncle Jon was talking with Aunt Magda who was feeding the chickens, acting as though he had just come out of the house.

Uncle Jon left Aunt Magda and went up to Josif. Josif turned to him and spoke quietly. "I don't want to sell the horses, but I see no other way."

Uncle Jon looked at Josif with understanding. "A man has to do hard things. Do not blame yourself too much, Josif. They all know that you are trying to do what is best for them."

Josif replied, "Who knows what is best? I don't know anymore. I thought that coming to America was best, but things here are not what we had hoped. 'America,' they said, 'that is the one place in the world where if a man works hard he can find happiness and security. He can own his own land. He can provide for his wife and children. He can save money for his old age.' I believed that, and I brought my family here, taking them from their homeland to this new country, taking them from the ways they knew, from their people, from their native soil. I thought I could change our fate. Once Izabella was happy. Now there is sorrow in her eyes...."

Uncle Jon grasped Josif's arm. "Give America another chance, Josif, before you turn against her. There must be some place in this land where you can find your dream."

Josif shook his head despondently. "I cannot believe it anymore. California will be as bad or worse than here. We will always work for some rich landowner. We will never own land of our own. My sons will only know how to pick oranges and strawberries. They will not be men. They will be landless peasants; even in America you cannot change your fate."

They went in together to eat their breakfast of bread and eggs. The family ate silently, sadly; their eyes cast downward, not looking at one another.

When he had finished, Josif slowly got up and put on his hat. "I am going now," he said quietly. "When I come back with a car, we will pack our things in it and go. Be ready, all of you. There is no reason to stay here."

* * *

Tyson was five miles from the farm. Josif let Peter and Paul set their own pace as they pulled the wagon along the dusty road. The team walked along so briskly that by 10:00 they came into the outskirts of the town. Josif drove first to

19

the high red Farmer's elevator by the railroad tracks and sold the corn and oats. Corn was sixty cents a bushel and oats thirty-two and he was given fourteen dollars for his load. He tied the team in the shade of some half-dead cottonwoods and walked across the railroad tracks and along a side street to Shorty Sundquist's Garage.

The garage was built of concrete blocks and had a gas pump and a greasy bench in front. Shorty led Josif out behind the building where an old Dodge touring car stood amidst piles of junk. "This ain't no spring chicken anymore," Shorty told him, "but she's still got a lotta miles in 'er if you treat 'er right. She'll get you to California if you keep oil in 'er and watch them tires. You know how to drive, I guess?"

"I drive truck in army." Josif sat in the driver's seat behind the black upright steering wheel and looked out the two-piece windshield. The car smelled of old upholstery and oil. He looked into the back seat and saw the tar paper roof of the garage through two oval windows in the back. "How much you want for car?"

Shorty rubbed an oily hand across his chin. "Well, I was thinkin' maybe seventy-five dollars would be about right. Like I said, it ain't no spring chicken, but it'll get you there. That's the main thing, ain't it? I don't blame you none fer wantin' to get outta here. You just pile your family in this here Dodge and take off. Next thing you know, you'll be out in California, eatin' them oranges."

"That sound like fair price. You keep car, not sell to anybody else until I go sell horses?"

Shorty nodded. "Sure thing. She'll be here waitin' fer ya. I'll even fill 'er up with gas and throw in a coupla quarts a oil; soon you'll be on your way, just cruisin' down ol' Route 66."

Josif walked back to the railroad tracks and followed them to the depot. The waiting room smelled of coal smoke and varnished wooden seats, and a large picture of the Grand Canyon hung on the wall opposite the ticket counter. The lanky man behind the counter wore a green eyeshade, and around the sleeves of his white shirt were red armbands. He kept on working at the counter as Josif stood waiting. Finally he looked up. "Somethin' I can do fer you?" he asked impatiently.

"I look for Mr. Montgomery. You can tell me where I find him?"

"Maybe I can, and maybe I can't. Waddaya wanna see him for?"

"I want sell horses."

The man looked at him as if Josif were something he had stepped in. "So does ever'body else. Cain't make it, huh?"

Josif put his hand in the pocket of his overalls and made a fist. He said quietly, "Can tell me where I find him?"

"Sure, I can tell ya soon's I get finished with this here paperwork. I'm tryin' to run a railroad here, not some sorta guide service for people that cain't stick it out." The man bent over his counter again, ignoring Josif.

Josif stood at the counter, waiting for the man to finish. After what seemed like ten minutes, the man looked up at him. "You still here?"

Josif said nothing, looking at the man coldly.

"I suppose you're gonna stand here all day. You danged foreigners. Come over here and then y'all cain't make it." The man jerked his thumb back over his shoulder. "He's got a corral over behind the lumberyard. Now move along. Make room for the payin' customers." There was no one else in the waiting room.

"I thank you," Josif said to the man. "I never forget you."

The man glared at Josif. "Don't you go tryin' to threaten me, bucko. I happen to be real good friends with the town marshal. Suppose you just move along outta here afore I give him a call." He picked up the telephone that sat on the counter.

Josif gave the man a look that suggested what the man could do with the phone. "I thank you again for your expert help," he said sarcastically. "Goodbye." He turned slowly away from the man and went outside leaving the door open behind him.

Josif drove the team through the side streets to the lumberyard and guided them out behind it. A barbed wire corral with about thirty horses in it stood in the dry weeds near an old wooden windmill. A galvanized metal water tank sat inside the corral and a pile of poor-looking bales of hay rose outside the fence. Some horses stood near the hay, stretching their necks through the barbed wire toward a few wisps that lay on the ground. A battered Ford truck was parked on the other side of the windmill. Josif climbed down from the wagon and walked around the windmill to the truck.

A man was sprawled out on an old tarpaulin which lay on the ground in the shade of the truck box. He held a bottle in one hand and a cowboy magazine in the other, while his head was propped up on a black saddle. He wore fancy cowboy boots with red stars on the sides, a red and blue shirt, tight blue denim pants with a tooled leather belt, and by his side was a greasy cowboy hat with a snakeskin band. He lifted the bottle and took a long swallow before he spoke to Josif. "You're wantin' to sell them horses, I'll bet."

"They good horses," Josif said. "Five years old."

The man placed the bottle carefully against the saddle. "Oh, sure, they're all the best damn horses ever was. You never seen such good horses as people been bringin' here. 'Course I 'spect yours is the finest horses that ever could be. You prob'ly 'spect me to pay that kinda price fer 'em too."

"Only want fair price. You buy harness and wagon too?" Josif indicated the wagon. "Is not new, but everything strong."

The man got up off the tarpaulin, an acrid smell rising with him. "Lemme just take a look at your crowbaits an' rig. I don't buy no wagons, but sometimes I'll take a harness."

He walked over to Peter and Paul and pulled at their harnesses, then he opened their mouths and looked at their teeth. He had big hands, and he roughly twisted the horses' upper lips as he held their mouths open. "Well, you ain't lyin' too much 'bout their age." He stepped back and stared at the horses. "Sixty-five dollars fer the lot. That's my price. Take it or leave it."

Josif stroked the horses' necks to soothe them. "Good horses maybe seventy dollars each in horse sales two years ago."

"Well, this ain't no two years ago, and this ain't no horse sale. I'm buyin' up horses more like a favor to you people." The man walked back toward the truck. "Sixty-five dollars is my price. Don't take too long to think it over. I'm shippin' this bunch outta here in a coupla days."

Josif looked at the horses in the corral. Those closest to the fence were still trying to reach the wisps of hay, pushing their shoulders against the barbed wire, and there was a strained and nervous look about them that he did not like. Farther back in the corral other horses stood listlessly with their heads drooping and their eyes glazed. Every weed in the corral had been eaten, and those outside the fence were gone three feet from the barbed wire. Josif felt disgusted. "Horses look hungry."

The man turned back, facing him. "You tryin' to tell me how to run my business, mister?"

"No, but these horses starve. Not right do that. Horses can't get hay through fence."

The man stepped closer to Josif. "Listen, bucko, if you wanna walk outta here with any money a'tall, just keep yer trap closed. I ain't too goddamned sure I wanna deal with you anyhow. Matter a fact, I just lowered my offer down ta sixty bucks!"

Suddenly, Josif felt strangely happy. He turned his back on the man and walked over to Peter and Paul. He stroked their noses and patted their necks. He said to them in Romanian, "You knew, didn't you? That is why you came into town so fast. You knew." He climbed up into the wagon and clucked the team forward, moving them and the wagon in a tight circle away from the man and his truck.

The man stared at them. "Where the hell you think you're goin'? Cain't you take a little joke? Tell ya what. I'll make ya another offer on that team. Seventy bucks. Now you cain't say that ain't fair."

Josif looked down at the man from the wagon seat. "I do not want your money; I think I go buy some bells."

* * *

Alexander came running into the house. "Papa is coming down the road with Peter and Paul! They're coming home!" He was so excited that he almost crashed into the kitchen table. "They're coming home! Papa is bringing the horses home!"

Everyone poured into the yard, shouting with happiness, eager for a look at the horses, and they ran to meet Josif and the team.

Peter and Paul were trotting proudly with their heads up and their manes flying, and attached to each horse's collar was a string of tinkling bells. Josif stood erect in the wagon, smiling as he brought the team to a halt so that the family could caress the horses.

Everyone tried to talk at once, but finally they quieted enough so that Josif could be heard. "We're not going to California, and we're not selling Peter and Paul. I could not do it. They are part of our family. We are horse people, not car people.

"Tonight we will make plans to go somewhere else. It will not be our fate to be without land and horses. In America you make your own fate! We will find a direction to go that is not through a desert. Then we will celebrate. What do you say to that?"

Izabella was crying with happiness. She smiled up at Josif. "I prayed to God that you would not sell the horses. He has answered my prayers. Tonight we will celebrate and be glad, and I will thank God every day that you are a good man."

Josif held his hand down to her. "Come up into the wagon with me." He lifted her up and over the side of the wagon to stand close to him. "That you should be happy is what I pray for." He looked down at the rest of the family. "Come up with us. We will go together and make plans."

Uncle Jon boosted the children up and then helped Aunt Magda up and over the side. As he nimbly climbed in after her, he said, "Josif, tonight when we celebrate I will bring out a bottle of palinca that has been waiting for such a happening." He looked at the bags of grain that were lined up along each side of the wagon-box. "You did not sell the corn and oats?"

Josif laughed. "I sold them once. Then I bought half of them back again. The man at the elevator thought I was crazy. Maybe he was right; I felt crazy-like a wild man. I wanted to dance and sing right there in the office of the elevator." He pointed to the bags. "There is food there for us and for the horses. I took the corn to the mill and had it ground for our mamaliga. The oats will feed the horses. They will be better than gasoline for a car."

Uncle Jon looked at him, then burst out laughing. "Josif, you have it all planned, don't you? We are going on the road!" He pounded Josif on the back. "Like Gypsies!"

The children leapt up and down on the floorboards of the wagon. "Gypsies! Gypsies! We are going to be Gypsies!"

Josif cautioned them. "Settle down, children. We will not be Gypsies. We will just travel like Gypsies until we come to the right place to stop. We will work hard and get land of our own. Then we will be true Americans. We will have our own land, our own home."

"Josif, where will we go?" Aunt Magda asked him. "Where will we find such a place?"

Josif smiled at his family. "That is what I will decide tonight." He lightly slapped the reins, and directed the horses into the barn.

Everyone climbed out of the wagon and watched as Josif and Uncle Jon unhitched Peter and Paul, took their harnesses off, and watered and fed them. They all helped curry and brush the horses, and when the family left the barn, Peter and Paul nickered softly to them, as if saying their thanks.

It was after 6:00PM, and the women quickly put their supper of bread, cheese, fried pork, and sliced tomatoes on the table. Uncle Jon got out the bottle of their home-made *tuica*, and all the adults had their customary drink before dinner.

When they had eaten and cleared the table Josif spread the map out on the oilcloth and pointed to Oklahoma. "Here we are. Which way should we go?"

The adults bent over the map, studying it. They read the names of the states aloud, marveling at the strange sounds. They traced the routes of the highways with their fingers, following them as they led from town to town, from city to city, from one part of the continent to another. They exclaimed over the long rivers that seemed to all come from the north and flow south.

Josif said, "Maybe this is something."

"What, Josif?" Uncle Jon asked. "What do you see?"

Josif rubbed his chin. "The rivers. If they come from the north..."

Uncle Jon saw at once. "Water! The water comes from the north in this country!" They bent over the map again, making sure. They looked up at each other, realizing that here was something important, something that could be of fundamental value in their decision.

Uncle Jon pulled at his mustache. "We should have a map showing the mountains. Maybe the rivers come from mountains. We know how hard it is to farm in mountains."

They looked on the other side of the map, but there was nothing to show mountains. Alexander spoke up hesitantly, not wanting to interrupt the adults, "We studied geography last year in fifth grade." He approached the table and traced on the map with his finger. "I think the Rocky Mountains are here, through Colorado. There are other mountains farther west. I think there are some to the east, too." He pointed to West Virginia and North Carolina. "Here are the Appalachian mountains. I think there are more mountains north of them, but it was a funny name I couldn't pronounce."

Josif studied the map. "What is here, north of us?"

Alexander replied, "I don't know, Papa. The teacher called it the Great Plains. He said that buffalo used to live there." Alexander backed away from the table.

The adults crowded around the map again, looking carefully at the states in the north central part of the country. They traced the course of the Mississippi River and painstakingly followed the smaller rivers that were shown on the map.

Josif pointed. "See this river, the Missouri? It flows from far up in Montana across North Dakota and South Dakota, then down between Nebraska and Iowa, across Missouri, and joins the Mississippi River. It goes from the north edge of the United States right down to the south coast. It must be one of the longest rivers in the world." He put his hand on the Dakotas. "What water there must be here to feed it!"

As Josif spoke the wind howled around the house, and red dust blew across the barnyard and by the windows of the house, darkening the room as though a heavy cloud had swept across the setting sun. The kitchen door was closed, yet through the keyhole a tiny stream of dust came into the room and onto the floor.

Aunt Magda shuddered and crossed herself. "This dry dust is like a strigoi, sucking the life from the land and creeping into our house, into our souls." She looked up at Josif. "Take your family from here, Josif, take them to a place where there is rain. Where there is water. Where there is cool shade and where green grass and flowers grow."

They were all silent, looking at him, looking at the

map. Josif pointed down at the map. "We want to go where there is water, where there is rain. We agree it should be north. I think we should go on until we come to that long river, the Missouri. I say we just go north, go north from here, keeping to the back roads so there will be few cars. It should be harvest time now; maybe we can find work in the fields as we go. We will just keep going north until we come to the place. We will know it when we come to it. Then we will stop." He looked around confidently. "We will go see this Missouri River and the land that feeds it."

Tuica Still

Everyone took that name to their hearts, the Missouri River, the river that would bring them fertile land and a future. Now it was the family's special river with their private tie to it and a fierce hope of deliverance from the drought and sadness of Oklahoma. Now they felt strong with Josif's plan and leadership, and determined instead of fearful.

* * *

Shortly after dark, Josif and Uncle Jon began packing the wagon with a very important piece of their essential equipment: their small still. *Tuica*, a moonshine-like alcohol made from fermented plums, was a daily aperitif in Romania, and the Dacias considered it part of their meal rather than the illegal alcohol of prohibition. Life without *tuica* wasn't normal and the Dacias never considered not making it; they just took precautions to keep its production private.

Josif and Uncle Jon quickly constructed a wooden seat at the back of the wagon which exactly concealed the parts of the still, and packed tools wrapped in burlap around them. Then they returned to the house for their last dinner at their first home in America.

That night even though it wasn't Sunday, God's day, with church in the morning and relaxation the rest of the day, they played the instruments they had carried with them from Romania. Violin, panpipes, and Uncle Jon's tambal – an instrument like a hammered dulcimer with a strap that goes around the player's neck and holds the instrument in place for playing – were all brought out.

Uncle Jon, as promised, brought out a bottle of *palinca*, twice distilled and twice as strong *tuica*, and poured the adults each a small glassful. They toasted the house and the future and clinked and drained their glasses. Then they picked up their instruments.

First they played wild and exuberant songs of joy to celebrate the decision not to go to California and to keep their horses, and also the new plan for becoming landowners in America. Songs of hope and joy.

Then they played the *doina de jale*, a mellow and sad song which that night expressed their feelings of leaving, of departure. Uncle Jon played the tambal; Josif played his violin, lovingly stroking the bow across the strings of the old instrument to bring to the doomed old house one last evening of beauty and love; and Alexander played the melodic panpipes.

The women sang in plaintive voices and the younger children joined them, singing and clapping in time to the music, while outside in the darkness the hot, dry dust swirled around the old house and covered every surface, sucking out all moisture and smothering all life.

Chapter Two
Tornado

The next morning the Dacias prepared for the journey north. The women had harvested all the vegetables from the little garden the day before. They had sliced the tomatoes and peppers and dried them in the sun, while the potatoes, onions and garlic had been carefully bagged. They had kept the garden alive through the heat and drought by bringing every drop of waste water to it and by doling out what little they could spare from the shallow well.

The rooster and the six hens were placed in a wooden slatted cage which was tied to the back of the wagon and shaded from the sun with an old piece of burlap.

The family's other possessions were few, and they were easily packed into the wagon. A hinged wooden box held their cooking and eating utensils, while their clothing was packed in an old trunk. They made four bedrolls from their blankets and old canvas, one for Josif and Izabella, one for Uncle Jon and Aunt Magda, one for the two boys – and one for the three girls. Their most precious possessions–the violin, tambal, panpipes, and their native folk costumes–were packed in a trunk which was carefully wrapped in oilcloth and stored securely beside the big trunk under a canvas cover.

The men and Alexander made a covering and sunshade for the wagon from a tarpaulin and three big iron hoops which they fastened to the wagon-box. They threaded ropes through the tarpaulin so it could be rolled up at the sides or closed against the dust, wind, or storms. When the rest of the family saw what a snug home the wagon had become, they could hardly wait to leave.

Three big canvas water bags were hung on the sides of the wagon. They had carefully stowed their two lanterns, axe, shovel, two pitchforks, a box of tools, a coil of rope, the clothes line, some baling wire, and the thermometer from the porch around the insides of the wagon. A can of kerosene, a small pail of axle grease, and two water buckets were fastened below the wagon, and finally, the big round washtub was hung on the side of the wagon-box.

They fed and watered Peter and Paul, harnessed and hitched them to the wagon. Josif looked over the wagon and back at his family. "We are ready," he said with finality. It was 11:00 in the morning.

The nine family members climbed up into the wagon. They sat on the bags of grain, on the trunks and bedrolls which were along each side of the wagon, and on the new bench seat at the rear.

Uncle Jon spread his arms and laughed. "We will lead the Gypsy life. There is no one more free. The open road is our home, the sky is our roof, the whole world is ours."

Josif clucked to the team. "Now, Peter and Paul, take us north."

All the rest of that day they moved slowly northward. Josif guided the team along the country roads past weathered farm houses and fields of withered crops. The heat was so intense that the air rose in shimmering waves above the land, and the sky held a dull coppery look that was depressing to the family. They worried about the horses and rested them every two hours. When they came to farms with windmills and stock tanks they asked to water their horses and refill the water bags, for water was their greatest concern.

The temperature in the wagon was one one hundred and five degrees in the mid-afternoon, but the family merely looked at the thermometer and shrugged. "People can stand anything," Josif said. "But tomorrow we will start early in the morning, and when the sun beats down in the afternoon we will rest the team in some shady place until it cools off. Then we will go on until dark."

They camped that night in a field, and after they had eaten, they discussed the day's journey as they sat around the fire.

The silver crescent of the new moon appeared in the west, and as they crawled into their bedrolls by the wagon, the beauty of the night and the open sky above them seemed to make up for the heat of the day. The stars came out, large and brilliant in the night sky, and the Milky Way stretched from one side of the horizon to the other. The horses moved quietly in the darkness, softly stamping their feet.

Alexander spoke from the bedroll which he shared with Michael-Joseph. "How long will it take us to come to the Missouri River, the place where the green farm is, Papa? Will we get there this summer?"

"We should," Josif replied. "I think it is maybe seven hundred miles to the Missouri. The team can travel around twenty miles a day, but we will try to find work in the fields as we go north. I think maybe we will come to the river before winter."

"Will it be green there, Papa? Will it be green by the river?" the girls asked.

"It will be green by the river." Josif rolled over onto his side. "Now everyone go to sleep. We will start early in the morning, before the sun comes up."

* * *

The farms in this area of Oklahoma were still occupied by their owners or tenant farmers who hung grimly on, hoping for rain, for a crop, however small. The Dacias found themselves welcomed when these people saw the children. Often they were given milk from some thin cow, or a cup of flour from an almost empty bin.

"Poor little things," said one elderly woman in a sun-bonnet, "Bring them into the shade of the porch with your washtub. You can bring water from the well and everyone can have a nice cool bath. The mister and I can make ourselves scarce 'til you're done."

The water was wonderful, and when all had finished and put on clean clothing, the woman said to Izabella, "Get your scrubbing board and wash your things out, dear. While they dry you can all have a glass of buttermilk."

When the Dacias drove away from the farm the woman and her husband waved from the porch, watching as the team pulled the wagon northward. Izabella's eyes shown. "They were so good to us..." She hugged Michael-Joseph. "Doesn't it feel good to be clean again?" she said happily.

They went on, across the state line into Kansas, always northward. They found work in wheat fields where they shocked bundles behind the farmers' horse-drawn binders, the whole family laboring under the sun, earning enough money to buy food for themselves, more hay and oats for the horses, axle grease, matches, and even to save a little. The layer of dollar bills in Josif's wallet began to thicken.

One day Josif led the family into a mercantile store in a little town, and in the fruit and vegetable section in a back corner, shining golden and round between the apples and the potatoes, was a pyramid of oranges. "Look, Michael-Joseph," he said, "oranges here in Kansas!"

Michael-Joseph was speechless. He reached out his hand and gently touched an orange, then looked up at Josif, then back at the oranges. A sign by the oranges said, "Fresh California Oranges at sixty cents/dozen."

A plump woman wearing glasses came over to them. A pencil protruded from the bun of her hair, and she wore a blue apron over her dress. "These just came in yesterday by truck, all the way from California." She looked down at the children. "I bet your Papa would buy some of these if you asked him."

Josif felt the wallet in his overalls pocket. "How much we pay for one orange?"

The woman smiled. "They're five cents each."

Josif pulled out the wallet and took out a quarter. "We buy this much please."

The woman looked down at the children again, then at the rest of the family. She took a paper bag from behind the counter and put six oranges in it "We have a special price today. Half a dozen for a quarter." She handed the bag to Michael-Joseph. "Do you think you can carry this, young man?"

Michael-Joseph clutched the bag against his chest. He looked up at the woman, then at Josif, then ran to Izabella and held the bag open for her to see. Izabella knelt down by him. "What do you say to the nice lady?"

Michael-Joseph looked up shyly at the woman and smiled at her. "I like you."

They traveled on, slowly crossing Kansas during the month of August. The heat in the wagon was intense, but the family members were so toughened now that they paid little attention to it.

Even the chickens had become accustomed to their new way of life. They foraged near the horses at each campsite, and when the family worked in the wheat fields the rooster led the hens in hunting expeditions through the stubble, finding shelled out grain and chasing grasshoppers. The hens laid two or three eggs each day, and each night the little flock perched on the wagon tongue, each in their own place, the rooster at the top.

One afternoon in late August, as the team pulled the wagon toward the Nebraska border, the family noticed a change in the light. Uncle Jon peered up at the sky. "There is something going on up there, Josif. I don't like the looks of it."

Josif leaned out the front of the wagon, looking up into the brassy sky. Something was forming there, a gathering of energy that he could feel but not see. Alexander spoke from the rear of the wagon with some urgency. "Papa, there are big clouds coming up behind us!"

Josif stopped the wagon and they all got out to better see the sky without the canvas top over them. Black clouds were billowing up in the southwest, forming so rapidly that as the family watched, the clouds boiled upward and toward them, filling half the sky. A green light was everywhere, an icy green, thick and ominous. Now the bottom of the clouds began to drop down in sagging round pockets, gray-green and threatening. An eerie stillness hung over the land, yet it seemed that far in the distance a ghostly wind moaned.

Peter and Paul shook their manes uneasily, tossing their heads and showing the whites of their eyes; the chickens crouched in their cage and looked fearfully around them.

Josif kept his voice steady. "A tornado is coming. People who have lived here long say that a great funnel comes from the southwest. We cannot outrun it if it comes toward us. We must get down in a ditch or low place."

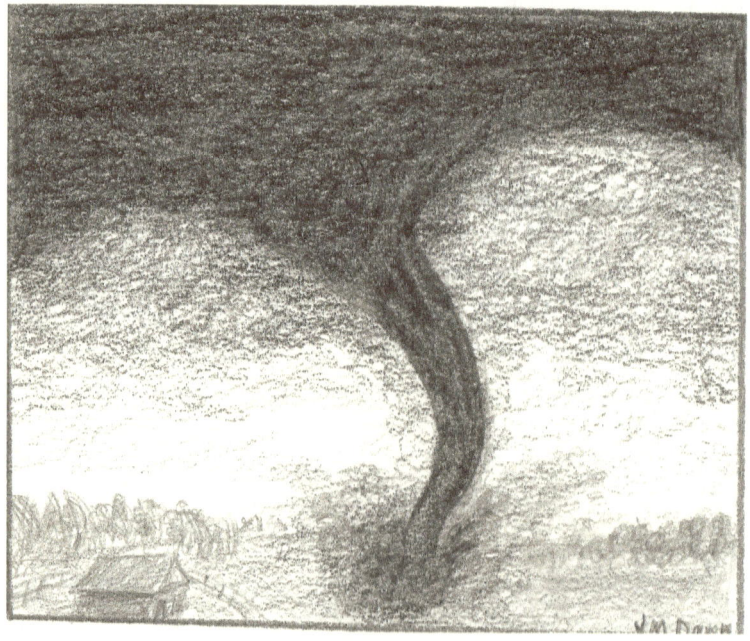

Only shallow ditches lay on either side of the road, but about a quarter of a mile ahead the road cut through a low bank in the earth. The family hurried into the wagon and Josif slapped the reins on the horses' backs. Peter and Paul broke into a gallop, and the wagon bounced on the rough road as they raced the storm to the cut in the earth.

The clouds swept toward them, and the gray pockets dropped lower and lower, like hanging drops of viscous liquid. Then one huge slate-colored pocket dropped toward the earth and formed a sinuous, whirling spiral.

A roaring sound like a dozen trains came out of the whirling thing, and it widened out as it touched the earth, becoming an immense black funnel that tore the earth up into itself and fed on it, gaining in monstrous strength as it came swaying and lurching across the fields.

Josif lashed the team to a dead run, and just as they charged into the deep ditch below the embankment, the hungry black thing leapt upon them.

An immense roaring, awful and thunderous, filled the world, the universe. Dense blackness and a deafening, screaming thing tore at them and battered them with terrible intensity. No time, no space–nothing but the roaring, the blackness, and the fierce hammering and tearing existed.

Then it was gone. It had swept over them like the end of the world and now was gone and they were alive.

Slowly, they looked up. Izabella lay facedown with the three girls clutched in her arms beneath her, Josif held Michael-Joseph and had thrown himself over Alexander, and Uncle Jon and Aunt Magda were sprawled over everyone, like mother hens over their chicks.

Uncle Jon rolled stiffly off Josif's legs. He sat up and tried to wipe the dirt out of his eyes. "Holy Mother of God, Satan himself must have come roaring over us!"

"God has protected us," Izabella said with relief.

Dirt covered them; it was in their hair, in their eyes, inside their clothing, even in their shoes. The canvas top that had been over the wagon hoops was gone, the ropes that had held it were broken as though they had been bits of string.

Peter and Paul stood in front of the wagon, still alive, their sleek bay coats so covered with dirt that they looked like two rough-furred black bears.

The chickens and their crate were gone, torn from the end of the wagon without a trace. A wound, a wide scar, marked the earth just behind the wagon, leaving a torn path of destruction almost a quarter of a mile wide that led across the land in the same sinuous course taken by the black whirling funnel.

The family climbed slowly out of the wagon. They brushed the dirt from one another and inspected each person for injuries. Miraculously, they were unhurt. Josif pointed to the path of the tornado just behind the wagon. "If it had been one foot closer, we would be up in the sky with the chickens now."

The children had not spoken since the wagon had started its wild race behind the horses. Now they looked at the place where the chicken crate had been, and tears began to make muddy tracks down their faces. "Are the chickens up in heaven, Papa?" Marie asked.

Josif knelt down by the children. "They are up in heaven." He wiped their faces with his fingers. "I think the rooster is showing the hens some nice grasshoppers right about now."

"Are there grasshoppers up in heaven, Papa?" Caroline asked.

Josif looked to Uncle Jon for help, then to Izabella and Aunt Magda. He said to the children, "Now there are. There are lots of grasshoppers up there now. Those chickens are never going to be hungry again."

They tried to wash the dirt from their faces and to brush it out of their hair and clothing. They currycombed and brushed the horses, but it was impossible to remove all of the deep, hard-packed soil from their coats.

Uncle Jon laughed, "I think I will use one of these currycombs on myself when we are through with the horses. Half of the state of Kansas must have blown down my neck."

They all had to laugh when they looked at one another, for their faces were so grimy and their hair so wild-looking that they hardly resembled human beings. Izabella and Aunt Magda combed at the children's hair with their fingers and at their own, but it did little good.

"We will have to find water—a place where there is enough to wash ourselves and our clothing, even Peter and Paul," Josif said.

Uncle Jon agreed. "This dirt will never comb or brush out, and it's bad for the horses."

When the team pulled the wagon out of the ditch and up onto the road, the Dacias saw what devastation had been left by the tornado. A wide path went from southwest to northeast across the dry fields, and in that path nothing remained except raw, torn-up earth. Where lines of trees had stood in the tornado's path there were huge gaps. Fences had been ripped out and either wrapped into tightly-bound lumps of posts, barbed wire, and crushed woven wire, or they had simply disappeared.

The mass of clouds from which the tornado had dropped still boiled in the sky to the northeast, and the ominous rumbling of thunder still came from it. Izabella shuddered and crossed herself. "There are people there. May God protect them as He did us."

Terrible destruction lay ahead of them—a flattened mass of wreckage over which the splintered trunks of trees stood like towering gravestones. The horses raised their heads and snorted apprehensively as they approached the place. Aunt Magda touched her cross. "There is death here," she said grimly.

Josif stopped the team, and he and Uncle Jon climbed down from the wagon. "Wait here," he said to the others. "Keep the children in the wagon." The two men walked slowly toward the wreckage. It was the remains of a house, collapsed into a broken tangle of boards, shingles, and beams. Beyond it were the smashed shapes of a barn and some sheds. A wooden windmill lay by the barn, twisted and broken.

Josif and Uncle Jon went to the front of the house where three concrete steps still stood. Josif pulled a broken two-by-four out of the debris and pried the flattened roof upward about six inches. Uncle Jon knelt down and looked under the section that Josif held up. He thrust a short piece of broken beam vertically under the roof to keep it raised and then looked up at Josif. "There are people under there. I can't tell if they're still alive."

They both knelt, peering back under the section of roof. Dimly, they could see the still forms of a woman and two children huddled together, far back under the wreckage.

Josif called, "Lady, you hear us?" There was no sound from the forms. He looked at Uncle Jon. "We have to get them out."

Uncle Jon nodded. "If we can pry the roof up a little higher, I think we can crawl back in there. We maybe could use the rope to pull them out."

"We will need Alexander and the women to pull on the rope." Josif studied the roof. "Maybe we could use the team to pull this part of the roof away." They peered into the darkness under the roof again.

Uncle Jon shook his head. "We could pull it away with the team, but it would be too dangerous for the people under there."

Josif agreed. "It would scrape right over them. We have to go in."

They pulled more two-by-fours out and pried the creaking roof upward, bracing it precariously with broken boards until they could raise it no higher. They looked in once more. The huddled forms now had a few inches of space above them where the roof had been lifted, but there was a feeling and look of instability about the wreckage, as though it might break apart and all come crashing down again.

They went back to the wagon, and Josif spoke quietly to the women. "We need you to help us; Alexander too." He lifted the coil of rope and the clothesline out of the wagon. "Marie, you stay in the wagon with the children. Do not come out of the wagon until we tell you to. Do you understand?"

"Yes, Papa." Marie bit her lip. "Are there people under the house?"

Josif looked up at her. "There are people under there," he said gently. "They may be alive. We have to bring them out."

"Be careful, Papa," Marie said with concern on her face.

"We will be careful. You take care of your sisters and brother, Marie, and we'll be back as soon as we can." They went back to the wrecked house with the rope and the clothesline. Alexander, Izabella, and Aunt Magda knelt down and looked back under the propped-up piece of the roof. When they stood up their faces were pale under the dirt, and Izabella's eyes were dark with sorrow. Josif put his hand on her arm. "We will go in and fasten the rope around them, one at a time. When we call, you, Aunt Magda and Alexander must pull them out."

Josif gave the clothesline to Uncle Jon and then took one end of the rope and knelt down by the opening. "Alexander, if anything goes wrong, help your Mother and Aunt Magda and take care of the family."

They crawled back under the wreckage of the roof, moving slowly and cautiously over splintered boards, broken plaster, and smashed laths. The sagging, propped-up roof swayed above them, and the farther in they went, the lower the space under the roof became. Uncle Jon looked sideways at Josif, barely able to turn his head in the cramped space. "Josif, let me take the rope in from here."

Josif shook his head. "Uncle, by all the ways of our people, I should obey your wishes. But talk no more about taking the rope. It will not be."

They squirmed forward on their stomachs, pushing and pulling themselves forward with their knees and elbows toward the woman and the two children. Uncle Jon drew in his breath. "I wondered where the man was."

The man's body lay to one side of the woman and children. His hands were pushed up against the roof, straining to hold it away from his family, even in death. He was a young man, not as old as Josif.

They went to each of the bodies and searched for any sign of life. "The women knew. They have gone to God." Uncle Jon said quietly.

They pulled the family out, one by one. Each time that the women and Alexander untied the rope from a body the men drew the rope back in with the clothesline and tied it to another body. When they crawled out from under the roof, the men saw that the dead family lay in a row on the ground: the father, the mother, and two little boys, about six and eight years old.

Because of the heat, they dug a grave in the front yard of the house and lowered the bodies gently into it, covering them with their tablecloth before they shoveled the dirt back in. They made a cross from two pieces of broken planks, and Josif carved on it with his knife the words, "Father. Mother. Two Little Boys. With God."

They left the devastated farm, continuing north on the country road. Four miles from the farm they approached a small town, and Josif brought the team to a halt by the first store they came to, a false-fronted wooden structure with, Al's Feed and Seed painted above the door. A woman wearing a faded calico dress stared at them from the doorway.

Josif climbed down from the wagon and walked across the rickety board sidewalk to the woman. "We come to tell you. Family about four miles south here all die in tornado. We want you should know."

The woman looked vague. "So many died in the tornado. So many... My man is out there now trying to dig 'em out. So many dead out there."

Josif rubbed his fingers through his hair. "We bury these people. We want to tell somebody."

The woman stared at him.

Josif said, "I thank you. We go now. Please, you tell people about family. They just four miles south. Father, mother, two little boys."

He went back to the wagon and climbed up over the wheel into the box. He spoke quietly to the family. "We had better tell someone else. I think that poor woman does not hear us."

He drove the team along the main street. The little town seemed deserted; not a living soul was in view. Josif stopped the team in front of a drug store and went in. One person was in the store, a man behind a counter at the rear.

Josif walked back to the counter and spoke to the man. "We come to tell you. Family four miles south from here all killed in tornado. We find under house. We bury them in front yard because of heat. Is marker there. We want tell someone. You know them?"

The man stared at him. "You look like you've been in the tornado yourself. Four miles south, you say? That must be young Ed Slocumb and his family." He shook his head sadly and wrote on a sheet of paper that had a list of names on it. "I'm keepin' a list for the sheriff. Everybody's out there now, tryin' to help." He looked closely at Josif. "I don't believe I've seen you around these parts before."

Josif shook his head. "We come from Oklahoma with team. Go north."

"Well, you sure look like you came awful close to that tornado, or it came close to you." The man looked out toward the street. "Is that your family out there in the wagon?"

Josif nodded. "Tornado blow away wagon cover. You tell us where could maybe find old binder canvas and place wash dirt off horses and family?"

The man rubbed his chin. "John Martin's Implement Store is right down at the end of the street, on your way outta town. He might have some old canvas lyin' around there, but he's prob'ly out with one of his tractors, tryin' to pull roofs offa people. As far as washing' up goes, if you cross over into Nebraska, the Republican River is about four or five miles further along. It's still got some water in it they tell me. Maybe you could find a place where you could get your horses down in and clean 'em up." He looked out at the wagon again. "You sure you folks don't need some help? Those kids a yours look pretty tuckered out."

Josif looked back at the wagon. "Today they see death first time. See little boys dead on ground. They not talk about it yet."

The man came out from behind the counter. He went to the front of the store where candy was displayed in big glass jars, and scooped red and white peppermints into a paper bag. "You give this to them fer me. That was a good thing you did fer Ed Slocumb. I want you to know that the people around here are gonna appreciate it when they find out about it." He held out his hand to Josif. "I sure wish you folks good luck."

Josif shook the man's hand. "We thank you. Kids be all right. They never have so much candy before." He looked at the man with compassion. "This storm is terrible for you and your neighbors. We hope you find many of your friends alive and that town can get better." The man smiled sadly at Josif.

They drove to the implement store, and when Josif went in, he found an elderly man who had been left in charge. The man pulled some old binder canvas out from a shed at the rear of the store. "I dunno know why he keeps this stuff. It ain't no danged good to nobody no more. Far as I'm concerned, you can take all you want."

Josif took out his wallet. "We pay for it. You tell us how much."

"I don't want anything for it, but if it'll make you feel better, you can give me about two bits."

"What is *two bits*? Is money?" Josif asked.

The man stared at Josif. "Say, where you from, anyway? Twenty-five cents. That's what two bits is."

Josif gave him a quarter. "We come from Romania. I sorry I not speak English good yet."

They selected three of the old tarpaulins and tied them over the wagon hoops with pieces of the clothesline. The wooden slats riveted to the canvas gave the wagon more of an appearance of a Gypsy caravan than ever, and the man stared after them as they drove away. He shouted, "You folks have a good trip, wherever you're goin'."

* * *

It was almost 6:00 when they left the town, and darkness came before they found the river. They spent an uncomfortable night on their dusty blankets, and in the morning, after about two hours' driving, they came to the river.

A narrow channel of water flowed in the river bottom, and downstream they saw a wide pool. Josif guided the team down off the road and along the riverbank through dry patches of sunflowers, cockleburs, and brush until they were just above the pool. He shouted jubilantly, "Now we wash!"

They scrubbed themselves, their hair, their clothing, and their blankets with yellow soap, kneeling in the shallow water in the morning sunshine, the women at one end of the pool, the men at the other, their backs turned for privacy.

The late summer smell of wild roses and plums perfumed the air, and red-winged blackbirds trilled from the cattails. When they finally forced themselves to come out, the women dressed in clean clothing from the trunk and then spread their washed clothing and blankets over the low shrubs to dry.

While they were doing this, the men brought the horses down into the water and poured bucket after bucket of water over them until their coats were clean.

While they waited for the clothing and blankets to dry, Uncle Jon wandered off into the bushes. He came back bearing a double handful of ripe wild plums. "Plums by the thousands! Taste them!" he said jubilantly.

The others tasted the sweet fruit, and eagerly went into the bushes with their buckets and cooking pots, filling them with the red and purple fruit.

When they left the river and started north along the road once more, they were clean and comfortable, the horses' coats shone in the sunshine, they had the wonderful gift of free wild plums, and it seemed that soon now they would come to the place of their dreams.

* * *

That night in Chicago, there was a special dinner at the Lake Front Inn. The inn was closed to all except the invited guests. Ten men sat at a long table, four Italians and four Irishmen, each group with their own guard. They drank red wine and ate Italian food in honor of the guests: antipasto, lasagna, crusty bread, and salad. Italians of the South Side and the Irish of the North Side were there to make peace.

The host was a stocky, powerful-looking Dublin man who smiled and toasted the guests of honor. "Good evening to all of ya. Here's to an end to the warfare. Enjoy yer dinners!"

When they had eaten the food and drunk the wine, the host signaled to the waiters to bring dessert and coffee. As the dessert was being served, one of the waiters leaned around the Italian guard, and while setting his plate down with his left hand, shot the guard in the back of the head with his right. The other waiter smoothly pulled out a pistol, and the two quickly dispatched the Italians.

"Take that, you fuckin' wop sons-a-bitches!" the host yelled at them during the slaughter. "You think this is over between us? You bleedin' gobshites; I only wish I could kill ya twice!"

Chapter Three
Traveling North

September came, and as the Dacias crossed Nebraska, the goldenrod glowed yellow in the fence rows, and a warm, dusky, end-of-summer feeling permeated the air. The nights and mornings grew cooler, and during the days the sun's rays became less intense.

They met children who were on their way to or from school, carrying lunch pails and books, and Alexander and the girls watched them wistfully, knowing that they too should be carrying these items and going to school.

Josif and Uncle Jon found it harder now to get work, for in that golden empty time between small grain harvest and corn-picking when nature seemed to drowse, farmers made fences and shoveled manure and thought about getting one last cutting of hay, but had little need of extra help.

Uncle Jon scrounged three one-gallon glass jugs, and they rode in the wagon, full of ripe plums and sugar. *Tuica*, he said. "That's what it will be. It should be ready about the time we come to the green farmland by the Missouri River. We will set up our still and make next year's supply when we find our new home."

They came to the Platte River, and finding that it was not the Missouri, crossed it and continued north. The weather grew steadily cooler and the fields now had good crops of corn ripening in them.

In October Josif and Uncle Jon were hired to pick corn with the team and wagon on a big farm near the Elkhorn

River, and they worked for two weeks there. They were given an old house on the farm to live in, and it seemed strange and wonderful to the family to be under a roof again.

They moved their belongings into the house in order to free the wagon for the corn-picking, and Izabella and Aunt Magda used the opportunity to wash and mend the family's meager supply of clothing.

The farmer's wife saw their patched and worn things hanging on the clothesline and came to talk with the women. She was a big woman with a loud, jolly voice.

"If you folks are headin' up north into Dakota for the winter, you're gonna need warm clothing, 'specially for these kids a yours. It gets about forty below up there." She tousled Michael-Joseph's hair. "How old are they? It looks like this young fella must be about four."

Izabella spoke shyly and haltingly in English. "He turn four in August. Caroline is six, Rose is eight, Marie is ten, and Alexander is twelve."

The woman chuckled. "Every two years, was it?" She winked at Aunt Magda. "I wish my man was that easy to handle. Six we had, one every year for six years after we got married. Then I had to just put my foot down." She raised her eyes to the heavens. "You never heard such complainin'. I says to him, 'Six is enough. I'm not havin' anymore, and that's final.' Course it wasn't, but at least it slowed him down a little."

She pointed to the clothes on the line. "Don't you folks have any warm stockings or underwear or sweaters and coats? You're gonna freeze to death up there in those things."

Izabella looked at the ground. "We come from warm place, Oklahoma."

The woman patted Izabella's shoulder. "Now, honey, you don't need to be ashamed a those clothes. Lotsa us started out poor. You can be proud that you manage to keep everything patched and clean. Now, I've got a trunk full a things up in the attic that our family grew outta. There's even things that might fit you, what with you bein' such a slender little thing – clothes our girls had when they were in high school and such."

Izabella looked up at her. "I thank you, but Josif, my husband, I don't think he let us take clothes."

The woman smiled at her. "He's that kind is he? Proud. You can tell that from those black eyes and that mustache. Well, we'll just fix him."

She went to the clothesline and touched one of the embroidered blouses that hung there. "Did you do this embroidery?" she asked appreciatively.

"Yes," Izabella said shyly.

"Well, I've never seen anything so unique and pretty. Those Bohemians over around Wilber do real pretty work, but I think yours is nicer." She smiled at Aunt Magda and Izabella. "Now how would you two like to embroider a tablecloth for our Ladies' Aid sale while your men are pickin' corn? I think a nice tablecloth done as beautiful as this blouse would be a fair trade for some warm, used clothes for you folks."

Izabella shook her head in disbelief. "Tablecloth could not be worth same as clothes..."

"You just let me decide that, honey. I know what good embroidery is worth, and the ladies in our church are just gonna fall all over themselves to have your tablecloth when they see the kinda work you do. And don't you worry about that husband a yours – I'll explain to him in no uncertain terms that it's a fair trade."

The woman went to the house and brought back a plain white linen cloth and rolls of colored thread. "If there's any other colors you need, just tell me, and we'll pick 'em up in town on Saturday night."

Izabella spoke with Aunt Magda in Romanian, then said to the woman, "My aunt says that she is afraid we will not do it the way Americans like. She is afraid that you may not like Romanian designs."

"Now, don't you worry about that, either of you. You just do it the way you would in your country and use designs

49

that you like. If it looks half as pretty as the designs on that blouse, I'll be happy."

When the woman had left them, Izabella and Aunt Magda excitedly discussed what designs they should use. "It must have the *House Spirits* and the *Tree of Life*, but what else should we put in it?" Aunt Magda asked. "It must be something very good for these people who are so kind to us."

Izabella smiled. "I think the *Lily Tree* and *Fairy Queen*; they are so pretty."

"That will be perfect," Aunt Magda responded, smiling. "They are good, strong symbols for these people, and I have patterns for them."

They got their needles and patterns from the trunk and threaded the needles with red and black thread which the woman had brought. "Now," said Aunt Magda, "I feel that I am back home. Back in Romania!"

* * *

Near the end of the second week, the farm woman and her husband came to the old house one night after supper and chores with big armfuls of clothing.

"I've had such fun pickin' these things out for you folks that I couldn't hardly stop," the woman said, smiling. "Now Mr. Dacia, I don't wanna hear one word outta you about not takin' these things. They're no good to us anymore, and goodness knows, our own kids don't want 'em, what with them havin' their own farms and husbands and wives and whatnot. Besides that, I made a bargain with your wife and aunt about them makin' that gorgeous tablecloth, so don't get me mad by gettin' up on your high horse." She spread the clothing out on the table. "Now everybody gather 'round and we'll see if this stuff fits or not."

The woman had warm clothing for everyone, the men included. Woolen socks, warm underwear, flannel shirts, sweaters, mittens, head scarves and neck scarves, coats, ear-flopper hats, heavy skirts for the women; all were there.

"The only thing we couldn't find was decent shoes. Those kids of ours just wore 'em out," the woman said. "Besides, no one wants to wear somebody else's old shoes. You kids are all comin' into town with us Saturday and get fixed up." She glared at Josif. "And I don't wanna hear any backtalk from anybody about it. This is gonna be a present from the Ladies' Aid. When I showed them that tablecloth, they wanted to buy shoes for your whole family. We sent barrels of things to those heathen people in Timbuktu or some place, and they prob'ly never even heard a shoes and won't wear 'em anyhow." She turned to her husband, a big, red-faced man in a red-checked mackinaw. "Isn't that right, Henry?"

Henry nodded. "Sure is."

"Well, that settles it then. You folks try these things on and let me know if they don't fit." The woman headed for the door. "And don't forget, we're takin' all you kids into town on Saturday for your new shoes."

* * *

That Friday the men finished picking the corn. The farmer figured with a stub of pencil on the wall of the granary. "Twelve days at two dollars a day comes to twenty-four. For two of you, that makes forty-eight." He peeled five ten-dollar bills out of his wallet. "You two been danged good workers. You keep the extra two dollars." He gave them another bill, a five-dollar one. "This is for the work that boy of yours did. He was right out there all the time workin' with you."

Uncle Jon and Josif thanked him. "You been good to my family," Josif said. "You give us warm clothes, nice house to live in while we been here, feed for horses, even milk for kids. We remember you always."

"Well, it ain't very often we get men that work as hard as you two did, and your wives sure did make a pretty tablecloth," the farmer said. "I think we're 'bout even all the way around."

Before they went in the house for supper, Josif, Uncle Jon and Alexander swept the wagon out and put the iron hoops and the binder tarpaulins back on. They brought the wagon up close to the old house with the team and then took Peter and Paul to the barn where they unharnessed and fed them.

When they went in the house, Josif said to the women, "We will load everything in the wagon tonight. Everything but our blankets and the cooking box. We are leaving before sunrise tomorrow."

Izabella stared at him. "You are not going to let them buy shoes for the children?"

"No. They will not buy shoes for our children."

Aunt Magda put her hands on her ample hips. "Josif Dacia! You are enough to make me forget what a peaceable woman I am. These good people want to give a present to the children, and you won't let them."

"We have been given enough *presents* by these people. We are not taking any more!" Josif struck the table with his fist. "We are not beggars or some savages waiting for a barrel of shoes from the Ladies' Aid."

Izabella bowed her head. "We will load the wagon."

Aunt Magda glared at Josif. "Josif, you are as stubborn and as proud as old Michael Dacia, your grandfather. And what did he get for his pride and his stubbornness? A little patch of rocky ground and a bullet in the back!"

"Yes, but he was a man. He owned his land, and he came to no one begging for shoes. He bowed down to no man." Josif pointed to the trunk that held their native costumes. "His knife is there, the knife he won in a fight with a Turk, passed down to my father to me; no man dared to start a fight with him. My sons will be men, as he was, not beggars holding out their hands."

Uncle Jon nodded. "Josif is right. Either a man is a man or he is nothing. It is better to go barefoot in the snow than to bow down. Not to the rich. Not to the king. Not to the church. Only to God."

Aunt Magda narrowed her eyes and stared at Josif. "That is fine for a man to say, but what about his family? You both know that these children cannot go north into the winter with bare feet. Not when it is forty degrees below zero!"

Josif sat down at the table. He took his wallet from his overalls and put the money from it on the tabletop. "We were paid today, even Alexander, who worked like a man; fifty-five dollars." He spread the bills out. "We already had earned one hundred and fifty-three dollars on our way here. We have two hundred and eight dollars! We can buy our own shoes!"

Aunt Magda laughed and shook her finger at him. "You are wicked, Josif, making us think that you are a tyrant. I'm sorry that I spoke sharply to you."

After supper they loaded their things into the wagon, packing them neatly, making room for the big bundle of their winter clothing which was wrapped in a sheet of canvas given them by the farmer. Then the women cut the men's and boys' hair, and they all took baths in the big washtub which they placed in front of the kitchen stove.

They got up at 5:30 in the morning, and by 6:30 they stopped the wagon in front of the big house. Josif went up to the door and knocked.

The farmer came to the door, smelling of bacon and coffee. "I knew you weren't gonna let Myrtle buy them kids shoes." He shook Josif's hand. "She ain't too happy about it, but she'll get over it. You folks have a good trip up north. Watch out for them people in Dakota, they get some real strange ones up there."

He came out to the wagon with Josif and shook Uncle Jon's hand. "I sure wish you folks good luck." He handed Izabella a paper bag. "This here's some biscuits Myrtle just baked. She's too mad at your man here to come out and talk, but she wanted you to have these anyway."

As the team pulled the wagon out into the road, the farm woman came out and joined her husband at the end of the sidewalk. They both waved at the family until the row of trees along the road hid them from sight.

At noon they stopped to water the team at a farm and then drove on down the road for another half-mile to eat their lunch. They spread their piece of canvas on the ground in a sunny spot by the roadside and all gathered around Izabella as she opened the paper bag the farmer had given them.

Izabella's face was pink with surprise. She reached in the bag and took out nine hardboiled eggs, a dozen biscuits, a glass jar of strawberry jam, and a sealed envelope with writing on it.

Izabella studied the envelope silently, then she handed it to Marie to read. "It is for you, Mama, but it says that Aunt Magda should keep it until tomorrow. We are not to open it until then." Marie looked puzzled.

Aunt Magda took the envelope and slipped it into the bodice of her dress. She smiled at Izabella. "I will be happy to keep it for you."

Josif scowled at the women. "There is no use hiding it. I will not take the money of the Ladies' Aid."

Aunt Magda's eyes flashed. "It is not your money to take or not take. It belongs to Izabella. Besides, how do you know what is in the envelope?"

"It is money. Why else would the woman seal it and ask you not to open it until tomorrow?"

Uncle Jon peeled the shell from a hardboiled egg. "Josif, you might as well give up. There is no way to fight against women when they band together. The big woman of the farm has beaten you, and there is no loss of your honor." He took a bite of the egg. "I salute the big woman. She would make a good colonel in the army."

Josif pushed the food away. "Give me some *mamaliga*. I will not eat the big woman's food, nor will I use her money. At the first town we come to you will all have new shoes, and they will be bought with our money, not with the money of the big woman, not with the money of the Ladies' Aid, but with our own money – money we have earned, not begged."

The next day they crossed the Niobrara River in the late afternoon and camped on its far side. The nights had become cold, and they slept in the wagon for the first time. They closed the ends of the wagon canopy by lacing more canvas into place, and they slept crowded and almost warm between the sacks of corn and oats.

The morning air had a sharpness that spoke of the coming winter, and all of them, except Josif, put on the warm sweaters they had been given, and as the coffee boiled, they hovered around the morning cooking fire, thankful for its warmth, and eating their breakfast of bread and smoked meat.

After traveling for several hours, they came to a small town, and Josif brought the whole family into the only shoe store. The proprietor, a large balding man wearing a leather apron, was hammering nails into a shoe at the back of the store. He looked up in surprise as the family trouped in, then he took a small handful of nails from between his lips and came to the front of the store, carefully looking everyone over as he approached.

"Somethin' I can do for you folks?" The man stared at Izabella as he spoke, his eyes going slowly from her face down her body to her feet.

"Everybody need new shoes," Josif said looking at the man with narrowed eyes. "Kids, women, men."

The man whistled. "Everybody?" He counted. "All nine of ya?"

Josif nodded. "Everybody. Want good shoes, strong shoes. Made good leather. Not cost too much."

The man looked at Izabella again. "Something in a dress shoe, maybe? Good-looking, but built to last."

"What you mean *dress shoe*?" Josif asked. "Can show us?"

"Sure, mister." The man pushed a wheeled ladder along the track that ran above the shelves of shoe boxes. He climbed up the ladder and brought down two boxes. He opened them and showed the shoes to the Dacias. One box held a black, shiny pair of men's low oxfords; the other, a pair of lady's patent leather high-heeled pumps.

Izabella gently touched one of the pumps' slender heels. "They are beautiful," she said softly.

"They're size 6," the man said. "Should just about fit that little foot of yours." He had Izabella sit down in a low chair as he squatted on a little stool before her. "We'll just try these on." He reached his hand out toward her foot.

Josif said harshly, "No. We want shoes for work." He pointed to his dilapidated work shoes. "This kind of shoes."

The proprietor looked quickly at Izabella. "Even for the ladies?" He smiled at her. "This little lady doesn't wanna be wearin' ugly shoes, do you?"

Josif scowled at him; he leaned toward the proprietor with clenched fists. "You do not tell me what my woman want!" He stepped between the man and Izabella. "How much shoes cost? You tell me now before we look at more shoes. Maybe we go different place. Not get cheated."

Izabella spoke up softly behind Josif. "He mean no harm, Josif. He not understand what we want."

Josif whirled around and slapped Izabella across the face, knocking her back in her chair and almost tipping it over, his face dark with rage. "Do not take the side of this stranger over me!" he spat at her in Romanian. He turned slowly back to the shoe salesman. "That slap meant for you, only harder, but if I hit you I have to kill you and I cannot take time to go to court over killing man like you."

The proprietor's face reddened as he stood up. "No one asked you to come in here. You better git outta here before I go get my shotgun in the back."

Josif spit on the floor, "Everybody get back in wagon." He hustled the family out the door, then turned back to the man, his eyes narrow with anger. "I always remember you, even if I see you ten years from now, I will know you!"

The man stepped threateningly toward him. "Get outta my store, mister. We don't need your kind around here."

Josif smiled at him. "I go." He went out, leaving the door open, and climbed up into the wagon where the family members stood silently, not looking at him. He clucked the team forward past the shoe store where the red-faced man glared out at them.

Josif could feel the shame and embarrassment of the family, but he said nothing to them. He drove down the main street of the town, looking straight ahead. A hot anger burned in him, an anger that grew as the silence in the wagon deepened.

He drove the team to the side of the street and stopped them. He pushed his way past the family and went to the end of the wagon where the oilcloth-wrapped trunk stood. He took off the oilcloth and opened the trunk. His hands searched under the embroidered blouses, the vests, the flowered skirts, the boots.

Uncle Jon said quietly, "Josif, don't do it."

Josif's hands found the knife. The feel of ancient death was in the gold-plated handle, in the curved sheath. He brought the knife out of the trunk. "He insulted me. He made free with my wife."

Izabella's face was pale. "It was my fault, Josif. I should not have touched the shoes. The man thought I wanted them. There was nothing more."

Josif looked around at the others. "The man should die. It is my right."

Uncle Jon came slowly toward him. He put his hand on Josif's arm. "The man is not worth killing, Josif. He does not know our ways."

The anger was heavy in Josif, heavy and cold now, like a stone. The knife was calling out for blood, for vengeance.

Uncle Jon held out his hand. "Give me the knife, Josif."

Josif felt the eyes of the family on him. "You know the ways of our people. If a man touches another man's wife, he may be killed."

"He did not touch Izabella, Josif, and we are in a new country. The ways are different here."

A stillness, a waiting, hung in the wagon.

We are in a new country. Uncle Jon's words rang in Josif's ears. He put the knife in Uncle Jon's hand. "I will not kill this man, but if ever again a man tries to touch my wife as that man did, I will kill him."

They moved then, silently, carefully around him, not wanting the terrible anger to return. Uncle Jon put the knife back under the clothing and wrapped the oilcloth around the trunk again, then went to Josif. "I was saving that *tuica* for when we got to the Missouri River. This might be a good time for a little taste."

Josif shook his head. "It is not *tuica* that I need. It is for people to not treat us like beggars, or like peasants whose women they can make free with."

Uncle Jon put his hand on Josif's shoulder. "It has been a long road. I think we have almost come to the place we seek. Things will be better then."

Josif did not look at the women where they knelt below the wagon-box, hiding themselves from the gaze of an old man who watched the wagon from the board sidewalk. "I hope so, Uncle. I hope so. But I should have killed the man."

* * *

Verne Lamb blamed the Centerford bank when he learned that his wife, Belle, had terminal cancer, and his anger grew.

The same day that Josif Dacia took his grandfather's knife from the trunk, Verne received a letter from his Uncle Clarence in Chicago. The letter read:

Dear Vernon,

I might be bringing some big equipment back your way in the spring. If I do, Vincent will come with me, and we will set up an operation that will expand your business considerably. I expect you to cooperate in every way. Keep this aspect quiet. If anybody talks I will be very unhappy.

Your Uncle, Clarence

Verne read the letter twice, then tore it up and threw it in the kitchen stove. He went out to the big hay barn which held his still, and he looked at his still and cursed, the anger and frustration in him about to explode.

He did not want to see his uncle and brother again, and resented their intrusion into his life. He would not be turning over his farm and operation to the likes of them. Verne eyed his shotgun on the wall, and thought that he might soon have to use it.

The Dacias went on to the north. Strangely, the weather grew warmer, and a golden haze in the air made it seem almost like summer again.

Without knowing it, they crossed into South Dakota, only finding out when they came into the small town of Colome. They found a shoe store run by an old couple who fussed over the children and fitted them with sturdy lace-up oxfords.

Izabella would not come into the store, and Aunt Magda had to carry shoes out to the wagon for her to try on, both of them finally choosing for themselves low-heeled *sensible* shoes with cross straps. Uncle Jon and Josif bought heavy work shoes, high-topped with hooks for the top laces. At the recommendation of the white-haired owners, they bought high, four-buckle rubber overshoes for everyone.

"If you folks plan to spend the winter around here, you have to keep your feet protected, or you'll freeze your toes right off. Thirty or forty below, it gets," the woman informed them. "And keep your ears covered up. Once they start to freeze, you don't even feel 'em, and then it's too late." She shook her finger at the children. "You watch each others' ears. If they start to turn white, get into a house right away. Then rub snow on 'em 'til they thaw out."

Josif took out his wallet. "We pay for things now, then we go find Missouri River."

The man totaled up their bill. "That'll come to forty-nine dollars and forty cents." He rang the money up in the cash register. "Any particular part of the Missouri River you folks are lookin' for?" he asked.

Josif pulled the map from his overalls' pocket. "We look for good farmland by Missouri River. You tell us which is best way from here to find good land?"

"You mean black dirt farming? Corn, hogs, oats? You wanna raise crops?"

Josif nodded. "That what we want. Good soil, nice and black. Plenty rain. Everything green."

The man looked curiously at Josif. "What gave you folks the idea that you would find that kinda land around here, if you don't mind me askin'?"

"We look at map. We saw how Missouri River come across whole country. Must be much water in it. Everything green. Good farmland."

The man looked quickly at his wife, then back at Josif. "I don't wanna discourage you folks, but I'm afraid that isn't quite the way it is." He pointed to the map. "This country here west of the river is more cattle country than it is farmland. The soil isn't that rich, and we don't get a whole lotta rain. People come out here and try to raise corn and oats, and it just don't work. Some wheat is raised west a here, but it has to be a pretty big operation to succeed."

Josif stared at him. "Not green farms here?"

The man shook his head. "Not here. There's plenty a water in the Missouri River, but it just flows on down into the Mississippi and into the Gulf of Mexico." He pointed to the map again. "There is pretty good farm country over east a the river, south a Sioux Falls, and on east into Iowa. The Corn Belt, they call it. They tell me there's black topsoil maybe ten feet deep in some places there. When they get enough rain, they get maybe fifty or sixty bushels a corn per acre."

The Dacias looked excitedly at the map. "How far is to this place? Josif asked, "I think we go there right now."

The man traced a line of roads on the map with his finger. "It's about thirty miles over to Lucas, and another ten to the Smoke Creek ferry where you cross the Missouri. From there, it's prob'ly another hundred miles or more before you get into real good farmland. If I were you, I'd head straight east from Platte, or go down to Lake Andes, here, and then head east."

"We look for farm to rent. You think any in this place where soil so good?"

"There should be. Trouble is, most farms rent from about the middle of March. Everybody sorta stays put durin' the winter." The man looked up at Josif. "Before I started out goin' very far this time a year, I'd sure think about the weather. I'd have some place in mind to stay if an early blizzard came along."

Josif looked out through the store window at the clear blue sky and the sunshine. "We go east, hope find nice farm empty now." He shook hands with the man and his wife. "You nice people. We thank you."

They went out with the packages of their new shoes and overshoes to the wagon where Aunt Magda waited with Izabella.

They climbed up into the wagon, and Josif clucked the horses forward. As Izabella admired their new shoes, and as Uncle Jon told the two women about the conversation with the shoe store owner, Josif guided the team out of the little town and east toward the Missouri River.

They came to the river around noon two days later. It flowed between eroded bluffs, winding in a broad, sinuous path through the prairie. It held a somber beauty that was strange to the family; the water was a flat brown, almost the color of the sloping banks. Sandbars and small islands gave it the appearance of shallowness, yet a feeling of hidden power came from the swift-moving, muddy water.

They waited with other wagons for the ferry to slowly cross the river to their side. When Josif had driven Peter, Paul, and the wagon on-board, the whole family came down out of the wagon to watch the water sweep by the bow of the ferry.

Izabella hugged the girls to her. "Now we will soon come to the green farm where you can have tea parties in the trees and where we will have flowers and green grass. It will be beyond those hills to the east, waiting for us." It was the first time since Josif struck her that her voice sounded happy.

Aunt Magda took her hand. "And you will have a house of your own. A house where there will be music and singing and happiness."

Josif stood alone by the horses, holding their bridles, not wanting to be with the others. Ever since the time of his anger he had felt a sense of shame, guilt, and solitude. The rest of the family were careful not to offend him in any way or get too close to him, as though he were an angry bull, and none of them except Uncle Jon would look directly at him. Even Michael-Joseph seemed afraid of him, and at night Izabella was silent and motionless beside him in the blankets.

Uncle Jon came to stand beside him. "We have come to the river we sought. You have done well to bring us all here safely, Josif. Soon now the long journey will be over."

Josif stared out at the water. Uncle Jon touched his arm. "Josif, Izabella saved you from killing that man. She took your anger upon herself. Not for the man, but for you."

Josif looked at Uncle Jon. "I know that now. Then, I thought only of my honor, of how the man looked at her, of how he spoke to her. Now it is done, and there is more sadness in her."

As they spoke, the ferry approached the east bank of the river, and the family members came back to the wagon. Alexander and Michael-Joseph were wide-eyed with excitement. "A man told us there are Indians camped on the hills south of here. Can we go see them, Papa?"

Josif shook his head. "There is not time. We must still travel a long way to the east. Remember what the man said about the winters here."

A man standing near the wagon spoke to Josif. "Tell your boys the Indians ain't worth seein', mister." He was a little, whiskered man with beady eyes. He spat tobacco juice over the railing of the ferry. "Back in 1890 the cavalry took care of about three hundred of 'em over west a here. Place called Wounded Knee. Wiped 'em out with Hotchkiss guns. Good riddance, if ya ask me."

They drove off the ferry and up the long slope of the bluff, and as they came up onto the level ground, they saw waving prairie grass stretching ahead of them as far as they could see.

They came to the town called Platte and studied their map, looking for the best way to travel east. Lake Andes, Josif said. "The man mentioned that town. We will camp near there tonight, for if the bad weather comes, it would be best to be close to shelter." He folded the map and put it back in his pocket. "We will go east about seven miles, then south, then east again."

When they were about five miles east of Platte they saw a low bank of clouds rising up behind them in the northwest. The day was warm and the sun shone brightly down upon the prairie, yet now a strange chill came into the air. Uncle Jon studied the clouds. "They are not like the tornado. These clouds look cold." He spoke reassuringly to the women. "They are moving fast, but maybe they will not even come this way."

But the cloud bank did come toward them. It quickly filled the western sky, moving like a ragged gray blanket over the earth. The air became cold, and as the sun disappeared behind the approaching cloud bank, an icy wind swept out of the northwest.

Aunt Magda crossed herself. "It is like the winter wind from the Carpathian Mountains."

They put on their warm coats, caps, and scarves, and Uncle Jon and Alexander tied shut the canvas flap at the rear of the wagon to keep the wind from sweeping through.

Tiny flakes of snow appeared, moving almost horizontally, so small that they could hardly be seen. A heavy grayness filled the air, and Peter and Paul tossed their heads uneasily.

Josif took the map out and looked at it as he drove, trying to find the shortest route to the town of Lake Andes, while the snow grew heavier, so thick that as it swept past the wagon it obscured the low hills on either side.

Until now the snow had not stuck to the ground, but swirled over it; now it began to cover the road and whiten the prairie grass. Gradually the ditches, the road, and the land on either side of the wagon took on the same appearance as the swirling snow-filled air so that it seemed the wagon, the horses, and the people were not moving, but instead hung suspended in a world of blowing snow that had no boundaries, no limits, no end.

The wind became a howling demon that shrieked through the canvas cover, and the wagon rocked and shook like a ship in a heavy sea. The snow was so thick that Peter and Paul were barely visible, and the deep cold began to bite into the family.

They put on the woolen socks and the heavy shirts, sweaters and coats that had been given to them by the big Nebraska farm woman. They pulled their new overshoes over their shoes, thankful that they had them. But still the cold drove into them, and they wrapped blankets and tarpaulins around themselves, the adults holding the children sheltered in their arms.

And all the while, the snow drifted deeper. Josif strained to see beyond the horses, to see the road, the ditches, the fence lines, but there was only the roaring whiteness. Peter and Paul moved more and more slowly, their heads down, laboring to pull the wagon through the high drifts of snow that now blocked their way. Finally, the horses stopped. They stood motionless ahead of the wagon, almost invisible in the driving snow.

Josif gave the reins to Uncle Jon. "I will have to lead them." He climbed out of the shelter of the wagon cover down over the wheel, and was immersed in an icy, blinding, screaming whiteness that tore at him with furious strength.

Uncle Jon shouted down to him, his voice almost lost in the howling wind. "Come back in, Josif! You can't live out there!"

The wind sucked the air from Josif's lungs as he tried to answer, and the snow drove against his eyelids like birdshot as he turned into the wind to look back at the wagon. He groped his way forward along Paul's side, clutching the harness for support until he came to the horses' heads.

"Come. We will go together." He took the horses' bridles in his mittened hands and pulled them forward, and Peter and Paul followed, slowly, plunging in the deep snow. They went forward with the wagon, struggling for each yard gained, but going forward.

There was no end. There was only whiteness and wind and cold and struggling. No time or space, only the swirling whiteness through which they moved and did not move, forever the same. Then it seemed to Josif that a dark form walked before him, leading him, moving always just ahead of him, blurred and indistinct in the snow.

His mittens struck a solidness. He forced his ice-encrusted eyelids open. The thing was flat, a wooden wall with long, snow-filled, horizontal grooves.

He pulled himself back along Paul's side to the wagon, and Uncle Jon and Alexander came down to him. He shouted against the roar of the wind. "A building! We have come to a building! We need the rope!"

The women held the rope down to them and they struggled forward along the horses to the building. Josif tied one end of the rope around Alexander's waist, and the other end to the wagon tongue. Then they groped along the side of the building, around a corner, and along another side, and around another corner, and miraculously they were out of the full force of the wind.

They found a door and desperately pounded on it, but the only answer was the howling of the wind. Josif shouted to Uncle Jon, "We will have to break it down!"

Suddenly the door opened. A huge, bearded man looked down at them as if they had come from out of the earth. His eyes quickly softened and he threw his arms open in welcome. "God has brought you through the storm to us," he said warmly. "Willkommen."

Big, bearded men, moving strongly and quickly in the blizzard, brought the team and wagon and the women and children around to the sheltered side of the building. They helped the family into the house and had them sit near a great tile stove, giving them hot milk with pepper in it to drink.

With Josif, Uncle Jon and Alexander, they took Peter and Paul into a huge barn. They put the horses in a stall with clean straw on the floor and hay in the manger, and they gave each horse a bucket of warm water and a warm mash of ground barley. The barn was filled with other horses, and it held a homey animal smell and warmth.

Josif sensed only goodness here and was overcome with humble gratitude for their rescue. He realized that his entire family could have died, and thanked God from the deepest place in his heart.

The bearded men brought Josif, Uncle Jon, and Alexander back into the house, where they gave them hot milk with vodka and warmed them in front of the stove beside the women and children.

Other people were in the house now: more bearded men, and women; quiet, capable-looking women dressed in somber dresses and aprons, with polka-dotted scarves covering their hair. The women gently rubbed the hands and feet of the children until they were warm and pink, then shielded Izabella and Aunt Magda from the men's view with blankets and warmed them as they had the children. The men saw to

Alexander, Uncle Jon, and Josif, making sure they were not frostbitten.

"You have saved us from the storm, and warmed and cared for us," Josif said. "You speak a language that we know from our homeland in Romania. Will you tell us who you are so that when we thank God for your help we may know your names?"

The man who had first opened the door smiled at them. He gestured toward the people in the room. "Ve are the Hutterites."

Chapter Four
The Hutterites

Martin Vogel, the man who had first opened the door to Josif, came with four elders to the Dacias on the evening of their arrival.

Martin introduced the men: "This is Michael Schmitt, our assistant minister; David Sachs, our householder; Eli Rahn, our field manager; and Jacob Miller, our councilor. I am head minister."

The men shook hands with Uncle Jon and Josif, moving slowly with dignity, but with friendly eyes.

"Ve haf prayed to God," Martin Vogel said, "and talked seriously in council about your coming to us. It is our opinion that you should be allowed to remain viz us for the vinter, sharing our food and shelter, but ve must bring the matter before our membership."

"We cannot take your food for all the winter," Josif replied firmly.

Martin Vogel smiled at him. "Our leader, Jacob Hutter, said, 'You should gather in ven it is summer, so that in the extremely cold and dangerous time of vinter you will haf something to draw upon; ya, that you are clad and prepared and can draw out the treasure of your hearts.' Ve haf been diligent and haf done God's vill, and there is food in abundance in our store house, so you vould be no burden to us. Because you are not members of our Leut, our people, you vould not be allowed to vorship in our service, or take part in our decisions, but in all other vays you vould share our lives. This, of course, if you desire to do so, and if the membership approves."

"We thank you for your kindness" Josif said to the men. "If you had not taken us in we might have died. But we cannot repay you. When the storm is over, we will go east again."

"My dear friend," Martin said, "ve do not even think of payment. But you should be told the vays of our people. Here all vork together, sharing all that ve haf, all caring for one another. If you and your family stay viz us for the vinter, ve vill expect all of you to share in the vork of our colony, doing the daily tasks assigned by the leaders, living according to our vays. These may seem strange to you and your family, but they are just and goot. Even the children vill live as our children do, learning to love God and obey His vill."

Josif looked at Uncle Jon and the two women. He said to Martin, "We are true believers in the Holy Church. We believe in the seven mysteries, the seven sacraments. You should know this before you ask us to live with you."

Martin's face was unsmiling now. "Ve haf seen the crosses that you vear, and ve recognize that your beliefs are different from ours. This is a most serious matter, and for this reason ve must bring it before our entire membership." Then he smiled. "But ve know that you believe in God and in his son, Jesus Christ, as ve do. Between us, therefore, can be no great differences, ja? If this is of concern to you, however, please know that our people vill make no attempt to convert you or your family to our religious beliefs."

"It is important that our family talk about this before we decide," Josif said.

Martin nodded. "Ja, of course. Ve need decide nothing now, since you cannot possibly leave vile this blizzard rages outside. For the present, you vill be our guests. Ve haf varmed an apartment in one of our houses for you, and you vill haf your food brought to you. Your horses are varm in the barn, and our men haf brought your belongings in from your vagon. Now, to rest from your journey is all that you should do."

The householder, David Sachs, took the Dacias out through the blizzard to their apartment in one of the long houses near Martin Vogel's house. It consisted of an entry room, a kitchen, two bedrooms, and an attic. The kitchen contained a table and chairs, a washbasin, cupboard, and a stove. Two double beds stood in each of the bedrooms, each bed covered with a thick down-filled comforter.

"The rising bell vill be at 7:00," David Sachs informed them. "The breakfast bell vill be at 7:15. Because it has not yet been decided how you vill live in the colony, your food vill be brought to you here." He gestured to the table. "If you vill be seated here, the vimen vill bring your evening meal in just a few minutes." He left them, and went out into the storm.

Aunt Magda looked uncomfortable. "They are Anabaptists! Once they lived in Transylvania. There are terrible stories about them. They are said to steal children!"

Uncle Jon shook his head. "Those are tales told by old grandmothers in the chimney corners while the wind howls around the house. These are good people who have saved our lives."

A knocking sounded at the entry room door, and when Josif opened it, two women came into the kitchen along with a blast of frigid, snow-filled air. The women were bundled in heavy coats and scarves, and red-cheeked with the cold, but their faces were smiling and happy-looking. Each of them carried two large covered baskets.

"I am Katie; she is Jennie. Ve haf food for you," said the first one. "And you still haf your coats and overshoes on!" She shook a finger at them. "Surely you cannot leave in this storm. Now take your things off and sit down and eat."

Katie and Jennie took covered dishes from their baskets and put them on the table: two roast ducks on platters, serving dishes filled with mashed potatoes, gravy, string beans, and rolls, butter, a pitcher of milk, a dish of preserved plums, and two dusky bottles.

Katie smiled at the Dacias. "One is grape, one is rhubarb. Rhubarb is supposed to be the vine of the poor Bruderhof, ja? But ve like it better here."

She went to the cupboard and brought plates, glasses, and silverware.

"Now don't let your food get cold. Ve vill come back in an hour to get the dishes." The two women went out, pulling the doors shut against the wind and snow.

Uncle Jon picked up one of the bottles and pulled the cork from it. He sniffed the opening. "Josif, I think we have gone to heaven!" He put the bottle back on the table and took off his coat, scarf, and overshoes. "Now, ducks, watch out! A man comes to the table who three hours ago would have eaten his overshoes. Now you wait there all juicy and brown, swimming in your own sauce. I will wash you down with this wine from God, and then you will be followed by these potatoes, beans, bread and butter, plums, and milk."

Aunt Magda stared at the children and the ducks. She said softly, "Would the Lord forgive us if we ate their food?"

Izabella replied, "We have drunk their hot milk when we were freezing. Now the children and all of us are hungry. Surely God would not have us starve."

Josif smiled at her affectionately. "I think we should eat the food too, some of everything, all we can eat. Now, let us do as the lady said, take off our coats and overshoes, and sit down to the table!"

Later, they slept warm under the feather comforters, hearing the wind howl outside, knowing the ancient security of having shelter in a sturdy refuge during a storm. Izabella slept in Josif's arms, and they made love quietly and passionately while the blizzard tore at the house and shook the empty wagon. The snow drifted ever higher, and the deep cold made the bare trees crack in the darkness.

The family was awakened by the morning bell. A thermometer which could be seen from the entry room showed twenty degrees below zero, and the wind blew the snow in a blinding ground blizzard that almost hid the nearby buildings in the Hutterite community.

Each family member made the freezing visit to the nearby outhouse, Alexander going with Michael-Joseph to keep him from being lost in the storm, while Izabella and Aunt Magda took the girls.

At 7:15AM Katie and Jennie appeared with their baskets and placed a pot of hot coffee, a pitcher of warm milk, a platter of fresh rolls, a platter of fried eggs, and a great kettle of oatmeal on the table.

Katie was as happy and cheerful as she had been the night before. "Such a storm, and so early in the vinter! But it vill be goot for the crops – all this snow yet." She smiled at the family. "The members met last night. I think they haf decided to let you stay." She patted Michael-Joseph's head. "They are so serious about everything, those men. If ve vimen had anything to say about it, ve vouldn't even haf had to haf a meeting; ve just vould haf known that you could stay."

Aunt Magda raised her eyebrows. "The men make all the decisions?"

Jennie, answered. "Vimen are the veaker vessels. Ve cannot expect to make decisions. Only the council and the membership can do that."

Aunt Magda sniffed. "And only men can be on the council or in the membership, of course."

Jennie nodded. "Ja, of course. That is the vay it has always been. That is the vay it always vill be. It is best for the colony that vay."

Katie smiled. "Some of the vimen don't like it, but it keeps the men happy. Ve can still tell them vat ve think, so it vorks out for the best." She gestured toward the food on the table. "And here ve stand talking vile your coffee gets cold, and these poor little ones vait for their eggs and oatmeal! Come on, Jennie, ve must get back to the kitchen."

Later that morning Martin Vogel came to visit them. He stamped in out of the snow and sat down at the table with Josif and Uncle Jon. He was beaming with satisfaction.

"The membership has decided. You can stay viz us for the vinter!" He spread his arms as if to encompass the whole Dacia family. "The little ones vill go to our kindergarten, the older children to our English school, and to our German school if you vish them to. And you grown folk can vork viz us here in the colony, doing things of use to all." He smiled at them. "Now you need haf no feeling of being un-paying guests. You vill be almost like our own people."

Josif spoke slowly. "We thank you for your kindness. You are good people. But we are outsiders; we can never be truly part of your colony. We have talked among ourselves about this, and we will go on to the east when the weather improves."

Martin's face showed his disappointment. "My dear friends, I'm sad that you feel yourselves to be outsiders. Believe me, you vould not be treated as outsiders if you stay viz us. And vhere vill you go if you leave us? Haf you anyone you can stay viz if you do go east? The vinter has hardly begun, and your children may suffer greatly if you leave us. I ask you to reconsider, please."

Josif shook his head. "Is not right that we should eat your food when we did not help raise it. We will go when the weather clears."

Martin considered Josif over the top of his gold-rimmed eyeglasses. "Vill you promise me one thing? Vill you promise not to take your family away from here in your vagon if the veather is threatening? Ve vould never forgive ourselves if ve let you go out into a storm."

Josif looked at his family. "We will not go out into a storm. We promise you that."

"Goot!" Martin stood up. "I vill send the householder,

the field manager, and the head cook to talk viz you. As long as you are here, you vill become part of our community." He put his heavy coat back on and pulled on his overshoes. "I haf seen vinters here that vere one long blizzard. It may be that you vill be viz us until the end of March. Who can say? It is all in God's hands."

David Sachs, the householder, came first. He explained to the Dacias how the community operated. "Grownups eat in one dining hall, men on the left, vimen on the right. Children eat in another hall. Those below the age of six eat in the kindergarten for the morning and noon meal. The men vill be assigned vork by the field manager; the vimen by the head cook, Amanda Hofer. If you haf any questions or problems, see me."

"What about the school?" Josif asked. "We want our children to learn how to be good Americans, and to learn about America. Mr. Vogel talked about a German school and an English school. Can you explain that to us please?"

"The English school is the same as any rural school in South Dakota. The teacher is selected and paid by the school board, and the same courses are taught here as in other schools in the state. Ve feel that it is important for our children to know arithmetic and to know how to use the language of this country, and how to read. Ve allow no dancing in the school, nor may any pictures be on the valls. The German school is under our own supervision. Its function is to teach our children the ritual of life. I cannot discuss it further now vizout the approval of our head minister."

Josif considered this. "We want our children to go to the school where they will learn what is required in this state. We cannot let them go to the German school if it teaches a religion different from our own."

Later in the day, the field manager, Eli Rahn, came and explained to Josif and Uncle Jon how and where they would report for work assignments each morning.

"In vinter, it is easier. Ve repair the machinery, take

care of the animals, milk the cows, build furniture, clean seed for spring planting, and do anything else that is needed. I haf seen how you care for your horses, and it might be vell to start you both out in the horse barn." He nodded toward Alexander. "If your boy is not in the German school, he could help viz the horses too, or maybe vork viz the men on the machinery. It vould be good experience for him."

* * *

The head cook, Amanda Hofer, was a cheerful, plump woman. She brought coffee and rolls when she came to talk with Izabella and Aunt Magda, and as they sat at the table together she explained the work system.

"The men haf it easy in the vinter. Ve vimen vork hard all through the year, cooking, baking, vashing dishes, butchering ducks and chickens, caring for the children, vorking in the kindergarten, vashing clothes, sewing and scrubbing floors; but it is not more than ve can stand." She sipped her coffee.

"Ve rotate the vork each veek so that no one is too long on the hard jobs, like the bun maker who must be up at 4:30 each morning. Ve all do our family vashing and ironing together on Mondays, everything is scrubbed on Fridays, and everyone bathes on Saturday to get ready for the Sabbath. You vill be supplied viz cloth to make clothing for your family, and there is even a cobbler who makes and mends shoes." She smiled at the two women. "I'm sure none of the tasks vill be new to you, ja?" Izabella and Aunt Magda nodded in agreement.

Martin Vogel had been right about the weather. Blizzard after blizzard roared over the Hutterite colony through December, January, and February – huge storms that swept down from Canada and across Wyoming, Montana and the Dakotas. The temperature dropped as low as forty degrees below zero, and for a period of six weeks it never rose above zero, so that the Hutterites would not hear of letting the Dacias take the children east in the wagon.

* * *

On February 14, 1929, Saint Valentine's Day, a black Cadillac stopped at the door of the SMC Cartage Co. warehouse in North Side, Chicago. Four men went inside. Two were dressed as policemen. The policemen carried Tommy guns and the men in suits carried shotguns. Seven of Bugs Moran's men had been lured there and were lined up against the wall. The phony policemen tore them into bloody horrors with their submachine guns, then the two men in civilian clothes shot them in the faces with their shotguns.

TOMMY GUN

As the real police arrived, the fake police escorted the men in suits out at gunpoint, and into a waiting car.

None of the four were ever identified, and to keep it that way, C.D. Lamb decided Vince and he should visit his nephew's farm near Centerford, South Dakota, as soon as possible.

As the Lambs were not Italian, they would never be *made men* and absorbed into a *family*. They were only *associates*, and therefore expendable. They had made good money with the mob, but now it was time to break ties, and leave.

C.D. had sweetened his departure from the South Side Italians by stealing a lock-box of gold, jewels, and cash from Primo Moretti, who was currently in Leavenworth Federal Penitentiary. Primo was the boss of a mob family, and had many resources at his disposal. The sooner C.D.'s and Vince's trails went cold, the better.

* * *

With each new storm, the Dacias became more restless. They were treated well in the colony, yet the restrictions under which the people lived seemed oppressive to them, and they longed for the freedom of the open road, or the chance to make their own decisions on a farm of their own, however poor it might be.

Josif spoke to the field manager about finding a farm, and Eli let him borrow a farm magazine to which the colony subscribed. Advertisements in the back of the magazine told about land for sale or rent, and the family eagerly studied and discussed each one as they sat around their table after the day's work. One advertisement became of particular interest to them. It read:

> *For rent, with possibility of purchase: Quarter section farm in eastern South Dakota, near Centerford. Buildings, four-bedroom house with some furniture and two stoves. Farm machinery on premises. P.O. Box 39, Centerford, S. Dak.*

Josif obtained an envelope and paper from the house-holder, and with Alexander's and Eli's help, wrote a letter to the address in Centerford.

On one of the rare days when it was possible to go into the town ten miles away, Eli and one of the younger men, David Hofer, drove the colony's big truck in for supplies. They took Josif with them so that he could mail the letter.

Eli let Josif out at the post office. As Josif was buying a stamp from the man behind the counter, the man looked closely at Josif and remarked, "You Hoots don't get into town much, do ya? We ain't seen ya all winter."

"I not speak English good. What you mean 'Hoots'?"

The man stared at him. "Hoots. Hutterites. Ain't you heard that before? I seen you get outta that Hoot truck. Ain't you one of 'em?"

78

"They good people," Josif said. "We lost in blizzard, they take us in their house. Children freeze if they not help us."

"I'll bet they took you in. You'd better watch out for your kids. Them Hoots'll try to get 'em into their colony. Damned shirkers, wouldn't fight in the war."

Josif paid the man for the stamp. "Letter come for me here, you keep? I come back, maybe week from now."

"How the hell am I supposed to know it's for you? Is it gonna have your picture on it?" The man pushed a scrap of paper and a pencil toward Josif. "Here, write your name on this. You can write, can't ya?" He winked at a big farmer standing at the next counter. "I ain't too sure about anybody that would live with them Hoots."

On the way home Josif mentioned the man in the post office to Eli Rahn and David Hofer. Eli's face was stern as he explained to Josif.

"Our people haf been persecuted in every country ve haf lived in because of our faith and principles. Moravia, Hungary, Transylvania, Vallachia, Russia, and now America. People cannot understand our views of the Christian life. In America it vas not so bad until they expected our young men to kill for them in the var. Var is a violation of Christian principles. Our young men died in army prisons, but they vould not give in. Ve haf never been forgiven or accepted because of this," David Hofer said bitterly. "They vere tortured to death. My Uncle Michael vas one of them. He died in Fort Leavenworth, but he never gave up his Bible."

Josif said no more about the matter to Eli and David, and when they were back at the colony, he did not speak of it to the family, but there was a feeling of anger in him that the good people who had saved their lives should have been so persecuted in America, the land of the free.

The family waited each day for a reply to Josif's letter, hoping that someone from the colony would be able to get into town again to ask at the post office. Finally, in late February, the weather cleared and Eli took the big truck into town once more. When he returned, he had a letter for Josif. The return address on the envelope read, The First State Bank, Centerford, S. Dak.

The whole family gathered around Josif at the table as he opened the envelope. The letter inside was typewritten on stiff, white paper. Alexander read it slowly out loud to the family:

> *Dear Mr. Dacia,*
> *I have received your letter of February 17, 1929, and am pleased to tell you that the farm with buildings and machinery mentioned in your letter is still available for rent or sale. Rent would consist of one-half (50%) of the crops raised on the farm each year. The owner, The First State Bank of Centerford, will pay the annual taxes of two hundred dollars ($200) per year. The renter will furnish all seed, labor, and horse or tractor power, and is required to work the land according to accepted practices of good farming. If you desire to purchase the farm, the present price is thirty-two hundred dollars ($3200) cash. The First State Bank is prepared however, to offer a mortgage for purchase of the farm at terms mutually acceptable to the bank and the purchaser. Please contact me as soon as possible if you wish to rent or purchase the farm. Moving date is March 15.*
>
> *Sincerely yours,*
> *Alan W. Johnson, President,*
> *First State Bank of Centerford*

The family stared at the letter. It was if they could see the farm in the paper, a green farm with black earth and fields of golden grain. They had Alexander read the letter again, to make sure there was no mistake. They brought Eli Rahn in and had him read the letter, watching him with eager eyes, fearful that he would find they had misinterpreted the letter's meaning.

Eli read the letter twice through, slowly. He sat back in his chair and studied the envelope, then he read the letter again. Finally, he looked up at them.

"There is no telling vat kind of farm it is, how goot the land is, how old the buildings, vat shape the machinery is in. It sounds to me like a farm that the bank has foreclosed on and is having trouble renting. You should be very careful. Bankers can take every penny a man has, and squeeze him for more then."

He frowned, thinking. "There is not much time before March 15th. It is not goot to decide such things too quickly, but you vill haf to let the banker know soon if you vant the farm. Still, I vould be very careful."

"What if we only rent the farm?" Josif asked. "What could we lose then, except our work?"

Eli nodded. "That vould be safer. Find out how good the farm is before you buy. The rent is fair enough; it's vat people pay around here if they haf no machinery." He looked at the letter again. "The bank president himself is handling this. Either it is a very small bank, or he has some personal interest in this farm. Something seems a little strange about the whole thing, but I can't quite say vat it is."

"Do you think we should look for another farm?" Josif asked with some trepidation.

Eli shook his head. "It's too late in the year now, ja? This heavy snow has blocked roads all over the state, and ven it melts, there's going to be mud. By the time you can get over into the corn country viz your family, most of the farms vill be rented already."

Eli had given the family a battered map of South Dakota, and they spread it out on the table and bent over it, studying the roads between the colony and Centerford. Uncle Jon looked thoughtful. "Is there a railroad?" he asked. "Somehow, the mail must have come through. Josif could go and look at the farm, then we could decide."

Eli answered, "There are railroads. Josif could take the train to Sioux Falls, and then go down to Centerford from there. It vould be expensive, but it could be done."

Josif shook his head. "We will need every penny to buy seed. A letter is cheaper. All we have to do is make up our minds." He looked around at the adults. "I think we should rent this farm. It has machinery, buildings, a house, and the bank president himself has written us this letter offering us the farm."

Uncle Jon agreed. "What more could we want? The land is there, waiting for us."

Izabella and Aunt Magda agreed. "Yes! Rent the farm! Write a letter, tell the bank man we are coming!" Aunt Magda said gleefully.

Josif looked at Eli Rahn, "What do you think? We are new in this state, in this country. Will we make a mistake if we rent the farm?"

Eli scratched his chin. "Who can say? Ve of the colony vould never rent or buy land vizout seeing it. But it is different for you and your family, because you may haf to agree to take this farm in order to haf any farm at all." He thought for a moment. "Suppose you write to the man at the bank. Tell him you vould like to rent the farm, but until you can come to see it, that it vill not be for certain. He should understand about the veather and the roads. Tell him that you vill come as soon as the roads are clear."

Josif agreed that this was the best plan, and with Eli's help wrote another letter to the bank president. Two days later, Eli took the letter into town and mailed it. It was the twenty-seventh of February.

Chapter Five
Making for Home

On March second the spring thaw began. The temperature rose to fifty degrees above zero, and the high drifts of snow that stretched to the southeast from every building, tree and fence row began to soften and melt. The sun shone down in dazzling brightness on the white landscape, and black earth started to show through in the fields. The creeks and rivers rose and lifted the thick sheets of ice which had covered them, so that there was the sound of grinding, cracking ice, and flowing water both day and night.

The Dacias were like geese waiting to migrate. Each day they walked out to the road testing its firmness, and they went over their wagon and gear, greasing the wheels, tightening loose bolts, replacing worn or weak ropes, oiling their harnesses, trimming Peter and Paul's hoofs, sorting their sacks of corn and oats, and collecting their tools and equipment.

By March 11th they could wait no longer, and they hitched the team to the wagon and loaded it early in the morning, before breakfast. As soon as they had eaten, they said goodbye to Martin Vogel and the other Hutterites, and went out to the wagon.

They could not believe what they saw. A red and white cow stood tied behind a small two-wheeled cart which had been attached to the end of the wagon, a crate of chickens was lashed to the tailgate, and in a stout pen in the cart a fat young sow grunted excitedly. A large pile of hay and sacks of grain lay in the cart along with the sow's pen.

Twelve bottles of wine in a box with straw tucked around the bottles and four thick feather comforters nestled in the wagon by the Dacias' trunks and boxes.

All of the people of the Hutterite community gathered around the wagon, smiling. Martin Vogel spoke. "The cow is for milk for the children. The chickens are for the ones the tornado took. The sow is for the future, for she should haf a litter of pigs in late April. The vine and comforters are for varmth and health." He beamed at them. "You are like a new colony setting forth, and ve always see that they are provided for."

Josif tried to protest, but Martin would not hear him. "You haf all earned it. You haf vorked hard vile you vere viz us. Besides, ve haf so many cows, pigs, and chickens that ve can hardly count them, and these vill not be missed." He shook Josif's hand, then Uncle Jon's. "I hope the farm you go to is a good one." He handed Josif a bag. "Here is some seed corn. Let us know how it does in that black soil."

Katie came forward from the group of women. She gave another bag to Izabella. "These are garden seeds. Some seed potatoes and onions and garlic too. Think of us ven you harvest them, ja?"

Izabella's eyes filled with tears as she hugged Katie. "How can we ever forget you? You have been so good to us."

The other women and the Hutterite girls came then and hugged Izabella, Aunt Magda, the girls, and Michael-Joseph. The boys shook hands with Alexander; they were sober in their black hats, saying little, but their eyes showed their friendship.

The Dacias climbed up into the wagon and Josif clucked the team forward. The family members waved at their new friends as they went out between the orderly rows of buildings and into the road, the same road down which Josif had blindly led the horses through the blizzard almost four months before. They went west for half a mile, then they turned south onto the county road which would bring them to the main road leading east toward their new farm.

The Hutterite settlement with its rows of houses, barns, and sheds grew smaller behind them, but it seemed they could still see the people waving to them, even when the buildings were so far away that they looked like a collection of tiny dollhouses in the distance.

The Dacias traveled east for five days. They were so used to the regimentation and sober discipline of the Hutterites that at first they journeyed silently, keeping track of the time with Josif's nickel-plated watch, half-expecting the rising bell and the meal bell to summon them, almost afraid to raise their voices.

Finally, Uncle Jon could stand it no longer. "They were good people, but it was hard not to be able to play our instruments, or to sing or dance. Now we are like Gypsies again; it is time to sing!" He began the folk melody by George Enescu called *Maidens Fair* and the others joined in, their voices blending with the jingling of the horses' harness bells:

> *The maidens fair, we love them all.*
> *Tra la la, la la la la.*
> *No matter whether short or tall.*
> *Tra la la la la la la.*
> *To all maidens let us sing,*
> *Sing until the rafters ring!*
> *Tra la la la la la la la. Tra la la la la la.*
> *The sweetheart that I love the best,*
> *tra la la la la la,*
> *Is nicer far than all the rest.*
> *Tra la la, la la la la.*
> *When she says she'll marry me,*
> *Oh, how happy I will be!*
> *Tra la la la la la la la. Tra la la la la la.*

As the family sang, the horses pricked up their ears and walked more briskly, and even the red and white cow came more willingly, not pulling back on her halter rope, but stepping along behind the wagon as though she too looked forward to their new home.

They camped at night along the road, sleeping in the wagon together for warmth, snug under the featherbeds the Hutterites had given them. The weather stayed mild, but a blustery March wind blew out of the west, reminding the family that the weather could still turn bad.

As they went farther east the farms became more prosperous looking: bigger barns and houses, most with a freshly painted look, more cribs of yellow corn, stacks of hay, big straw piles, cattle, horses and sheep in the pastures, and in general, an appearance of well-being and abundance.

On the sixth day, at about 1:00 in the afternoon, they sighted the town of Centerford. It lay on the dark land ahead of them in the midst of farms and fields, a wide grouping of buildings surrounded by bare maple and cottonwood trees, with a tall water tank and grain elevators rising above the trees.

As they came closer they could see the letters, "CENTE" on the side of the water tank facing them, and as they approached the outskirts of the town, a sign by the side of the road announced in large letters:

> "WELCOME TO CENTERFORD
> THE BIGGEST LITTLE TOWN
> WEST OF THE MISSISSIPPI
> POPULATION 3043"

Josif guided Peter and Paul into the town and down the main street which ran north and south between two long rows of false-fronted wooden and brick buildings. The street was paved with concrete, and the horses' hoofs clopped loudly as they pulled the wagon and the cart along between the lines of automobiles that were parked on either side.

Because of the warmth of the morning, Josif and Uncle Jon had taken the canvas cover off the wagon, and people stared at the Dacias from the sidewalks and store entrances. There were farmers in work clothes, but also well-dressed townspeople, the women in short, colorful skirts and coats, with shiny silken legs and high-heeled shoes, the men in business suits, or in fancy jackets and pants with wide-brimmed hats and flowered neckties.

Izabella and Aunt Magda sank down behind the shelter of the wagon-box, so ashamed of their appearance in their drab coats, long skirts, kerchiefs, and muddy overshoes that they tried to hide from the view of the townspeople.

They went by the buildings, searching for the bank. Signs on windows and storefronts said: Miller's Variety Store; Al's Cafe; The Egyptian Theater; The Corner Drug Store; Harold's Grocery; and Thompson's Shoes.

A big man with a prominent stomach stepped off the sidewalk ahead of the Dacias and walked into the middle of the street, holding up one hand importantly. A shiny metal star glittered on his chest, and he wore a white cowboy hat, a black leather vest, striped pants, and cowboy boots. A heavy pistol in a black leather holster hung low on his right hip. His thick, pugnacious-looking face, heavy-jowled like a bulldog, scowled at the Dacias.

"Where're you people from, a zoo? You can't bring all this livestock down Main Street. There's a law against it. This street's for cars and people." He stared at the horses, the chickens, the pig in the cart, and finally at the cow. "There's a place for teams over behind the blacksmith shop. Now get this circus off the street before they mess it all up!"

Josif nodded. "We do that right away, soon as we find bank first."

"You ain't finding any bank first. I want this menagerie moved off the street, now!" The man tapped his star. "Maybe you ain't noticed this. I happen to be the town marshal."

He smacked his hand down on Peter's hip. "Now move this outfit."

"You not should hit Peter," Josif said. "He will make mess in street."

It was true. Peter looked back at the marshal, then he raised his tail and deposited a long series of juicy yellow turds on the pavement at the marshal's feet. Josif clucked to the horses and slapped the reins lightly on their backs.

"Every time he get excited, he do that. We better go before Paul get excited too, and maybe cow." He looked back at the marshal as the wagon moved forward. "We thank you for telling us about street. We not bring horses here again."

The marshal stared down at the horse manure spattered on his boots, then ran after the Dacias, pulling his revolver from its holster. He aimed the gun at Josif. "You're under arrest. I told you it was against the law to bring livestock down Main Street. Now climb down offa that wagon. There's a ten dollar fine or you can spend the night in jail."

Josif stopped the team. "I not know about your law."

"It don't make no difference whether you knew about it or not. What'll it be? Ten dollars or jail?"

Josif spoke in Romanian to the family. "I will never give this man ten dollars." He gave his wallet to Uncle Jon. "Take the team to the blacksmith shop and go with Alexander to buy what food we need, then get out of this town. When I get out of the jail tomorrow, I will meet you by the blacksmith shop."

The marshal shouted, "Don't think you're pullin' anything on me with your foreign gabble. Now hand over ten dollars or climb down outta that wagon!"

Josif handed the reins to Uncle Jon and climbed down over the wagon wheel. He said to the marshal, "I come to jail."

The jail was downstairs in the courthouse. The marshal slammed the door of the one big cell behind Josif. "You damned foreigners think you can come in here and do any damned thing you feel like. Not in my town you can't. Now just shut up and behave in there or I'll keep you in till you learn some manners."

A small man lay on one of the wooden benches in the cell. When the marshal had gone, he sat up and looked at Josif. The man made Josif think of a friendly squirrel, a squirrel with a round brown face and brown almond eyes. He had shaggy eyebrows pointed upward like a squirrel's ears over his eyes. The man smiled at Josif. "I'm Crazy Conklin. Why'd Fat Fred put you in here?"

Josif sat down on the bench next to Conklin. "We bring horses down street. Peter make manure on marshal's boots."

Crazy Conklin was silent for a moment, then he said to Josif, "I like you and your horse. Fat Fred doesn't like me 'cause I get drunk. I wish I'd seen your horse crap on Fat Fred's boots." He smiled. "Fat Fred's prob'ly down in Elmer Eggert's barber shop right now gettin' 'em polished." He looked up toward the small barred window in the cell. "I can hide where nobody can see me. I can hide like a fox." He held out his hand to Josif. "I like you. We'll be friends."

Josif shook Crazy Conklin's hand, "My name is Josif Dacia. I glad be your friend."

The marshal opened the door from the outer office. "I been listenin' to what you two been sayin' in here, and I don't want any more of it." He gestured angrily to Crazy Conklin. "Get over here. I'm bootin' you out; settin' here gabbin' with this here foreigner." He opened the cell door and helped Conklin out with a kick.

"Get on out. You get drunk again I'm gonna have you sent up to Redfield to the insane asylum." He glared at Josif. "Now shut up. I don't want to hear any more outta you."

Josif was released from the jail the following day at 1:00. Before he left, a big man dressed like a farmer but wearing a star came to the cell. He handed Josif a safety razor, a bar of soap, and a towel.

"The blade's a new one. Get cleaned up before you leave, and keep outta the marshal's way if you plan to be in town long."

When Josif came out of the courthouse, he hurried to the blacksmith shop. The family was there, behind the shop, waiting for him in the wagon. They had put the cover back on, and they all watched him from its shelter as he came toward them.

The look of relief and happiness on their faces made Josif's heart swell. Uncle Jon and Alexander came down out of the wagon and ran to him, and Uncle Jon shook his hand vigorously. "You are out of the jail! Holy Mother of God, that fat marshal should have his throat slit! These women have been mourning all night, sure that you would never get out. Tell us, Josif, have you killed the marshal? How did you get out so soon?"

"I have not killed the marshal, but I would have liked to. Another man, a good man, gave me a razor to shave with and then let me out." He smiled at all of them. "Now I will go to the bank of Mr. Johnson and find out about the farm." He left the family and went back to Main Street, looking for the First State Bank.

The bank stood two blocks down from the courthouse corner, a two-story brick building with white stone trim around the wide doorway and the windows. The steps leading up into the doorway were also of white stone, hollowed just a little where people's feet had worn them down on either side of a shiny brass railing mounted in the center.

Josif entered the lobby, and it smelled of ink and paper, floor wax, and polished wood. Marble tables with pens on them lined one wall, and behind a marble counter and iron grillwork Josif saw two women.

One woman had a stern face and stiff-looking waves in her hair. The other woman made Josif think of a flower, her blue eyes and lovely face the center, her short golden hair the petals. She looked up at Josif. "May I help you?" she asked.

Josif took off his hat and held it in both hands. "Mr. Johnson send us letter about farm. I am Josif Dacia."

The woman's eyes widened, just for a moment, then she smiled at him. She had good teeth, and she was even more beautiful when she smiled. "Mr. Dacia! Mr. Johnson was just asking this morning if there had been any more letters from you. I'm sure he will want to talk with you."

She came out through a little door at the side of the marble counter, and Josif detected a delicate scent of wildflowers. "Let me just go and tell Mr. Johnson you're here."

She tapped on the door and partly opened it, then went into the room, quietly closing the door.

In a moment, she came out, smiled at Josif again and came toward him. "Mr. Johnson will see you now, Mr. Dacia. Please come with me." She led him to the open door, her heels tapping lightly on the polished floor. She smiled at him. "Please go right in."

A man rose from behind a huge mahogany desk as Josif came into the room. He was big, tall, and broad-shouldered, with a look of youth and strength about him. His face was not what Josif had expected of a banker; it was dark and hawklike, handsome as a Hungarian dancer. He wore a clean white shirt with a dark blue necktie and dark trousers. His eyes were dark blue under straight black eyebrows, and his dark hair was combed back.

He came around the desk, moving easily, his hand held out to Josif, a clean hand with neatly trimmed fingernails.

"Mr. Dacia! I am Alan Johnson. We have been hoping that you would make it through the snow drifts and mud!" He moved a chair forward. "Sit down, please. Tell me about your trip, and how is your family?"

Josif hesitated, then sat down."Trip was slow, but no problems came. Family is all healthy."

Mr. Johnson went back behind his desk and sat down in the big leather chair. He smiled at Josif. "And now you are here." He opened a drawer in his desk and took out several sheets of paper. "Let me give you this county map. I have marked the location of the farm so that you can find it." He laid the map on the desktop and traced on it with his finger. "This will keep you off the main roads. Go north out of town a mile, then four miles west, then three miles north. The farm buildings are just on the other side of a small creek, here, on the east side of the road." He made a small "X" mark with a pencil.

Josif studied the map. "Farm is still for us, then? We can rent it?"

Mr. Johnson nodded. "The offer is still open. The farm is yours to rent or buy, whichever you prefer."

"We think we like to rent first. Find out how farm is."

"Very wise, Mr. Dacia, very wise. Too many farmers are not so prudent. They buy land that they know nothing about, they overextend themselves in securing loans and in buying machinery; they do not use good judgement. That's the secret, Mr. Dacia, good judgement. I'm pleased to see that you and your family have it." Mr. Johnson glanced toward the door. "Speaking of your family, did you bring them with you here to the bank?"

Josif shook his head. "They stay in wagon behind blacksmith shop."

"That's too bad. I'd like to meet your wife and those children. And you have your aunt and uncle with you, too, don't you?"

"We do, but excuse please, how you know so much about us?"

Mr. Johnson smiled. "Mr. Dacia, I'm a banker. It's my business to protect the interests of the bank. I've learned much about you from correspondence with Martin Vogel, the leader of the Hutterite colony in which you spent the winter. He has told me only good things about you and your family." He indicated the other papers he had brought from the desk drawer. "These letters are the finest recommendations you could have."

He got up from his chair and went to the door of his office. "Miss Olson, will you bring in the lease papers for Mr. Dacia, please?"

Josif turned his hat in his hands. "I think we see farm first, before sign."

Mr. Johnson smiled down at him. "Of course you should. I just want to go over the papers with you while you're here." He looked at his watch. "I think there's time for you to get out to the farm before dark. You can make yourselves at home there tonight and look over the farm tomorrow. If you decide not to stay, just stop in here at the bank and let me know. Otherwise, as soon as the roads dry, I'll drive out to the farm with the papers and we can sign them there."

He looked up as a light tap sounded at the door. "Come in, Ellen. Mr. Dacia and I would like to look over the papers before he goes out to the farm."

The golden-haired woman came into the office, exuding the aroma of flowers again. She gave the papers to Mr. Johnson, smiling at him, then at Josif.

Mr. Johnson smiled at her. "Ellen is my right–hand man here. I don't think we could get along without her."

We? Josif thought. *I think you mean "you" couldn't get along without her.* Then he quickly focused on the papers.

Mr. Johnson explained the lease papers to him. "They are the standard conditions for farm rental in this area: two-fifths of the crops to the owner, three-fifths to the renter. However, if the renter has no machinery, and if that machinery is supplied by the owner, as in this case, the crops are shared equally, half and half. You will be expected to maintain and repair the machinery, of course." He looked up at Josif. "Does that seem fair to you?"

Josif looked at the agreement, studying it. "It look fair. If we like farm, I sign it."

"Good!" Mr. Johnson opened his desk drawer again and took out two keys on a ring. "Here are the keys. If all of you go out of the house for any length of time, it would be wise to lock the door. There are some people in the neighborhood who might just walk in, otherwise." He stood up and shook Josif's hand. "Good luck, and say hello to that family of yours for me. Tell Mrs. Dacia that the big stove in the kitchen is brand new. The one that came with the place had to be replaced; I think she'll enjoy using it."

As Josif left the office and walked through the lobby to the door, Ellen Olson smiled at him. "Goodbye, Mr. Dacia. Maybe I'll come out with Mr. Johnson sometime to see you."

* * *

The family still waited for him behind the blacksmith shop, and again everyone watched him as he came toward them. He saw a look of hope in their eyes, but also a look of caution against expecting too much, a look of being prepared for disappointment.

Josif took the keys out of his pocket and held them up. "We have a farm!"

* * *

The team and wagon and the cart and cow moved slowly north, then west, then north along the muddy roads past prosperous-looking farms. As each new set of buildings appeared, the family gazed at the well-kept yards, the huge red barns, the big square white houses, the corn cribs, the stacks of hay, and the yellow straw-stacks, and at each place the children asked, "Is this it? Is this our farm?" And at each place, Josif shook his head, saying, "No, no. Wait. It is another few miles. There is a creek and a bridge. Then the farm."

Michael-Joseph spoke quietly to his father, "Papa, I have to pee."

Josif looked down at him. "Right now? You can't wait until we get to the farm?"

Michael-Joseph pulled at his overalls. "I'll try, Papa."

"Whoa." Josif brought the team to a stop. He climbed down out of the wagon into the muddy road. He held up his hands to Michael-Joseph and lifted him down, then he helped him unbutton his coat and overalls. He looked up at the rest of the family as the sound of falling liquid came up from the mud.

"Now I suppose everybody has to go?"

Marie spoke for the girls. "No, Papa, we can wait. We can wait until we get to the farm."

Josif looked at their faces. "I think we had better find a place where we all can go. It has been a long time."

Alexander pointed ahead. "There's a big grove of trees up there, on the west side of the road."

Josif stretched, trying to look over the horses.

"Any house? We have to be careful not to insult people by going on their land in front of their house."

"I can't see a house." Alexander stood up on a sack of oats. "There's a big building, way back beyond the trees. I think it's a barn. There's a silo. There might be other buildings behind the barn."

Josif bent down and helped Michael-Joseph button up. He lifted him back up into the wagon, then climbed in himself and clucked the horses forward. "We will all stop. If it's only a barn, no one should mind."

When they were opposite the grove he stopped the team, and the rest of the family climbed through a barbed-wire fence and went into the grove. Josif waited with Michael-Joseph until the others could come back to be with the team.

Alexander came back first, and Josif left him with Michael-Joseph and the team while he went through the fence and toward the woods. He met Izabella and Aunt Magda at the edge of the grove as they were coming out. They were laughing and talking, walking easily and gracefully in spite of their heavy coats and overshoes, and he thought that he had never seen Izabella look happier.

They smiled at him, and Izabella said, "The buds on the trees are swelling; soon there will be new leaves. I hope there will be trees like this at our farm; they are so beautiful."

"We will have trees." Josif looked up at the tall, old cottonwoods. "Many trees, like these. Eli Rahn said that all the people who settled here in this state planted such trees to shelter them from the winter storms." He touched Izabella's arm. "We will have trees. You will see."

When he came back to the wagon, they started north again, eager to come to the farm. As they approached the next road intersection, a team of black horses pulling a buggy came toward them from the west, moving fast. A man in the buggy lashed the horses with a long whip, forcing them forward at a gallop through the mud; their feet slipping and sliding, their eyes white and wild.

As the team drew nearer, the family heard the man cursing at the horses as he struck them with the whip. Crouched in a half-standing position in front of the buggy seat, dark-faced, scowling, angry-eyed, dressed in a black hat, black coat, black moleskin trousers, and muddy black boots, the man lashed the plunging horses into the intersection. Just in front of Peter and Paul the man hauled viciously back on the reins, bringing the buggy to a stop so as to block the road in front of the Dacias.

"You people were trespassin' on my property! Who the hell gave you permission to climb through my fence?" The man's voice was thick with anger as he jerked savagely on the reins of his panting horses. "You damned Gypsies think you can walk right into anybody's property anytime you feel like it. What the hell were you doin' in there?"

"We should not go through your fence," Josif said. "Was wrong to do, but we been in wagon long time, needed to get out."

The man scowled fiercely at them. "I don't care how long you been in your goddamned wagon. You trespassed on my property. I seen you Gypsies before. Steal anything you can get your hands on."

Josif spoke in Romanian to Uncle Jon. "I should kill him for what he has said, but we are in a new place – a place

96

where we will live, and we were wrong to go on his land."

Uncle Jon touched the knife in his belt. "Any man who treats his horses as this man does should be lashed with his own whip, and any man who talks as this man talks should be taught some manners. But we are in a new place, as you say. I think we should not kill him now. Someday we may have to, but if we do it now, it is not a good way to come into our new home."

The man glared at them. "You can gabble away all you want to in your damned Gypsy language, it don't make no difference to me. You went on my land without my say-so, and I ain't gonna stand for it. I got half a mind to turn you over to the county sheriff."

Josif spoke quietly to the man, "We sorry we go on your land. We want be good neighbors."

The man snorted contemptuously. "I'll bet. Well, you ain't gonna be any neighbors of mine. Just keep on headin' north and get the hell outta here. We don't want your kind around here."

Josif replied calmly, "We move to farm north of here. We will stay there."

The man stared at him. "What farm north a here? How far north?"

Josif took the map from his pocket. "Maybe one-half mile."

"Half a mile!" The man's face grew ugly with anger. "You mean you're gonna move onto the Ariosto place? Did that son-of-a-bitch from the bank rent you Gypsies that farm?"

Josif smiled at the man. "I think we be neighbors."

The man struck the butt of the whip on the buggy seat. "I'll kill 'im, that bastard! Thinks he can pull that on me does he? Puttin' a bunch a goddamned Gypsies on land that belongs to me!" He spat on the ground. "You ain't gonna be on that farm long. We'll see who that land belongs to." He shook his fist at the family. "Don't you ever come onto my land again, or I'll fill you fulla buckshot."

He lashed his horses with the whip and pulled the rearing animals around in the road intersection in a tight circle, then he sent the team galloping back the way they had come.

Aunt Magda crossed herself. "He is the type of man who will become a *strigoi* when he dies. He is evil in life; he will be evil in death. We must all carry garlic and hang many garlic braids in the house and buildings of our new farm."

Uncle Jon shook his head. "He is not a *strigoi* yet; only a crazy man who will someday die under his own horses' hooves or by our knives." He put his hand on Josif's shoulder. "But you did well not to kill him now."

Josif folded the map and put it back in his pocket. "The knife was calling from its resting place. I think maybe someday it will taste his blood. But now we come near to the farm. Let us forget that man and find our land!"

Ahead of them a long curved line of trees and brush extended across the land from west to east. They stared at it eagerly as the team drew the wagon forward, and they heard a faint roaring sound that grew louder as they approached the line of trees. It was the sound of flowing, rushing water.

The family members leaned forward, looking up at the tall budding cottonwoods and willows, staring ahead of them toward the sound of the water, not yet daring to believe that they might be near the end of their journey.

They went down a slight incline in the road where they entered a low marshy area filled with willow saplings, their swollen tips red in the late afternoon sun. The sound of the water grew louder, and a rich smell of budding life emanated from the marsh.

A low stone bridge appeared ahead of them, and Josif brought the team onto it, stopping them with the wagon in the middle of the structure. They rolled the canvas cover up over the wagon hoops so that all of the family could see the creek.

From the narrow bridge the Dacias could look almost

straight down into the rushing water. A primeval force moved in the creek, an ancient power which called to the family, reminding them of another land and time where mountain streams cascaded down rocky glens, and campfires gleamed in the dusk under shadowy pines.

On the other side of the creek, on the right, beyond the marsh, stood a thick grove of trees. In the midst of the grove, almost hidden by the branches, a wooden windmill towered between farm buildings and a low white house.

"We are here," Josif said. "This is the place."

* * *

Clarence, aka C.D., and Vince Lamb plotted with two hit men, Angelo Moretti and Lou Fallucca, to leave Chicago profitably. They brought two very modified cattle trucks to Moran's distillery in the North Side. Among other things, these trucks had removable roofs, which were currently off.

The four men crept silently into the building and shot the still operators. Then they backed the trucks in through the big double doors and, with the use of the overhead cranes, loaded the stills, retorts, and tanks through the tops of the trucks.

They loaded bags of sugar, yeast, and malt into the spaces between the stills and covered the trucks with dark canvas.

They drove the trucks to a special warehouse where the roofs of the trucks were lowered into place and bolted on, then both trucks were recovered with the dark canvas. When this was done, they headed for Detroit, Clarence leading in his Model A.

Vince followed in his big eight-cylinder Studebaker, but before he left, he did something which brought him excitement and pleasure. He poured fifteen gallons of gasoline over the bodies of the still operators and around the interior of the building, and led a trail of it out through the big doors.

Then he tossed a match into the thin river of gasoline.

Vince was not able to stay and watch the fire as he had loved to do on other jobs, but when he was well outside the city he pulled the Studebaker to the side of the road and looked back in the direction from which he had come. Black smoke billowed up a 1000 feet into the sky, and even at the distance he was from Chicago, Vince seemed to hear the crackle and roar of the flames, and he was happy.

Chapter Six
Hearts Delight

Josif slapped the reins gently on the horses' backs and they started forward. The family made no sound, for they were so overcome with emotion at having finally arrived that they could not speak. The horses pulled the wagon up the incline on the other side of the bridge, on through the marsh, and along the road that led to the grove and buildings. When they came to the narrow driveway that led to the house, Peter and Paul turned into it without guidance from Josif, stepping briskly with their heads up, whickering softly, as though they had come home.

The red and white cow that had plodded along silently and patiently behind the cart for so many days now arched her neck, and with her head up, bellowed a long, drawn-out moo that broke the silence of the family as though a spell had been lifted from them. They began to talk and laugh, and as the wagon rolled down the long driveway beneath the arch of tree limbs, they exclaimed over each part of the farm, praising the beauty of the trees, the nearness of the creek, the rich-looking soil, the lay of the land, and the feeling of home about the place.

Josif stopped the team on the south side of the house, and everyone became silent again as they looked at the building.

It was of a strange design, completely unlike the big square houses they had seen on the other farms. It consisted of four low buildings of varying size which had been joined

together in a line: on the west end sat a small square structure, attached to its east side was a slightly bigger one, attached to the east side of this stood an even bigger one, and
attached to the east side of this stood a smaller structure
with a porch on its south side. The line of buildings lay like
an opened telescope made of roofed cubes, with its eyepiece
to the west and its objective lens to the east.

The once-white paint on the elongated house was
cracked and peeling, each of the four roofs sagged in the
middle, the wooden shingles curled with age, and the crum-
bling putty around the small-paned old windows gaped with
empty sections like missing teeth.

The door and windows of the largest structure held colored glass in their upper halves, which caused the girls to
exclaim with delight. The door appeared to have been little
used, for no step stood below it, and rank old weeds and
snow-flattened long grass filled the area in front of the door.
The only entrance appeared to be through the rickety porch
on the farthest east section of the strange old house.

Beyond the house, to the east, stood an old red barn, a
granary, several decrepit sheds, rusty machinery, the wood-
en windmill, some broken wooden fencing, and a wooden
stock tank. The buildings and equipment spoke of age and
neglect in a farmstead which might have once been tidy and
well-cared for.

A rough path of flat stones led from the driveway
through the weeds to the porch of the house. The family

climbed down from the wagon and walked single file along the path to the rusty screen door which sagged at the entrance to the porch.

Josif pulled the door open and they stepped into the porch, taking off their muddy overshoes and carefully placing them against the inner wall. The girls stood on tiptoe to see through the window into the house.

"A stove, Mama! A big stove with shiny things!" They made space for Izabella so that she could see into the room.

Josif looked through the dirty glass pane in the upper half of the kitchen door. "That big stove is brand new. Mr. Johnson at the bank said the old one had to be replaced." He took the keys from his pocket and unlocked the door, then he touched Izabella's hand. "You go first into your new house."

Izabella tiptoed silently into the room, slowly, reverently, as though she were entering a cathedral. The others followed her, walking on their tiptoes, hushed and silent with awe.

The house smelled of old things: old wooden floors; old window sills with dead bees on the cracked and dusty paint; old stovepipes and brick chimneys; old linoleum and oil-cloth; and old plaster, laths, and wallpaper. But it was not an unpleasant smell, for the house also smelled of bees' nests and honey, of seasoned old wood warmed by sunshine streaming through wavy glass, and of faded flowers and memories.

The room they entered was the kitchen: square, high-ceilinged, and homey-feeling. Faded yellow wallpaper with a floral pattern of pink roses covered the walls, while the smoke-stained ceiling paper had once been white. A worn linoleum rug covered the floor, so dirty that the pattern could not be distinguished. In the west wall a door led into the next room, and farther along, a wooden cabinet or cupboard, once painted white, leaned against the wall. In the north wall a narrow door led into a small pantry or storeroom which appeared to have been added to the north side of the room as a sort of appendage. Shelves hung along its walls, and a small window looked out to the north.

To the right of the pantry door stood the main feature of the room, a great nickel-trimmed black kitchen range. Izabella stood in front of the stove and touched it lightly with the tips of her fingers, her face filled with joy.

Over five feet high and four feet long, the stove was a thing of majesty and grandeur. Scrolled in the nickel trim of the great oven door and the doors for wood and ashes were beautiful floral patterns, and in the middle of the oven door gleamed a huge medallion, richly scrolled. Most wonderful of all, in the center of the medallion was the face of a clock. At the top of the stove loomed a large warming oven, below it the flat cooking surface with six covers, one with a nest of little covers, and at the right end was the hot water reservoir. At the top of the oven door, beautifully written in nickel trim, was the word ACME, and at the bottom, the word REGAL.

Izabella gently opened the oven door. The massive door swung slowly down to rest in a horizontal position on its supports, and the huge oven became visible, almost two feet wide and deep. The Dacias held their breaths at the sight of it.

"Now we can cook many things at the same time! See all the places for kettles..." Izabella touched the covers of the hot water reservoir, then lifted one, looking down into the cavity. "Imagine! Hot water – all we want!"

Marie and Rose peered down into the reservoir, Aunt Magda held Caroline up so that she could look in, and Izabella held Michael-Joseph up. Then Alexander and the two men came, and Uncle Jon whistled in amazement. The reservoir was lined with a smooth, glassy material, and it had a clean elegance that strangely affected the family.

Izabella's eyes sparkled. "It will be so easy now when we wash clothes, and we can put the tub right here in front of the stove when we bathe."

Beyond the stove, against the east wall, was a lead-lined sink in a wooden cabinet, with a hand-operated water pump at its south end. A window above the sink looked toward an outside cistern pump and the farm buildings beyond. A big, round kitchen table and four rickety chairs stood against the south wall.

"Look, Mama!" Alexander worked the handle on the pump over the sink with a squeaking, chugging sound; then, miraculously, a thin stream of rusty water came from the spout. Alexander pumped harder, and the stream thickened and cleared, running into the sink in a steady flow.

"Where does the water come from?" Aunt Magda asked, peering out the window.

"From that cistern, I think." Alexander pointed out the window at the green metal pump that stood on a little cement platform. "Or it could be from a well."

Izabella ran her hand softly over the pump handle. She pumped it once, smiling at the stream of clear water. She looked up at Josif. "We will want for nothing!"

The girls and Michael-Joseph were fascinated by the pump, and Josif helped each of them work the handle. "We had better stop now," he said finally, "or we will pump all the water out of the cistern. Even though there has been much snow and rain, we must always be careful of water."

They went into the big central living room. A black potbellied stove stood in the middle of the floor with a stovepipe rising up from it almost to the ceiling, then turning and running back to a chimney in the north wall.

The room was papered in a faded pattern of purple birds on cherry blossoms with a plain white ceiling. The wallpaper sagged over the kitchen door, and behind the door a patch of white oilcloth replaced the paper.

The floor consisted of old narrow pine boards so worn that little islands of higher wood surrounded shiny nail heads which testified to the original height of the surface.

In the southwest corner of the ceiling, near a trap door, a large yellow stain indicated that something in the attic had leaked through. Josif sniffed under the stain. "Honey!" He pointed to the bodies of several bees on the window sill. "This is a honey house! I could smell it when we came in. We can go up through that trap door into the attic and fill a bucket with honey!"

At the back of the living room, two small sleeping rooms had been partitioned off, each just big enough for an iron bedstead and a cheap dresser. Against the walls of the living room sat four battered straight chairs and an old wooden rocker.

To add to the wonders of the house, the stained glass in the upper portion of the windows and door of the living room consisted of purple grape clusters and green leaves, and as the setting sun shone obliquely across them, they glowed with a pastoral beauty that was beyond belief for the family.

Aunt Magda hugged Izabella. "It is the farm of the green leaves we have dreamed about."

They went into the two west rooms – strange, bright little rooms, one leading into the next, each with an old iron bedstead. They had a cozy warmth as the sun shone in through the bare branches of the trees and the small windows. The first room was papered in a rose trellis pattern, making the room so much like a flower garden that the girls were ecstatic. "It's your room, Mama. Here are your flowers!"

"It is like a garden of roses." Izabella said, smiling at

them. "But I think it is a girls' room. A room for three little girls."

The girls could not believe it. They hugged her, all three at once, their arms tight around her, saying, "Thank-you, Mama, we love our room."

The two boys had already gone into the end room and the rest followed them in, the nine of them almost filling the little cubicle. Sunlight flooded the room through two windows, one in the south wall, and one in the west, giving the room a warm glow.

The wallpaper in this room had a pattern of little green pine trees on a light green background, and the effect of this coupled with the sunlight and the views through the windows of the grove made it seem that they were in a forest.

Michael-Joseph said nothing, but he gazed with wide eyes around the little room, then up at Josif and Izabella.

Josif laughed, tousling the little boy's hair. "What do you think, Michael-Joseph? Could you and Alexander get along in this room? It's just about big enough to turn around in."

"It's too nice for us," Alexander said. "You and Mama should have it, Papa, or Uncle Jon and Aunt Magda."

Josif smiled at Alexander. "You boys will have this room. Your Mama and I will have one of the rooms at the back of the big room, and we will be happy."

Aunt Magda agreed. "They are good rooms. Besides, they are closer to the stove. When winter comes again, you will see who the clever ones are."

Uncle Jon nodded his head in agreement, then said, "I think we men should go out now and take care of the animals. You women have too much to do in here to also tend to them." He looked at the women and winked. "When we come in again, be ready for music and singing. This is a night to celebrate!"

Before they went out, Josif pulled the little pins in the sides of the windows so they could be raised and locked in place. As they raised the windows, the March wind swept in. "Now we will sweep and mop the house, and the wind will carry the dust right out!" Isabela noted happily. "We'll carry our things in and fix a meal while you men take care of the animals."

"We'll unload all the house things onto the porch," Josif said. The two men and Alexander pulled on their overshoes and brought the trunks, boxes, and house goods from the wagon and stacked them on the porch. Then they led the team and wagon, with the cart and cow trailing behind, into the barnyard.

An old granary leaned toward the barn, and they drove the team into the granary's open alleyway, stopping them so the wagon with its sacks of grain was sheltered under the roof.

They unhitched the horses and led them and the cow to the stock tank by the windmill where the animals drank long and deeply. The tank, an old wooden one with edges that had been badly chewed by previous horses, was full of water, but a round chunk of ice floated in the center of the tank, a reminder that the water had been frozen solid during the winter.

They investigated the barn before taking the horses into it. The roof sagged, but the old building looked structurally sound. The roof was a shed type with the side facing south being the shortest, resulting in a high exterior wall on the south side and a low one on the north. Three doors sagged in the west side, the side facing the house.

The Dacias went in through the middle one, entering a central alleyway which extended through the building. Five double-horse stalls with mangers and feed-boxes lined the left side of the alleyway, while on the right side a grain bin, a small pen, and stanchions for six cows stood opposite the horse stalls.

The rough plank stalls and partitions were mellowed and worn by age and use, and an accumulation of old manure in the horse stalls and the milking area covered the floor, as did chaff and old straw in the alleyway.

A vertical ladder of rough boards led up into the haymow through a square opening in the ceiling. Ancient rafters and the roof and hayrack high above in the mow were dimly visible in the last light of the sun which penetrated the cracks in the board walls.

The barn smelled of old manure and harnesses; of old planks and beams; of horses, colts, cows, and calves of years past; of milking in winter nights when the frost cracked outside and the barn was warm and cozy; of great loads of fragrant hay tumbled into the mow to smell of summer when snow whirled through the bare tree branches.

They brought Peter and Paul in through the door on the horse side and haltered them to the manger of the first stall, closest to the house. Josif and Uncle Jon took off the horses' bridles and harnesses, and hung them on pegs against the back wall; then Josif blew the dust out of the two feed boxes and poured half a bucket of oats in each.

He spoke to the horses. "You did a good job. That was a long haul from Oklahoma." He patted their necks. "As soon as we get the cow, pig, and chickens settled and fed, we will give you both a good grooming with the currycombs and brushes. How will you like that?"

The horses stamped their feet and rolled their eyes in appreciation as they chewed their oats. Uncle Jon patted them. "We will even bring you some hay and some clean straw to sleep on. You deserve the best. You are good horses."

They led the cow into the other side of the barn and fastened her head into one of the wooden stanchions. Josif brought her a forkful of hay from the cart.

"Now you can eat and rest. That was a lot of mud we made you plod through."

The cow took a mouthful of hay, then she spread her hind legs and raised her tail. The urine gushed out behind her in a steaming arc that splattered down into the old manure like a small waterfall. They watched in amazement as she kept on for what seemed like five minutes. Finally she stopped, then she hunched her body and sent out two more short bursts. She lowered her tail with such an air of relief that Uncle Jon slapped his thigh in delight.

"She has shown us what she thought of that trip: 'Piss on it!" He pulled gently at her ear. "You must have drunk half the water in the tank. Now you better make that much milk!"

The three of them carried the pig in its crate into one of the small sheds, and while the men opened the crate, Alexander brought a bucket of water and one of oats. He poured water into one of the pig's pans, and oats into the other. The pig sampled the oats; then it drank briefly from the water pan, put its snout under the edge of the pan, and rooted it over.

Uncle Jon glared at the pig. "She is going to make good pork roast with sauerkraut if she doesn't behave. If she wasn't supposed to have a litter in April, I would say we should butcher her right now." The pig snorted and rooted around in her straw.

They left the sow and went to the wagon to get the chickens and their lanterns. The sun had set behind a bank of clouds, and with the approaching darkness and a cold night wind came a feeling of the need for shelter for both men and animals. The lanterns cast dim pools of light in the barnyard, their smoky glow familiar from the nights of camping on the trip north.

They carried the chickens in their crate to a small shed that had apparently once been a chicken house. A rusty chicken-wire fence formed a small yard outside it, and the lantern light revealed roosts of rough poles inside. They pulled the rooster and his harem of hens from the crate and shut them in the building with pans of water and oats, carefully latching the door against the night.

They returned to the barn with forkfuls of hay for the horses and the cow, and they brought straw for bedding from an old pile near the barn.

While Alexander milked the cow, Josif and Uncle Jon currycombed and brushed the horses in the lantern light. The barn had become a cozy place with the solid bulk of the horses; the warm sweet smell of the milk; and the cow lazily munching her hay, all warmly enclosed in the shadowy beams and planks of the old building with the comfortable light of the lanterns illuminating the rustic interior. The feeling of warmth and security in the old barn was intensified by the cold wind and darkness outside, and when they left to go to the house, it was with a feeling of satisfaction that the animals were well cared for.

As they crossed the barnyard with the lanterns and the pail of milk, the warm glow of a lamp in the kitchen window guided them. When they came into the porch to kick off their muddy overshoes, they saw that the traditional bunch of garlic had already been hung over the kitchen door, and a pile of stove-wood from the grove lay stacked against the wall of the house.

As they opened the kitchen door, a wave of warm, fragrant air struck them. A fire crackled in the big stove beneath steaming kettles, and the rich aroma of cooking tomatoes, garlic ,and peppers permeated the kitchen.

The table had been placed in the middle of the room with all the chairs around it, and the kerosene lamp burned brightly in its center. Izabella and Aunt Magda were bustling around the newly-polished stove, the three girls were setting the table, and Michael-Joseph stood on one of the chairs, banging the back of it with a large spoon and singing. The kitchen had a freshly-scrubbed look; even the old linoleum on the floor gleamed clean and shiny with its pattern of squares and flowers revealed. The whole atmosphere of the house was of warmth and shelter, of good cooking, and of happiness.

But most marvelous was the appearance of the women and children. Their change from muddy and bulky-coated travelers was even greater than the change in the house.

They all turned toward the doorway to greet the men and Alexander as they entered, and Uncle Jon and Josif smiled in appreciation and gratitude for having made it to their new home with their beautiful and happy family intact.

The girls had changed their overalls for pretty embroidered blouses and colorful skirts, their faces were washed, their hair was freshly braided and tied with ribbons.

Michael-Joseph was also scrubbed and combed. He wore a flowered vest over a hand-sewn white shirt, and had on new dark trousers made of the Hutterite cloth.

But the two women caused Josif's and Uncle Jon's eyes to widen in delight. Izabella and Aunt Magda had put on new skirts and blouses that they had made in the Hutterite colony and had been saving for this moment. They looked fresh and crisp and full of joy. The women's cheeks were flushed from the heat of the stove, and their eyes were filled with happiness and a relaxed contentment that made the rest of the family feel secure and truly home.

The men and Alexander washed at the sink, using basins of hot water from the reservoir of the stove. They went into the other part of the house, and when Izabella called them to come to the table they appeared in their own new clothes that had been made for them over the long winter. They looked lean, handsome, and satisfied. Relief was beginning to settle on them, and their shoulders lowered and their faces softened.

They all gathered around the table where steaming dishes of goulash, *mamaliga*, and boiled potatoes waited. Uncle Jon's eyes gleamed as Aunt Magda placed four glasses and a bottle on the table.

"Now is the time to celebrate!" he said smiling at her, then at all the family. "Our own *tuica* to welcome the new house and home of Josif and Izabella and their family!" He filled the glasses, and the four adults raised them in salute to the new home. "Let all who live here know happiness, freedom, and prosperity!" They clinked glasses and drank, then let each of the children have a tiny sip, for it was their new home, too.

They had eaten only cold *mamaliga* and apples for lunch, and the chilly March wind and long ride had made them ravenous. The steaming food was heaped on plates and passed to each person, and it was as if they were in heaven. Uncle Jon filled the glasses again with rhubarb wine from the Hutterites, and while the family ate and drank and laughed, the fire crackled cheerfully in the stove, the lamp shed its warm light on them, and the walls of the old house sheltered them from the night, the wind, and the darkness.

Finally they sat back in their chairs and laid their forks and knives on the empty plates. Uncle Jon's eyes were moist with emotion. "That was as fine a meal as the best restaurant in Bucharest could serve!"

Izabella and Aunt Magda blushed with pleasure. Aunt Magda touched the bottle. "It is the *tuica* speaking." But she smiled at Uncle Jon, and her face was especially beautiful in the lamplight.

Josif took Izabella's slender hand in his, looking into her eyes. "You and the others have traveled far on a hard road, without complaint, to come here. Now you have made this old house into a good house, a happy house, a home. I will always remember this night."

Then he spoke to Uncle Jon and Alexander. "Our animals are safe and warm. Tomorrow we will look at our fields and make plans for the spring planting. But now..." he clapped his hands once, lightly. "But now, we will tune up our instruments while the women clear the table, and then we will play music of celebration! Even though it is not a Sunday, this moment needs to be recognized and remembered; we have found our own home in America today!"

The men took their chairs into the living room and lit the kerosene lamp that stood on a box by the stove. The warm glow of the lamp transformed the old room, hiding the stained ceiling, the loose wallpaper, and the worn floor, and causing the colored glass in the windows to sparkle like precious jewels.

Alexander and Michael-Joseph followed the men into the room, and they watched eagerly as the instruments were brought from the bedroom cubicles.

Josif sat down in a chair and opened the violin case slowly and carefully. The violin glowed in the lamplight, beautiful and perfect, the golden varnish and the mellow wood rich and lustrous, its shape as beautiful as a lovely woman.

He lifted it from its case, holding it gently, turning it, inspecting it for any damage that might have occurred during the trip. Then Josif tuned it, tightening the strings with sensitive fingers, listening to the singing life as it began to awaken in the instrument.

Meanwhile Uncle Jon was unwrapping the tambal from the canvas that had protected it on its journey from Romania to America. The wood was dark and worn around the corners, and the neck-strap was a rich, chestnut leather which had become supple with much use. Uncle Jon hefted up the heavy instrument, and Aunt Magda helped place the strap around the back of his neck.

Uncle Jon leaned back to balance the instrument, and struck the taut strings with a small wooden hammer with one hand while adjusting the tension of the strings with the other. When he was done he played a few tantalizing notes from *Invertite*, a song of joy and celebration.

Alexander had already unwrapped the pan-flute and was playing softly, a sweet haunting sound which would carry the tune in most songs.

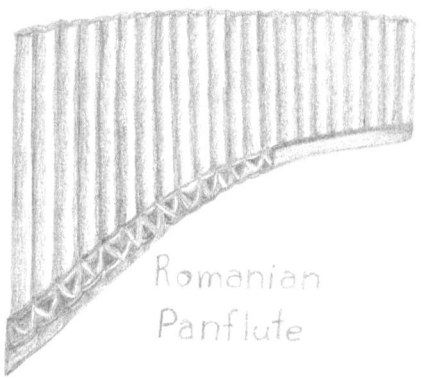

Romanian Panflute

Josif adjusted his bow and rosined it, then placed the violin beneath his chin and drew the bow across the strings. The sound resonated in the room, a low rich tone that had the quality of a woman singing. The three began slowly, playing *Maidens Fair*, softly, gradually awakening the spirit of each instrument, calling it from its slumber in the seasoned wood.

The women and girls came from the kitchen, their eyes soft and excited in the lamplight, watching the men, listening, letting the sound embrace them. Without a change in their slow tempo, the men began the *Hora Fetelor* from Ardeal, in Romania. Eyes were soft with memories in the adults, and the children knew that this music belonged to their family and would always be associated with happy times which had their roots in Romania.

Then the violin changed to a different rhythm and melody, the powerful and exuberant *Invartite*, and Alexander and Uncle John joined in. The women sang, their voices strong and barbaric, filled with a primitive joy and strength. The children joined in also, singing and clapping.

Finally they stopped and put down their instruments, and as Uncle Jon called for a restorative, they heard a loud pounding on the kitchen door.

They looked at one another in amazement and alarm. The three girls went behind Izabella like baby chicks fleeing a hawk, and Aunt Magda sprang from her chair to Izabella's side, while the two men, with the boys behind them, leapt to either side of the door leading into the kitchen. Josif and Uncle Jon each held a knife in one hand.

Through the glass in the upper part of the kitchen door they saw a dark form, its face partly lighted from below, the light and shadows giving it the appearance of some horrible and unearthly apparition that had come from the darkness.

Chapter Seven
Meeting the Neighbors

Uncle Jon muttered a hoarse incantation against evil and shifted his knife into fighting position, low, with the blade up.

"Wait!" Josif said and stepped into the kitchen. He took the lamp from the table and held it up in front of the glass, illuminating the porch.

A man's face glowered in the lamplight, heavy-featured and coarse, a long bony face with a lantern jaw and fierce dark eyes. The man wore a cloth cap and a sheepskin coat, and he looked as wild and rough as a herdsman from the Carpathians. Behind him loomed another figure, sinister and hulking in the dim light.

Josif put the lamp back on the table. He said in a low voice to Uncle Jon, "Keep your knife out of sight, but ready." He opened the door.

"We saw lights." The man's voice was loud, and like his face, coarse and heavy. "Thought we'd come over."

Josif groped for the American words. "You are... neighbors?"

"Course we are. We live right northa here. Everybody knows that." The man turned back toward the figure in the darkness. "They didn't know who we was!"

The voice from the darkness was younger-sounding than the first man's, but it had the same loudness and coarseness. "They didn't know who we was?" Heavy feet stamped on the porch floor and snorting noises came from the shadows.

"They didn't know who we was?"

"That's what they said."

"They didn't know who we was?"

"Nope."

"Well, I'll be...."

The man turned back to face Josif. "You just move in?" His eyes looked past Josif, into the kitchen.

"We come...we came... today."

"You havin' a concert or somethin'?"

Josif nodded. "We play music because are in new home. Is way of our people."

"We seen you through the window. What kinda music was that? It sure wasn't like anything I ever heard."

"We play *Invartite*."

"What kinda tight? I ain't never hearda that."

"Is from our country."

"What country you from?" The man's eyes narrowed. "You ain't Mexicans?"

"Mexicans?"

"Yeah, Mexicans. Wetbacks. Greasers."

Josif turned back toward Alexander. He spoke in Romanian. "What are wetbacks?"

"I don't know, Papa"

Josif looked at Uncle Jon. "What is he talking about?"

Uncle Jon shrugged. "I can't understand half of what he says; are you sure he is speaking English?"

"I think so, but I don't recognize the words. Maybe they have a different dialect up here in South Dakota." Josif turned back to the man. "We are from Transylvania."

The man fumbled with the word. "Train's Hill Vania?"

"Transylvania. We are from Transylvania, also called Ardeal, is part of Romania."

The man shook his head. "Never heard of anybody like that." He looked into the kitchen again. "In this country when you visit the neighbors, we generally get asked in for a cuppa coffee and a little pitch."

ROMÂNIA

Josif looked back at Alexander. "What does he mean, *pitch?*"

"I think it's something that comes from pine trees." As Alexander spoke, Josif saw the door that led into the living room softly close.

He said to the men, "We not have pitch, but we be glad have you come in for cup coffee. My name is Josif Dacia. This is my Uncle, Jon Dacia. This is my son, Alexander. Please, you come in."

The man seemed almost to smile. "Well, I'm Fritz Wagner, and that's my brother, August. By God, me an August thought you was gonna leave us out here all night."

The two men took off their muddy overshoes, blew out their lantern, and came into the kitchen. They were big. Big-handed, big-boned, big-footed, tall, and as strong-looking as two rangy plow-horses. They seemed curiously ill at ease now that they were in the house, and as they took off their caps and coats their eyes looked quickly at the closed door, then around the kitchen.

119

The first one appeared to be about twenty years old, while the second one, August, seemed younger. They had thick brown hair, and their brown eyes had a stolid, ox-like look as though nothing that happened could surprise or excite them. They wore striped blue and white bib overalls with blue work shirts, and a smell of sweat, cows, and manure hung about them. But there was also another smell, a vinegary aroma of pickled cabbage.

"You folks sure have warmed this place up in a hurry," Fritz remarked. He sat down in one of the chairs at the table. "There ain't nothin' more miserable and cold than a empty house."

August agreed. "Cold and miserable is right. You remember, Fritz, that time that Louie Vanderplanck tried to drive down to Sioux City in January and got his rear end froze off in that blizzard?" He looked at Josif and Uncle Jon. "Grandpa and us had to go into his house to get his Sunday suit for the undertaker. The fire had been out for about a week, and we just about froze in there."

Fritz nodded. "It was forty below outside. Musta been fifty below in Louie's house. He had a jug a water on the table and it froze so hard the glass all broke away leaving the water froze in the shape a the jug with the cap sittin' on the top. Funniest thing I ever seen."

He took a cloth bag of tobacco and a packet of cigarette papers from the pocket in the bib of his overalls, blew a paper loose, and carefully shook tobacco into it. He rolled it, licked the edge of the paper, and sealed it, then put one end in his mouth. He took a big wooden kitchen match from his pocket and snapped it alight with his thumbnail. He lit the cigarette, took a long drag on it, then shook out the match and put it in the wide cuff of his overalls, blowing smoke out through his nose.

"Course, any fool that don't know how to handle a car shouldn't take one out in the winter-time, anyway." Fritz took another long drag on the cigarette. "Specially when a blizzard's blowin' in." He blew more smoke out of his nose. "Louie didn't know a damn thing about a car. Never shoulda had one."

August was busy building his own cigarette, but he looked up from it. "Like the time he wanted to see how much gas was in the tank." He spoke to Uncle Jon. "It was gettin' kinda dark, and old Louie couldn't see down inside the tank, so you know what he did? He took a match and held it down in the hole!" August looked around to make sure that they were all listening. "Kaboom! It blew Louie about ten feet up in the air. Took off all his hair, and his face was so black he looked like a darky for about two months."

Fritz crossed one leg over the other and tapped his cigarette ashes into the cuff of his overalls. "Never shoulda had a car." He shook his head. "Old Bent Nelson is another one." He stretched out in the chair, putting both hands behind his head, letting the cigarette wobble from the corner of his mouth as he talked.

"He come over to our place once, to see Grandpa about somethin' or other. When it got time to go home, he got in that old Star a his and got the engine goin' full speed with the clutch in and the gear shift in high. All of a sudden he jerks his foot offa the clutch." He looked at Uncle Jon. "That old Star jumped straight up in the air with the wheels spinnin'. When it come down it took off like a billy goat with a corn cob up his rear end, hittin' the ground 'bout once every fifty feet. Old Bent took it around the barnyard 'bout three times with the dirt and chicken crap flyin' every which way afore he got it headed out into the road, and you know what he was yellin'?" Fritz took the cigarette out of his mouth and tapped the ashes into his cuff. "'Whoa!' That's what he was yellin'. 'Whoa!' He thought he was drivin' a team a horses!"

Fritz and August did not laugh at this, but instead looked at Josif, Uncle Jon, and Alexander belligerently, as if daring them to doubt the story.

Uncle Jon looked perplexed. He spoke to Josif in Romanian, "What in the name of Christ are they talking about?"

Josif shook his head. "I'm not sure. Maybe Alexander can tell us tomorrow." He spoke to Fritz and August in English. "You like cup of coffee?"

"I wondered if you was ever gonna ask," Fritz said looking at August with a raised eyebrow as Josif went to get the coffeepot from the back of the stove.

"In Romania only people who live in cities drink coffee, but we see in Oklahoma that everybody drink it and we learn to like it too," Josif said to the brothers.

Fritz spoke to Josif. "You got that right! Everybody in America drinks coffee. If you wanna fit in here, you gotta drink it morning, noon, and night. It's what keeps everybody goin'. Without coffee everything grinds to a halt!" he said with finality. "It just wouldn't be these United States of America without coffee!"

Not wanting to think about such a sorry state, Fritz quickly changed the subject, and addressed August. "You bring that deck a cards like I told you? We can have a game a pitch."

August felt in his overalls pockets. "I ain't got no cards. I thought you was gonna bring 'em."

"Well, Jesus H. Christ!" Fritz glared at August. "I told you to bring them cards!"

"Well, I ain't got 'em. If you wanted them goddamned cards so bad, why didn't you bring 'em yourself?"

"I'm gonna take a two-by-four to you when we get home." Fritz turned to Uncle Jon. "This dumb cluck is gettin' so he thinks he could maybe whup me in a fight." He jerked his thumb toward August. "Why, he ain't even outta grade school yet." He looked at Alexander. "What grade you in?"

Alexander tried to speak, but only a squeak came out. He tried again. "The sixth."

"The sixth! A little runt like you?" Fritz stared at him. "How old are ya? You look like you're about nine."

"I'm twelve."

"Twelve! When I was twelve, I was twice your size, and I could pick up a two-hundred-pound calf." Fritz spoke to August in a pitying voice. "Them kids at school are gonna just plain beat the stuffin' outta him."

August agreed. "Specially when they find out what his name is. I never hearda such a name."

"Well it ain't his fault he's got a funny name." Fritz spoke to Alexander. "You better learn to fight quick, or them kids at Mount Faith are gonna beat hell outta you."

Josif put the coffee cups on the table. "Kids fight with knives at school?"

"Knives? Not that I heard about. Clubs maybe. Them kids are mean bastards."

"They ain't so damn mean," August said. "I can lick any two of 'em with one hand tied behind me."

Fritz scowled at August "No you can't. That big Jensen kid is gettin' strong as a goddamned bull, and Julius Lamb is gettin' mean as his old man."

"Junior Jensen ain't so strong. I kicked him in the nuts yesterday, and he doubled up like a damn worm on a gol dang fishhook." August looked at his knuckles. "Julius Lamb ain't no problem either. I can beat the hell outta him any-time I feel like it."

Fritz tapped more ashes into his pant cuff. "Well, no-body ever could lick any of us Wagners, but you ain't the best damned example I could think of if I was gonna men-tion fightin'. When I was in the eighth grade there wasn't any two kids in school that dared even look cross-eyed at me, and I was only fourteen."

"That ain't so, Fritz, and you know it. You was almost sixteen when you graduated." August looked to Uncle Jon for understanding. "He always acts like he's the smart one in the family, just 'cause he only flunked one grade. I'm just as smart as he is; it's just that I got other things to think about 'steada studyin'."

"Oh, sure you have, like peein' in the modeling clay.

Why, you ain't got sense enough to pound sand down a rat hole or pour piss out of a boot." Fritz glared at August, then watched as Josif poured the coffee. "You got any cream for that coffee? Coffee ain't fit to drink without cream an' sugar."

"Cream?" Josif was apologetic. "I think cream from morning all used up. Have milk."

"Well, I suppose if you ain't got any cream, milk'll have to do, but it ain't gonna taste right." Fritz looked around on the tabletop. "I don't see any sugar. I hope you ain't outta that."

"I get sugar, Alexander bring milk." Josif brought the family's supply of sugar to the table. The sugar was in a fruit jar, about half-full.

Fritz dipped the spoon into the sugar and ladled three heaping spoons-full into his cup. "Now if it ain't got too cold." He poured milk from the pitcher that Alexander brought, shifted his spoon to one side, and took a long slurp. "Well, it ain't too bad. It ain't quite hot enough and it shoul-da had straight cream, but it ain't too bad."

August, meanwhile, had been spooning sugar into his cup, four teaspoons-full. He poured milk into the cup un-til the liquid quivered at the edge, threatening to overflow. He left the cup on the table and, carefully maneuvering the spoon handle away from his eye, bent his head down. He brought his mouth to the surface of the coffee, inserted his lips into the liquid, and sucked in. The sound was long and loud, like that made by a cow pulling its foot out of the mud, and the level of the coffee in the cup went down a full inch.

August lifted his head and wiped the back of his hand across his lips. "Didn't spill a goddamned drop!" He spoke confidentially to Alexander. "I been practicin' that. There ain't nobody can suck coffee up out of a cup the way I can."

"What's so wonderful about that? A stupid horse could do that." Fritz turned to Josif. "He ain't got no more man-ners than a pig. I been tryin' to teach him, but it don't do no good." He shook his head. "Grandma's been makin' him go to church to get confirmed, but she might as well be sendin' one of the horses." He tapped ashes from his cigarette again. "I got a feelin' that preacher is gonna just plain puke from desperation."

August made no reply, for he was busily emptying his cup. The coffee was now below the reach of his lips, and he lifted the cup and let a long stream of half-dissolved sugar drip into his mouth. He used his spoon to scrape out the last of the residue, then wiped his mouth with his hand. "I could use another cup."

As Alexander brought the coffeepot from the stove and refilled the Wagner brothers' cups, Fritz spoke to Josif and Uncle Jon. "Ain't you havin' any? Jesus Christ, I sure hate to have to drink all by myself." He looked hard at Joseph. "In America everyone drinks coffee together."

Uncle Jon said to Josif in Romanian, "What is he saying? It sounds as if he is praying."

"He is not praying, Uncle Jon. He wants us to drink coffee with him."

Uncle Jon looked at the sugar jar with its brown balls of coffee left by the Wagner brothers' spoons from their repeated dipping into the sugar. "I have learned to drink sugar in my coffee, not coffee in my sugar. I will have mine *black*."

Josif spoke to Alexander, "Bring cups for us. Three cups."

"Three cups, Papa?"

Josif spoke in English. "Yes, three cups. You have coffee too, as man should, with new neighbors."

Fritz slapped the table. "Now you're talkin', Joe! Make a man outta him while havin' a cup a coffee with the neighbors. That's how we do things in America!" He scowled at August "You sure you ain't got those cards? I sure feel like a good game a pitch."

"I felt in every goddamned pocket. They're sittin' home, right on that table by the piano." August slurped his coffee. "Right where you left 'em."

Fritz ignored this. He looked around the kitchen. "Why

in hell didn't somebody think of this before? We'll use your cards. Everybody's got a decka cards stashed away somewhere." He spoke to Josif. "Get out your cards, Joe, and we'll have us a game."

"We have no cards," Josif said to Fritz.

"Well hell," Fritz replied. " Everybody's got cards. Didn't you ever play cards in the army in your country durin' the war? Grandpa says everybody played cards in the army."

Uncle Jon spoke to Fritz. "I know cards you mean. We had in army. But no cards like that here, we married men now."

"You sure you ain't got no cards?" Fritz stared dejectedly at the table. "I sure did wanna have a game a pitch." He watched Alexander as he filled the coffee cups, then he helped himself to sugar and milk again. "How many heada horses you got?"

Josif was beginning to understand Fritz better as they talked, and for some reason it seemed that it was easier for him to speak English. He replied, "We have two horses."

"Two! How you expect to farm with only two horses?"

"Are good horses."

"It don't matter how good they are, you can't farm a quarter section with only two horses." Fritz turned toward August. "Did you hear that? They only got two horses!"

August was showing Alexander his coffee-drinking technique again. He completed a long slurp and raised his head. "Course I heard it. Waddaya think I am, deaf?"

"Well, with all that horse-drinkin' noise you're makin', nobody can hear." Fritz spoke to Josif again. "How in hell you been farmin' with only two horses?"

"We had farm in Oklahoma. Same two horses only."

"Oklahoma, huh? Them crazy galoots down there don't know anything. They wouldn't know what to do with a good farm if they had one, not that this farm you got here is any prize." Fritz looked thoughtfully at Josif. "How'd you get up here all the way from Oklahoma with a team?"

"We drove team with wagon."

Fritz stared unbelievingly at him. "You came up here in a wagon, with all them kids?"

"Yes."

"Well I'll be a S.O.B.!" Fritz looked at the closed door to the living room. "And your womenfolk too? In a wagon? How'd you get through all them blizzards we had?"

"We came in summer. We live with people west of here in winter."

"Oh, I got it. You had some of your relatives to stay with. Some of them *Train's Hill Vanians*."

"Not relatives. Just good people."

"Well, it don't make no difference; you still can't farm a quarter section with only two horses, unless maybe you're plannin' on buying a tractor. Now that would be the way to do it."

"Goddamned right," August said. "Soon as I sell them hogs this spring, I'm gonna buy me a John Deere."

"You ain't buyin' nothin' until I say so. And who the hell gave you the idea them hogs was yours to sell?"

"Well, I have to take care of 'em. They oughta be mine."

Fritz scowled at August. "Well they ain't yours, and don't keep buttin' in when me and Joe here are tryin' to talk." He turned back to Josif. "How many acres did you farm down there in Okyhoma with them horses?"

Josif conferred with Uncle Jon and Alexander. "Was eighty acres. This farm not same?"

"Hell, no. Every farm here is a quarter section, a hundred and sixty acres. Everybody knows that."

"This farm one hundred and sixty acres?"

"It sure is. Take away that part where the creek goes and your buildings and barnyard here and you still got a hundred and forty. 'Course it ain't the best land in the county, and that low spot ain't good for nothin' much, and you got one great big patch of creepin' Jenny, and there's sunflowers all through the place, but even so, if you try to work it with just one team, you ain't gonna make it. Why, you won't get your corn planted 'til the middle of June, and what the hell kinda crop is that gonna make? Plus the fact that that lazy galoot that was here last year didn't do any fall plowin'." Fritz took another long slurp of his coffee. "Plus another fact that the fields is so wet from all this snow and rain that you couldn't get into 'em now unless you was a goddamn duck."

Josif spoke to Uncle Jon and Alexander, quietly, but so excited that he mixed English and Romanian. "We have a one-hundred-and-sixty-acre farm!"

Uncle Jon stared at him. "You are sure? Twice what we had before?"

"Yes! Fritz says that all of the farms here are that size. We will have to get more horses!"

Uncle Jon's eyes gleamed with excitement. "Ask him where we can get good horses, Josif."

Josif turned to Fritz, "We thank you tell us about this big farm. You good neighbor."

Fritz was rolling another cigarette, and he licked and sealed it before he answered. "Oh, that wasn't nothin'," he said modestly. "Anybody with any brains coulda told you that."

"Could tell us where can buy good horses?"

"You mean good horses? Not some broken-down crow-baits?"

Josif nodded. "Want good horses."

Fritz licked the cigarette end, thinking, pushing the wet end in and out of his mouth a few times. "Alfred Anderson's got a pair a three-year-old geldings he was tryin' to sell..."

"Hell," August said, "them horses of Alfred Anderson's never did get broke right. Them stupid Swedes ain't got any more sense about horses than a dang frog!"

Fritz glared at August. "Well, let me finish, for Christ's sake. I was just gonna tell Joe and his uncle here about that till you came buttin' in." He took a long pull on his cigarette. "Now, of course, they would be a damned good buy for somebody that knows how to handle horses, but I 'spect you folks want somethin' more broke-like that ain't gonna kick hell outta everything."

"We have raised horses in our country. Could you please tell where Alfred Anderson live?"

"Why, hell, everybody knows that. Just the other side of old Bent Nelson's. You musta almost gone by the place."

"How many miles?"

"Miles? Why it ain't no miles. You just go down across the bridge to the road south a here and go three-quarter-mile east. All a them Swedes live over that way."

August interrupted again. "It ain't any three-quarter-mile. Three-quarter-mile would take you right into that fence line by the slough. Alfred Anderson's driveway is another ten rods further east."

"No it ain't, damn it. Ten rods further east would take you right smack into the middle of his hog yard."

August banged his coffee cup down. "The hell it would! You count the fence posts from the east corner down to the edge of his woodlot and see where you get!"

Fritz brought the front legs of his chair down to the floor with a crash. "Listen, you dummy, don't you think I know how to count fence posts? You go down to that fence line just across from Carl Croat's mailbox and head on east. Alfred Anderson's driveway is just seven fence posts further on. Now that ain't any ten rods!"

"Well, what the blankety blank does Carl Croat's driveway have to do with it anyway? Besides that, it ain't seven fence posts, it's eight."

"The hell it is," Fritz argued. "It's seven. I oughta know. I helped old Carl put them in just a week before he went crazy with that shotgun and they shipped him off to the puzzle factory. Back in '27 it was, June."

"They didn't come get 'im 'till July. Old Hannah stood 'em off with that old twelve-gauge shotgun for pretty near a week." August lifted his cup and poured more syrupy dregs into his mouth. He spoke to Uncle Jon. "She woulda blowed their heads off, too."

"For cryin' out loud!" Fritz said with exasperation. "Don't you think I know that? June was when they came and tried to haul him off. That's what counts – not how long old Hannah stood out there with her shotgun."

"You said they hauled him off in June. It wasn't 'til July." August spoke to Uncle Jon as if the matter were settled. "There was more damned commotion than a chivaree. Ol' Marshall Fat Fred Franklin was scared shitless tryin' to nail Carl."

Fritz could stand no more."Why you dumb little S.O.B., you ain't got one thing straight about that whole mess. First, I know for a fact that they hauled him off in June because at the 4th of July celebration in town everybody was so damned worked up about it they didn't even watch the damn fireworks. Second, ol' fat Fred didn't have any say-so 'bout it 'cause Carl plugged that lawyer outside the city limits. That made it the sheriff's business. It was Frank Ariosto that came out and took that gun away from Hannah and hauled Carl off. On top a that, if you keep interuptin' me when I'm tryin' to talk with Joe here, I'm just purely gonna beat the shit outta you."

There was an uncomfortable silence while the brothers glared at each other. Josif said, "I think we go see Mr. Alfred Anderson Sunday about horses."

Fritz turned away from August. "Sunday! I sure as hell wouldn't if I was you. Them Swedes spend just about all day Sunday in church, and if they was home, they wouldn't talk no business with ya." He drained the last of his coffee, put out the butt of his cigarette between his thumb and forefinger, and placed the butt carefully in his overall's cuff. "If we ain't gonna play any pitch, me and August might as well go home. Grandpa'll be routin' us out to milk them cows 'bout the time we get to bed."

"You milk many cows?" Josif asked.

"Many! Sixteen every mornin' and night."

August spooned out the last of the sugar from his cup. "Yeah, and soon as those heifers come fresh the end of the month, we'll be milkin' till our dang fingers fall off." He gave the spoon a last lick. "Soon's I get a few bucks a my own, I'm gonna take off for California. Pick a few oranges out there and spend the rest of the time layin' in the shade of a palm tree, eatin' oranges. I ain't gonna stick around here all my life freezin' my balls off every winter and fryin' my ass every summer and milkin' a buncha friggin' cows on any friggin' farm."

Fritz glared at August. "I told you not to use them god-damned words in the house, and you ain't goin' to no California. We got too much work to do to have you runnin' off to California suckin' oranges." He held out his hand to Josif, then to Uncle Jon. "Next time I'll bring them cards myself, and we'll have us a game a pitch."

The Wagner brothers put on their caps and coats and went out into the porch, stamping into their overshoes, lighting their lantern. They went off into the darkness like two ogres from a fairy tale, the swinging lantern casting its dim and smoky light on their tall, heavy-coated bodies and in a little circle on the dark, wet ground around them.

The kitchen was blue with cigarette smoke, and Josif left the door open and raised the windows to let fresh air blow through the room. The quiet after the loud profanity of the Wagners was so intense and pleasant that Josif, Uncle Jon and Alexander stood silently for a few minutes without speaking.

Finally Uncle Jon spoke, his voice a whisper. "What in the name of all the saints, were they shouting and blaspheming about? I could only understand them when they talked about land or horses."

Josif put his hand on Uncle Jon's shoulder. "Uncle Jon, you are a lucky man. They are worse than drunken soldiers; they have no manners at all."

When they went into the living room they found Izabella and Aunt Magda sitting fully dressed on the two chairs. The lamp was turned low, and three embroidered table cloths hung over the windows and the glass in the door. Each woman held a small knife in her hand. Aunt Magda's eyes were as fierce as a mother eagle's. "What terrible men! How could you let them in the house? Who were they? They sounded like madmen!"

Josif smiled at her. "They are our neighbors. Their names are Fritz and August. I think their family name is Wagner."

Aunt Magda sniffed. "If they are our neighbors, I hope they live a long way off." She looked suspiciously at Uncle Jon. "You weren't drinking *tuica* with them were you? It sounded as if they were drunk."

Uncle Jon crossed himself and raised his right hand. "Believe me, I was not drinking anything but coffee with them, and that was enough. I think maybe Alexander learned some new ways to drink coffee, though."

"And some terrible words!" said Aunt Magda. "With all that horrible cursing and slurping, I think they must have been raised by wolves. They should not be allowed in public!"

Izabella laughed. "Michael-Joseph wanted to come out to talk with them, but we were afraid he might also learn bad words."

"He might have. But we also learned some good words!" We have one hundred and sixty acres here, and we are going to buy more horses! This will be a good farm!"

Chapter Eight
Getting to Know the Neighbors

Izabella awoke early the next morning and made loaves of bread for the day, stoking up the fire in the stove and sending the age-old scent of home wafting through the house like a friendly spirit as the bread baked. Aunt Magda and Marie next appeared in the kitchen, returning from the barn where they had milked the cow and cared for the animals, as in Romania it is traditionally the job of the women to take care of the animals while the men farm.

The rest of the family was also soon up, eager to see more of their new home. Josif led them to the barn.

A warm and pleasant smell of animals and hay greeted them in the barn, and Peter and Paul nickered a soft welcome from their stall.

They gathered around the cow. The girls fed her wisps of hay and stroked her neck, and Aunt Magda and Marie told her how good she was for giving so much milk.

They went to the shed where the pig rooted in the ground made damp from her watering pan. Uncle Jon studied the animal critically. "I thought she was supposed to have a litter in April. She still looks like a ballerina."

"Now that she has stopped traveling, she will get fat. A pig needs to relax and lie around," Aunt Magda said with the voice of experience.

They next went to the chicken house where they heard the chickens protesting their captivity inside the old building. Aunt Magda opened the door. "We will let them out," she said, "let them see their new home."

The family stood back so as not to frighten the flock. The rooster came out first, darting his head from side to side, his fierce red-rimmed eyes examining the new surroundings. He stepped slowly and deliberately, speaking deep in his throat, his comb and wattles quivering, his gaudy tail feathers ruffed out, his wings slightly raised like a boxer coming into the center of the ring. He looked around the barnyard, twisting his neck, looking up at the old windmill, the barn, the cottonwood tree by the tank, the granary, the house. He listened to the creek, cocking his head.

He called to the hens and they came out slowly, timidly, one by one, hesitating at the door, looking with fearful eyes at the new things around them.

The rooster stood up on his toes and flapped his wings; he crowed a wild cry of defiance at all things in the universe, challenging the gods to battle.

Far away across the fields another rooster sent back the challenge, and the rooster shook his feathers in rage. He stood up on his toes and crowed again, shouting back with such anger and strength that his feet left the ground, and his body shook and quivered like some exotic dancer. Then he walked calmly away from the chicken house, pecking at the ground, leading the hens to a pile of horse manure, all of them busily talking to one another.

Josif propped the door open with a stick. "We will make nests for them and fix this broken fence. We may have to keep them in if there are skunks in the woods."

They left the chickens and went across the barnyard to the windmill and the tank. Josif released the catch on the long wire that led up the wooden tower of the windmill, and the wheel and fan screeched and opened into the wind. The wheel began to turn, slowly, then faster, and the long wooden rod connecting the pump to the gears above began to jerk up and down. A thumping, clanging noise came from beneath the old straw and boards covering the pump.

Alexander ran to the end of the rusty pipe that led into the tank. "Water is coming, but it is slow. I think the pump needs new leathers."

Josif walked to the tank. "Where did you learn so much about pumps?"

"From Mr. Rahn. He knows how to fix any kind of machinery. He taught me about them while the other boys were in German school."

"Uncle Jon and I thank Mr. Rahn. I think we will need all the help we can get on the farm machinery." Josif spoke lightly, but deep inside him there was a small feeling of resentment that Alexander had spoken so highly of Eli Rahn.

The machinery lay scattered among the box elder and ash trees north of the barn. The family gathered around each implement, examining it with hopeful eyes, discussing its condition.

They came first to a handheld *walking* plow which consisted of a large single plowshare with handles behind for a man to hold and an iron bar in front to which a team could be hitched. An iron-seated *sulky* plow with two plowshares stood nearby. The moldboards and plowshares on both plows were rusty and had obviously not been greased since their last use. Uncle Jon shook his head. "A bad farmer was here before us."

Josif agreed. "The Wagner brothers said the man had done no fall plowing; these must have stood here for almost a year, rusting. But we will soon wear the rust off, and the plows look strong enough otherwise."

The other implements appeared to be just as neglected as the plows, but they were so buried in old weeds that it was hard to tell their actual condition. They found an old drag, a disc, a long wooden small-grain seeder, two single-row corn cultivators, a two-row corn planter, a mower, a manure spreader, a rickety hayrack, a wagon, and an old binder whose tarpaulins had been left on and were weak and rotten from the rain and snow.

A warped, wooden grain elevator ran up onto the roof of the granary and under a sheet-metal hood which had come loose and appeared to hang by one nail. The *horsepower* mechanism for operating the elevator was almost buried under old corncobs and dead weeds, and the wagon hoist tilted crazily on a broken sill.

Piles of junk lay everywhere in the old weeds around the buildings, and the family marveled at such waste.

In one of the empty bins in the granary they found an old hand-cranked corn sheller and a wooden fanning mill, and when Alexander turned their handles, they screeched from lack of oil.

The granary smelled of mice and dust, and in the empty corncrib side, the diagonal wooden slats were chewed away and broken at the bottom in several places as though something had gotten at the corn from the outside.

Uncle Jon sighed. "Whoever was here before was a bad farmer. He had no pride in the land, buildings, or machines...."

Josif nodded. "It looks that way. But these things can be repaired. We have wrenches, hammers, nails, oil, and grease. While the fields dry, we will fix these things and get the machinery ready."

They walked counterclockwise around the farm, first going south from the house through an old and neglected orchard toward the creek. Uncle Jon pointed delightedly to the fruit trees."Plums! See how many! Magda, you can make tuica by the barrel!"

He pointed to the other trees. "Look! Apples, cherries, pears, peaches, apricots! If we prune these trees and clean out the weeds, this orchard will feed us by itself." He came to stiff attention. "I, personally, will take responsibility for this orchard. It will bloom again, and be the envy of all the neighbors."

Izabella beamed. "We will make *dulceata* and jams and preserves and filled pancakes with the fruit, and this orchard will be like our home in Romania, moved here to this new land."

Aunt Magda smiled happily. "It will be good to have an orchard again." She touched Uncle Jon's arm. "If any of those cherry trees are sour cherry, I will make Visinata, our sour cherry brandy! It is good for coughs in the winter and for sipping!"

The adults agreed. "If there is not a sour cherry tree in our orchard, I will make room for one," Uncle Jon said with determination. "In a few years it will be a good producer, and we will have everything we love right here on our own farm!"

They walked down to the creek. The winding course and the cottonwoods and willows lining both banks gave the stream the charm of a painting, and the memory of mountain torrents in their homeland caused the adults to gaze at the flowing water with delight. "We have truly come to the place of water and green fields," Josif said.

Alexander pointed. "We could have a pond in this low place if we built a dam; and we could have water lilies, and a boat, and a place to swim!" The girls jumped up and down in excitement.

Josif cautioned them. "Field work comes first. Ponds and water lilies do not feed us or our livestock."

"We could raise fish in the pond," Alexander said. "Eli Rahn said that bullheads and catfish grow well in ponds."

Josif frowned. "Eli Rahn will not tell us how to farm." He regretted his words as he said them, but they were said and he could not take them back.

They followed the course of the creek on east as it flowed along the south edge of their farm. Remembering the words of the Wagner brothers, Josif pointed out the surrounding farms.

"The one just south of us must be where Bent Nelson of the Star car lives, and east of that must be the land of the Swedish Alfred Anderson of the horses. East of our farm must be the farm of Carl Croat of the shotgun and the fence posts who is now for punishment in a factory where they make puzzles, which I cannot understand."

As they walked around the perimeter of the farm they found the fields so filled with weeds that it was difficult to determine what had been raised in each area the previous year. They saw evidence of corn stalks in one big field, and in another there seemed to be the stubble of small grain; but the whole appearance of the farm was one of neglect and poor management.

They tramped through soft mud and water, realizing how difficult it would be to get into the fields with any machinery.

The northeast corner of the farm was completely covered with water, and as they sloshed around the edges of the huge pond with the mud sucking at their overshoes they saw wild ducks swimming in the center, busily feeding in the shallow water.

The sun shone down from the washed blue March sky, and with the rich smell of the wet earth and the pond around them, the family experienced a kind of ancestral memory – a feeling of a warm, wet world where life slowly unfolded in an infinite expanse of water, earth ,and sun. A sound came from the south, a faint gabbling, a low wild crying of something primeval and mysterious moving toward them.

They gazed upward into the sky, shielding their eyes from the sun. Far to the south, tiny specks appeared – a wavering, undulating line, shifting slowly in the clear blue air. The sound became clearer as the line approached, and it was the voice of wild geese, the voice of hundreds, of thousands, a sound so immense, so filled with the force of life that the family could not speak, but stood in silent awe as the geese approached.

They came in a ragged V formation which had no visible end. A single bird led them, a powerful point of life flying strongly and confidently northward with its flock behind it, the whole immense column moving as a single being, an organism whose will and instinct converged in the leader. But there was a mobility and fluidity in the being which spoke of another mystery – of the individual will of each cell of the organism.

Effortlessly and smoothly, almost unseen, geese shifted positions in the V; individuals dropped back or surged forward in the new line, new Vs branched off from the main line as others merged with it, whole groups moved and attached to the ends of the short lines. Yet always the organism remained intact, the basic powerful V moving steadily northward in a single unit.

The flight was at least two miles long, and the family members were affected more and more strongly as the undulating formation passed over them.

Michael-Joseph stretched his arms upward toward the geese, and Josif lifted the little boy onto his shoulders to bring him closer to them.

Marie, Rose, and Caroline stared silently upward, their hearts so connected to the geese that it seemed they flew with them, and the wild, free flight called to some ancient knowledge in their spirits. Tears came to their eyes, tears for something beautiful and wonderful, and they felt that God was close to them.

Alexander watched the geese with a deep inner excitement that was like a wild wind. It seemed that he flew with the geese, above them, beyond them, swift and straight toward the sun, moving with such speed and power that the earth swept by underneath him in a dazzling blur of fields and trees and water that receded and grew smaller and fell away beneath him.

Uncle Jon stood near Alexander with his hat against his chest, looking up at the geese with his fierce old warrior's face raised to the sun and the sky as though he were in a cathedral.

Josif felt the living warmth of Michael-Joseph on his shoulders. He thought: *Thank you, God for helping me get my family here, and please let these children's fate be to live a good life here. Let them see and find happiness in this new land, safe and free from oppression.* And he thought again, *If I had killed that man yesterday my family would not be here, in this field, with the geese and the sunshine and the water. The old ways of our people call for blood, death, and revenge on our enemies, but I will not be a son of Vlad the Impaler. Here, in this new land, we should live like the geese, free and happy, forgetting blood and death, forgiving our enemies, giving up old hatreds, old ways.*

The end of the long line of geese appeared. The family felt a sadness then, for it seemed that the geese should have gone on always, their wild voices filling the sky, their waving, changing, undulating line forever moving northward through the clear, bright sky.

A break, a weakness, showed at the end of the line. One goose flapped wearily along behind the others, the distance between it and the flock increasing. The goose saw the water in the field, and it dropped down toward it, but the flock members called to it and it struggled upward, its wings moving frantically as it tried to regain its altitude and position. But it was too late, for the others were already beyond it, their voices growing fainter as the long dark line flowed into the northern sky.

Then a goose from the flock turned back. It circled out and down toward the struggling one and came to it, and the two geese dropped down together toward the flooded field and the people.

The family watched in awe as the geese came down, seeing the miracle that a part of the mysterious and magical line was coming out of the sky and down into their own field. The geese flew down to the pond at a steep angle, then at the last minute they held their great wings out and forward gliding just above the surface of the water, and then settling down onto the pond. They floated on the water in the sunlight, as beautiful and wonderful to the family as if two angels had come down from heaven.

The girls were ecstatic. Marie spoke quietly not to frighten the birds. "Will they stay with us, Mama? They are so beautiful."

Izabella said softly, "They have come to our pond to rest, but they are wild creatures. They may fly after the others when the tired one is strong again."

"But it could hardly fly, Mama. Maybe they will stay?"

"Maybe. They will stay awhile. While they are here we must not frighten them."

"We won't, Mama."

They continued their tour of the farm, quietly skirting the north end of the pond, watching the geese as they went.

The Wagner farm lay to the north, and they noticed the weed-free fields, the fall plowing, the tight fences, and the general appearance of good husbandry about the place. A huge red barn and a square white house were visible through the trees, and above the buildings towered a tall red silo and a steel windmill, all as solid and strong-looking as the Wagners themselves.

The northwest corner of the Dacias' farm rose above the surrounding flat fields, and from this elevation the family saw the countryside around them to better advantage. Several miles to the east, the white spire of a church pointed to the sky, and the whole landscape was dotted with groups of farm buildings set amidst their groves in the black fields, each farmstead about half a mile from the others along the grove that grew north and west of the buildings. Tall, old cottonwoods grew along the outer edge; then a mixture of soft maples, ash, and box elder in the center; and just behind the house, great clumps of lilac bushes, some ten or twelve feet high.

Everywhere lay fallen branches and trees, so thick that it was hard to walk through the grove. Josif lifted a heavy piece of broken branch. "Always we will have enough wood here to cook our food and heat our house. It is a gift from God."

A sharp smell of spring filled the grove, an aroma of swelling buds and damp earth and trees that was so pleasant to the family that they stood silently enjoying it, looking up at the trees, hearing the faint murmur of the wind in the upper branches, feeling the peace and serenity of the place.

Izabella said softly to Josif, "It is a beautiful grove, just as you said it would be. In the summer when the leaves are green we will have picnics here. It will be like heaven."

The walk around the farm had taken most of that Saturday morning, and the family returned to the house hungry for their noon meal. While the women reheated the remains of the night's meal and sliced the bread, the men sat around the kitchen table and discussed what must be done to bring the rundown farm into working condition.

"The fence around the animal yard is first," said Josif. "The horses cannot stand in the barn all the time. Next we will repair the machinery so we can plow the fields and plant our crops."

Uncle Jon reminded Josif, "For that we have to get the new horses."

"The new horses!" Josif felt the excitement growing inside him. Getting new horses was like a miracle – like birth – a special happening in life that renewed and invigorated man. It was a challenge and a fulfillment. A challenge to train the horse so that it became part of the man, not breaking the horse's will, but guiding it so that it would join its strength and spirit with that of the man. A fulfillment because man and horse were meant to be together, each incomplete without the other. The magic in the bond between horse and man strengthened both of them.

Uncle Jon and Michael-Joseph were as excited about the horses as was Josif, but he was not sure about Alexander. After he had worked with Eli Rahn, the boy seemed to care more about machines than horses. Josif spoke to Michael-Joseph, "Do you want to come with us when we go to look at the horses?"

As Michael-Joseph nodded happily, the girls, who were setting the table, protested. "Papa, we want to go see the horses, too!"

Izabella spoke from the stove. "Aunt Magda, the girls and I will go for a walk this afternoon after we have brought in firewood. Perhaps we can see the horses in the field at Mr. Anderson's farm."

Josif stared at Izabella. Ever since they had set foot on the farm he had seen a change in her and in the girls, too. It was as if having land and a house of their own had given them more spirit, more life. "What will these Swedes think," he said, "seeing women and wild girls on the road?" He shook his head. "I don't know. I think the women and girls had better stay home and not bother these Swedish people."

"We'll be good, Papa." Marie spoke for the girls. "We won't bother the Swedish people."

"What if you meet the man in the black buggy? The man with the whip."

"God will protect us," Izabella said. "We will carry garlic and our knives. The man will not harm us."

Josif felt some apprehension, yet he was pleased that Izabella seemed more like the laughing and independent dancer he had courted in Romania.

After they had eaten, the men went to work on the fence while the women and girls brought wood from the grove and piled it in a small woodshed between the house and the privy. They went to talk to the men before they started on their walk.

"We will go as far as the church so we can find out what kind it is," Izabella said to them. "It would be so wonderful if it were Orthodox. The children could be blessed by the priest."

"It's probably Lutheran," Josif replied. "Fritz said that the Swedes lived south of here. I don't know what kind of people live to the east, but there is little chance that they are of our faith."

The men watched the women and girls go out the driveway, then returned to their fence repairs. The fence between the barn and the tank was built of old wooden planks, some splintered and broken, while the fence which enclosed about an acre behind the barn was of woven wire with three strands of rusty barbed wire above it, all stapled to rotten and fallen wooden posts.

They mended the plank fence first by splicing the broken pieces with old boards from the piles of junk that lay about the place. The wire fence was more difficult. In places where the wooden posts had broken, only the sagging barbed wire held the posts in place, and the wire lay close to the ground.

"Whoever invented barbed wire should have been hung up on it," Uncle Jon said with disgust. "This will cut a horse right to the bone if he gets tangled in it."

They found rusty steel posts in a pile back of the granary, and made a temporary repair of the fence by driving a steel post into the ground beside each broken wooden one and then wiring the two posts together.

Before they turned Peter, Paul, and the cow into the little pasture they carefully removed all the old wire and junk that had been left by previous tenants, then went to look at the machinery to determine what repairs were needed.

The two plows, the drag, and the disc all seemed sound, but when they pulled the seeder, the corn-planter, and the cultivators out of the tangle of old weeds, they found that in many places the machinery was held together with baling wire instead of bolts. They searched through the junk piled around and in the buildings, but found only a few bolts that could be used. Josif opened his purse and took out three dimes which he gave to Alexander along with a rusty bolt. "Alexander, go to the Wagner's farm. See if they will sell us any old bolts like this one. Make sure you pay for them."

Alexander took the dimes and bolt, and set out for the Wagner place. The road was drier than the fields had been, so that the walking was easier, and as he strode along, he whistled *Maidens Fair* and looked happily at the fields of their new farm.

When he came to the Wagner farm, a strong smell of cow manure greeted him, and the huge red barn and the big square white house loomed over him like the buildings of giants. He briefly wondered if Fritz and August had really been raised by wolves and if he was in any danger.

As he got closer, he found August leaning over a wooden fence by the barn, idly throwing clods at a big black and white bull that pawed and snorted behind the fence. "Ain't he a pisser?" August said. "He's so damned ornery that nobody but Fritz can go in there 'cept on horseback and carryin' a pitchfork."

Alexander stared at the bull. "Fritz goes in there with him?"

"Oh, hell yes. He's meaner than the bull, and the bull knows it." August spit between the heavy planks. "Grandpa was the same way." He spit again. "Course, the bull ain't no dummy. He waited 'til, just once, Grandpa turned his back on him. Then, whammo! He woulda stomped Grandpa right into mush if me'n Fritz hadn't come runnin' with a coupla pitchforks."

"Your Grandpa must have been real glad you were there."

"Glad? He was so goddamned mad he ain't never got over it. Claimed he coulda licked the bull himself if we hadn't come buttin' in. He's got more ornery ever since." August threw another clod at the bull. "We was gonna shoot the bull, but Grandpa wouldn't let us. Said as soon as his leg got better he was goin' in there and teach him who's boss."

"How long ago was that?"

"Bout four years ago. Grandpa was in the hospital for a month, up in Sioux Falls. They finally kicked him out, he was so ornery." August threw another clod. "They said if the bull ever got him again, they wouldn't let him in." August spit again through the fence. "You walk up here just for fun, or you got somethin' on your mind?"

"Papa needs some bolts to fix the cultivator and other machinery. He needs some like this." Alexander held out the bolt and the three dimes on the palm of his hand. "I brought money to pay for them."

August snorted. "Jesus Christ, we ain't gonna charge for no old rusty bolts. Grandpa's got a whole barrel of 'em over in the toolshed. Come on over and we'll pick some out."

They went to the toolshed, and August tipped the contents of an old wooden keg onto the floor. He was pawing through the heap of old bolts, screws, bent nails, washers, nuts, rivets, and spark plugs when Grandpa Wagner appeared in the doorway like some terrible and gaunt apparition from the underworld.

He balanced himself on a scarred wooden crutch with a big gnarled hand gripping the cross bar. His fierce eyes glared out from under heavy eyebrows and an uncombed shock of thick gray hair, and his bristly jaw stuck out belligerently beyond his upper lip like the blade of a plow ramming through a stubble-field.

"Who's this?" His voice was so loud that the pile of nuts and bolts seemed to quiver and fall back toward the far wall. "Goddamn it, August, answer me when I talk to you!"

August looked up from the pile of junk. "This here's Alexander. They come to the old Ariosto place."

Grandapa lurched forward on the crutch. He balanced himself and swung the crutch at August, just missing as August leapt up and backward. "Who told you you could go dumpin' my bolt barrel on the floor?"

"Well, hell, Grandpa, we gotta find some half-inch bolts." August circled warily just beyond reach of the crutch. "They need 'em to fix that ol' hammock-seat cultivator and that other junk."

"Hammock-seat, huh?" Grandpa turned to stare at Alexander. "w

Why don't you use a piece a wire?"

Alexander swallowed. "Papa told me to buy some bolts if I could." He held out the three dimes. "We'll pay you for them."

Grandpa Wagner stared at the coins. "We ain't no blankety blank hardware store." He glared at Alexander. "How old are you anyways?"

Alexander's voice shook. "I'm twelve."

"Twelve, huh? You ain't no bigger'n a skinny spring chicken." Grandpa hopped toward the junk pile and prodded it with his crutch. "This here's my bolt collection. You know how long I been savin' it?"

"Fifteen years?" Alexander guessed reluctantly.

"Fifteen years? Forty-five years! that's how long!"

Grandpa swung the crutch at august again. "Goddamn it, August, i'm gonna clout you a good one if you don't leave my bolt collection alone!"

He scowled at Alexander. "You want a piece a cake?"

Alexander swallowed. "No thank you. I have to get back home." He started for the door, trying to circle around Grandpa.

A Plymouth Rock hen that had been cowering in a far corner of the shed came half-running, half-flying in a rush of gray feathers and yellow feet between Grandpa's legs and crutch, and out the door, squawking hysterically. Grandpa flailed after her with his crutch, whacking both sides of the door jamb. "Get me the Goddamned axe! Damn hen's been settin' on my bolts, crappin' on 'em!" He glared at the hen as she ran across the barnyard toward the cottonwoods by the tank. "Run off, Damn it! I'll get you yet!"

He turned back toward Alexander, hitching himself around on the crutch. "Ain't you gone in the house yet fer that cake?"

"No, sir."

"Well go on in. Tell her you want a piece a cake!"

"Yes, sir." Alexander stepped cautiously around Grandpa and went to the gate and concrete sidewalk that led up to the house. He opened the gate and walked hesitantly up the walk to the big screened porch that circled the house on three sides.

A group of wild-looking, half-grown kittens stared at him from under the porch, and from a low shed near the cyclone cellar came the muffled chugging of a gasoline engine. He went up the porch steps and tapped on the frame of the screen door.

August yelled from the toolshed, "Go on in. She can't hear nothin'."

Alexander slowly opened the screen door and went up onto the porch. Two old kitchen chairs with flower-embossed cardboard seats stood next to the door of the house, and beyond them on the gray-painted porch floor stood a row of huge mud and manure-covered overshoes and rubbers. Through the glass pane in the door of the house he saw a tall, spare woman working at a cream separator with her back to him. Alexander tapped on the door. "Hello?"

The woman kept on with her work at the separator. She wore her gray hair in a bun and she had a long blue and white checked apron over her dress. She was placing a stack of shiny, metal, cup-like discs in the separator, and on the table next to the wall were pans of milk and a stack of milk pails. Embossed on the side of the cream separator was the name, DeLaval.

Alexander tapped on the door again, but the woman kept on with her work. He looked back, toward the barn; Grandpa was lurching up toward the house on his crutch. "Go on in!" Grandpa yelled. "Tell her you want a piece a cake!" His bellow made the screens shake.

Alexander opened the door and stepped fearfully into the room, trying to move past the woman, wishing he'd never come.

Grandpa banged up the porch steps. "Move around where she can see ya! You ain't gettin' any cake that way!" He whacked his crutch back and forth against the door

148

frame. "He wants a piece a cake!"

The woman straightened up and looked back at Grandpa, then saw Alexander. She was a sweet-faced old lady with kindly light blue eyes, and her face made Alexander think of the Madonna on an icon, except that she was much older. She smiled at him. "Why, boy, where did you come from so quiet-like?"

Alexander wished he could disappear. "Grandpa Wagner told me to come in."

Grandpa shouted, "He wants a piece a cake!"

"Oh my goodness! All that way!" Grandma Wagner placed her hand on Alexander's shoulder. "Come in the kitchen and sit down. You must be tired."

Grandpa hobbled close to Grandma and placed his jutting chin next to her ear. "He ain't tired! He wants a piece a cake! He come after a bolt!"

Grandma led Alexander into the kitchen through a wide door. "He isn't interested in colts now. He's tired after his walk."

She sat Alexander down in a big straight chair at a huge oak table. "You just sit there and rest." She felt his shoulder. "Why you poor boy, there isn't enough meat on you to hold you together. I'll just bring you a nice piece of cake and a glass of milk to fatten you up." She went to a big cupboard that covered one wall.

Alexander looked around the room. The table was massive, built of wide oak planks, the chairs were wide and high-backed, and the row of dark-doored wooden cupboards against the wall extended right up to the ceiling as though whoever used them must have been able to reach that high. It seemed like a giant's house in a fairy tale.

Grandma brought a shiny, dark chocolate cake to the table and cut out a thick wedge which she placed in front of Alexander then brought him a glass of milk. "Now you just rest and have a good bite to eat."

Grandpa came thumping into the kitchen. He stuck a

finger out toward the cake, his eyes greedy. Grandma pulled a long-handled spoon from her apron pocket and whacked him across the knuckles. "Keep away from that, Gerhard. It's for supper."

Grandpa jerked his hand back. "Dag nab it, i want a piece a cake!" He banged his crutch on the table leg. "Right now!"

Grandma looked up at him. "Don't try to sweet talk me, Gerhard. It won't work." She took a curved ear trumpet from a drawer in the table and put it to her ear. She smiled at Alexander."What's your name, son?"

Alexander spoke timidly into the ear-trumpet. "Alexander Dacia."

"You have to speak up. Sometimes my ears just fill up with wax, and I can't hear a thing. Then, I just use this ear-trumpet until I get a chance to go into town to have Dr. Sinclair flush them out."

Grandma touched his shoulder. "Poor boy, you're so thin it's no wonder you can't make yourself heard." She brought a pencil and a pad of paper out of the table drawer. "Write your name here."

Alexander printed his name in big block letters. Grandma studied the paper carefully. "Alexander." She turned to look at him with her mild blue eyes. "You look like an Alexander."

Grandpa reached in his overalls pocket and pulled out a rusty half-inch bolt and a nut "You give me a piece a cake and he can have this bolt."

Grandma looked disdainfully at the bolt. "You've been sorting through that old keg of yours again. I don't want any of your old bolts."

"i didn't get it for you!" Grandpa banged on the table leg. "This boy wants it!"

Grandma shook her head. "Take it back outside. I don't want the rusty old thing here in my clean kitchen."

Alexander wrote on the tablet, "I came to get some

bolts. We need them for the machinery."

Grandma read what he had written. "Well, my land, why didn't somebody say so?" She spoke severely to Grandpa. "Gerhard, you get those bolts for Alexander. The very idea!"

Grandpa backed away, his eyes crafty. "Not until i get some cake! Then he can have the bolts!"

Grandma frowned. "I declare, Gerhard, all you think about is horses. Now give Alexander those bolts."

She cut another piece of cake. "Poor boy, you still look hungry."

Alexander wrote on the tablet, "I think you should keep the cake for Grandpa."

Grandma read what he had written. She smiled at him. "Land sakes, what a thoughtful boy you are. 'Keep the cake for Grandpa.' But Gerhard wants you to have the cake, don't you Gerhard?" She shook her finger at Grandpa. "Now just you forget about those colts."

Grandpa's face was as red as the comb on a rooster. He hopped up and down on his crutch. "No I don't want him to have it! Leave some of the blankety blank cake for me and I'll give him the bolts!" He shook the bolt under grandma's nose. "Bolt! Bolt! It ain't no colt, it's a bolt!"

Grandma's smile was beatific. "There now, we've got that settled." She put the piece of cake on Alexander's plate. "There you are, Alexander, just what Gerhard wanted you to have." She cut a thin wedge of the cake and placed it in front of Grandpa. "And there's a nice piece for you, Gerhard, for being so thoughtful about this poor, thin boy." She patted Alexander on the head. "When you finish your cake, you just go right out to that toolshed and have August help you pick out all the bolts you want."

* * *

The men and boys were in the barn finishing the chores before the women and girls came back around 5:00PM. The women appeared on the long driveway and joined the men in the barn. They were pink-faced and excited from their walk and eager to tell of their adventures.

"We saw horses, Papa! In Mr. Anderson's field! They are beautiful!" The girls all spoke at once, dancing around Josif and Uncle Jon. "And we walked all the way to the church!"

"Settle down, girls," Elizabeth said gently.

"What kind of a church is it?" Josif asked.

"It is Lutheran," Izabella replied. "As you thought."

"What about the horses? How big are they, what color?"

"The horses we saw are about sixteen hands, chestnut with white manes, tails, and feet, part Belgian, I think. Almost as beautiful as Peter and Paul."

"If they are the ones Fritz talked about, they sound as if they are worth looking at. We will go see Alfred Anderson tomorrow or the next day. If we have enough money, maybe we will buy them."

Izabella went to the manger and stroked Paul's nose. "Maybe Mr. Anderson will wait until after harvest for the money."

Josif shook his head. "We will not owe anybody." He looked to Uncle Jon for confirmation. "My grandfather, your father. He had three rules to live by."

Uncle Jon nodded.

"Owe no one. Fear no one. Get horses and land and a good wife. Those were his rules." Josif looked at the children. "You all hear that? Owe no one. Fear no one. Get horses and land and a good wife. That is what your great-grandfather, Michael Dacia, said. Remember that."

Aunt Magda sniffed. "It is interesting that a good wife is the last thing Michael Dacia thought was of value."

Izabella smiled. "Maybe last is best." She looked out at the barnyard. "See how the men and our two boys have fixed the fence! It looks like new."

Michael-Joseph took her hand. "We fixed the fence behind the barn too, and Alexander went to Fritz and August's, and Grandma Wagner and Granpa Wagner gave him two pieces of chocolate cake, and Grandpa sent some bolts. Can we have cake sometime, Mama?"

Izabella lifted him in her arms. "Of course we can." She looked at Alexander. "It was nice for you to meet Grandpa and Grandma Wagner. What good neighbors they are! What nice old people they must be."

Alexander scuffed his toe in the dirt. "They are, Mama."

* * *

Sunday night, after supper, Izabella and Aunt Magda brought the big washtub and a small tub into the kitchen and put them in front of the stove along with towels and a cake of Hutterite yellow soap. "Tomorrow, you go to school," Izabella said to the children. "It is time for baths."

The children went into the hot, soapy water one-by-one, in order of need to be clean in public and of who had the most dirt to wash off, so it was usually the girls and women before the boys and men. Each rinsed off in the small tub with warm water from the stove reservoir after their sudsing. When the children were finished, Izabella cut their fingernails and toenails with the big scissors and shooed them into bed.

"Tomorrow you all go to your new school. Is important for you to make good impression," she cautioned. "So you must all sleep well and put on your nicest school clothes tomorrow. Tomorrow you will meet new children, just like yourselves, and will make new friends. It will be happy day!"

Chapter Nine
School: the First Day

Today Alexander and the girls would start in their new school.

Izabella packed their lunches, placing an apple and a thick slice of *mamaliga* and white cheese in each of their syrup pails. The cover of each pail had been perforated by driving a nail through it to form the owner's initials with the holes. All of the pails except Caroline's were dented and rubbed shiny by use, and they smelled of metal and apples and school.

Josif decided to take the children to school in the wagon that first morning so that he could introduce them to the teacher. He had a lurking suspicion that the teacher used only the Swedish language in the classroom, and he intended to speak man-to-man with the fellow. Americans expected to be taught in English, not Swedish.

He also carried the children's report cards and a letter from the "English" schoolteacher at the Hutterite colony.

They left early, wanting to be at school by 8:30 so there would be time to talk with the teacher before school started. Peter and Paul were full of energy after their Sunday rest, and Josif let them pull the wagon at a brisk trot over the drying road. Josif and the children all stood up in the wagon, swaying easily with its motion, the cold morning air fresh and sharp on their faces. The clear, bright morning and the early sunlight gave a dark richness to the flat, wet land, and the transparent air allowed them to see every detail of grass, field, and fence. The sky above them glowed in a pale blue radiance that extended forever into space.

A meadowlark gave its clear melodious call from a wooden fence post, blending it with the jingle of the harness bells, and Josif and the children listened happily, feeling that life would be good in the new land.

From the wagon they saw the wide pond in their northeast field, and in its center two gray and white forms floated gracefully in the water. "They stayed!" Rose and Caroline stood on sacks of oats to see better. "Our geese stayed in our field!"

Marie asked, "Can we take them some oats after school, Papa?"

Josif slowed the team to a walk so as not to frighten the geese. "There is plenty for them to eat in the fields. We need all our oats for seed and to feed the horses."

"What will they do when the pond dries up, Papa?"

"They will move on to the north." Josif slapped the reins lightly on the horses' backs, letting them trot again. "Don't you kids interfere with the geese. They will do what is best for them by themselves. Right now, we have to get to school so we can talk with the teacher."

They went past the Wagner place, and Alexander pointed to the pen where the bull pawed at the dirt, and to the tool-shed where Grandpa Wagner kept his bolt barrel. From a long shed and fenced lot north of the barn, a herd of black and white Holstein cattle stolidly watched the Dacias as they went by.

The schoolhouse stood about a quarter of a mile beyond the Wagner buildings, on the west side of the road, just south of an east-west crossroad. The white one-story building looked to be about forty feet long and twenty feet wide. It had a gable roof, and a low platform jutted from its eastern end. A metal flag pole and a pump stood at one side of the platform.

Behind the schoolhouse crouched a small shed, a low barn, and two outhouses, one on either side of the barn.

Swings and teeter-totters stood in a skeletal line south of the schoolhouse, and a thin row of trees partially enclosed the schoolyard: cottonwoods on the south, box elders on the west and north.

Josif stopped the team in front of the platform and sent Alexander to the door. Alexander knocked timidly on it, then tried the handle. He looked back at Josif. "It's locked."

Josif unbuttoned his coat and pulled out his watch. "It's almost 8:30." He frowned at the building. "Probably the Swedish teacher isn't up yet."

As he spoke, a woman came around the north side of the building, and she stopped so suddenly upon seeing the Dacias that some of the coal fell out of the bucket she was carrying. The Dacias were so surprised to see her, and the woman appeared to be so taken aback by the sight of the Dacias, that for a moment no one spoke.

The woman was large, about forty years old. She wore her brown hair done up in a bun, and her long, intelligent-looking face had a prominent nose upon which perched a pair of rimless eyeglasses with a brown ribbon hanging from one side. Her mouth, which could have been pretty, seemed to tremble, as if from fright. She wore a heavy, knitted, brown coat-sweater over a white blouse, a red ribbon necktie, a heavy brown skirt, thick brown stockings, and brown, laced oxfords. Her pale blue eyes stared apprehensively at the Dacias, and her whole posture spoke of readiness for flight.

Josif took off his hat and made a little bow to the woman. He spoke to her in English, quietly, as he would to a skittish horse. "We not mean frighten you. We look for schoolteacher. You know where he is?"

The woman continued to stare at the Dacias, but a little of the fear left her eyes. "I am the teacher. What did you want to see me about?" Her voice was surprisingly beautiful. Josif dropped his hat. He bent and picked it up from the floor of the wagon. He stared at her. "You are schoolteacher?"

"Yes. I am Mrs. Horsefall."

Josif looked around at the children. He asked them in Romanian, "They have Swedish women teachers in America?"

"I don't think she is Swedish, Papa," Alexander said. "She speaks English too well."

Josif turned back to the woman. "I am Josif Dacia. These children of my wife and me. Are Alexander, Marie, Rose, and Caroline. They come to school. At home is Michael-Joseph. He come next year."

"They want to come to school here? Now?" Mrs. Horsefall asked incredulously.

Josif nodded, smiling at her to make her less frightened. "That right. Here to this school. We just move to farm south of here, first farm other side of Wagner farm."

"Good morning, children." She looked at Josif. "Mr. Dacia, there must be some mistake. I have had no notice that your children would be coming to this school. I cannot accept them without an official transfer from their previous school. I would also need their report cards from that school."

"Have report cards and letter. Children have good grades."

Mrs. Horsefall stared up at Alexander and the girls. Her eyes held a look of desperation. "I cannot admit these children without proper authorization from the County Superintendent of Schools."

"You read letter, please. Teacher in other school say everything be all right." Josif came down from the wagon and held out the letter to her.

Mrs. Horsefall took the letter. She opened the envelope, adjusted her glasses, and read the letter. When she had finished she looked up at the children, then at Josif. "It seems that I will have to accept your children," she said with resignation. "Please come into the schoolhouse with your report cards. You may come too, Mr. Dacia."

Josif smiled at her. "We thank you. Children be good. You see." He spoke to Alexander. "You bring coal bucket in for teacher."

Mrs. Horsefall smiled uncertainly at him. "Thank you, Mr. Dacia." She went up onto the platform and unlocked the door with a key she took from the pocket of her sweater. "Please come in," she said to the group, "I was just going to start the fire."

They went through a central entryway with a cloakroom on either side, and into the schoolroom, straight ahead.

A large, round, black stove sat at one side near the door, rows of battered wooden desks lined either side of a central aisle, a pump organ stood against one wall, and at the far end of the room blackboards loomed above a desk which sat on a small wooden platform. A long wooden bench stretched on one side of the desk, and a faded American flag rose on the other side.

Above the blackboard the faces of the American presidents Washington and Lincoln looked sternly down from their framed portraits, and on the south wall hung a picture of a beautiful young man in armor, leaning on his sword.

On the north wall, above the organ, hung a picture of many horses, some rearing up, with men holding their halters.

Mrs. Horsefall opened the door of the stove and arranged paper, kindling, and coal in the fire-box. She adjusted the damper and draft, then lit the paper and quickly closed the door. A thick cloud of smoke poured out into the room from around the door, and she frantically readjusted the draft and damper until the smoke began to pull back into the stove, leaving a dark cloud under the stained ceiling.

She sighed and walked up to the desk on the platform and sat down in the chair behind the desk. She took out her keys and opened a drawer in the desk, then placed a grey ledger precisely in the middle of the desktop. She looked up at the Dacias. "Please have your children come to the front of the room with their report cards, Mr. Dacia," she said resignedly.

Alexander and the girls stood by the organ, looking up at the picture of the horses. Josif gave them their report cards and motioned them forward. "Report cards good. You see," he assured Mrs. Horsefall.

Mrs. Horsefall laid the report cards in a neat row on her desk. Then she read them, one by one, glancing up periodically to look at each of the children. When she finished, she spoke without looking up from her desk.

"The report cards are quite acceptable, even excellent. For that reason, Mr. Dacia, I suggest that you enroll your children in another school. Pleasant Valley School in the Swedish Vikstad community is only five miles south of here. It would be a good school for your children."

Josif and the children stared at her in disbelief. "We not want children to go to Swedish school," Josif said. "Why you not want them to come here?"

Mrs. Horsefall looked up at him. "We have seventeen pupils in Mount Faith School. All but a few are good children. But the others are the worst, the most unteachable, the most stubbornly bad, the most delinquent pupils I have ever tried to teach. The older boys are ignorant and depraved monsters who are completely beyond any hope of discipline or learning, and who exert their evil influence on the other children. You would be wise, Mr. Dacia, to send your children to another school."

Josif tried to understand her words. He said to Alexander in Romanian, "Tell me what she said, in our language."

Alexander repeated Mrs. Horsefall's outburst as well as he could, and the girls added their own interpretation, inserting words as he hesitated. Josif listened, then he said in Romanian, "I think this lady is like a mare getting ready to crash into a fence. Maybe we can calm her down before she gets too excited."

He said to Mrs. Horsefall, "Not worry about Alexander

and girls. They not let other kids make them bad. You see."

Mrs. Horsefall looked into Josif's eyes as she spoke. "You insist, then, on sending your children to this school?"

"Yes," he said returning Mrs. Horsefall's gaze. "I want children to go to this school."

"Very well. I have tried to warn you. If any harm comes to your children, Mr. Dacia, remember what I have said." She placed the report cards and the letter beside her ledger. "I suggest that you see to your team before the other students arrive."

Josif smiled at her. "We thank you. Not worry about team; I go now." He hesitated. "You like horses, Mrs. Horsefall?"

"Horses?" Mrs. Horsefall stared at him. "Yes, I do. Why do you ask?"

Josif pointed to the picture over the organ. "Because you have horses' picture on wall, and you think about our team."

Mrs. Horsefall's eyes grew less apprehensive. "Do you like the picture, Mr. Dacia?"

"I like. The man who paint that was good horseman. He love horses."

"The one who painted that picture loved horses, but it was not a man. It was a woman." Mrs. Horsefall smiled at the girls.

"Her name was Marie Rosalie Bonheur. Sometimes she is called Rosa Bonheur. The picture is called *The Horse Fair*." She gently touched Caroline's head. "Do you like the picture, Caroline?"

Before Caroline could answer, the sound of loud voices and scuffling came from the platform in front of the schoolhouse. Something crashed hard against the door and it flew open, banging against the cloakroom wall, and August Wagner and two other boys came bursting through the doorway, shoving and elbowing each other. They stopped just inside the doorway, staring at Alexander and the girls.

One of the boys was a big, thick-bodied, red-faced

161

blond; the other was a dark-haired, mean-eyed, rat-faced individual who looked strangely familiar to Josif.

August spoke to Josif, "These dumb galoots was gonna unhitch your team and turn 'em loose. It's lucky I came along, huh, Mr. Dacia?"

"They touch our horses?"

The dark one sniggered. "We was just gonna have a little fun, Mister."

The blond one added, "Sure. What if we was?" He had little pig-like blue eyes and a big cold sore on his lower lip. As he spoke, he wiped with his sleeve across a wet dribble under his nose.

Josif asked August, again. "They touch our horses?"

August's face had a pious look. "They didn't touch 'em, Mr. Dacia. I stopped 'em."

Josif looked hard at the boys. "I hope you tell truth. What your names?"

August jerked his thumb at the blond one, then at the dark one. "This here's Junior Jensen, this one's Julius Lamb."

The dark one scowled, and his eyes burned with a vicious, almost insane fire. "My pa's gonna knock hell outta you if you touch me. Big Jens Jensen will too."

Josif's eyes were cold. "Listen, Junior Jensen and Julius Lamb. If you ever touch my horses, I get mad. You tell that to your Papas."

He turned and spoke to Alexander and the girls. "You be good kids in school and mind teacher." He said to Mrs. Horsefall, "I happy to meet schoolteacher who like horses."

Alexander watched his father as he walked down the aisle and out the door. He could feel the eyes of Julius Lamb and Junior Jensen staring at him. A feeling of resentment hovered somewhere in his head, yet at the same time he knew that his father had done the best thing, the only thing that he could do. "If you ever touch my horses, I get mad." Not, "If you ever touch my kids, I get mad." The horses were gentle, trusting creatures, dependent on the family for their food, care, and safety, and they had to be protected. With him it was different. Any word from his father to protect him would only make it worse. It was going to be bad. He knew that from those mean eyes, but it was the only way.

Mrs. Horsefall unlocked a drawer in her desk and took out a large, brass bell. She relocked the drawer, then placed her record book and the Dacias' letter and report cards in the top drawer and locked it. She said to Alexander and the girls, "You will sit in these four desks at the side of the room. Place your lunch pails, coats, and overshoes in the cloak-rooms, then go to your desks."

She went out with the bell, and the Dacias went down the side aisle and around behind the three boys to get to the cloakrooms. When Alexander came back he took the fourth seat back in the row Mrs. Horsefall had indicated. Only Julius Lamb and Junior Jensen were in the room.

Julius and Junior came to stand by Alexander's desk, staring down at him. Julius worked his lips and spat on the desktop. "Hey, kid, look what you done to your new desk. Don't you know that's school property?"

Alexander did not speak or look up. He could hear the school bell ringing outside. The spit lay in a slimy, bubbly pool in the center of the desktop. Someone had carved the initials, F.W. in the wood and the spit was running down into the cuts.

Julius cuffed Alexander on the side of the head, hard, his knuckles tight and mean. "You better clean that up, you little bastard, or I'm gonna kick the shit outta you at recess."

Junior Jensen moved closer. He hawked long and nois-ily, then he spit a thick yellow gob next to Julius's. "Jesus Christ, kid, you done it again!" Junior stepped heavily on Alexander's foot and leaned against him. Junior smelled like a pig – rancid, like old fat. He ground his knuckles down on top of Alexander's head, pushing hard and twisting. "How you like a Dutch rub, kid? It'll kill your cooties."

Mrs. Horsefall came back into the room, moving fast,

the bell in her hand, a crowd of children behind her. She went up onto the platform where her desk stood and locked the bell in the desk. She turned to face the students. "Go to your seats. We will now pledge allegiance to the flag."

Julius and Junior moved away from Alexander, going somewhere behind him. He could feel their eyes on him as Mrs. Horsefall spoke from the platform.

"Everyone rise." She turned to face the flag and placed her hand on her bosom.

I pledge allegiance...

Alexander said the words, looking at the flag, feeling the eyes on his back,

...to the flag of the United States of America...

Hoarse snickering came from behind him.

and to the Republic for which it stands...

Something whooshed through the air and splatted against the blackboard, a fresh yellow ball of horse manure that spread out on the smooth surface and then slid slowly down, leaving a wide, wet track until it came to rest in the chalk trough at the bottom of the blackboard.

... one nation, indivisible, with liberty and justice for all.

Mrs. Horsefall swayed slightly. She did not look at the blackboard, but turned to face the students. "Now we will sing. This morning we will sing *America the Beautiful*." She looked at the Dacias. "New students will share the songbooks with those beside them."

A dark-haired girl stood by the seat next to Alexander, and she opened her songbook and held it so that he could see the pages. Her hand was square and strong-looking with short nails that looked as though they had been chewed to the quick. There was a smell like fresh milk about her, and there were little blue flowers on the white background of her dress.

Mrs. Horsefall seated herself at the organ and placed her songbook on the music rack. She pumped the organ pedals, struck the first chord, and began:

Oh beautiful, for spacious skies
For amber waves of grain
For purple mountain majesties
Above the fruited plain.
America! America! God shed his grace on thee
And crown thy good with brotherhood
From sea to shining sea.

Another ball of horse manure splatted against the blackboard, but Mrs. Horsefall continued pumping and playing the organ and singing, her voice rising in a soaring contralto that lifted to the smoke-blackened ceiling and hung quivering there.

Oh beautiful, for Pilgrim feet...

A loud stamping reverberated from the back of the room.

Whose stern impassioned stress
A thoroughfare for freedom beat
Across the wilderness...

Desktops pounded like gunfire.

America! America! God mend thine every flaw
Confirm thy soul in self-control Thy liberty in law...

Snickering and loud thumps from the back seats.

Oh beautiful for heroes prov'd In liberating strife
Who more than self their country lov'd
And mercy more than life.
America! America! May God thy gold refine
Till all success be nobleness
And every gain divine...

The students' singing grew more and more discordant and ragged as they swiveled around to look at the back of the room where the snickering was growing louder. The smell of horse manure permeated the room now.

Oh beautiful for patriot's dream
That sees beyond the years
Thine alabaster cities gleam
Undimmed by human tears...

Mrs. Horsefall played grimly on, her voice soaring now like an eagle, and the Dacias' voices joined with hers so that it was as if there were two choirs in the room, one a howling caterwauling mob of students, the other a musical and harmonious chorus composed of Mrs. Horsefall and the Dacias.

America! America! God shed his grace on thee
And crown thy good with brotherhood
From sea to shining sea!

Mrs. Horsefall slowly lifted her hands from the keyboard. She sat motionless, her back stiff and straight, then she rose, took her songbook from the rack, and walked slowly back to her desk. She unlocked the desk drawer and put the songbook safely inside.

"August Wagner!"

More snickering came from the back seats. August's

voice was innocent-sounding. "What, Mrs. Horsefall?"

"Come up here!"

"I didn't throw no horse manure."

"Come up here!"

August came slowly up the aisle, grinning, his heavy shoes clumping on the wooden floor, his hands in his overalls pockets.

"Hold out your hands!"

August tugged. "They won't come out."

Mrs. Horsefall's eyes were becoming wild. "Hold out your hands!"

August tugged again, grunting and grinning. "They're stuck."

Now there were tears in Mrs. Horsefall's eyes. "August Wagner, I am going to tell you once more. If you don't take your hands out of your pockets, you will be expelled from school!"

"Grandpa ain't gonna like it if you expel me."

"I hope that he doesn't like it. I hope that your brother doesn't like it. I hope that they both horsewhip you." Mrs. Horsefall's face was white. "Now take your hands out of your pockets, or I will expel you!"

August looked back at Julius and Junior. "Maybe I don't feel like bein' expelled."

Mrs. Horsefall spoke to a big plain-faced girl. "Anna, go to the Wagner farm. Tell Fritz Wagner that I must see him right now."

August scuffed his feet. "Aw, look at my hands if you want to. They ain't too clean, though. I been milkin' a lotta cows." He pulled his hands out of his pockets.

Mrs. Horsefall looked quickly at his hands. "That looks like horse manure. Get the coal shovel and paper towels and clean up the manure that you threw."

Julius Lamb spoke from the back of the room. "Teacher, it wasn't August that done it. It was that new kid. He spit on his desk, too. Take a look at it."

Mrs. Horsefall came to Alexander's desk. She stared at the gobs of spit on its top. "Alexander, did you spit on this desk?"

"No, Mrs. Horsefall."

"Then who did spit on it?"

"I don't know."

"You don't know who spit on your desk?"

"No, Mrs. Horsefall."

Mrs. Horsefall's shoulders slumped, and she spoke with resignation. "Get paper towels from the cloakroom and clean it up. Put them in the stove when you're through."

She went back to her desk and stood behind it. "While August and Alexander clean the blackboard and the desk, we will begin our studies. But first, I will introduce our new students, the Dacia children. They are Alexander, Marie, Rose, and Caroline." Alexander felt the eyes of Julius and Junior on his back as he stood up.

Mrs. Horsefall brought arithmetic books to each of the Dacias and showed them their assignments. Then she said loudly, "Everyone do your arithmetic problems. Eighth grade reading class, come forward." She spoke to August, who was slowly coming toward the front of the room with the coal shovel and paper towels. "You will join the class, August, as soon as you have cleaned the blackboard."

The big girl called Anna came to the front of the room along with Junior Jensen and Julius Lamb. They sat on the bench, facing Mrs. Horsefall and the blackboard, scuffling and kicking at one another.

"You may read first, Anna," Mrs. Horsefall said. "Please start at page thirty-two in our book."

While Anna slowly and painfully read out loud, Alexander cleaned the spit from his desk with the paper towels, and August clumped up the aisle to the blackboard and began to wipe the wet smear from its surface. He worked with deliberate slowness, carefully studying the blackboard after every wipe, sniffing it, stepping back to admire his work, turning and grinning at the other students.

The smell of horse manure became even stronger in the room as he began to scrape noisily at the chalk trough with the coal shovel, pushing the manure out and down onto the floor. Every student except Anna watched as he daintily flicked half-digested oats into the shovel with the corner of a paper towel. Mrs. Horsefall finally could stand no more, and she signaled Anna to stop reading. "August, get the broom and sweep that manure up from the floor. Then come to the bench."

August protested. "But I ain't done yet."

"You never will be done, the way you are going about it. Now get the broom and sweep that manure up immediately."

August held his nose. "It stinks up here. I can't hardly stand it."

Mrs. Horsefall came to her feet. "If you do not have that manure swept up, and if you are not in your place here in two minutes, I will send for your brother!"

August stared at the clock on the rear wall. "I can't work that fast. It ain't good for me."

Mrs. Horsefall's voice was close to breaking. "It is now twenty minutes after nine. You have until twenty-two minutes after nine."

August grinned at the watching students. "Watch this!" He ran down the aisle, lifting his knees high, his big work shoes slamming the floor like mallets. He seized the broom from its place in the corner and ran forward again to the blackboard. He swept the manure toward the coal shovel so hard that chunks went flying by on either side of the shovel. He circled, sweeping harder, and the manure spread farther over the floor with each stroke of the broom.

He looked up at the clock. "Whoo-ee! Time's almost up!" He made one more futile swipe with the broom, then raced down the aisle with the broom, shovel, and a wad of paper towels.

There was a bang as the outer door crashed open against the wall, a clattering of the shovel, another bang, and he came charging up the aisle and hurled himself onto the bench next to Anna, almost pushing Junior Jensen off the other end. "Here I am, teacher. Just made it!"

Mrs. Horsefall was almost crying. She stared down at the book on her desk; her shoulders quivered. Finally she looked up at August. "August Wagner, I hope and pray every day that you will leave this school. There are only eight weeks left in this term, but they seem like eight years to me. You were sixteen years old last month, and the law does not require you to be here any longer. Why, why do you keep coming?"

August looked up at the ceiling. "Because I wanna graduate. I wanna get a diploma same as Fritz did."

Mrs. Horsefall shuddered. She slowly closed the book in front of her, and sat rigid and silent while the students stared at her. Finally, she said, "Julius, you may read."

Julius lifted his book, wet his finger, and flipped the pages so fast that the paper bent and crumpled. He dropped the book on the floor, then kicked it as he bent to pick it up so that the book sailed across the floor and hit the wall. He retrieved the book and opened it again, pulling hard at the binding. He began to read, fast, mouthing the words so quickly that they were barely understandable.

Alexander knew the passage that Julius was reading, and as he listened, he realized that Julius was reading correctly, but so fast that there was no meaning to the words. When Mrs. Horsefall held up her hand to signal that he had read enough, Julius ignored her and read another paragraph before she could stop him.

She said, "Julius, can you tell us what happened in the part of the book that you just read?"

Julius looked at Junior as he answered. "You asked me to read it, not memorize it." Junior snickered.

Mrs. Horsefall ignored Junior. "Do you know why we read, Julius?"

Julius yawned. "Oh sure, teacher. To learn."

"That is correct. But how can you learn if you read so fast that the words have no meaning?"

Julius nudged Junior. "I don't wanna learn this book. It don't have no spice in it."

Mrs. Horsefall's face turned pink. She fumbled with the ribbon on her glasses before she spoke. "That will be enough, Julius. Junior, please read."

Junior cleared his throat, and Alexander had a mental picture of another thick yellow gob. When Junior began to read, his voice sounded as though he had a mouthful of mush that he was talking around. He read slowly and ponderously, often halting in the middle of any word containing more than one syllable to repeat the sound.

The gob in Junior's mouth was getting bigger and more unmanageable, and saliva was beginning to drip from one corner of his mouth. Mrs. Horsefall held up one hand. "Junior Jensen, go put whatever you have in your mouth in a paper towel and throw it in the stove!"

Junior swallowed. It was a long, audible gulp. He wiped the back of his hand across his mouth. "Why, teacher?"

August snorted. "Jesus Christ! That sounded like a dish a rotten eggs droppin' down a drainpipe!"

When the sixth grade was called up, Alexander found that the dark-haired girl who had shared her songbook with him was his classmate.

Mrs. Horsefall handed him a worn, red book. "Have you read this yet, Alexander?"

He looked at the book. The words *Treasure Island* were barely visible on the faded cover.

"No, Mrs. Horsefall."

"You will begin reading on page one, please."

He opened the book. Ink and crayon marks were scribbled over the cover pages, and the back of the book was broken and limp so that the pages hung loosely by white threads. "Julius Lamb" was written in ink on the top of the

first page in huge letters. He looked at the opening sentenc-
es. They were in English, but so strange that he could make
no sense of them.

Mrs. Horsefall was watching him, waiting for him to
start.

He began, sounding the words out in a low voice.

*Squire Trelawney, Dr. Livesy, and the rest of the gentlemen
having asked me to write down the whole particulars.*

It was like a foreign language, and he wondered if it
could be Swedish,

*...about Treasure Island from the beginning to the end,
keeping nothing back but the bearings of the island...*

Suddenly the words were beginning to make sense,

*...and that only because there is treasure not yet lifted, I
take up my pen in the year of grace 17—, and go back to the
time when my father kept the Admiral Benbow Inn, and the old
brown seaman, with the sabre cut, first took up his lodging under
our roof.*

He was reading fast now, the words coming easily.
There was a beauty and an excitement in them that drew
him on, a magical and continuous dream that waited in the
old book.

Mrs. Horsefall smiled at him. "That's enough, Alexander." She spoke to the dark-haired girl. "Alice, you may read
now, please."

Alice bent her head over the book.

*Fifteen men on the Dead Man's Chest, Yo Ho-Ho and a
bottle of rum!*

Her voice was low and clear, and she read quickly and easily.

In the high, old, tottering voice that seemed to have been tuned and broken at the capstan bars…

The words made little sense to Alexander, but as Alice read them there was music and poetry in them.

Mrs. Horsefall raised her hand. "Thank you, Alice." Her eyes were different now – not frightened, but eager and pleased, almost shining. "You have both read well. We will read all of *Treasure Island* during the next few weeks. I think that you will enjoy it, for it is an excellent book."

Other classes recited, and as the fourth grade finished, Mrs. Horsefall stood up and faced the students. "It is recess time. Come in promptly when I ring the bell." She looked toward the Dacias. "The new children will stay until I have given them their books and assignments."

The classroom emptied in seconds with a crashing of desk covers, a wild trampling of feet, a slamming of bodies against walls and doors, shrieks, yells, and laughter. The teacher and the Dacias were left alone in the room.

Mrs. Horsefall brought them spelling books, and she gave Alexander a big geography book. When she had shown them their assignments, she said to them, "Now you have seen the students here. Are you still certain that you want to stay?"

They looked at one another. Alexander said, "We will stay."

Mrs. Horsefall slowly shook her head. "I cannot understand why your father wants you to be here. Very well. You had better go to the outhouses now. Boys on the north, girls on the south."

As Alexander came out of the building and through the schoolyard, he found that Junior Jensen, Julius Lamb, and a white-haired boy from the seventh grade were waiting for him behind the barn.

Junior spoke, "This here's Harry. Him and you's gonna fight now."

Julius reached forward and grabbed Alexander's cap. "Listen, kid, don't you know enough to take your stupid Gypsy cap off when you talk to us? Now I'm gonna hafta hang it up for ya." He opened the door of the boys' privy and dropped the cap down one of the holes. August was sitting over the other hole.

"Oops, it slipped." Julius looked down the hole. "Right in a pile of shit. You oughta know better'n that, kid."

August raised a foot and drove it into Julius' stomach, sending him flying backward out the privy door. "Damn it, Julius, get the hell outta here!" He slammed the privy door shut.

Junior stepped hard on Alexander's foot. He ground his knuckles into Alexander's scalp. "I think I missed a coupla them cooties." He stepped back. "Get 'im, Harry."

Harry rotated his fists around each other in a fast motion like a turning wheel. He ran forward into Alexander with his fists turning so fast that they were a blur. Hard knuckles struck Alexander's nose, his mouth, his eyes, his cheekbones, his forehead; then he was falling backward with Harry on top of him, Harry's fists still rotating, hard and hurting.

Alexander brought his knees up behind Harry, hard. They struck Harry in the buttocks, sending him forward, sprawling over Alexander, and Alexander slid his shoulders out from under Harry. In the same motion he brought his legs around Harry's middle and locked his ankles together. He squeezed hard, and Harry yelped, his stomach caught sideways between Alexander's knees. Alexander squeezed harder, feeling his knees sink deeper into Harry. Harry thrashed on the ground, kicking and hitting toward Alexander, but Alexander hung on, squeezing tighter.

Julius kicked at Alexander's feet. "Unhook, you little son-of-a-bitch." He kicked again, hard. "Goddamn it, I said unhook!"

August came out of the privy. He hit Julius in the stomach, a short jab that sent Julius flying backward, his arms and legs stretched out, his mouth open.

Junior Jensen bent down, reaching for Alexander's legs, and August's heavy foot caught Junior in the side, lifting and rolling him away like a pole-axed pig.

"Let these two little bastards fight, goddamn it. You wanted 'em to fight, now let 'em, or I'm gonna beat the shit outta both a you." August glared down at Julius and Junior.

Julius sucked for air. "I'm gonna kill you some day, August. Hell, Harry was knockin' the shit outta him till he got that leg hold."

"Well, the goddamned fight ain't over till one of 'em says *uncle*," August said. "Now keep away and let 'em fight, or I'm gonna kick your balls off."

Harry was breathing hard. He struggled one more time, kicking and hitting, cursing at Alexander. Finally, he stopped. "I don't wanna fight no more."

Junior crawled to his feet and hawked and spit in disgust. "Jesus Christ! You was knockin' the shit outta him. Now you wanna quit?"

"This damned little bohunk ain't any fighter," Julius said. "Get up and kill 'im."

Harry said nothing. He lay still on the ground, looking at Alexander. Alexander loosened his legs a little, letting Harry breathe.

The school bell rang from the front of the schoolhouse, loud and commanding.

"Jesus Christ, there's Mrs. Horseballs ringin' her bell, and you little bastards ain't even finished your fight yet." August's voice was unbelieving. "Well, I ain't gonna stand around here all day watchin' you lay there. I never seen such a goddamned fight." He leaned over and looked down at Alexander. "You gotta learn how to use your fists and you might not be too bad a gol dang fighter."

175

The three bigger boys slouched away toward the school-house, kicking at one another half-heartedly.

"I'm ready to quit if you are, "Harry said quietly.

Alexander unhooked his ankles and let Harry roll out. He got up and wiped tenderly at his nose. There was blood, but not too much. He opened the door of the privy and looked down in the hole. His cap was lying just to one side of the piled-up mound of turds in a wet mess of urine. There was no hope of recovering it.

Harry looked down through the other hole at the cap. "That damned Julius is a mean son-of-a-bitch." He looked up at Alexander. "You better wash that blood offa your nose, or Mrs. Horsefall is gonna faint."

Alexander washed at the pump and he and Harry went back into the schoolhouse and took their seats just as Mrs. Horsefall was about to take the roll. Julius Lamb stared at Alexander from his seat, his eyes like a snake's, cold and venomous.

After the recess, grades three, two, and one had reading class, then grades eight and seven had arithmetic, each class at fifteen-minute intervals. Alexander kept his bruised face hidden behind his book, glad that his class was not called up for arithmetic before noon. At noon, Mrs. Horsefall dismissed them for lunch.

When Alexander came into the boys' cloakroom, his lunch pail was gone from the shelf. He went outside and found that all of the boys except August were sitting on the south side of the barn with their lunch buckets. Julius Lamb had Alexander's bucket in addition to his own.

"Well, if here ain't the damned little bohunk!" Julius pried the lid off Alexander's pail and looked inside. "Let's see what the hell you Gypsies eat." He pulled out the piece of cold *mamaliga*. "What the hell is this? It looks like something a dog threw up. Jesus Christ, it's alive! I better kill it!" He leapt up and threw the *mamaliga* on the ground and stamped on it, then he slowly ground his heel in it, smearing it out on the dirt. "There, I think I killed it!"

He reached in the pail again. "What else you got, kid? He pulled out a large piece of white cheese. "What the hell is this?" It looks like a piece a white rubber! Hell, kid. You don't wanna eat that! You eat that and your turds are gonna bounce! They'll bounce right up outta the shitter and hit you in the ass! I'd better help you out and get rid of this too." Julius flung the cheese far away into a tangled clump of weeds.

Julius stared at Alexander defiantly, daring him to try to stop him from destroying his lunch. He reached in the pail again. "One lousy apple!" He rubbed the apple on his shirt and took a bite. He chewed, then spit on the ground.

"That apple ain't any good. You don't wanna eat that apple, kid. It wouldn't be good for you." He tossed the apple to Junior Jensen. "Whaddaya think, Junior? This apple any good?"

Junior took a bite. "Jesus no. That apple ain't no good." He tossed it back to Julius.

Julius threw the remains of the apple over the roof of the girls' outhouse. "There now, kid. You oughta thank us. You ain't gonna get sick from any of that lousy stuff somebody put in your bucket. Prob'ly some fat, greasy Gypsy woman." He kicked the lunch pail out into the area by the swings and sailed the lid after it. "From now on, kid, you'd better remember who's boss around here. I want you to bring your lousy lunch to me every day so's I can inspect it. If you don't, I'm gonna kick hell outta you. You understand?"

August came around the corner of the barn. "Who the hell did you say is boss around here, Julius? Here I am, takin' a good piss, an' I hear you spoutin' off about bein' boss, an' I hear you tellin' this new kid that he's gotta bring his lunch bucket to you every day. I think I'm just gonna pound the shit outta you right now."

He took Julius by the collar with one hand and back-handed him across the face twice, hard. Then he hit Julius in the stomach with a short jab similar to the one he had used at recess, and Julius went flying backward as he had before. He lay on the ground gasping for breath, then he turned over on his stomach and threw up, retching and heaving with his face against the dirt.

August sat down with his back against the barn wall and opened his lunch bucket. "Soon's I get through eatin' my san'wiches, an' Julius gets through pukin', we're gonna have a game a ball," he said to Alexander. "I sure hope you can play ball better'n you can fight."

* * *

When Alexander and the girls came home from school that afternoon, they found the rest of the family behind the barn making further repairs on the fence. The men were pulling the wires tight while the women hammered staples into the wooden posts, and Michael-Joseph carried a pail of staples from post to post. Aunt Magda took one look at Alexander's face and shrieked. "Holy Mother, they have killed him!"

Izabella went to him and gently touched his nose and mouth. "There is nothing broken?"

"I don't think so, Mama."

By this time Josif, Uncle Jon and Michael-Joseph had gathered around. "How did it happen?" Josif asked.

"It was just a fight, Papa."

"Was it that Julius Lamb, or that Junior Jensen?"

"No, Papa."

"It was Junior Jensen's brother," Marie said. "His name is Harry and he's in the seventh grade and he's bigger than Alexander and he has white hair. He's thirteen years old."

Rose added, "Claude Dordoine said that Alexander almost made Harry say *uncle*. Claude can talk in French and he can make his ears pop out."

Caroline said, "Gladys Wample has seven sisters, and their names go like the alphabet: A, B, C, D, E, F, G, H."

Marie spoke again. "August threw horse manure at the blackboard, and Mrs. Horsefall made him clean it up or she was going to send for Fritz."

Aunt Magda turned to face Josif. "You should not let the children go back to that school. They will be torn apart."

"We are in America now and my children will be Americans. They will go to the American school," Josif said firmly.

Izabella spoke quietly to Alexander as she examined his bruised face. "Your cap, Alexander. Did you leave it at school?"

Alexander looked at the ground. He replied in a low voice, "No, Mama."

She touched his hair. "The March wind is still cold. There is another cap in the clothes the woman in Nebraska gave us. I will get it for you."

"I'm sorry, Mama."

She said no more, but carefully cleaned his face with a cloth from her pocket, touching the bruised places so lightly that there was no pain, only the good feeling of her hands. She smiled at him when she finished. "Now the first day is over. I am proud that you fought well."

That evening at supper the girls continued their description of the Mount Faith students and families. Marie began. "Nobody knows why it's called Mount Faith. Ella Wample and Ernie Deerfield and Jackie Gunn are in my class. Ernie Deerfield picks his nose, and Jackie Gunn made it smell. Ella Wample says her mother is gonna keep on having babies until she gets a boy."

Rose added, "Flora Wample is in my class. So is Claude Dordoine. I can say all the Wample girls' names. Anna, Bella, Cora, Dora, Ella, Flora, Gladys, and Hester."

Caroline took her turn. "Gladys Wample is in my class. So is Bobby Deerfield. The first-graders don't know hardly anything. Little Timmy Flanahan and LeRoy Dordoine and Hester Wample are all first-graders. LeRoy peed on the floor."

Aunt Magda hands shot up from her sides. "Spare us!

Anna, Bella, Cora, Dora, Ella, Flora, Gladys, and Hester Wample! Those names will come at us in our sleep. They are never to be forgotten. And someone makes it smell, another urinates on the floor, another picks his nose, horse manure is thrown at the blackboard!"

She spoke to Alexander. "You have not said one word about school, and these girls are telling us about Wamples until our brains are like scrambled eggs. Besides that, you are eating like you are starved, yet I saw your mother pack you a good lunch. Is it possible that anyone can learn anything in that school?"

Alexander looked up from his plate. One lip was so swollen that it was hard for him to speak and there was a strained look in his eyes. "Mrs. Horsefall is having our class read a book called *Treasure Island*. I read part of it before arithmetic class."

"What is the book about?" Izabella asked him gently.

"It's about pirates and buried treasure." Alexander's eyes lost some of their strained look. "It's about a boy named Jim and a man called Long John Silver."

Izabella said to Josif, "Maybe if we get good crops this year, we can buy that book."

Josif considered this. "I was in a house once in Cluj. A big house. A man lived there who was a professor at the University, a very smart man. In one room there were books. There were more books there in that room than in ten schools, in twenty schools. All in polished wood cases behind glass doors."

Uncle Jon nodded. "I have heard about that house, and those books. They are a wonder. All the knowledge of the world must be in those books."

They all were silent, picturing the house in Cluj with the books.

"We have no books," Izabella said. "But even that professor was not born with books. He must have started with one book. We can start with one book."

Alexander's face had been happy and excited-looking as they talked about the books. Now a look of doubt came. "A book would cost too much."

Josif looked at Izabella, then said to Alexander, "We have a one-hundred-and-sixty-acre farm. Maybe someday we can buy it. We have two good horses, and we will try to get more. If we get good crops, we are going to buy that book." He spoke to all the children. "We will buy more books. One for each of you!"

The children were speechless, their eyes round with wonder. Josif said to them, "Tell us more about the school, but not about the sisters of the eight names. Tell us what you learned."

Marie spoke first. "After arithmetic we had spelling and writing, and then citizenship."

"Palmer Method writing," Rose added. "We made big circles and we had to move our whole arm."

"Spelling is fun," Caroline added. "Mrs. Horsefall let us write on the blackboard with chalk. If we made it squeak, the Wample girls screamed."

"What is citizenship?" asked Izabella. "Is it about how to be a good American?"

Alexander replied, "I think so. We learned today about President Hoover's cabinet. He just appointed them."

"His cabinet? What does a piece of furniture have to do with being an American?" Aunt Magda raised her eyes to the ceiling. "Such a school!"

Alexander explained, "They call the people that help the president his 'cabinet'. They are people that know all about certain things. They are called *secretaries*. The Secretary of State is Henry L. Stimson."

The girls recited, and Alexander joined them: "State, Stimson; Treasury, Mellon; War, Hurley; Interior, Wilbur; Agriculture, Hyde; Navy, Adams; Commerce, Lamont; Postmaster General, Brown; Attorney General, Mitchell."

Uncle Jon pulled at his mustache. "They have generals for postmaster and attorney? What a brilliant country. They have finally found a use for generals." He looked around at the family. "But it will be a catastrophe! A letter will be three years in going from one town to another. There will be orders and counter-orders. The letter will be sent out and then it will be recalled. It will be marched in one direction and then another. It will rush to one place and then wait there for months. It will be inspected every morning, five minutes after latrine duty. It will polish its stamp until it is worn away, while it waits for orders. And then, finally, when the letter, by accident, limps into the town of its destination, it will be court-martialed by the other general for having frayed edges. And the generals will make speeches in the town square, and statues will be erected of them." He raised his glass. "I salute our new President Hoover. With such men to help him, he cannot fail."

"Mrs. Horsefall told us that President Hoover is an engineer, and he fed millions of people, and he is going to help the farmers, " Marie said happily.

Izabella agreed. "He is a great man. All over Europe, after the war, starving people were fed because of his work." She smiled at Alexander and the girls. "You are lucky to have a teacher who knows about these things, and we are lucky to be in a country with such a man as president."

Alexander looked down at his plate. "I think Mrs. Horsefall will not keep on being teacher at Mount Faith school."

Josif nodded. "She is like a violin string that is stretched too tight. I do not think she can stay that way until those Iron Guard boys are finished with school."

"She cried at noon." Marie's eyes were sad. "We could hear her."

"I feel so sorry for her," Izabella said. "Is there no one who can help her? No family?"

"Ella Wample said that she was married once, but the

man she was married to got killed in the war," Marie answered. "She stays at the Bowman's. All the teachers stay there."

"And who are the Bowmans?" Aunt Magda asked. "The parents of some of these criminal children?"

Marie shook her head. "Ella said that they are old. She said that Mrs. Bowman is head of the Ladies' Aid and the WCTU, and that she tells the minister what to do in church. Ella said that Mrs. Bowman told her mother she should stop having so many babies, and Mr. Wample got real mad."

"What is the WCTU?" asked Uncle Jon.

"I don't know. I don't think anybody knows. It's something secret," Marie replied.

Aunt Magda frowned at Uncle Jon, then said to all of them, "I think we should have poor Mrs. Horsefall come to visit us sometime, maybe for a good Romanian meal. It might make her feel better."

Izabella gasped. "Oh, we couldn't!" She blushed and looked down at the table. "I would like to have her come, but our furniture and dishes are not right for entertaining the schoolteacher. We should have chicken for such a guest, and we do not have many yet. We would shame the children. Our food would be too strange for her, too poor."

"Not at all!" Uncle Jon replied. "A little *tuica*, garlic, and peppers would put strength in her spirit."

Aunt Magda glared at him. "Alcohol is illegal in this country; how can you think of giving the schoolteacher *tuica*? Izabella is right, the children would be shamed. I'm sorry that I even mentioned it."

Josif held up his hand. "Now, wait. I do not think it is such a bad idea. If someone doesn't help that woman, she may fall apart. I think we should have her come."

"But what could we give her to eat?" Izabella asked. "All we have are eggs, *mamaliga*, cheese, bread, potatoes, onions, garlic and dried tomatoes and peppers. We cannot give such a meal to the schoolteacher!"

"What we have will be good enough," Josif said. "We do not have to be ashamed of good Romanian cooking. We will ask the schoolteacher to come. I have decided."

Aunt Magda placed her hand on Izabella's. "It will be all right, you will see."

Izabella looked up at her, then at Josif. "I'm afraid the meal will not be very grand, but we will do our best and have her come. The important thing is to help her feel better."

Chapter Ten
Company for Dinner

Tuesday afternoon Alexander and the girls walked home from school with Claude and LeRoy Dordoine and the Wample sisters. As the Dordoines and Wamples continued down the road and the Dacias came in the driveway, they found the rest of the family standing by Peter and Paul and the wagon in the barnyard.

"Now everybody climb in!" Josif said. "We're going to Alfred Anderson's to look at the horses!"

Alexander ran with the lunch pails to the porch and put them inside the screen door, then ran back to the wagon and climbed in behind the others. As the team drew the wagon out the driveway, the Dacias saw the Wample girls and the two Dordoine boys ahead of them on the south road, looking back at the team and wagon.

The girls waved eagerly as they came abreast of the Wamples and Dordoines, and called, "We're going to go look at horses at Alfred Anderson's! Maybe Papa will buy them!"

Josif stopped the team and spoke to the Wamples and Dordoines. "You kids want ride? Where you live? If we go by, we take you there."

They all stared up at the Dacias. Claude and LeRoy Dordoine had broad, pale faces, curiously handsome, with high foreheads and light blue eyes. The Wample sisters were as alike as eight minks, differing only in size. There was a wild, woodsy look about them, as though they might sleep at night under the willows that lined the creek. Their green eyes shone otherworldly as foxes'.

The biggest Wample sister answered, "Pa says we ain't to ride with anybody, case we get dragged off in the bushes an' get you know what."

Claude Dordoine pointed to the west. "We live over there. It's only a mile if you wanna take us."

Josif looked at Uncle Jon, then back at the Wamples and Dordoines. "We go to east. We sorry can't take you, but glad to meet friends of Alexander and girls." He clucked to the horses, and they moved on past the Dordoines and Wamples, down the slope, and across the stone bridge and through the swamp to the east-west road that led to Alfred Anderson's place.

"Now," Aunt Magda said, "when the Wample girls of the alphabetic names come to my dreams, I will see their green eyes shining in the night. It was thoughtful of you, Josif, not to insist that they ride with us. There would have been only nineteen of us in the wagon."

Uncle Jon smoothed his mustache. "It would have been an interesting ride. Girls with green eyes like that could make a man wild. Their Mama and Papa must be careful to watch them and keep them out of trouble."

Aunt Magda looked at him sternly. "You heard what their father said. He is probably a huge giant of a man who carries an axe."

Marie's eyes were wide. "Ella said that her father has a shotgun. He gets real mad if they don't do what he says."

Uncle Jon coughed. "We have come to look at horses, not to talk about wild girls. Let us say no more about them." He counted as they went along the road, pointing a finger at each fence post.

Aunt Magda stared at him. "What on earth are you doing?"

Uncle Jon held up a hand for silence, counting fence-posts as they went between the fence line of Bent Nelson's farm and the first gatepost of Alfred Anderson's driveway. "One hundred and nine!" He smiled triumphantly at the family. "Now when the Wagner brothers start to argue about how far this driveway is, I will be the possessor of facts. It is necessary for a South Dakota farmer to know these things."

Aunt Magda sighed and lifted her hands in despair. "He has finally done it. He's gone mad."

* * *

The Anderson farmstead possessed the typical big square white house and huge red barn of the Swedish community. A lanky man in new-looking blue overalls came out of the barn as the Dacia's wagon circled around in the barnyard. The man's pale blue eyes stared curiously at the Dacias from under straw-colored eyebrows.

Josif introduced the family. "We new neighbors. I am Josif Dacia, this is my Uncle, Jon Dacia. These wives and children. Fritz Wagner tell us you have two horses, three year old, might sell to us."

The man continued to stare at them. "Oh, yah, I have horses."

"Are good horses? Calm and gentle?"

"Oh yah, they wery calm, wery jentle."

"You sell? We maybe buy if horses and price good."

The man studied the Dacias' wagon. "Where'd you get a big wagon like dat? I ain't seen one like dat before."

"We buy in Oklahoma."

The man looked up at the family. "I seen some of you people walking on da road last Sunday." He reached in his overalls pocket and took out a flat can of snus. He put a big pinch of it inside his upper lip. "I was in Oklahoma once. Didn't like it."

Josif tried to bring him back to the topic of the horses. "We pay cash for horses."

The man studied the windmill. "Oh, yah, dat's da only way. I wouldn't sell horses to nobody didn't pay cash."

"Could look at horses?"

"You could, but I ain't gonna sell you any."

The family looked at him in disbelief. Josif said to Alexander in Romanian, "Did he say he wouldn't sell us horses?"

"I think that's what he said, Papa."

"You tell us why you not sell horses to us?" Josif asked.

"I don't mind tellin' ya," the Swede said looking Josif in the eye. "Is yust because you rented the old Ariosto place. I ain't sellin' horses to nobody dat lives dere."

"Why you say that?"

"Because I ain't havin' any of my family or horses gettin' shot or killed. Dere's lots of bad feeling about dat place, and I ain't gettin' mixed up in it. If you folks knew what was good for you, you'd pack up and move."

"We have come long way to find farm. Is too late find other farm now."

"Prob'ly is. Even so, you'd be better off to yust move along."

Josif spoke to the family in Romanian. "This man is not going to sell us horses. We might as well go home."

"Why won't he sell us horses?" Uncle Jon asked with some indignation.

Josif shrugged. "I don't know exactly. It seems to have something to do with our farm; maybe with our neighbor, Verne Lamb. He has made his mind up. There is no use talking any more to him."

He turned to the Swede, "We thank you for talk to us. We go home now." He clucked to the horses, and they moved forward with the wagon.

The man stared silently after them, then he went back into the barn.

They spoke little on the way home. Josif drove silently, and the others were subdued and quiet. There was a feeling of disappointment among them, but more than that, a sense of foreboding. They had seen the black fury of Verne Lamb, and now this Swede spoke of the killing of families and horses. Their farm came with more than a price tag, it seemed; it had a history that was not settled, and they were right in the middle of the turmoil.

Josif wondered what it would take to make the farm feel like theirs and what price his family would have to pay to get there. He squared his shoulders and drove home with a feeling of grim determination.

In spite of their dejection, the Dacias sent a note to Mrs. Horsefall the following morning asking her to come to supper with them that coming Friday evening. Alexander wrote the note according to Aunt Magda's and Izabella's directions, and it was decided that he should be the one to give it to her.

Mrs. Horsefall read the note silently when Alexander gave it to her at the morning recess. Her eyes were moist when she looked up at him. "Tell your parents that I will be very pleased to come. Please thank them for their kindness."

* * *

Friday morning when the girls went to let the chickens out, they found the rooster and two hens dead on the floor of the chicken house. Only seven terrified hens remained alive, crouched high on the roosts.

The family gathered around the bodies, unable to believe what had happened. The rooster's throat was torn and his bright feathers were bloody and broken; he had been mostly eaten. He had fought with something, for the straw on the floor was blood-soaked and tossed in piles. Something terrible had come into the chicken house in the darkness.

The two hens were mostly eaten also, and their torn bodies were scattered across the floor. "He was so brave...." Izabella gently stroked the rooster's gaudy tail feathers. "What could have done it?"

"Something very fierce," Uncle Jon said. He looked around at the walls and floor of the chicken house. "But how could it have gotten in?"

189

"Things that come in the darkness...." Aunt Magda crossed herself. "We must hang garlic over the door of every building!"

Izabella's eyes were wide. "The horses, the cow, the pig – are they all right?"

Josif reassured her. "They are not harmed." He pointed at the cracks in the old building. "These are not wide enough to let anything in. It must have come in some other way." He stepped outside, looking at the old foundation of the chicken-house, circling around the building with the family following him.

A little pile of fresh dirt lay by the north wall. Between it and the foundation a hole opened in the earth, a small opening about four inches in diameter. Josif stopped and pointed at the hole. "Here is where it came in."

"A snake!" Aunt Magda leapt backward, her hands holding her skirt tight against her.

"No, Magda, not a snake." Uncle Jon poked in the hole with a stick. "It had claws. See where it left marks in the dirt."

Josif pointed at the foundation. "It can dig anywhere around these walls and get in. Unless we can kill it, there won't be a chicken left."

"How could a thing so small kill the rooster?" Alexander asked.

"It is something so fierce," Uncle Jon said, "that it kills like a tiger. We need a gun. I could shoot it if we had a gun."

"We have no money to spare to buy a gun, but we have to think of some way to protect these chickens." Josif looked at his pocket watch. "You kids get ready for school. Tonight the teacher comes to eat with us, so you had better be on time."

Mrs. Horsefall told Marie that the Bowmans would be going to a church meeting that evening and would drop her off at the Dacias on their way.

Alexander and the girls were home from school by four-thirty. The family members had almost finished getting into their best clothes for the teacher's visit when Fritz and August Wagner drove a wild-looking pair of rangy, buckskin horses pulling a loaded manure spreader into the driveway. Josif, Uncle Jon, and the boys went out to talk with them.

Fritz spoke from the high iron seat. "By God, Joe, we heard that stupid Swede wouldn't sell you them horses, so we brought this team down for you to look at. They ain't exactly broke yet, but they ain't goin' anywhere very fast with this loada cow shit hooked on behind 'em!" Fritz jerked a thumb at the pile of manure. "We was gonna take this out in the field, and then I says to August, I says, 'Why in hell don't we take this team down and show 'em to Joe and his Uncle Jon. It might be that these horses is just what they're lookin' for."

August spoke from where he stood on the mound of manure behind Fritz. "We got 'em from some horse traders last fall. I told Fritz there wasn't no damned sense buyin' 'em if we was gonna buy a tractor this spring, but he had to go ahead, bullheaded as always."

"Well, Jesus Christ," Fritz said, "I just decided this week to maybe buy a tractor. We needed these horses, right up till two days ago when I got to thinkin' about a tractor." He looked at Josif, "It's a good thing you didn't get them horses from Alfred Anderson, Joe. He woulda' charged you to hell and gone for 'em."

"Them Swedes," August added, "will screw you every which way if they get a chance. This team here now ain't gonna cost you a arm an' a leg."

Fritz scowled at August. "For Christ's sake, let me do the talkin', will ya? Me an Joe here can figure this out without you stickin' your nickel's worth in."

Josif had been studying the horses. They were as nervous and wild as jackrabbits, laying their ears back, rolling their eyes, shifting forward and back and sideways in their harnesses, biting at one another, stamping their feet, kicking back at the manure spreader. In addition, they were about as ill-favored a pair of horses as he'd ever seen: Roman-nosed, hip-slung, sway-backed, bow-legged, narrow-chested, and rat-tailed. He said to Fritz, "We thank you for bringing horses for us to see. Maybe we need horses a little bigger, little heavier. We have to plow much land when water dries up."

Fritz waved a hand. "Don't worry about these here horses when it comes to pullin' a plow."

"Yeah, and they're just about broke, too," August said. "There's only one thing that scares hell out of 'em."

The sound of a car came from the road, coming from the north.

Fritz stared toward the road. "Who the hell is out drivin' a car this time a night?" He took a firm grip on the reins. "I just hope to Christ they don't come bustin' in here."

"It might be schoolteacher," Josif said. "Mr. and Mrs. Bowman going to bring her here for supper."

August shifted position on the pile of manure and grabbed the back of the iron seat. "Jesus H. Christ, Fritz, get these bastards down behind the granary, quick!"

It was too late. Even as Fritz urged the horses forward with a stream of obscenities, the car came snorting in the driveway.

What happened next was a combination of violent movements, actions and reactions that were thrown together in a simultaneous yet unfolding series of events that blurred together as when a pack of cards is flipped through with each card showing for an instant.

There was the team and the manure spreader going at breakneck speed down into the barnyard, circling and heading straight out the driveway toward the approaching automobile.

There was the bouncing of the manure spreader, and the slipping forward of the lever that activated the apron and spreading gears so that a thick wave of manure came whirling up behind the spreader while August leapt for his life, and Fritz, like an ancient charioteer in the Circus Maximus, stood wide-legged on the footrest of the manure spreader, swearing at the runaway horses in a voice that shook the pigeons out of the granary.

There was the Bowman's high black Overland touring sedan with its ising-glass curtains open and its two-piece slanted windshield, coming down the driveway toward the racing team and the flying manure.

There were the faces of the people in the car: Mrs. Bowman, the social leader of the neighborhood, done up in her fancy new pheasant-feathered hat from Sioux Falls and her beaded alpaca dress that the ladies of the Orkadallen Lutheran Church Sewing Circle had practically swooned over; Mrs. Horsefall, seeing as in her worst nightmares the Wagner brothers hurtling toward her in a cloud of manure; and Mr. Bowman, a gaunt, red-nosed, black-eyebrowed Abraham Lincoln grasping the steering wheel of the Overland with elbows high, staring down the newly-polished black hood and over the motor-meter at the oncoming manure spreader.

Josif and Uncle Jon leapt into the driveway, waving their arms and shouting, and the wild-eyed team swerved to the left, looped down toward the creek, swerved back onto the driveway, and galloped at full speed out into the road with the emptying manure spreader bouncing behind and the wave of manure rising grandly up into the rays of the setting sun.

As the Bowman's car skidded to a stop, August came limping from the barnyard. "That was the thing I was gonna tell ya about, Mr. Dacia. Them horses are so damned afraid of a car that they just plain shit shingles when they hear one." He grinned politely at the people in the car. "Howdy, Miz.Horsefall. Howdy, Mr. and Miz Bowman." He waved a hand at the Dacias. "Well, I s'pose I might as well be gettin' on home. We got cows to milk."

Mrs. Bowman sat stiff and white-faced in the front seat

193

of the Overland with one hand pressed to her bosom, the other to her forehead. Her feathered hat had fallen sideways so that the long pheasant tail feathers pointed rakishly up toward the roof of the car. Mr. Bowman bent solicitously over her, patting her shoulder as Josif, Uncle Jon, and the boys came to the car.

"By gracious, I think she's going to faint." Mr. Bowman looked back at Mrs. Horsefall. "Are you all right, Viola?"

Mrs. Horsefall nodded grimly. "Those awful Wagners! We had better get Beatrice a place to lie down!" She looked out at the Dacias. "Mrs. Bowman is about to faint. We must bring a chair out from the house and carry her in to a bed or couch. Please hurry."

Alexander ran to the kitchen and brought back a straight-backed chair, with Izabella, Aunt Magda, and the girls coming anxiously behind him. Mr. Bowman and Josif lifted Mrs. Bowman carefully from the car and sat her in the chair. With everyone helping, they carried her into the house, through the kitchen and living room to the girls' bed where they laid her down and put a blanket over her.

Izabella brought a basin of water and a washcloth, and Mrs. Horsefall sponged Mrs. Bowman's forehead while the family watched in dismay.

"Maybe little sip wine help her," Uncle Jon suggested.

Mr. Bowman shook his head. "Mrs. Bowman is death on alcohol.... WCTU, you know."

Mrs. Bowman stirred and raised a weak and wavering hand to her forehead. She smiled bravely at the anxious faces above her, tried to raise her head, gave a little gasp, and let her head fall back on the pillow. Her voice was a weak whisper. "Please, don't concern yourselves about me. Just let me lie here a few minutes; 'I'll be all right," she said.

"We certainly shall concern ourselves!" Mrs. Horsefall said. "Poor gallant woman! Frightened half to death by those terrible Wagner brothers, and now wanting no help!" She looked up at Josif and Uncle Jon. "If it hadn't been for your heroism in leaping in front of those horses, I hate to think what might have happened. How can we ever thank you?"

Uncle Jon smiled at her. "Was nothing." He waggled a finger at Josif, speaking in his best English. "Josif, you have not tell us about beautiful schoolteacher."

Mrs. Horsefall blushed and looked down at Mrs. Bowman to hide her embarrassment.

Aunt Magda said sweetly, "Maybe brave men go out now, let women take care sick lady."

"By gracious," Mr. Bowman said, "I think Beatrice will be all right now if she just rests a bit. I'm afraid we're going to have to miss that church meeting, though. We'll just go on back home as soon as she feels better."

Izabella said shyly, "We will... would... be happy to have you stay, eat with us, but maybe you would not like our food...."

Mr. Bowman looked at the still form of his wife on the bed. "That is real nice of you to ask us, Mrs. Dacia, but I always leave those sort of things for Mrs. Bowman to decide." He said to Josif, "If you and your uncle are going out to see to anything, maybe I'll just come along, give the ladies a chance to decide about eating."

"Chores done," Josif replied, "but maybe we look at Peter and Paul, make sure they not scared by wild Wagner horses."

Mrs. Horsefall smiled at him. "It's good to see a family that cares for their horses." She patted Michael-Joseph on the head. "Do you like horses, too, Michael-Joseph?"

Michael-Joseph had been looking up at Mrs. Horsefall in fascination. He said, "I sure do. Papa's gonna get us a pony if we get good crops." He turned to follow Josif, Uncle Jon, Mr. Bowman, and Alexander, then looked back at Mrs. Horsefall. "I got to go out with the men. Come on, Mrs. Horsefall, I'll show you the farm."

Mrs. Horsefall beamed at him. "Not now, thank you,

Michael-Joseph. I had better stay with Mrs. Bowman until she feels better."

The men and boys went into the barn. As they checked on Peter and Paul, Mr. Bowman took a flat bottle from his inside coat pocket. "Mr. Dacia, I believe I heard your uncle mention wine a little while ago. This is a little stronger than wine, but would you both join me in a small libation?"

Uncle Jon's eyes gleamed as he saw the bottle. "We have good neighbor here." He took the offered bottle and drank. "Hoo ha!" He did a little dance step in the straw. "That is good drink!"

Mr. Bowman nodded happily. "By gracious, it isn't too bad, is it?" He handed the bottle to Josif. "See what you think of it, Mr. Dacia."

Josif took a small sip, then a bigger one. It was not as fiery as *tuica*, but had a more mellow, yet heavier taste. He handed the bottle back to Mr. Bowman. "That melt ice off roof. What you call it?"

"We call this cough medicine. It was prescribed for me by an old friend, John Barleycorn." Mr. Bowman took a long swallow with his eyes half-closed, then he licked his lips and handed the bottle back to Uncle Jon. "My good wife doesn't exactly believe in this kind of medicine, but I have found it to be of considerable benefit and comfort over the years."

Uncle Jon drank again, then Josif, then Mr. Bowman. There was a warm glowing feeling in Josif's middle, and the old barn seemed a comfortable and cheerful place. Mr. Bowman passed the bottle around again, and Uncle Jon and Josif took it politely, not keeping it too long, carefully thanking Mr. Bowman after each drink. Mr. Bowman appreciated their politeness, and he offered the bottle again, not holding it back, but generously sharing it with them.

A feeling of friendship and camaraderie grew between Mr. Bowman and the Dacias, and it seemed that they had known Mr. Bowman for a long time. Mr. Bowman admired Peter and Paul and said that he had never seen more likely-looking horses, and he could have said nothing that would have endeared himself more to Uncle Jon and Josif.

When the bottle was empty, Uncle Jon led them to the granary where he reached deep in a sack of oats and brought out a bottle of the Hutterite rhubarb wine. Mr. Bowman licked his lips in deep appreciation after tasting it and said that he had never tasted better rhubarb wine. Uncle Jon agreed and explained how the old orchard would be put to good use when the fruit was ripe and Magda would make sour cherry brandy, called *visinata*. Mr. Bowman smiled in anticipation and said that he looked forward to trying that brandy when it was ready, if there was enough to share. Uncle Jon assured him that Magda always made plenty, and that he would be sure to provide her with lots of fruit from the orchard. Uncle Jon was now the host, and he passed the bottle around in gracious old-world style until it too was found to be empty.

It was beginning to grow dark in the granary. Suddenly, Josif slapped his thigh. "The chickens! Uncle Jon, we so busy with machinery we forget about chickens!"

Uncle Jon placed one hand on the granary wall to steady himself. "The chickens! Holy Mother of God!" He grabbed a piece of board that leaned against the wall. "The thing may be killing them right now!"

They ran to the chicken house, with Alexander leading and Michael-Joseph and Mr. Bowman bringing up the rear. Alexander opened the door and then turned back toward the others with a look of disbelief on his face. "They're all gone!"

Josif and Uncle Jon squeezed through the doorway together, each with a raised piece of broken board ready for clubbing the marauder. The chicken house was empty. There were no chickens; there was no marauder. The roosts were empty.

Uncle Jon banged his club on the dirt floor. "It's taken all of them!"

Josif saw the stricken look on the faces of Alexander and Michael-Joseph. "Maybe they roosted up in those old lilac bushes. Chickens are smarter than we think."

They went through the dusk to the huge old lilac bushes that grew between the house and the privy. The gnarled branches rose twice as high as a man's head, jungle-like against the cold twilight sky, a perfect chicken haven in times of trouble. But there were no chickens in the branches, only a pair of small owls that hooted and flew silently off into the dark grove behind the house.

Josif and Uncle Jon looked at one another. Uncle Jon shook his head, "Josif, we are in trouble."

Josif agreed. "We will have to tell them."

"Not tonight, Josif, not tonight. Maybe the chickens will show up in the morning." Uncle Jon pointed to the grove and then to the thick growth of willows and cottonwoods along the creek. "They could be up in any of those trees."

They went through the grove, stumbling over the fallen branches in the darkness, looking up against the last light in the sky in the hope of seeing the flock perched on the branches, but there were no chickens. They went along the north side of the creek, searching the branches of the big cottonwoods, but again, there were no chickens.

Josif spoke to Alexander and Michael-Joseph, "We say nothing about the chickens to your Mama, Aunt Magda, or the girls tonight. We wait until tomorrow in case the chickens come home." He explained to Mr. Bowman as they went back toward the barnyard, telling him of the loss of the rooster and the two hens.

Mr. Bowman was puffing from the chicken hunt, but he spoke cheerfully. "By gracious, I wouldn't worry, Josif. Chickens can hide in strange places." He rubbed his hand across his mouth.

Uncle Jon saw Mr. Bowman's gesture, and he led them to the granary again and brought another bottle of wine up from a sack of oats. Half an hour later they came into the house.

The women and girls were all in the kitchen, even Mrs. Bowman. She was sitting in a chair near the stove where Izabella and Aunt Magda were busy with steaming kettles, while Mrs. Horsefall was helping the girls set the table. A delicious smell of cooking filled the room: onions, garlic, chicken, tomatoes, fresh rolls, and something else that Josif recognized but could not believe.

Mrs. Bowman seemed recovered from her fainting spell, for her cheeks were pink and her eyes sparkled in the lamplight. She smiled coyly at the men and boys. "There you are, you naughty men. Leaving us poor women alone while you talk outside!"

Uncle Jon clicked his heels and bowed. "Is wrong of us. When beautiful ladies wait, men should come."

Mrs. Bowman tittered like a wren and looked archly at Uncle Jon. "Oh, Mr. Dacia, what a flatterer you are."

Aunt Magda looked suspiciously at Uncle Jon. "It took much time to see to horses only."

Josif interceded, "We show Mr. Bowman farm buildings, old lilacs, grove, creek." He looked hard at the boys. "Had nice walk."

Mrs. Horsefall took Mr. Bowman's arm and led him to the stove. "You must see this wonderful recipe that Mrs. Dacia is preparing. What do you call it, Mrs. Dacia, chicken *tocana?*"

Izabella smiled shyly and stepped aside so that Mr. Bowman could see into the kettle. "Is nothing. Just old-country food. I hope you like."

"Nothing, indeed!" Mrs. Horsefall exclaimed. "You should see what went into this kettle! Tomatoes, potatoes, butter, garlic, these plump beautiful pieces of chicken, dried parsley, paprika, and just now roasted flour. But before that, something secret!"

Mr. Bowman bent over the kettle and inhaled deeply.

He looked up at Izabella, and his eyes had a glazed look of ecstasy. He passed his tongue over his lips. "By gracious, Mrs. Dacia, I can hardly wait to taste this!"

Josif came to the stove and looked into the kettle. Thighs, drumsticks, breasts – all swam in the rich sauce like ducks in a pond. He spoke to Uncle Jon and the boys, "We put on other shoes. Come into living room."

They followed him into the living room and he shut the door behind them, then led them back into the boys' room where they could not be heard from the kitchen. He spoke softly in Romanian.

"Listen. The women have killed at least three of the hens for this meal. They must have hidden the rest somewhere. Say nothing about the chickens being lost. Do you understand?"

The boys nodded. "Yes, Papa."

A noise came from under the bed.

Uncle Jon hiccuped. "The ghosts of those hens must be prowling the house. I could swear that I heard a chicken cluck!"

The noise came again. They looked at one another in disbelief. Josif pulled the blankets away from the side of the bed and they all knelt down and looked under it as Josif held the lamp.

The hens clucked softly in their crate, staring out at the men and boys, their eyes yellow in the lamplight.

Uncle Jon hiccuped again. "Santa Maria! Those women are going to drive us crazy. Here we beat the bushes trying to find these chickens, and all the time they are here, warm and snug under the bed." He fumbled unsteadily with the hasp on the door of the cage. "They didn't even fasten this right."

Aunt Magda called from the kitchen doorway, and they hurriedly stood up and adjusted the blankets on the bed. They put on their good shoes and came back into the kitchen where the others were gathered around the table. Josif was about to close the kitchen door when Aunt Magda stopped him. "Please, Josif, it is too hot in here. Leave it open."

Later on, Josif thought how a combination of little things could amount to something more than their sum: the dirt floor of the chicken house; the thing that killed the rooster and two hens; the fact that he and Uncle Jon had been so busy with the machinery that they forgot about the chickens; the Wagner boys with their crazy horses; Mr. Bowman's bottle; Uncle Jon's wine; Uncle Jon's unsteadiness in fastening the hasp on the chicken cage; and Aunt Magda asking him to leave the door open. These little things added together to make the catastrophe.

The meal had gone well – not only well, but magnificently. The Bowmans and Mrs. Horsefall exclaimed repeatedly over the chicken *tocana*. Mr. Bowman and Uncle Jon engaged the ladies in lively and animated conversation, only slurring their speech a little. Mrs. Bowman accepted every compliment with gracious titters, and Mrs. Horsefall seemed as relaxed and happy as a schoolgirl.

Then the four hens came walking in from the living room. They came in single file, walking slowly and cautiously, talking softly to themselves, looking up with cocked heads at the wonders of the house and at the twelve people seated at the table.

Mr. Bowman saw them first, and he stared at them speechlessly as they entered the kitchen. Other heads turned to follow the direction in which Mr. Bowman's eyes were fixed – all except Mrs. Bowman, who had her back to the living room door.

Then, before anyone could cry out a warning, the hens leapt onto the table with much wing-flapping and squawking. Two of the hens landed within inches of Mrs. Bowman and looked her in the eye. Mrs. Bowman screamed and fainted, this time for real.

Even the next morning, Uncle Jon was still in disgrace with Aunt Magda. His explanations were met with cold eyes and silence; his apologies were ignored. But it came out finally that not only Uncle Jon was to blame; everyone was guilty in one way or another, even Aunt Magda, and some of the burden was taken from Uncle Jon.

The men and boys had erred in forgetting to fix a safe place for the chickens, and they were certainly at fault in not fastening the hasp on the chicken cage securely, and they should never have let Mr. Bowman lead them astray with his bottle; but otherwise, as Uncle Jon pointed out, they were blameless. They had merely tried to be good hosts.

The women and girls, on the other hand, had enticed Mrs. Bowman into staying for dinner by letting the tantalizing smells from the kitchen creep into the room where she lay, and they should have told the men that they had put the chickens under the bed in the boys' room.

It also came to light that Mrs. Bowman's pink cheeks, bright eyes, and tittering were not exactly normal for her, but that Aunt Magda, in an effort to revive Mrs. Bowman from her first fainting spell, had let her taste the something secret ingredient that went into the chicken *tocana*. Mrs. Bowman had liked the ingredient, and had tasted it several times, finding that it did wonders for her faintness.

When all of this had been revealed and discussed, the family felt better, almost as cleansed in spirit as though each one of them had confessed his or her sins to a priest. But the catastrophe lingered in their minds like a splinter in a finger. No one but themselves was to blame, and they did not feel good about it.

Josif's head did not feel good either. The mixture of Mr. Bowman's cough medicine and the Hutterite wine seemed now to have become almost lethal. In addition, he was worried about finding good horses in time to get the spring work done.

When Alexander said that he would go out and work at repairing the cultivators, Josif stopped him, "It is time you learned to handle horses, not play with machinery. What good are these machines if we do not have horses to make them move? Today you will start becoming a man. Come out to the barn with me. You will learn to put the harnesses on Peter and Paul by yourself."

Izabella looked quickly at Alexander, then at Josif, "The horses are too big for him to harness, Josif. He's only twelve years old."

He frowned at her. "It's time for him to start being a man. A man must be able to handle horses."

Aunt Magda spoke gently, "Josif, let him grow a little more. How can he lift those heavy harnesses up onto those big horses?"

"He can stand on a box. I did that when I was his age." Josif spoke to Alexander. "It will make muscles, then you can fight better at school."

Alexander looked at the floor. "Yes, Papa."

Josif stared at him. "Horses are more important than machines. When will you learn that? Always, you want to work at the machines. A man can throw seed with his hand, but he cannot pull a plow or a disc. You will learn to put the harnesses on today. Now."

Uncle Jon reached for his hat and coat. "I think I will take a little walk."

Michael-Joseph looked pleadingly at his father, "Can I come with you, Papa? I want to help put the harnesses on Peter and Paul."

Josif tousled Michael-Joseph's hair. "Good boy. Soon you will be big enough to put the harnesses on. You will be a man."

As Josif and the two boys went across the barnyard, Aunt Magda said to Izabella, "Something has changed with Josif. It is true that a father must be tough with a son, but he is being harder on Alexander than usual."

Izabella looked through the window at the three figures as they went into the barn. "He cannot forget the man in the black buggy. The man insulted Josif in front of his family. In Romania, he would have killed the man. He does not know what to do with his anger."

Aunt Magda spoke from the other window. "Izabella! A big car is coming in the driveway! A big shiny car!" She drew back from the window so as not to be seen. "There is a strange man in it, and a woman!"

Chapter Eleven
A Dream Come True?

The car came slowly down the driveway and stopped in front of the house, then it went forward again toward Josif, Uncle Jon, and the boys as the driver saw them come out of the barn. Aunt Magda, Izabella, and the girls watched from the east window as the car stopped in the middle of the barnyard.

A tall dark man dressed in a fine, dark blue suit got out of the car and shook hands with Josif, then with Uncle Jon, Alexander and Michael-Joseph.

A woman got out of the car, a beautiful golden-haired young woman wearing beautiful clothing – a tailored, light blue coat over a blue skirt, with silken stockings and small high-heeled blue shoes. She smiled at Josif and shook hands with him, Uncle Jon, and the boys, then knelt and hugged Michael-Joseph, talking to him, smiling at him.

As they all came toward the house, Izabella and Aunt Magda fled into the living room with the girls behind them, fearful and ashamed that the beautiful woman and the tall man might see them in their handed-down and mended clothing.

They heard the kitchen door open, then light footsteps and the woman's voice, then the tall man's voice, then Josif, asking them to please sit down. There was the sound of scraping chairs, of Uncle Jon and the boys coming in, of the beautiful woman's voice again, talking to Michael-Joseph, then to Alexander.

Josif opened the door into the living room and came in, shutting the door behind him. The girls peeked out from their room, while Izabella and Aunt Magda looked apprehensively from the doorways of their cubicles behind the stove.

"Mr. Johnson from the bank is here," Josif said. "He wants to meet all of you. Come into the kitchen."

"Don't make us come, Josif," Izabella entreated. "Her clothing is so beautiful, we would be ashamed."

Josif pointed to his overalls and work shoes. "There is no shame in honest work clothes. Farmers do not dress like bankers. Come out now." He came to the door of the cubicle where Izabella stood. "I will be more shamed if you hide here."

"I will come then," Izabella said quietly.

"You will not go alone, Izabella," Aunt Magda said. "We will all come with you."

They went into the kitchen behind Josif. There was a good smell of spring flowers in the room, light and fragrant. The tall man stood up as they entered, as did the beautiful woman.

The man was handsome and strong-looking, so like the Hungarian dancer Izabella had known that the name "Franz" almost came to her lips. He smiled at her and took her hand, his hand big and warm around hers.

"Such a pleasure to meet you, Mrs. Dacia." His eyes looked into hers, and she felt a stirring somewhere inside her. He introduced her to the beautiful woman, "Miss Ellen Olson, my assistant at the bank." The woman smiled at her, her blue eyes like flowers. There was friendship in the woman's eyes and in the firm grasp of her hand.

Josif introduced Aunt Magda and the girls, and the man and the woman spoke to each of them, with sincere respect to Aunt Magda, and as equals to Marie, Rose and Caroline.

Izabella felt the shame leaving her, for the people did not look at her old dress, and when they smiled at her it was as if she were dressed as well, as beautifully, as the golden-haired woman. She said shyly, "If you like, we will make coffee."

They drank coffee and talked, and it seemed as if they were in Romania with good friends sitting around the kitchen table together, laughing quietly, knowing that good feeling of friendship, liking one another.

Mr. Johnson took some folded papers from his coat pocket and laid them out on the table. "Now that you've been here a week, what do you think? Do you like the farm? I know the machinery and buildings are old and not in very good shape, but I have something in mind that may help on that point."

Josif said slowly, "We like the farm. We like... we like... to stay."

"Good. Now let me tell you what the bank can do about the buildings and machinery." Mr. Johnson took a silver pencil from his vest pocket and wrote carefully in big characters on a clean sheet of paper as he explained to them.

"As I told Mr. Dacia in the bank, if renters have their own machinery, they keep sixty percent of the crops and pay the landowner forty percent. If the landowner supplies the machinery, as in our case, the renter gets fifty percent of the crops and the landowner gets fifty percent." He looked up from the paper at them and smiled.

"Now, since the machinery, buildings, and fences here need considerable repair, the bank is prepared to advance the money for necessary repair parts and material if you will supply the labor for such repairs. In the event that you should ever wish to buy the farm, a fair settlement would be made for the labor you had put into the repair work." He smiled at them again, "Does that sound fair to you?"

Josif and Uncle Jon spoke rapidly in Romanian. "It seem fair," Josif replied.

"Good." Mr. Johnson set the top piece of paper aside. "That is one possibility. There is one other I would like to discuss with you. That is the sale of the farm to you now."

"We talk of that in bank, but is not possible." Josif spread his hands. "We have little money – only enough to buy team of horses if we can find any."

Mr. Johnson held up a hand. "That need not be a problem. As stated in our letter to you, the bank is prepared to let you assume a mortgage for the entire amount of the purchase price."

"In letter, price $3200. We never have that much money."

"With a mortgage, it isn't necessary for you to have the money. You simply make monthly payments to the bank as you would pay rent."

Thirty-two hundred dollars.... It was still all the money in the world. Josif felt sweat forming on his forehead. But to own land – that was his dream, and now this farm of one hundred and sixty acres was offered to him if he would take a mortgage. He did not dare look up at the others. He studied the paper Mr. Johnson had been writing on, not seeing it. *Owe no one. Get land.* Old Michael Dacia's credo, and there was no way to do both. He wanted the land so badly he could already feel the pride of ownership. He looked up at Mr. Johnson, hoping to find a way to decide. "Must be some charge to owe money?"

Mr. Johnson smiled. "I'm afraid there always is. That's one reason why we banks are in business. Four percent – that's what mortgage rates are now. Four percent on the unpaid principle." He showed them on the paper.

That would be just one hundred twenty-eight dollars the first payment, plus whatever amount of the principle you agreed to pay."

"What happen if could not pay?" Josif asked.

Mr. Johnson waved a hand lightly. "We have to consider that possibility, of course." He smiled again. "That brings in many different courses of action. The worst one we would hope to avoid." He looked around at the family. "Banks may seem like cold, unfeeling institutions, but they are made up of human beings. Human beings with compassion, with feelings toward their fellow human beings."

"We not like to borrow money," Josif said. "We not like to owe anyone. But we like to own land. Is dream for us."

"I understand how you feel, Mr. Dacia. No one likes to owe money. But think of it not as borrowing, but as a way of buying the farm with money that otherwise you would pay as rent. The bank simply handles the transaction in an orderly way over the years until the farm is paid for."

"Is not borrowing?"

"You are a good businessman, Mr. Dacia. In a way, it could be called borrowing, but in another way, it is simply a promise to pay. You would not actually receive any money from the bank." Mr. Johnson smiled at all the Dacias. "Why don't you think it over for a few days before you decide?" He looked at Ellen Olson. "What about it, Ellen? Would you like to come out again in about a week?" We don't want to hurry the Dacias in their decision."

She smiled at them, and it was like sunshine in the room. "I would love to come out again."

Michael-Joseph took her hand. "Two geese came down in the water in our field. Come out and we can look at them. It's only half a mile."

Miss Olson looked down at her shoes. "I'm afraid these wouldn't be very good for hiking through the fields, Michael-Joseph. Maybe next week I could bring some rubber boots along and we'll go see the geese."

"You not have to come out again because of us," Josif said. "I come to bank."

Mr. Johnson shook his head. "No need, Mr. Dacia. We have to come out this way next week anyway. It'll be no problem to stop in here."

All the family went out to the car with the visitors, and there was much shaking of hands. Miss Olson hugged all the children except Alexander, and he blushed when she shook hands with him.

When Mr. Johnson and Miss Olson were seated in the big car, Josif mentioned something that he had been thinking about. "When we bring team and wagon out here week ago, we meet man in black buggy with black horses. Very angry man against us, against bank, about this farm. You should know."

"That sounds like Verne Lamb," Mr. Johnson said. "I'm sorry that you happened to meet him. He's a violent man, and someday he may end up in prison." He put the car in gear. "Don't worry about him. If he causes any trouble let me know and we'll have the sheriff pay him a visit." He smiled at Josif and the family. "Meanwhile, please consider the possibility of owning this farm."

Mr. Johnson and Miss Olson waved their goodbyes, and as the car pulled out of the driveway, the Dacias looked at one another in wonder. The farm could be theirs, not by borrowing money, but by having a mortgage. They walked silently back to the house looking at the farm in a different way now, looking at the trees, the old buildings, the windmill, the lilac bushes, the house, knowing that it all could be theirs.

When they went back into the kitchen, the fresh flower scent of Ellen Olson was still there, and on the table were the sheets of paper Mr. Johnson had written on, reminding them that the tall man and the beautiful woman from the bank had really been there, and that their dream could come true.

Chapter Twelve
Dream or Nightmare

That night after supper, the Wagner brothers appeared on the porch. Josif opened the kitchen door to them.

"I brought the goddamned cards myself," Fritz announced. "Now we can have us a game a pitch!"

"Hell, I coulda brought 'em," August said. "But Fritz had to make a big fuss about it."

The women were caught in the kitchen by the Wagner's unexpected arrival, and there was no time for them to flee to the living room. As Josif brought Fritz and August into the kitchen they stared drop-jawed at Izabella as Josif introduced them to her and Aunt Magda, and they suddenly became almost inarticulate. Fritz turned his hat in his hands and mumbled, "Nice to meet ya," and August said, "Same here."

"We are happy to meet you," Izabella said to them. She smiled at August. "You are good friend to Alexander at school. We thank you."

August scuffed his big work shoes on the floor. "Aw, it ain't nothin'."

Aunt Magda gave them her brightest smile. "We happy you help children learn English so they not use terrible swearing words like some people."

Fritz turned his hat some more. "Well, it ain't easy. I been workin' on August here, but like I said, it ain't easy."

"You like cup of coffee?" Josif asked, changing the subject.

Fritz and August still stared at Izabella. Fritz dragged his gaze away for a moment. "Well, that sure would be good." He looked back at Izabella. "'Specially if the ladies join us."

While the women made coffee and set the cups out, Fritz and August took their coats off and sat down at the table. Fritz turned to Josif. "Say, what about that team we brung over last night? Ain't they a pair a humdingers?" He started rolling a cigarette. "They're just a little bit spooky yet, but they'd sure make you a good pair a plow horses."

Josif dared not look at Uncle Jon. "We thank you for showing to us," he said, "but I think we need team same size as Peter and Paul; might put all four together on big plow."

"Well, you think it over," Fritz said. "We'll hold 'em for ya as long as we can, but I 'spect soon as the news gets around that we might sell that pair we're gonna have people climbin' all over us tryin' to buy 'em."

The women served the coffee, but while they sat at the table with the men, the Wagner brothers seemed unable to speak, as ill at ease as if they were in church. Finally Izabella and Aunt Magda refilled the men's cups and excused them-selves, explaining that they had to put the children to bed. After they had closed the living room door, Josif suggested that it might be best if they didn't talk too loudly, since the walls of the old house were so thin.

Fritz took out the deck of cards, "Well, we might as well have a game a pitch. "You guys ever play pitch in the old country? Aces and deuces is the important cards."

"In army," Josif said, "we play game learn from Ameri-cans. Is called acey-deucy. Maybe is same game?"

"Well, sure. You won't have no trouble learnin' pitch then. Course, we play accordin' to the rules around here."

"Oh sure we do. Your rules." August nudged Uncle Jon. "He makes 'em up as he goes along."

"Jesus H.—" Fritz looked at the closed door to the living room, then lowered his voice to a whisper. "August's only tryin' to be funny." He gave August a hard look. "He ain't gonna try to interrupt me no more tonight, are ya, August?"

August took a long slurp out of his coffee cup and wiped the back of his hand across his mouth. He whispered back, "Not if you don't go tryin' to cheat. I know all your tricks."

Fritz glared at him. "Well, just keep your trap shut while I explain the rules. Then we'll see who does the cheatin'." He spread the cards out face up on the table. "These here are the points: ace; jack; jack; joker; joker; high; low; game."

"High is the same thing as the ace," August protested. "There ain't no other high if the ace is high."

Fritz's neck started to turn red. "God–" He looked at the door again, then whispered, "Listen, August. If the ace ain't dealt out then the next highest card is high. I've explained that to you a million times."

"No, you ain't explained it, 'cause it ain't right. If you say 'ace is high,' then that's the only high card there is. If you say, 'high card is high,' then a eight spot might be high."

"Well, I know that," Fritz whispered fiercely. "That's just what I said. Now shut up and let me explain things." He picked up the cards and dealt them around, three at a time, until everyone had six cards. "Now we bid." He studied his hand. "Three," he stated looking around at the others.

"You can't bid first," August whispered. "The dealer don't bid first; it's the guy this side of 'im."

Fritz scowled at August. "I know that," he whispered. "I'm tryin' to show Joe and his Uncle Jon here how to bid. That's why I'm biddin' first."

"Well, I'm supposed to bid first." August slapped his hand on the table. "Three," he said defiantly.

Fritz stood up and leaned over August. He whispered, "I've already bid three. If you wanna bid, you gotta go up to four!"

"I don't neither. You wasn't supposed to bid, so your bid don't count." August looked up at Fritz's fist that was just in front of his nose. "Oh hell, four."

Fritz sat down, "That's more like it." He looked at Uncle Jon and Josif. Now you guys bid. If you can't bid you say 'pass'."

Uncle Jon studied his cards, then he looked at Fritz and August. "Pass."

Josif nodded. "I pass too."

Fritz slapped the table. "Four."

August threw his cards face down on the table. "Whaddaya mean, four? I bid four!"

"That don't make no difference. The dealer gets to take the bid."

"The hell he does," August whispered. "Ain't you heard of the gol dang rules? The dealer only gets to take the bid if it's less than four."

Fritz threw down his cards. "Listen, you stupid jerk," he whispered, "who the hell taught you to play pitch? I'm tellin' you, the dealer gets to take a four bid." He picked up his cards and threw the queen of spades in the center of the table. "Spades is trump."

August whispered, "You can't do that! You ain't got the damn bid. I got it." He threw down the ace of hearts. "Hearts is trump!"

Fritz reached out and picked August's card up from the table. He tore it in half and threw it on the floor. He whispered, "There's your blame ace a hearts! Spades is trump!"

August took Fritz's queen of spades from the table. He tore it in half, then he put the pieces together and tore them in half. He threw them on the floor. "There's your damn queen a spades." He threw the king of hearts on the table. "Hearts is trump."

Fritz picked up August's card. He tore it in half, then put the pieces together and tore them in half, then put those pieces together and tore them in half. He threw the pieces on the floor. "There's your dad gum king a hearts." He threw the ace of spades on the table. "Spades is trump."

August picked up Fritz's card. He tore it in half, put the pieces together, tore them in half, and put those pieces together. He grasped the pieces between his big thumbs and forefingers and and slowly tore them in half. "There's your goddamned ace a spades." He threw the deuce of hearts on the table. "Hearts is trump."

Fritz picked up the card. He tore it in half and put the pieces together. He tore them in half and put those pieces together, then he tore them in half again and put those pieces together. The stack was almost as thick as it was wide.

Fritz stood up and gripped the stack with the tips of his thumbs and forefingers and took a deep breath. Slowly, as the Dacias watched in awe, the stack began to bend. Fritz's face turned red and two large veins on his forehead stood out like ropes as he strained. Then with a spurting sound the card fragments shot from his fingers and flew over the table and floor.

Fritz quickly changed his look from one of startled surprise to one of defiance. "There's your goddamned deuce a hearts," He threw the ten of spades on top of the pile. "Spades is trump." He glared at August. "If you touch that ten spot I'm gonna tear you up and throw you on the floor like them cards."

August threw the rest of his cards down. "Damn you, Fritz," he whispered. "You cheat every goddamned time." The brothers glared at one another.

Uncle Jon spoke to Josif in Romanian. "If they keep on like this, something is going to explode. Tell them about the chickens–it will give them something else to think about and maybe get them outside where they can swear out loud at each other."

Josif nodded in agreement. "Something kill rooster and two hens," he said to the Wagner brothers.

Fritz and August appeared not to hear him. Then, slowly, they turned to look at him. "What'd you say?" Fritz asked.

"In chicken house. Rooster and two hens dead, mostly eaten."

Fritz looked at Josif. A look of dawning hope appeared on his face. "We better get the hell out there and look at it." He motioned to August. "C'mon, get that lantern lit and we'll go see."

They all got into their coats and overshoes and, with their lanterns, went through the darkness toward the chicken house.

The full moon was low in the east, partially hidden by black ragged clouds, and there was a feeling of wildness in the air. They went behind the chicken house and Josif held his lantern near the hole in the earth. "Jesus Christ," Fritz said. "It's a goddamned weasel."

"Yeah," August added. "Them damned little bastards can kill more chickens in one night than a bunch a damn bulldogs."

"What best way to get rid of?" Josif asked.

"Get rid of? Jesus Christ, ya gotta kill 'em! There's prob'ly a pair." Fritz held his lantern up, looking at the foundation and walls of the chicken house. "This building's so shot to hell anything can walk right in and grab your chickens. August," he directed, "go on home and get three of them little traps. We might as well catch these little bastards right now, tonight."

"Jesus H. Christ," August said. "Them little traps ain't gonna do it. You don't know any more about trappin' than you do 'bout pitch. Them medium-sized traps is what we want."

Fritz threw his cigarette down and stamped on it. He set his lantern on the ground. "Now goddamn it, I'm gonna beat the shit outta you, August. You been talkin' back to me all night, and I ain't gonna take no more of it." He lunged at August, barely missing him as August leapt backward.

August groped on the wet earth in the lantern light and lifted an old piece of broken two-by-four. "Keep away, goddamn it, or I'll bust you one."

Fritz put his head down and charged toward August like a bull, slamming into him as August brought the two-by-four down on his head. The wood broke with a loud crack, and the brothers rolled on the ground with fists, arms, and legs flailing as their bodies thumped on the earth. They cursed and grunted as they struggled, and they thrashed around so wildly that Uncle Jon hurriedly moved the lanterns back to a safe distance. Finally the rolling, tumbling mass was still, and Fritz sat on top of August, pinning his shoulders down with his knees.

He backhanded August twice across the face. "Now, goddamn it, are you gonna shut up and not go interruptin' me?"

August glared up at him. "If that blasted two-by-four hadn't broke, you wouldn't be so goddamned smart."

"Ain't no two-by-four gonna stop me, you dumb shit. You oughta know that." Fritz backhanded August once more. "Now say 'uncle' before I get mad."

"I ain't sayin' 'uncle' for nobody. Go ahead with your damn hittin'. I ain't sayin' 'uncle'."

Fritz looked up at Josif and Uncle Jon in disgust. "He's so goddamned bullheaded I could pound away at him all night." He climbed off August. "I sure feel better now. I was gettin' kinda tense-like in the house fer some reason."

August came up off the ground and wiped at the blood around his nose and mouth. "Me too. There ain't nothin' like a little good rasslin' ta unlax ya." He picked up the lantern. "Well, I guess I'll go get them traps now."

Fritz watched August as he went down the driveway with the lantern bobbing beside him in the near darkness. "He just needs a little convincin' sometimes." He sighed. "August ain't never gonna make a good fighter, though." He kicked at the broken two-by-four. "Anybody oughta know that damned two-by-four would have to be half-rotten, layin' outside on the ground that way."

They went into the chicken house with the remaining lanterns. Fritz stared at the empty roosts. "Where in hell's the chickens? There ain't any use settin' traps in a empty chicken house."

"Only four hens left," Josif said. "We put in crate in safe place at night."

"Well, we sure as hell ain't gonna catch any weasels without chickens. On top a that, we gotta have fresh chicken blood."

Josif spoke to Alexander. "Go bring two hens from crate."

"Wait a minute," Fritz said. "You only got four hens. That ain't even hardly worth botherin' about." He rubbed his jaw. "I s'pose your womenfolk hate to lose 'em, though. I'll tell you what. Grandma's got more damned chickens than she knows what to do with. I'll just slip down and grab a few of them old roosters."

Josif raised his hand in protest. "No. We not take your chickens. Is not right."

"Why the hell ain't it? If Grandma wants to give you a coupla old roosters that's too tough to eat or sell, what's wrong with that? All them roosters do is lay around all day and eat and fight. They ain't worth nothin'."

Josif shook his head. "We not take anything anymore unless we pay for it. Too many people try give things to us. Try to say I cannot support my family."

"Well, hell, we're not saying that!" Fritz said. "It just don't seem right to take them few hens when they're all you got left."

"I thank you, but I not take anything without pay for it."

Fritz stared belligerently at Josif. "I ain't never seen nobody so damned stubborn. Okay, Joe, have it your way. I'll ask Grandma what she wants for them old roosters." He scuffed a line in the dirt floor of the chicken house.

"While I'm gone, you guys dig a trench here out from the wall through this hole they came up in. Make it about a foot deep and get some old boards to cover it with. Better bring your axe and a tin can too. Now I'll just take one of your lanterns and go get them damn roosters." He went off into the darkness as had August.

Josif watched him disappear into the darkness. "Those boys need to spend some time kneeling on corn," he said disgustedly. "I never heard such disrespect for their elders from Romanians. If this is the American way, it is not good. They use bad language and use our first names without permission. They are bad examples for our children." He turned to Alexander. "If you are ever not sure how to behave, just think what the Wagner boys would do and you do the opposite! They are worse than Turks and I will not have my children grow up to be like that!"

* * *

The Bowmans and Mrs. Horsefall had discussed the Wagner boys during supper the previous night before the hens came in. Mrs. Bowman had her own opinion as to why they acted as they did. "It's that Gerhard Wagner. He can't say two words without blaspheming. Poor Gertrude, to have to put up with him all these years."

Mr. Bowman had objected mildly. "By gracious, it isn't all Gerhard's fault. Those boys were wild as possums even before their folks passed away." He explained to the Dacias, "Henry and Agnes died of the Spanish influenza, both of them within a week. Fritz must have been about ten, August about six. Gerhard and Gertrude, Henry's folks, were living in town. Gerhard thought he was going to be able to spend the rest of his time down at the social club after he retired from the farm. Then they had to come back and run the farm and take care of those two boys."

"Social club indeed!" Mrs. Bowman had exclaimed. "It's nothing but a den of vice and wickedness where they play pool and gamble and worse! And poor Gertrude can't hear well. People say that the language Gerhard and those boys use in that house is perfectly shocking, and, thank heaven, poor Gertrude doesn't realize it."

* * *

While Fritz and August were gone, the Dacias brought the spade and axe from the granary and some old boards and a rusty tin can from the junk pile by the elevator.

As they finished digging the trench, August arrived with the traps. He opened and set them, and carefully placed them in the trench about six inches apart, the jaws wide and menacing in the lantern light.

"Them little bastards is tough as hell. I still think we shoulda used bigger traps, but ol' Fritz always knows everything." A metal spike and chain hung from each trap, and August drove each spike down into the floor of the trench with the blunt end of the axe. "This oughta slow 'em up a little."

A few minutes later Fritz came in with a gunnysack over his shoulder. "You're gonna need a rooster to satisfy them hens. I got one good one here and two scrawny ones and two hens. Grandma said she'd take a dollar for the good rooster and the hens, but she won't take nothin' for the scrawny ones. She's gonna get mad as hell if you try to pay her for 'em." Fritz scowled at Josif. "She's goddamned mean when she gets mad, and I wouldn't advise you to try and tangle with her."

Josif took a dollar bill from his wallet. "Tell your grandma we thank her and we don't want her get mad. Want to be good neighbors."

Fritz tucked the bill in the watch pocket of his overalls. "Now we're all even." He reached in the gunnysack and hauled out a squawking and ruffled rooster. "Gimme that axe. August, you hold that goddamned can steady." He kicked one of the boards to the edge of the trench and laid the rooster's neck across it, holding its feet with one hand, the axe in the other.

"Here goes." He brought the axe down and blood spurted from the rooster's neck, while the severed head bounced forward, the yellow eyes surprised and accusing in the lantern light.

"Get that damn can under it!" Fritz lifted the rooster's

flapping, struggling body and let the blood pour into the can that August held, splattering his hands in the process. Then he held the rooster over the traps, dripping the blood over the center of each one. He made a trail of blood from the hole under the foundation, along the bottom of the trench, over the traps, and up onto the straw on the floor to where August had set the can of blood.

"If that don't bring them little bastards across them traps, nothin' will." He gave the rooster's still-quivering body to Josif. "If your missus wants to make soup outta that it might be okay, but it'd sure be too damned tough to eat." He fished around in the gunnysack again.

"Now we'll get the other scrawny one out." He brought out another protesting rooster and tied it with a piece of binder twine to the roost support. "They'll hear this one movin' around in here, and when they smell that blood, they'll come under that wall and through this trench like shit through a goose."

August laid the boards over the trench, leaving an opening near the can of blood, then he shoveled the dirt from the trench over the top. "This way, they hafta go over the traps to get up to that can. They ain't gonna make it."

Fritz held the lantern up and looked around the chicken house. "Let's get the hell outta here." He leaned the axe and spade against the wall. "Might as well leave these here. One way or another, you're gonna need 'em tomorrow."

They went out, closing the door on the tethered rooster, the can of blood, and the trap-filled tunnel. Fritz handed the gunnysack to Josif. "This here ain't too bad a rooster and the hens are pretty young. I seen this ol' boy jump about twenty hens in one day, so he's prob'ly gonna kinda loaf around here with just six to take care of."

Josif hefted the sack. "These are big chickens! You want another cup coffee?"

Fritz looked up at the moon. "Jesus Christ, I didn't think it was that late. Me and August better get on home. We got all them cows to milk in the morning, and Grandma's gonna shove August off to church for confirmation class. 1 think we better git."

"I ain't goin' to no chickenshit confirmation class," August said vehemently.

"The hell you ain't. Grandma's made up her mind. You're gonna go." Fritz spoke to Josif and Uncle Jon. "Besides that, he ain't goin' to school on Monday. We're shippin' hogs to Sioux Falls now that the roads has dried up."

August grinned in the moonlight. "That part don't hurt my feelin's any. I'd rather sort hogs any day than set in that damn schoolhouse."

"I like ask you question," Josif said.

Fritz glanced at him. "Let 'er rip."

Josif tried to find the right words. "Alfred Anderson say he not sell us horses because of trouble over this farm. When we come here week ago, we meet Verne Lamb on road. Was real mad because we come here. Can you tell us why people mad over this farm?"

Fritz spit into the darkness. "Hell, yes. I can tell ya. It's them lawyers."

"An' them bankers," August added. "They're all so goddamned crooked, a snake couldn't follow their trail."

"For Chist's sake, let me tell this, will ya? Joe here asked me, not you." Fritz glared at August. "Now shut up an' let me tell Joe and his Uncle Jon what the hell all the fuss is about." He took the makings of a cigarette from his overalls' pocket.

"Three years back we had one hell of a poor crop around here. First it rained too much, an' then it didn't rain for the whole damned summer. Even so, there was a little stuff came through. Then, about the last week in August, a bugger of a hail storm came along an' cleaned everybody out for sure." Fritz licked his cigarette and lit it. "A lotta folks couldn't pay their taxes that year, and damned if them lawyers and bankers didn't get their farms."

222

He pointed to the east with his chin. "That's when ol' Carl Croat got busy with his shotgun." Fritz blew smoke out of his nose and looked around at the Dacias as though they should now understand.

"That's why Verne Lamb's so goddamned mad about this farm," August said. "He thinks he still owns it 'cause it belonged to his wife's folks."

Fritz scowled at August. "Jesus H. Christ, Joe and his Uncle Jon can figure that out. You don't hafta go puttin' your nickel's worth in."

"Is good you tell us," Josif said. "We want be good neighbors, even with Verne Lamb."

Fritz looked in the direction of the Lamb farm. "Verne Lamb ain't liable to be a good neighbor to nobody. Them Lambs is a mean bunch."

"Aw, hell," August said. "I can beat the shit outta Julius any time I feel like it."

"Julius ain't growed up yet. Verne's mean as hell, an he's gettin' worse, maybe even goin' crackers over this farm thing. If he ever starts wavin' that shotgun of his around, why head for the hills. But Verne ain't nothin' compared to his brother Vince.

"Vince's crazy as a hoot owl. Always settin' fire to things. Straw-stacks, chicken houses, barns full of horses…" Fritz paused. "That's prob'ly why ol' Alfred Anderson wouldn't sell you no horses, 'cause of Vince and his firebug ways. Only Verne's here now, but if Vince ever came back and got worked up about your farm, he might go back to his old evil ways."

Josif stiffened. "Where this Vince?"

August put out his cigarette. "Nobody knows. The law kinda run him outta here a couple years ago, and he ain't been back."

"Goddammit, August," Fritz said, "you got that all mixed up as usual. Frank Ariosto is Belle's uncle. He's not gonna run any of them Lambs out. It was them insurance guys that run Vince out, not the law." He picked up their lantern. "We gotta get home, or them cows'll meet us comin' in." He waved a big hand at the chicken house. "Don't none of you go lookin' in there till morning or you might scare them bastardly weasels away. When you do go in, lift them boards up with the spade an' be ready to knock hell outta 'em with the axe. They're mean as badgers when they get a leg in a trap."

The Dacias watched the Wagners lurch off into the night with their bobbing lantern. When they went back in the house they found that the women and children had waited up for them. The men told them of the Wagner's trap-setting and gave the dead rooster to the women to clean, then pulled the live one and the two hens from the sack.

The rooster was a huge Plymouth Rock, gray with barred black stripes, majestic and noble-looking. Izabella and the girls knelt by it, exclaiming over its size. The hens were beautiful Plymouth Rocks also.

"I knew they were good boys," Aunt Magda said. "They were so quiet and polite when they played cards tonight that we could hardly hear them."

Josif did not sleep well that night. He lay awake staring up into the darkness of the little room, hearing Izabella's soft breathing beside him on the old bed. There were too many things bothering him to sleep well. Lawyers and bankers taking people's farms. The Lamb family. Vince Lamb burning barns full of horses – the most horrible thing Josif could imagine.

There were things that bothered a man hardly at all in the daytime, but in the night they came creeping in. Not things like weather or wars; they were acts of God or of politicians and generals and could not be helped. It was people. People did things or didn't do things, or said things or looked a certain way. He wondered what the relationship was between Mr. Johnson and Ellen Olson. They spent the day together in the bank, and they came to the farm together in Mr. Johnson's big car. What did they do at night? He wondered where Ellen Olson lived.

They had gone by a fine big house in Centerford. It had tall pillars in front and many windows with white curtains, and a front door with a large oval glass in it. Ellen Olson would live in a house such as that. There would be fine things in the house: cabinets of books; dark, polished tables; soft rugs; and marble floors. Mr. Johnson would have a house like that too. He wondered if Mr. Johnson had a wife. He could not picture Mr. Johnson's wife; somehow it seemed that only Ellen Olson could fill that role.

When the first gray light came in the windows Josif got out of bed and got dressed. Izabella was already in the kitchen making bread and he greeted her with a grim look on his face as he headed out the door to the porch where he put on his work shoes. He went out to the privy and then to the chicken house, moving quietly behind the lilac bushes in the chilly morning air. He slowly opened the door and looked inside.

A strange smell filled the chicken house, musky and sharp, and from underneath the earth-covered boards came the sound of something moving–a quick scurrying sound. The tethered rooster crouched on the floor in helpless terror, as far away from the opening in the earthen floor as the twine on his leg allowed.

Josif took the axe in one hand and the spade in the other and went past the rooster and the can of blood to the long mound of earth over the tunnel. He carefully shoveled the dirt away from the boards and then flipped the largest one over with the spade.

Furious brown motion erupted from the trench, and two squeaking, darting things leapt up at him with red eyes and open mouths, held back by the steel jaws of the traps that clutched their bloody legs. Josif struck down with the

axe and the blade missed the brown furies and clanged on
the metal of the trap. He struck again, then again and again
into the squeaking things, struck until their bloody bodies
stopped their furious movement and lay hacked and broken
in the bottom of the trench.

Alexander stood behind Josif, pale-faced and wide-
eyed. He said, "I came to help you, Papa."

Josif drew back from the trench. "It is done." He felt a
strange anger toward the boy, for he had watched while his
father had smashed and chopped at the two tiny trapped
things.

Alexander looked down into the trench. Suddenly he
turned and ran out of the chicken house, and Josif heard him
retching behind the building. Josif dropped the bloody axe
and came around to where Alexander knelt on the ground.

"For the love of Christ, boy, get up and be a man."

"I'm sorry, Papa." Alexander wiped his mouth and slowly stood up. He kept his face turned away from Josif.

"Don't say you are sorry." Josif felt the anger rising up
inside him. "A man doesn't say he is sorry to anyone. Don't
you know that yet?"

"Yes, Papa." Alexander still looked away from him.

"Goddammit!" Josif hit Alexander on the side of the
head. "Look at me." He hit him again. "Look at me when I
talk to you!"

Alexander staggered sideways as Josif hit him. He still
did not look up.

"Look at me or I am going to hit you harder until you do."

Slowly, Alexander looked up at him.

"I am ashamed to call you my son. You come home
from school without your cap. You let a boy mark you in a
fight. You have no interest in horses; I think you are afraid
of them. Now you get sick at the sight of a little blood. You
puke like a girl at the sight of some dead weasels."

Izabella spoke behind him, her voice low. "Josif, stop."

He turned away from Alexander and toward her, the

anger growing stronger in him. "He has shamed me. Do not tell me to stop. Do not tell me to do anything. I am head of my family. I will not be shamed by my son."

She was silent a moment, looking into his eyes before she spoke. "There is no shame on you."

The anger rose even higher in him. He raised his fist toward her. "A woman who tells her husband he lies will feel this, and worse. You tell me there is no shame. No shame when a man can insult and threaten our family and drive away. No shame when we have to borrow money. No shame when our firstborn son will not be a man."

She did not move away from his fist. "Beat me if you will. But do not blame Alexander because the man still lives. Do not blame Alexander because we have to borrow money to get land. Do not blame him because he cannot fight boys bigger than himself." She reached out toward him. "Do not blame yourself because you let the man live. You obeyed the laws of our new country. There is no shame."

The anger was still strong in him, but he lowered his fist. "I feel the shame. Do not tell me again there is no shame." He turned away from her and spoke to Alexander.

"Bury those things in the grove. Then reset the traps and put the boards and dirt back. There may be more of them. If there are, you will kill them yourself, with the axe." He stared at the boy. "You will act like a man here or at school or anywhere. You will start becoming a man now. Every morning you will harness the horses, by yourself, without help. Do not come into the house until it is done."

Alexander's eyes widened, but he said nothing. Josif turned his back on him and faced Izabella again. "Now, woman, what do you say? Will you tell me I am wrong again?"

She said nothing, but only looked into his eyes, and he saw the sadness in hers. He felt his anger leave him then, and in its place came a new shame, a shame that he had blamed her and Alexander for his anger at the world. He heard in his mind the words that he wanted to say to them:

I do not blame you for these things. The blame is only on me, not on you, my wife and my first son.

Instead, he said to her, "I will start work in the fields today. Is it too much to ask that a man's son should harness the horses, or that a man's wife should not judge him?"

* * *

That night Clarence and Vince left Detroit. They brought Lou Fallucca and Angelo Moretti with them to drive the two trucks which had been modified to carry bootleg whiskey and which carried the huge still and equipment from Bugs Moran's Chicago distillery.

Clarence wished to throw off his track any more of Moran's hit men who might have come to Detroit. He also wanted to elude any of the Italian mob, as he had just stolen from Primo Moretti, a mob boss, and had forever broken that connection. He now also had to get rid of Primo's brother, Angelo, before Angelo learned of the theft.

A perfect opportunity to disappear arose when two panhandlers approached Vince and him as they walked from their cars to a store that sold ammunition and guns.

Clarence put the panhandlers in the back seat of Vince's big Studebaker at the point of his black pistol. He shot both of them, using a silencer. Then, in his Model A, he bought five gallons of gasoline from a filling station and led Vince in the Studebaker to a vacant lot in a seedy section of Detroit.

"You like fires, Vincent," Clarence said to him matter-of-factly. "Put these men in the front seat of your car. Pour the gasoline over them and touch it off."

Vince howled in rage. "I ain't burning my car!"

"The men will be you and me. Moran's people will recognize your car. Do it now, Vincent."

Vince looked into the barrel of Clarence's silencer. He hauled the bodies into the front seat of his Studebaker and poured the gasoline over the bodies, over the seats, the floorboards, the upholstery. He led a trail of gasoline out into the weeds, then he threw a lighted match onto the gasoline trail and ran to the Model A where Clarence waited with the motor running.

They left Detroit while sirens screamed and fire-bells clanged. They went southwest toward St. Louis and Kansas City in order to avoid Chicago; they would turn to the northwest toward Omaha and Sioux City and the farm in South Dakota near Centerford. Clarence calculated that they would arrive at the farm sometime Monday night.

He would have to eliminate Angelo there.

Chapter Thirteen
Alexander Holds On

Early Monday morning, before the Dacias were up, heavy guns fired to the north. Two shots, then two more came almost simultaneously.

Josif and Uncle Jon leapt out of their beds before the last shots had sounded, and Izabella and Aunt Magda were close behind them. "Shotguns!" Uncle Jon hopped on one foot, pulling on his overalls. "They sounded close!"

Josif ran to the kitchen and looked out the north window from the pantry. The grove partially blocked his view, but to the north, beyond the alfalfa field, a truck stood in the road, and two dark figures ran toward it from the direction of the flooded field. He ran back into the living room, almost colliding with the rest of the family, who were running barefoot into the kitchen. They struggled into clothes and shoes and ran out into the driveway just as the truck came fast from the north with its motor racing.

Just before they reached the road, the truck roared by in front of them, a dark and sinister shape in the early light. Two figures were in the seat, and yells and harsh laughter came from the truck as it hurtled down the road toward the bridge and the swamp. Something white in the box of the truck fluttered in the wind as the truck disappeared among the trees.

The children's eyes were wide. "Papa, what was that in the back?" Marie asked.

He looked down at her. "Some sacks, maybe."

"It looked like feathers, Papa." Marie's eyes held tears.

Izabella put her arms around the girls' shoulders, silently comforting them. Aunt Magda knelt and held Michael-Joseph. "What happened to the geese, Papa?" Michael-Joseph asked anxiously.

Josif replied, "Somebody shot the geese. I saw them being carried by the men as they ran to the truck. The geese are dead."

No one spoke. They stood at the edge of the road in the mud, half-dressed, their eyes and bodies showing their sorrow.

"They were not our geese," Josif said to them. "Wild geese do not belong to people. Here in America, anybody that wants to can shoot wild geese."

Marie looked up at him. "But they came down in our field, Papa. They came to us."

Josif spoke harshly. "It is not our land. Maybe if we owned the land it would be different, but it is not our land."

Izabella said quietly, "We will own land someday. We will own this land."

Josif's voice was bitter. "We have one team of horses and can only farm part of this land. Tell us how we will own this land."

Izabella put her arms more tightly around the girls. "God will help us. We have come here from Romania, Oklahoma, and from the Hutterites. Our path has led us here; this is our destiny. God will help us own land here in America."

When the Dacias came into school that morning, Mrs. Horsefall stared at the girls' faces. "You girls have been crying."

"The geese are dead," Marie said sadly.

Mrs. Horsefall took a step backward. "The geese in your field?"

"Yes. This morning somebody killed them."

"Oh, how awful!" Mrs. Horsefall put her hand to her heart and sank down in her chair.

Julius Lamb snickered from the back of the room. He said in a loud whisper to Junior Jensen, "I'll bet those Bohunks were scared shitless. They probably never heard a gun before."

Mrs. Horsefall rapped on her desk with a ruler. "That will be enough, Julius!" She checked the students in her attendance book. She stood up. "Is August Wagner here yet?" Her face held a faint expression of hope.

Julius snickered again. "Naw, they're shippin' hogs today. Hope Fritz don't get him mixed up with the pigs."

Mrs. Horsefall stood a little straighter. "Will he be gone all day?"

"Oh, sure. Time them Wagners figure out which end of the truck to load 'em in, it'll be past noon." Julius and Junior both snickered.

Mrs. Horsefall's eyes took on a new light. She stood as straight as her blackboard pointer. "Everyone stand while we pledge allegiance to the flag. Then we will sing Santa Lucia."

School went well that morning, but Alexander felt Julius looking at him from the rear of the room, and when they met face-to-face as classes changed, Julius scowled menacingly at him. At recess Julius ignored him, but at noon when Alexander joined the other boys beside the barn, Julius spoke from where he slouched against the wall.

"Get your bucket over here, kid. Time for inspection." He poked Junior in the ribs with his elbow. "If he's got any more of that yellow crap again, I think I'm gonna puke right in his lunch bucket."

Junior stopped chewing on his sandwich. "Jesus Christ, Julius, I'm tryin' to eat." He belched. "Go puke somewhere else if you're gonna."

Julius laughed. "Don't worry, I'm just gonna kill it again."

Then Julius came up onto his feet and pushed Alexander down. He began to kick Alexander. He kicked viciously again and again with his heavy boots, aiming at Alexander's stomach, his back, his head, his ribs.

Alexander wrapped both arms around the lunch bucket and held it to him. He held it as Julius kicked him, clasped it tight against him as the pain came, clasped it as he slipped into unconsciousness.

* * *

He awoke in the little end room of the house. The tiny pine trees on the wall were curiously bright, and bright pain gripped his body. Tightness and pain circled his chest, and when he breathed, the pain flared up under the tightness. His mother bent over him, her eyes soft and full of love. "Alexander, we are here. It's all right now."

There were other people in the room. Aunt Magda, the girls, Michael-Joseph, and strangely, Mrs. Horsefall and Mrs. Bowman. He tried to move and the pain in his chest flamed and cut. His mother's hand softly touched his face. "Lie still, Alexander. Soon the doctor will be here."

He whispered, "Where's Papa?"

"Mr. Bowman has gone to get him and Uncle Jon from the field. They are coming in now – I can hear them on the porch."

He tried to sit up, but the pain forced him back. "Help me up, Mama."

She touched his forehead, her fingers gentle and light. "It's all right, Alexander. Lie still."

They came into the kitchen, then the living room, then through the girls' room, men walking quickly and softly in their heavy work shoes, which they had not paused to remove. All of the women except Izabella squeezed out of the little room, making a place for Josif and Uncle Jon.

Mr. Bowman had told Josif what had been happening at school. He hadn't realized how bad it was. Now he looked down at his son who could be mortally wounded, all because he was trying to make his father proud and remove the shame his father felt.

In his mind Josif spoke to him: *I am proud of you. Not only for this, but for being a man when everything seemed against you. I was wrong. I put my pride above all else and that has resulted in this. You have behaved as a man, and I have shamed myself.*

In his mind Josif said what Alexander needed to hear, but Josif could not bring himself to say these things out loud, no matter how much his heart was aching. Men did not apologize and talk about their feelings; it was not done. Instead he said, "The doctor will be here soon and make you better."

The sound of a car came from the road. Mr. Bowman peered out of the window of the girls' room. "By gracious, here's Dr. Sinclair already!"

The doctor's car came down the driveway fast, a battered and mud-spattered yellow and green roadster. "Horace, you let the doctor in," Mrs. Bowman directed her husband. "It will be best for you to see him first in this terrible time."

"By gracious, he must have had that old Oakland up to sixty to get out here this fast!" Horace hurried toward the kitchen.

The doctor came into the girls' room ahead of Mr. Bowman. He dropped his hat and coat on the girls' bed and adjusted a gold-rimmed pair of pince-nez as he looked at the people in the back room. He put a finger under Michael-Joseph's chin. "Is this the patient? He looks well enough to me!"

He came to Alexander's bed. "What's this? Have our eyes open, do we?" He placed a black bag on the bed and opened it, taking out a stethoscope. "And how are you feeling, young fella?"

Alexander looked up at him. He said weakly, "Okay."

"You are, are you?" Dr. Sinclair drew back the bed covers. "Let's just take a look and listen."

He unbuttoned Alexander's shirt and underwear. He whistled softly. "Somebody gave you some pretty good licks."

He touched Alexander's chest lightly with his fingers. "Hold still now. I'm just going to feel your ribs and stomach. Tell me if it hurts real bad."

The doctor's gray hair was combed straight across a bald spot on his round head, and his baggy gray suit was wrinkled as though he had slept in it. His hands moved slowly over Alexander's ribs, first in front, then down the sides. He listened with the stethoscope, moving it from place to place on Alexander's chest. He pressed lightly on his stomach, palpating it gently. Then he had Alexander open his mouth while he looked in with a little flashlight and probed with a flat wooden stick.

"You must have inherited good teeth. Haven't had much candy, either." He smiled at Alexander. "What's your name, young fella?"

"Alexander."

"Alexander, is it? Well, Alexander, I want to examine you a little farther down, then your father and mother and I are going to roll you over onto your stomach, real slowly. Don't try to help us, just relax." He looked up at the people in the girls' room. " I think only Alexander's father and mother had better help now. Maybe the rest of you could wait in the other room."

They all went into the living room, and Uncle Jon closed the door to the girls' bedroom. Michael-Joseph asked, "Is Alexander going to die, Uncle Jon, like the boys in the tornado?"

Uncle Jon picked him up. "The doctor smiled. That is a good sign."

Aunt Magda put her arms around the girls. "The doctor will make Alexander well. You will see." Then she spoke to the Bowmans and Mrs. Horsefall, "Doctor is good man?"

Mrs. Bowman clasped her hands against her breast. "He will do his best. But we must all be ready when the Lord calls."

Mrs. Horsefall dabbed at her eyes with her handkerchief. "I feel so guilty. If only I had gone out there sooner..."

Mrs. Bowman tried to comfort her: "There, there, you couldn't have known, Viola. The Lord works in mysterious ways to call us home."

Mr. Bowman patted her arm. "And you did the right thing, by gracious, sending the Wample girl to tell us."

"But I never thought Julius Lamb would do such a thing. I thought with August Wagner away, everything would be fine." Mrs. Horsefall's voice shook, and her eyes looked from one person to another, seeking help.

"Come in kitchen, everybody," Aunt Magda said. "I fix coffee, then you feel better."

They filed into the kitchen and sat disconsolately around the table while Aunt Magda made coffee. No one spoke, and they looked frequently at the closed bedroom door at the other end of the living room as they sipped the coffee and waited. The girls and Michael-Joseph stood close to Aunt Magda and Uncle Jon, drawing comfort from the touch of their arms and hands.

They heard the occasional sound of the doctor's voice from the bedroom, but that was all. The hands of the clock on the stove seemed to hardly move, and the March wind made a little moaning sound as it swept around the corner of the porch.

The bedroom door opened partly, and Mrs. Horsefall gave a little cry as they all turned to stare at the door.

Doctor Sinclair came out of the bedroom and through the girls' room and the living room, into the kitchen. He smiled at them. "What's this? A tea party and such sober faces?" He chucked Michael-Joseph under the chin. "Your brother is going to be all right. He has some cracked ribs, a lot of bruises, and a concussion, but he should be all right."

Mrs. Horsefall gasped, "Oh, thank heaven!" She began to cry, holding her handkerchief up to her eyes.

Mrs. Bowman patted her shoulder. "There, there, Viola. Didn't we say everything would be all right?"

Uncle Jon had Marie translate what Doctor Sinclair had said. He held out his hand to the doctor. "We thank you."

Doctor Sinclair took his hand. "You must be Uncle Jon. Alexander spoke of you. Said he was sorry you and his father had to be brought in from the field."

Uncle Jon's eyes seemed to bother him. "He is good boy."

Josif and Izabella came from the back room as Uncle Jon spoke. "He is asleep," Izabella said. She spoke shyly to the doctor. "Will you have coffee with us?"

Doctor Sinclair smiled at her. "I would like to, but I should be on my way. I have another patient in the neighborhood who I should see as long as I'm out here." The smile left his face. "Poor woman, I'm afraid she can't last much longer."

Izabella gave a little sound of sorrow. "We would not keep you. I am so sorry."

The doctor placed his bag on the floor and put on his coat. "I'll have coffee with you when I come out to see Alexander on Wednesday. Now remember, have Mrs. Bowman call me immediately if he coughs up any blood or has trouble breathing or develops a high temperature. I don't believe there was any lung damage, but we can't tell for sure with broken ribs." He turned to Mrs. Horsefall, "Did you see the boy actually kicking Alexander?"

Mrs. Horsefall put her hands to her face. "It was terrible. Harry Jensen was trying to pull him away, and he just kept on kicking..."

"Who was the boy, Mrs. Horsefall?"

She looked up at him. "Who was the boy?"

"Yes. Who was the boy who did this? I should report it to the sheriff."

Mrs. Horsefall wrung her hands. "Oh, Doctor Sinclair, I thought you knew. It was Julius Lamb."

Doctor Sinclair stared at her. "My God. Poor Belle!" He

turned to face the Dacias. "I told you I was going to visit a dying woman?"

"Yes, Doctor."

Doctor Sinclair's face showed his anguish. "That woman is Julius Lamb's mother!"

* * *

From where Belle Lamb lay in her bed, she could see out the window to the south. The window came almost down to the floor, and she could see the familiar sight of the windmill, granary, hog house, and the big cottonwood by the tank. Beyond them she could see the fields. She could see far across the fields, out across the flat, dark land. The land stretched out forever, and there was a mystery to it. At night she could see a single light, far in the distance, so far away that she wondered if it could be Omaha. Verne had taken her there on their honeymoon, seventeen years ago. She could still see Omaha in her mind: the tall brick buildings, the paved streets, the big glass windows in the stores, the streetlights, the restaurants, the hotels.

There had been a bright light on the top of their hotel – a big electric globe on the very top of the spire. For the airplanes, they said. She often dreamed about that–an airplane fluttering through the dark air toward the light like a moth toward a flame. Sometimes she was the fluttering moth/airplane, flying toward the flame/light, fluttering nearer and nearer, feeling the warmth growing, a beautiful shining light coming ever closer.

A car was coming. Her ears were like her eyes, able now to sense things that were far away: a coyote howling in the darkness, the mournful wail of the night train, the wind sighing through the willows along the creek.

She recognized the sound of the car, and she felt on the nightstand by the bed for her comb and mirror. She pulled herself up on the pillow and combed her hair. The comb had become heavy and she used both hands to pull it through her hair. The mirror was a small one, for she could no longer lift the fancy one Verne had given her. The comb, mirror and brush were a set, all nestled in blue satin in the white and gold box. They had flowers on their backs, golden roses, heavy and beautiful. She could still lift the comb, but not the mirror or brush.

When she felt that her hair was right, she put the comb down and held up the little mirror. Her face was in the mirror, but she did not look at it, for it was not her face. Her hair was still beautiful, dark and heavy, with a natural wave. She fluffed it, her fingers feeling that it had not changed.

She looked around the room, making sure that it was still tidy. The furniture was still beautiful – the bird's eye maple dresser with its curved front and big mirror, the matching bed, rocking chair, and nightstand. She and Verne had picked them out in Omaha, and they had come all the way to Centerford by train, then out to the farm in the wagon.

She wondered why Dr. Sinclair had not come in yet,;then she heard the low rumble of voices in the barnyard and knew that he was talking to Verne. The voices grew fainter and she guessed that they had gone toward the cow barn. She lay back on the pillow; the doctor would be up soon, and she was ready to greet him.

* * *

Verne went back to the far end of the barn with Dr. Sinclair, past the cow stanchions and the calf pens. "She can't hear us back here," he said. "Now what's this damned stuff about Julius?"

Dr. Sinclair saw that a pitchfork leaned against the wall near Verne's hand. Verne had changed in the last ten years, and he could not be counted on to keep calm. The doctor said quietly, "Julius hurt a boy at school. You should know about it, because I'm going to have to report it to Frank."

Verne's eyes changed. The pupils became smaller as if he were looking at a bright light. "Kids are always gettin' hurt at school. What's so different about this damned kid that you have to go to Frank about it?"

"Julius hurt the boy seriously. He was a younger boy and Julius kicked him while he lay on the ground. The boy has three cracked ribs and a concussion."

Verne shrugged. "Julius came home from school already. He told me the kid jumped him first; tried to hit him with a lunch bucket." He spat behind him. "Hell, it was one of those Gypsy kids. Serves him right!"

"Verne, the boy was kicked at least fifteen times. They brought him home unconscious. I've just come from there and I've seen the damage. If the boy develops pneumonia he could die. I have to go to Frank about it."

Verne's eyes changed again. There was a darkness in them that worried the doctor. "Belle isn't gonna be bothered with this. If anybody tells her, I'll kill 'em."

Dr. Sinclair waited a little before he spoke. "I won't tell her, Verne, but if the boy dies, you're going to have to be prepared for her to find out. Once it gets in the hands of the law, the papers will find out about it."

"It's not gonna get in the hands of the law. The damned kid's alive all right now isn't he? If he gets pneumonia, that's none of the law's business. Frank isn't gonna cause any fuss over a Gypsy brat gettin' hurt." Verne's eyes looked to the northeast, toward the Dacias' farm, "The sooner those damned Gypsies get off my land, the better. This might help 'em decide to move along."

"I'm going in to see Belle now," the doctor said. "She won't hear a thing about this from me, I promise you."

"You can go in." Verne's eyes were coming back to normal now. "You've done all you can to help her, and she likes to have you come. She knows she's not gonna get better, but she talks like she is. You've helped her in that. Just see that she has enough of those pills, enough to see her through."

"I will, Verne. We aren't gonna let her suffer." Dr. Sinclair shook hands with Verne, then went back out through the barn and across the barnyard toward the house.

The smell of cattle and silage was strong about the place, a powerful odor that seemed to hang over the buildings like a fog. He saw a large herd of steers in the feedlot to the east, and near them were the silo and the other barn where Verne stored hay.

The doctor decided that Verne must have been doing well with the steers, since a new truck stood in the barnyard, and he could hear the muffled sound of the new engine that generated electricity for the farm.

Dr. Sinclair went up the porch steps and knocked on the kitchen door. The hired girl let him in, and after he had spoken to her he went up the stairs to the big room where Belle Lamb lay dying. "Hello, Belle," he said, smiling at her. "How's the prettiest girl in South Dakota doing today?"

Chapter Fourteen
Omens in the Night

That evening the Dacias put Michael-Joseph in his parents' bed so that he wouldn't disturb Alexander. After he was asleep, the rest of the family closed the kitchen door and sat at the table together. Josif was subdued, struggling under the weight of his part in Alexander's injuries and his frustration at not being able to take direct action against the Lambs. "Honor demands that I make this right," he said. "If I let this go then I am not a man, neither in Romania nor in America."

Uncle Jon replied, "Honor is sometimes all that a man can have, Josif. But it can be a hard thing."

Aunt Magda added, "Do not blame yourself too much. There is something evil here that we all must fight." She crossed herself. "If only there were a priest. He would drive it howling back into its grave."

Uncle Jon clenched his fist. "In the old country such a thing could be changed. We could take vengeance. Here in America it is harder."

Josif nodded. "This is even harder. We have been insulted and sworn at by the father. The son has almost killed Alexander. Yet we cannot take revenge when the mother is dying."

"If we had not learned about the mother," Uncle Jon said, "your knife or mine would be in the two Lambs tonight. Now they live."

"Now they live." Josif's eyes were cold. "We will wait until the mother is at peace in her grave."

Aunt Magda crossed herself. "May God bless her. To have such a son, such a husband. They are the kind who become strigoi, the evil living dead who drain all life from their victims. They are cursed; it will be their fate."

Izabella shuddered. "Do not speak of strigoi."

Aunt Magda's eyes darkened. "We must ward them off in every possible way. I will hang more garlic on the door. Tomorrow we will hang more garlic around the house and over the bedroom doors. And we must paint a cross on the door with tar."

"If Alexander dies," Josif said, "or if any others of you are harmed by these Lambs, I will not wait for the mother to die. I will have vengeance."

Izabella looked at Josif with determination. "The doctor will not let Alexander die. There has been no blood, and when I came from his room just now, he said the pain was less. This cannot be his time to die; he is too young and strong."

But even as she spoke the wind moaned around the house and the old shingles clattered as though something tore at them in the darkness. An owl hooted loudly and close by, almost as though it were perched on the roof.

At the sound of the owl, all the adults froze with a look of shock on their faces, then crossed themselves. Izabella fought back tears and looked with stricken horror at Josif. An owl calling was a certain sign of death in the family. She felt a pain shoot through her heart almost as if she had already lost Alexander.

But owls live in the grove, we have heard them before, she told herself frantically. *But never when one of us has been sick or hurt,* she replied to herself grimly, *and never so loudly and close to the house.*

Aunt Magda got up and began pulling the curtains closed on the windows. "Every room must have a cross. I will make them now from the sticks for the stove, and I will bring out the frankincense which I brought from Romania.

We will burn some at the door and in Alexander's room."

She paused at the last window listening; her face became pale. "Something moves in the night. Something growling. Something huge."

They held their breaths, also listening. A faint, roaring sound, deep, and menacing, came through the walls of the house. Suddenly there was the sound of something hitting the floor. Everyone looked at the source of the sound and was horrified to see that the icon of Mary and baby Jesus which hung in the living room had fallen on the floor. There was a large crack in the wood.

Elizabeth screamed and ran to Alexander's room.

Josif blew out the lamp. He said, in the darkness, "I am going out. Wait here, all of you."

Uncle Jon drew his knife. "I am coming with you."

The children clung to Aunt Magda and she to them. Michael-Joseph had been awakened by the owl and tore out of his parents' room squeezing between the other children to secure a spot next to Aunt Magda, who was looking fiercely around the room with her hand on her crucifix ready to fight man, beast, or demon to protect them.

The two men went out through the kitchen and porch into the yard. Dark, scudding clouds hid the moon, and the night wind rattled the tree branches in the black night. The sound came more clearly now, a low rumbling like distant thunder somewhere to the southwest. The menace and danger in it made the hair on the back of the men's necks stand on end. Dogs howled and barked from all the surrounding farmhouses.

Uncle Jon put his hand on Josif's shoulder. "Those are engines. Big engines. Tanks maybe or big trucks. Their vibration is what broke the icon. That was the cause and nothing more."

"Uncle, there have been three signs of death in this family. I cannot pretend otherwise. First the owl calling, then the icon breaking with no one near it, and now the dogs howling. You know they are signs. I grieve for Alexander already," Josif said softly, feeling a terrible sadness growing in his heart.

As they listened, the sound suddenly became less, faint as if suddenly muffled, then gone. Only the sighing of the wind in the trees remained. A feeling of malevolence filled the night air, as real and as threatening as an approaching storm.

Chapter Fifteen
The Bad Neighbors

As the truck engines died, the rumble of sound still vibrated for a moment in the barn like the roaring of a wounded beast. Verne Lamb closed the big double doors through which the trucks had entered, then lowered the steel crossbar into the heavy brackets on the walls and the insides of the doors, trapping a strong smell of diesel exhaust fumes. A lantern dimly lit the interior of the barn and made monstrous shadows of the trucks on the walls, but now Verne threw a switch on the wall and four bright, overhead lights came on.

The rigs were big army trucks, remodeled to look like cattle trucks, and with a made-up livestock hauling company name on their cabs. Dark canvas stretched over their loads, and they loomed in the harsh glare of the electric lights like two immense black juggernauts.

Vince Lamb came from the driver's side of the lead truck, stepping easily as a cat. He wore a wide-brimmed gray hat, a flowered tie, and a pinstriped, double-breasted blue suit with wide lapels. He carried a black pistol, and as he looked around at the interior of the barn, the barrel pointed the same direction as his eyes. He raised the barrel of the pistol. "Come on out, boys; it looks clean."

Two men came from the trucks. They were dressed like Vince and they carried submachine guns.

Vince quickly spoke to them, "This is my brother, Verne. He's okay."

The men stared silently at Verne. One of the men was short and broad with no visible neck. He was blue-jowled and thick-lipped, and the oily skin on his broad, dark face stretched tightly over the fat and muscle. His eyes were cold and suspicious. The second man was tall and powerful-looking, with a fighter's broken nose and a beefy face. Small, mean eyes glared from under dark eyebrows.

"This here's Angelo and Lou," Vince said to Verne with a cautionary look.

Angelo, the blue-jowled one, spoke. His voice was low and harsh. "Where's Clarence?"

Verne spat on the floor. "He took the car around to the house."

Angelo's eyes did not move from Verne's face. "Who's in the house?" The muzzle of his gun pointed at Verne's stomach.

Verne looked at the gun. "Just my wife. The hired girl's gone home and my kid's staying with the neighbors."

Angelo moved the end of the machine gun as if he were jerking his thumb. "Bring your woman out here."

"I'm not bringing my wife out," Verne said defiantly. "She's sick, and I wouldn't bring her out to see you even if she wasn't."

Angelo kept the machine gun and his eyes pointed at Verne. "You got a big mouth, clodhopper." He flicked the gun up so it aimed at Verne's face.

"Jesus, Angelo," Vince said. "His wife's got cancer. She can't walk out here."

Angelo stared at Verne. Without looking away from him, he said, "Lou, you stay here with Vince. Farmer, you come along with me. I'm goin' in and check out the house."

Lou motioned with his gun at Vince. "Over here, Vince baby. Put your gun on the floor."

Vince was beginning to sweat. "Say listen, Angelo, Clarence ain't gonna like it if you show up at the house."

"Fuck Clarence, he's not one of us, and neither are you."

Angelo moved his gun so it aimed at Vince's necktie. "Put the gun down, or Lou and I'll both plug ya." He watched as Vince laid his gun on the floor. "Lou, if you hear any shooting, take care of Vince. I'm gettin' tired of hearin' him talk." He swung the gun back on Verne. "Now, farmer, we're goin' up to your house."

Verne looked hard at Angelo. "This is my farm. I don't take orders from any stranger. We're not goin' anywhere 'til I see what's under that canvas. You coulda' brought a loada empty barrels for all I know."

Angelo's eyes shone flat and dark in the glare of the electric lights. He moved the muzzle of the machine gun in a little circle. "Lou, you and Vince take the canvas off." He stared at Verne. "You think you're a big man 'cause you own a little piece a dirt here and have cow shit on your shoes? If you tell me again that we're not men of honor, I'm gonna chop you up into hamburger with this gun so that your own kid won't even know you when they scrape you offa the floor."

Lou and Vince climbed up on the trucks and untied the rope lashings at the ends and sides of each box. Then they pulled the heavy, canvas covers off, letting them fall to the floor behind each truck.

Through the slats of the first truck's siding, large gleaming objects could be seen. Lou and Vince went to each inside end of the truck and released clasps near the top of the siding. Using ropes and small pulleys attached to the upper corners, they slowly allowed the sides to lean out, and then fold down to the floor.

"Look at it, farmer." Angelo gestured with his gun. "Go ahead. See if it's all there."

Verne climbed up the ramp made by the truck's side. The boiler, condenser, and retort gleamed under the ceiling lights, massive metal forms as perfect as gold coins. Packed around them, cushioning and protecting them like white velvet in a jewel case, lay big sacks of sugar.

Lou and Vince opened the side of the second truck. Two huge fermentation tanks stood in this truck, one tank filled with big, foil-wrapped cakes of yeast, the other with bags of malt. More bags of sugar filled the area around the two tanks.

Verne came down off the truck, and looked over the second truck. "Looks likes it's all here," he said curtly.

Vince edged away from Lou. "Damned right, it's all here. We cleaned out Bugsy's whole North Side place. We'll be truckin' ninety proof outta here in a month."

"You ain't gonna be able to peddle any of it anywhere near Chicago," Verne said. "You dummies took care of that."

"Hell, we don't need Chicago," Vince replied confidently. "We've got Sioux City, Omaha, Sioux Falls, maybe even Minneapolis and Denver."

"That mean these Dagos are gonna to be in on it?" Verne asked, looking at Angelo and Lou with disdain.

Angelo raised his machine gun. "Clodhopper, now I'm gonna shoot your face off along with your mouth."

There were two soft chuffs, then two more. Angelo and Lou slammed forward with their eyes just showing understanding of what had happened to them, then crumpled to the barn floor as though their bodies had come apart inside their pinstriped, wide-lapeled suits.

Clarence Lamb came through the narrow side door of the barn. He wore gold-rimmed glasses, and his carefully parted white hair and the pink and clean-looking skin of his face made him look like a kindly little grandfather. He wore a neatly pressed black suit, a stiff white collar with a small, black bow-tie, and high-top, black, laced shoes. He held his 1911 .38 with a silencer attached to the muzzle.

"Angelo was getting a little hot under the collar, Vernon," he said. Clarence knelt down and put the end of the silencer against the back of Angelo's collar. He spoke softly. "Angelo, this is Clarence." The pistol chuffed softly, and Angelo's heavy body jerked and then lay still.

Vince went to Lou and bent over him. "Lou ain't down for the count yet. Let me finish him off, Uncle Clarence."

Clarence stood up. "Go right ahead, Vincent. Just don't spatter him all over Vernon's clean floor."

Vince showed his teeth. He picked up his pistol from the barn floor and slipped a silencer on the barrel. He knelt down by Lou and pressed the end of the silencer against his thick chest. "You ain't gonna make it, Lou," he said smugly. "You ain't gonna answer the bell, and you ain't gonna use your brass knucks anymore. I'm gonna blow your chest apart."

Lou looked up at Vince. When he tried to speak, bloody froth came from his mouth. He whispered, "Fuck you, Vince."

Vince pulled the trigger and Lou bounced once on the barn floor. Vince shot him again, then stood up smiling sweetly at C.D. "Lou's hung up his gloves."

"So it seems." Clarence slipped the silencer off his pistol and put it in his coat pocket. He put a new clip of cartridges in the pistol, felt its barrel, then carefully put it in the shoulder holster inside his black suit-coat.

"Want me to take the car an' drop 'em off somewhere, Uncle Clarence?"

Clarence shook his head. "No, Vincent, that wouldn't be wise. I wrote to Vernon about a place. I assume he has it ready."

Verne prodded Angelo's body with his boot. "It's ready."

Clarence smiled at him. "Good, Vernon. Let's just go out and take a look at it first. I like to be certain that these things are done properly." He turned his smile on Vince. "Vincent, you please wait here until we come back. Keep an eye on things."

When Clarence and Verne had gone out with the lantern, Vince locked the door and then bent over Angelo. He took a silver cigarette lighter and a thick roll of bills from Angelo's coat pocket, then went to Lou's body, saying to himself, "This creep's prob'ly only got his brass knucks and

251

his gun." He fished in Lou's pockets and pulled out a thin leather wallet. "How about that! Two hundred bucks!" He chuckled to himself as he took a pair of brass knuckles from Lou's coat pocket. "He ain't gonna need these anymore."

He took Angelo's and Lou's machine guns and laid them inside the first truck, then waited by the side door.

In a few minutes, Clarence spoke from outside. Vince unlocked and opened the door, and Verne and Clarence came back into the barn.

"Vernon has done a good job," Clarence said. "Vincent, you help him with Angelo and Lou while I just scout around and make certain no one disturbs us." They turned out the lights in the barn and by the dim light of the lantern, Vince grabbed Angelo's legs and Verne grabbed his arms. They began to drag him out the barn door.

Clarence slid out the door first and quickly ran around behind the barn. He reached into the base of a thick clump of weeds and pulled out a metal box wrapped in a piece of oiled canvas, and tied with rope.

He hurried with the box around the back of the barn to a gaping black hole, and lightly tossed it into the bottom of the hole where it landed with a dull thud. He grabbed a shovel and threw dirt into the hole where the box had landed until he heard the sound of Verne and Vince approaching with their burden. Then he replaced the shovel and disappeared into the darkness.

Vince sniffed the air. "Jesus, it stinks out here, Verne. Don't you ever clean the shit outta that feedlot?"

Verne grunted with the weight of Angelo's body. "I do that on purpose. The smell of the feedlot and ripe silage keeps the damned neighbors from gettin' nosy."

Vince coughed. "A great idea, if you can stand it."

They came to a huge excavation in the raw, black earth; a dark pit that seemed bottomless in the dim light of the lantern. Vince dropped Angelo's legs so that the body dragged on the ground, bringing Verne to a halt.

"Holy shit! What you been diggin' here Verne? Looks like you could put a house in it."

"It's a silage pit, you dummy. I dug it out with the Fresno." Verne pulled on Angelo's arms again. "Keep going, damn it." He glared at Vince. "Don't let this wop fall on top of us. We're going down in now."

They slipped and slid down the slope into the pit with the body, and the black walls of earth rose up around them. The heavy and acrid stench of the feedlot had settled into the pit, mingling there with the vapors of the rotting silage that lay at the bottom to form a thick miasma that choked their throats and made their eyes water. Verne stopped at the bottom of the pit at the edge of a deep trench about three feet wide and seven feet long.

Vince swore hoarsely. "Let's dump him quick and get the hell outta here. I ain't gonna last in this stink."

Verne held the lantern up to illuminate the trench. "You city guys can't stand anything. Help me move this fat bastard over here, on the edge." They dragged Angelo to the lip of the trench so that he lay on his back with one arm dangling into the hole. Verne pushed him with his foot and Angelo rolled over the edge and thudded into the bottom of the trench. Verne held the lantern over the hole as they looked down.

Angelo lay face-up with his mouth partly open and his gray hat crumpled under his head. His eyes shone up at them like two flat gobs of dark spit in the lantern light. Verne took the shovel that was driven into the nearby pile of dirt and threw a half-dozen scoops-full down on Angelo's face. "You had a lot to say about us farmers and our dirt. Here's a little for ya, wop!"

They climbed back up the steep slope of earth and carried Lou out of the barn and down into the vaporous pit where they rolled him into the trench on top of Angelo. "Give me that shovel," Vince said. "I been wantin' to do this for a long time." He shoveled dirt in until both bodies were covered, then looked up at Verne. "How about you takin' this for a while? I can't hardly breathe in this stink."

Verne took the shovel. "What's the matter, have you gotten too puny living in the city to do man's work?" He shoveled dirt in until the hole was almost full, then stopped. "I just want to tell you one thing: Belle doesn't know anything about this business, and I don't want you to go shooting your mouth off where she can hear you. You understand?"

Vince sounded hurt. "Jesus, Verne, Belle always liked me. I ain't gonna do nothin' to upset her."

Verne threw more dirt into the hole. "Just seeing you in that damned gangster suit is bad enough, acting like you was some big shot in Chicago. I can't see why Clarence brought you along."

"To make good whiskey, that's why," Vince said defiantly. "I been runnin' this kinda still back in Chicago. It ain't everybody can handle a big still."

"I don't need any of you Chicago hoods to show me how to run a still," Verne said hotly. "I been turnin' out corn for two years now without any complaints. What the hell do I need you for?"

"This is different," Vince said. "Sure, you make a little corn, but this is gonna go to them places where they want high-class stuff. Not some dump down in Dakota City where they'll drink hair tonic or antifreeze."

Verne threw the shovel down. "Nobody's ever complained about my stuff. Where in hell's Uncle Clarence? We'll get this straightened out right now."

Clarence spoke from the darkness at the top of the pit. "Vernon, you are just as unreasonable as ever. Please shovel the rest of that dirt in and cover everything with the silage. Come back in the barn then, and I will explain things to you."

* * *

When they came in the side door of the barn, Clarence stepped out of the shadows behind the trucks. "Please lock the door, Vernon. Then both of you come into the still room."

A partition covered the far end of the barn. The partition looked like the wall of a grain-storage bin, but behind the partition, a twenty-by-forty foot room held Verne's still. Hinges on the partition allowed it to swing open to allow large equipment to be moved in on the hay track.

Verne led the way into the room through a small door and turned on the lights. Clarence looked carefully at Verne's still, then sat down on a chair that stood against the back wall, facing Verne. He said to Vince, "Vernon's been making corn whiskey here for two years. What do you think of his equipment?"

Vince studied the small still and the fermentation tanks. "I s'pose it's okay for the type of little jobs you'd get around here."

Verne snapped at Vince, "Damned right, it's okay. Built it myself. I don't need any of you Chicago sons-a-bitches comin' in here and tryin' to tell me how to make whiskey."

Clarence frowned at Verne. "Vernon, if we're going to work together we must have no more of such talk." He pointed to an axe that stood by a pile of wood. "Vincent, take the axe and break up the still."

Verne stared unbelievingly for a moment at Clarence. "If Vince touches my still I'll kill him."

Clarence took the black pistol from his shoulder holster and slipped the silencer on. He held the gun easily, not looking at it. The pistol chuffed softly three times, and the boiler and condenser shuddered and rang as the bullets slammed into them. Clarence shot once more and the retort shattered.

Verne stared at his still, then started toward his shotgun which hung on the wall.

Clarence said softly, "Don't move, Vernon, or I'll put three bullets in you before you take another step."

He spoke to Vince. "Vincent, put all of the money you took from Angelo and Lou on top of this barrel."

Vince was sweating again. "Sure, Uncle Clarence. I was just gonna give it to you."

"Of course you were, Vincent," Clarence said with narrowed eyes. "Now count the money."

Vince went through the bills. "Jesus! Twenty-six hundred. That Angelo had a wad on 'im!"

Clarence motioned with the gun. "Take ten of those hundred-dollar bills over to Vernon. Don't get between us." When Vince held the bills out to Verne, Clarence said, "See if that makes you feel any better about your still, Vernon. We have to keep everyone happy in our little group."

Verne took the money. "You didn't have to shoot it up, damn it all. That was a good still," he said sullenly.

Clarence smiled at him. "I understand how you feel, Vernon. But we want no distractions; we must put all our efforts into getting the new equipment working and distributing the product." He picked up the rest of the money and gave two hundred dollars each to Verne and Vince.

"This is really an unexpected bonus. You boys enjoy it. I do suggest, Vincent, that you follow Vernon's advice and rid yourself of your rather inappropriate attire. Remember, from now on you are to be a simple farm hand and truck driver." He sat down in the chair again.

Vince brushed the sleeve of his suit-coat. "Jesus, I just got this suit, Uncle Clarence. When I go down to the Pavilion this suit is comin' along. I ain't wearin' overalls when I go out for a little dancin'."

Clarence said mildly, "That is something I want to talk to you about, Vincent. We must all be as inconspicuous as possible. There must be no fights, no fires, no trouble of any kind. If you go out dancing, there must be no heavy drinking or arguments over the local girls. Whenever we talk with the neighbors we will be polite, and we will all give them the same information: I have retired here to the family farm to live out my last years in peace and quiet. You, Vincent, have returned to help Vernon with the cattle business."

"How the hell am I supposed to pass Vince off as a cattleman?" Verne said. "I bet he doesn't know the ass end of a steer from a corn-planter anymore, not that he ever did."

Clarence looked at Vince. "I think Vincent will do fine. Certainly much better than Angelo would have. That was a possibility, you know."

Vince snorted. "I can just see fat Angelo out there in the field in a straw hat and overalls, chewin' on a piece a hay and tryin' to act like a farmer!"

Verne glared at Vince. "Shut up, you dumb bastard. This ain't funny and it ain't gonna work." He threw the money Clarence had given him on the floor. "Take your damned money and go back to Chicago, both of you. I was doin' fine here until you guys came bustin' in. I don't need you and I don't want you here."

Clarence's pistol moved so it pointed at Verne's stomach. "Vernon, it would be very easy for you to have an accident with your shotgun. There would be no trace of one or two little holes from this pistol. Now listen carefully. There's a very large amount of money involved in this operation, and we're not about to lose it because of you. This farm is an ideal place for the production of our goods, and we are going to stay here, even if you, for some unfortunate reason, are no longer with us." He lifted the barrel of the pistol so that the silencer was aimed at Verne's chest. "Now, tell me, Vernon. Are you with us or are you not?"

Verne stared at the pistol. "You can shoot me, but I'd still get you."

Clarence smiled. "I don't think so, Vernon. I'll shoot you now or at any time in the future if you turn against us. It isn't hard to do, you know. Now, are you with me or against me?"

The shotgun would have to be pumped once before he could fire it. Clarence could put at least two shots in him in that time, and then there was crazy Vince. "I'm with you," he said angrily, "but there's too many things wrong with this. I don't like it."

Clarence let the muzzle of the pistol drop down a little. "Tell us what's bothering you, Vernon. These things can usually be worked out. But first, pick up the money."

Verne gathered up the money from the floor. "There's three things. First, I thought it was gonna be just the two of us. I told you I didn't want Vince back here startin' fires again. Second, I don't want Belle and Julius to get mixed up in this. Third, we got some goddamned Gypsy family livin' on Belle's folks' farm that the bank stole from us. It's right downwind from here, and if we get a big operation goin', they're gonna smell it and get nosy. Then we'll have the feds in here before we know it."

Clarence looked thoughtfully at Verne before he spoke. "Vernon, I understand what you're saying. Let me see if I can help you straighten things out.

"First, as far as running this operation with just the two of us, it would be nice, but we couldn't do it right. You have to keep the farm and your feed-lot going so that no one gets suspicious. Someone has to run the fermenters and the still, and it will take two people every time a truck goes out.

"As for your second point about Belle, I agree with you, and we will certainly not burden her with any of it. But there is no way we can keep Julius in the dark. He already knows about your own operation here; we will simply have to bring him in on this one. I think he should learn how to run the new equipment, and with Vincent's help, I believe he can.

"Your third point bothers me the most, and may require some corrective measures. You say these people are Gypsies?"

"They sure as hell looked like it. All piled together in an old wagon with a canvas top, trailing a cart and a cow, pigs and chickens and kids all mixed together. There musta been nine or ten of 'em. I caught 'em pissin' on my land, just a mile east of here, too damned close to the barn for comfort. That damned banker in Centerford has rented 'em Belle's farm. I'm gonna kill him some day, and them too if they don't get off my land."

Clarence held up one hand. "Now, Vernon, don't let yourself get all worked up. These things can be handled without getting excited."

"Well this hasn't been handled. You weren't around here when them goddamned lawyers an' judges an' bankers took Belle's farm away from me. I had to sit there in that courtroom an' watch 'em scheme an' simper an' finagle together until they got everything their way. I had to see Belle cryin' when her folks' furniture was sold at that damned auction sale. That's what's killin' her now, and it's the fault of that banker. She's dyin' because a him."

Clarence took the silencer off his pistol and put it in his pocket. He spoke soothingly to Verne. "Vernon, sometimes these things are hard to understand. I'm truly sorry about Belle, and I'm sorry I wasn't here to help you when the farm was taken away, but I am here now. I have found over the years that the decisions of judges are not always final. There are ways to change things." He put the pistol back in its holster. "This banker now. Would that be old Norman Johnson's boy, young Alan?"

"That's the one. The bank dropped right in his lap when old Norm died. He went to school down at Vermillion and then to some fancy damned business school back east. Married into a lotta money, so he thinks he can do any damned thing he pleases." Verne spit. "We hear he wants to start another bank, usin' old man Steadman's money."

Clarence smiled. "There must be a way to convince young Alan of the error of his ways without going to extremes. We really don't want that sort of publicity." He studied his high-topped shoes. "I think I will make a little visit to Centerford in a day or two. Maybe drop in at the bank and say hello to young Alan."

"What about those damned Gypsies? I want 'em off my land, right now!"

Clarence waggled a finger. "Patience, Vernon. That's

the secret. Patience. Never fear, they will be gone, but we must not hurry things."

Vince's eyes gleamed. "I'll just go in there some night and torch the place. The banker might see the light then."

Clarence looked up in surprise at Vince. "Very good, Vincent. I hadn't realized that you had such a sense of humor." He shook his head. "But no fires, Vincent. Not yet. Not until I tell you to. Do you understand?"

"Oh sure, I understand." Vince grinned, showing his teeth. "But it sure would make one hell of a good fire with about five gallons of gasoline, that old house and barn and granary would burn like a paper box factory!"

Clarence frowned. "Vincent, I have told you before. You must not set fires unless I tell you to. Now please mind." He spoke to Verne. "There is one thing I am concerned about. That is Frank. Can we be certain that he's with us?"

"He's with us. He'd better be, for Christ's sake; he's part of the family."

Clarence rubbed his chin. "Not really, Vernon. I have never felt that Frank considered himself part of our family. The Ariostos always thought themselves to be somewhat above and apart from us Lambs. Frank is somewhat of a question in my mind right now. I believe that I will have a little talk with Frank fairly soon."

"He's never even looked cross-eyed at my business here," Verne said. "But if you movin' in with this big still gets Frank turning owly, it ain't gonna be any picnic. Frank's a whole 'nother matter than that stupid town marshal."

Clarence smiled. "I appreciate your concern about Frank. If he does turn *owly*, as you say, he may have to be dealt with. There are many ways a sheriff might run into somewhat serious trouble in carrying out his duties."

Verne scowled. "I wouldn't be too damned sure about that. Frank's about as handy with that .38 of his as you are with yours. On top a that, he's got a new deputy–that little runt, Earl Snipes."

Vince perked up, "Hell, I know Earl. We used to go dancin' with them Ordstrom sisters. He ain't gonna be any problem if he gets his cut."

Clarence looked thoughtfully at Vince. "Vincent, I will decide who gets cuts and who doesn't. There is no reason why we have to share our profits with the local constabulary." He got up from the chair. "I think we have a pretty good idea now of what the local problems may be, and I believe they can all be taken care of. Tomorrow you boys will please start moving the equipment in here and setting it up. The sooner we get started, the sooner the money will start rolling in."

Verne looked at his smashed still. "You maybe think you can take care of everything. I ain't too damned sure. You wrecked my still, and if this new still don't work right we're gonna be up shit creek. On top a that, just how the hell are you plannin' to move big shipments out without some of these smart-aleck cops in places like Sioux City and Omaha gettin' nosy?"

Clarence smiled in such a kindly way that his face beamed. "Ah, Vernon, I have been waiting for you to ask about our plan for transportation. Come out into the big room; I want to show you something."

They went out of the still room and up to the trucks. Clarence pointed to the cattle boxes. "How do these strike you, Vernon? Anything look suspicious about them?"

Verne studied the trucks and their boxes. "Hell, yes. They're too damned clean for one thing. There oughta be steer crap smeared all over the planks, and straw in the beds

261

and hanging out through the sides. There should be mud all over these bodies and wheels. These trucks wouldn't fool the stupidest jerk cop in Yankton."

Clarence chuckled and winked at Vince. "Other than that, they look all right to you do they, Verne? Nothing different from a regular cattle truck?"

Verne scratched his chin. "The damned things do ride kinda high. Other than that, they don't look too bad."

Clarence frowned. "You think they ride high? Is that liable to bother our friends of the law, do you think, Vernon?"

Verne stepped back and studied the trucks again. "I guess not. Why? Why's that so important?"

"Vincent," Clarence said, "please show Vernon our little invention." He handed a key to Vince.

Vince went to the rear of the first truck and bent down under the box with the key. He opened a small metal door in the bottom of the truck bed and pulled out a metal nozzle attached to a hose.

"What the hell's that?" Verne asked.

Clarence smiled. "Vernon, under each truck bed, built right into the floor, is a reinforced, stainless-steel tank just six inches high, but as wide and long as the box of the truck. How many gallons do you think that would hold?"

Verne stared at Clarence. He did some quick calculating in his head. "Those boxes are about six feet wide and twenty feet long. That would be about sixty cubic feet. How the hell many gallons are there in a cubic foot? Two or three?"

"Precisely seven point four eight one," said Clarence. "And the truck boxes are twenty-three feet long." His eyes gleamed behind the gold-rimmed glasses. "Deducting for the thickness of the walls, the tanks are fifty-seven cubic feet each. That makes four hundred twenty-six point four gallons per tank. Multiply that by the price we receive per gallon and you see why this can be a profitable line of endeavor." He frowned. "But the fact that you detected that extra six inches worries me. The people in Detroit that fabricated these truck boxes for us said that it would never be noticed. I think I will have to have a little talk with them."

"Hell, Uncle Clarence," Vince said, "Verne just thought they rode a little bit high. You get a load a steers in there and the damn springs are gonna flatten out so's nobody would see the difference."

Clarence looked at him. "Vincent, you have just made my mind up for me." He knelt down and studied the axles and springs of the truck. "I want you boys to figure out a way to lower these boxes six inches. If you can't do it, we will take the trucks back to Detroit. This operation is not going to be jeopardized by the appearance of our trucks." He stood up and said coldly, "Not by our trucks. Not by anything."

Chapter Sixteen
Alan and Ellen

Alan Johnson found early in life that things came easily for him. He was intelligent and alert, and obtaining good grades in school was never a problem; he also inherited an athletic and vigorous physique form his parents. As a result, he was a four-year letterman and valedictorian in Center-ford High School, and at the University of South Dakota he was elected to the honorary scholastic societies Phi Eta Sigma in his freshman year and Phi Beta Kappa in his senior year.

He was an All Conference basketball forward for his last three years, the university's swimming and middle-weight boxing champion for all four years, president of the most prestigious fraternity, and also president of the senior class. After graduation he attended the Warburton School of Business and graduated with honors in 1917.

The United States declared war on Germany in that same year, and Alan volunteered for the army and was commissioned a second lieutenant in the Quartermaster Corps, serving his country in England and France, attaining the rank of captain.

After the armistice he returned to Centerford, where he learned the banking business in his father's bank and married his college steady, Norma Steadman, who had been elected Miss Dakota in her senior year at the university, and whose father was Charles Steadman, one of the wealthiest men in South Dakota.

When Norman Johnson died and left the bank to Alan, the young man was well equipped to run it, and the bank did so well under his guidance that by 1929 he was considering opening a branch bank in the nearby town of Haymarket. At age thirty-five he seemed to have reached the pinnacle of success. Yet at this same time he found that he and his wife had tired of one another.

While delivering the graduation address at his former business school, he was struck by the beauty of one of the graduates, and at the reception following graduation he convinced Ellen Olson that there was a promising future for her in his bank in Centerford.

Ellen was not only beautiful; she was intelligent, and this became a challenge to Alan. He set out to find a way to seduce her without offending her intelligence or good taste, and without the town or his wife knowing about it. In the process, however, and before the deed was accomplished, he found that he was in love with her.

This was a new experience for Alan, and in March of 1929, when the Dacias came to Centerford, he was, for the first time in his life, in an agony of indecision. He longed to divorce his wife and marry Ellen, yet in order to open the new branch bank, he needed a large sum of money, which was only available from his father-in-law.

In spite of his indecision, he continued to court Ellen. In banking terms, he had a plan of action that involved four steps; these were the *Four Cs* of banking: capital, credit, clearing, and collecting.

The first step, capital, was well underway. He showed Ellen every courtesy, he was always friendly and correctly polite, he was helpful, he gave her responsible and rewarding assignments, he paid her well, and he arranged it so that they were together as much as possible. The Saturday trip out to see the Dacias was such a case, and on the way back to Centerford that day, he laid the groundwork for the next step, credit.

He said casually as he drove the big Chrysler along the country roads, "Ellen, I have to drive up to Sioux Falls this afternoon on business. How would you like to come along? It would be good experience for you, and it would help me out. We spent more time at the Dacias' than I had planned, and my appointment is at 1:00. We could go straight over to Route 77 and be up there just about in time."

She looked at her wrist watch, then smiled at him. "Of course. If you took me back into Centerford now, you would never make your appointment."

He smiled back. "Good. Do you mind if we postpone lunch until after the meeting? I know a good restaurant up there where we can have a leisurely meal before we start back."

"Only if you let me pay my way."

"Oh, no. Not when I am practically abducting you. Remember, I'm the boss. I pay."

She laughed. "Yes, sir. Just as you say."

"I have been thinking about the Dacias," he said. "I believe we should help them in every way we can. They seem to me to be a deserving family."

She agreed. "Those children are so cute. That little four-year-old Michael-Joseph wanted to take us out to see the geese. I just loved him."

He laughed. "He wanted to take you out to see the geese, not me. I think he shows excellent judgment."

She blushed. "Thank you. You're too kind."

"I mean it. Just as I showed excellent judgment in hiring you."

He went back to the original subject so as not to embarrass her. "I don't think they have any money to speak of, but they do have their pride. Did you notice how Mr. Dacia reacted to the idea of borrowing money? I think he would rather die first."

"He does seem to be a very proud man," Ellen said. "His wife is beautiful, but she seems to be very shy, almost afraid of strangers. I wonder what their life must have been like in Romania."

"Pretty harsh, I imagine. The Balkan countries suffered a great deal during and after the war." Alan slowed the car as they approached Highway 77, the paved highway that led north to Sioux Falls. He stopped at the intersection and then carefully looked both ways before driving onto the highway. As the car picked up speed, he resumed the conversation. "I'm surprised that they were able to bring the aunt and uncle over, immigration quotas for that part of the world being what they are."

"I think the quotas are unfair," Ellen replied. "The people from Eastern and Southern Europe are entitled to the same rights and consideration as are the people from Northern and Western Europe. The Dacias are an example. They are fine people, yet they're discriminated against by many Americans and, even worse, by our own government."

Alan nodded. "Our beloved town marshal, Fred Franklin, certainly demonstrated that. I'm told that he paid for his sins, however."

Ellen's face began to turn pink. She said in a small voice, "I heard about that."

He looked quickly at her, then back at the road. "Do I hear a small giggle coming from the first assistant, second vice-president of our bank?"

"Don't look at me."

"Why not?" He kept his eyes straight ahead.

"Because if you do, you'll find out how awful I am."

"Awful? I find that hard to believe. What is this terrible thing?"

"I start to giggle and can't stop. If anyone I like looks at me, I can't stop."

He kept his eyes on the road. "Did you mean that?"

"About the giggling?"

"About the people who mustn't look at you. Did you mean that?"

She was silent for a moment. "I'm sorry. I shouldn't have said that."

Now he did look at her. "I'm happy that you said it. It means a great deal to me."

"I want to do well in the bank, but not that way. Please forgive me."

"There is nothing to forgive; saying you 'like' someone is no crime. It was my fault for teasing you about it. From now on, it will be strictly business between us. All right?"

She looked straight ahead as she spoke. "All right."

There was a long silence as the car hummed northward over the pavement. Alan drove expertly, passing slower cars and trucks smoothly and carefully, keeping the car at an almost constant speed. He said to her, "I should let you drive; you brought that Chevy of yours all the way from Minneapolis. How did you learn? Few women know how."

"My father taught me. He thinks girls should be able to do things for themselves."

"I agree with your father." He looked at her, then back at the road. "What else did he teach you? Camping and fishing, I'll bet, and not the easy way."

She smiled. "If you want a fire, chop your own wood. If you catch a fish, you clean it. If you get blisters, it's your own fault."

He laughed. "Just like my father. We used to go out to the Black Hills. He expected us to catch our breakfast, climb Harney's Peak, swim across Sylvan lake, and then hike to a new campsite before nightfall."

"Were you a Boy Scout?"

"I was. Ask me to tie a knot."

Now she laughed. "Not while you're driving."

He smiled at her. "Never." He pointed ahead of them. "There are the towering skyscrapers of Sioux Falls. Four and five stories, some of them." He assumed the accent and dialect of a rustic. "Ayah, by gonnies, thar she is, gal, the big city."

"If you start me giggling again..."

The meeting was over by 2:30. As they got into the car, Alan said truthfully to her, "You were a real help, and I think you learned a lot. If you think it's worthwhile, I'd like to have you come to this sort of thing more often."

"I'd like to come. It was a good experience, and I appreciate the opportunity you're giving me." She smiled at him. "Thank you." She stretched her legs out, holding her feet above the floor of the car.

"That was a long meeting. Are you tired?"

"Not tired. I just feel like having a good walk or run." She smiled at him. "You know how we Campfire Girls are. Full of vim and vigor."

"I have an idea. May I show you one of my favorite places here before we eat? I think it may interest you, and it's only about a ten-minute walk. We can leave the car right here."

"The walk sounds wonderful. Are you going to tell me what this place is, or is it a surprise?"

"A surprise." He came around and opened the car door for her. "I think you'll like it."

They walked down the main street, and he felt the people looking at them, admiring them. She walked with an easy swinging gait like a boy, and he suspected that she could out-walk most men. There was an erect grace about her body, like that of a trained dancer, and her face was radiant with the joy of movement. She exclaimed with pleasure at the store windows, and when they came to a toy store she wanted to buy something for each of the Dacia children, and he only got her to go past the store by promising to come back after the surprise.

They came to a large, granite building, and he said to her, "Don't look up. Look down at the steps so that I can surprise you." They went up the entrance steps and into the building, then up another flight of stairs. The steps were polished granite, and she said, "You're taking me into another bank."

They came to heavy metal doors, and he took her arm. "Close your eyes." He led her through the door, and she knew. She cried out in delight and opened her eyes.

The swimming pool was huge, and it was beautiful. They stood on a balcony above it, looking down at the brilliance of the water, at the blue tiles, at the sunlight streaming in from overhead windows. The smell, the sounds, the feeling were all there: the sharp clean smell of chlorine; the echoing sound of the swimmers' voices and movements, the bang of the diving board, and the splash of water; the feeling of space and water and air and light. She leaned forward over the railing as though she could dive in at that moment.

"Do you like it?" he asked.

She turned to face him. "Can we go in? Do they rent suits? Do we have time?"

He laughed, seeing her excitement and pleasure. "The answers are all yes. We can go in. They do rent suits. We do have time."

They ran down the stairs and down more stairs to the locker rooms. He insisted on paying for her admission, suit, and towel, and turned her over to the ladies' attendant, a jolly Swedish woman named Anna, who took one look at Ellen and wanted to adopt her. He went into the men's locker room and changed into his suit and showered.

When he came out into the pool area, he saw Ellen just coming in from the ladies' side. He knew that she was beautiful in her street clothes; in the plain, black swimming suit and white bathing cap, she was more than beautiful.

He met her by the diving board, and again, he felt the eyes of other people on them, admiring them. "I forgot to ask if you swim," he said.

She looked at him, smiling, "I'll race you down and back, free style."

He smiled back at her. "You're on."

They took the racing start together, and together they streaked down the pool. He was more powerful than she, but she moved through the water the same way that she walked, gracefully and effortlessly. They turned under and came back, and he knew that she might beat him. He concentrated and his body responded as it always had, and he beat her, his fingers touching the pool edge a fraction of a second before hers.

"You've swum before," she said, her eyes twinkling.

He laughed. "A little. Back in my college days." He stroked under the water so that he came a little closer to her. "You almost had me. You can't do that to the boss, you know."

"I held back on purpose. Wait 'til next time." She slipped under the water and came up ten feet away, treading water, smiling at him. "I suppose you dive, too."

He knew this would be too much – the former champion showing off. "I'm afraid this old body has lost its cunning. I'd probably come down belly first."

She came a little closer. "I was only teasing. This is wonderful. Thank you for the surprise."

He looked into her eyes. "Maybe we can do it again."

They swam laps, swimming easily now, varying their strokes, playing in the water like two seals. He kept a polite distance from her, never touching her, never offending her.

A clock hung on the wall, and at half past three they forced themselves to come out of the pool. She was happy and hungry, and when they had showered and dressed, they walked back toward the car talking of food like starving teenagers.

She forced him into the toy store, and he helped her pick out presents for the Dacia children. They found dolls for the three girls and a stick horse for Michael-Joseph, but they could find nothing that was right for Alexander. "You were a twelve-year-old boy once. What was your best present?"

He thought a moment. "A baseball glove I got for my birthday. But somehow, Alexander doesn't strike me as being much interested in baseball."

"He's so serious. He just doesn't have the look of our American boys." She looked up at the shelves. "There must be something...."

A model airplane kit lay on the top shelf, and she reached up for it. A picture of Charles Lindbergh and *The Spirit of St. Louis* was printed on the box. They looked at it, then at each other. She said, "It's perfect! He has the same serious face as Charles Lindbergh. It'll be perfect for him!"

They went to the car with the packages, and she was so pleased with the presents that she hugged them to her as they drove to the restaurant.

It was a Greek restaurant, downstairs below street level, and they sat at a table with a red-checked tablecloth. A tantalizing smell of good food filled the place, the room was dark and exotic, and Greek music played on a hidden phonograph.

The proprietor, swarthy and mustachioed, came personally to take their order. He beamed at them, "There should be wine. A beautiful woman should have wine. How can I have such a woman in my restaurant and not bring her wine?"

The music was strong, the dance music of warriors — men with shields and spears and horsehair plumes on their helmets. They ordered the stuffed grape leaves called dolmadakia, roast lamb with Greek salad, broccoli with oil and lemon sauce, and Greek bread.

The proprietor came back with two glasses of dark, red liquid. "It is grape juice. If the police should come, drink it quickly. I cannot serve such a lady without wine."

The wine was strong and resiny, and they sipped it with added pleasure, knowing that it was forbidden. The music was an intricate, twelve-beat rhythm now, and Alan saw that she responded to it by an almost imperceptible movement of her body. "You are a dancer," he said happily. "I knew it when we walked. When we swam."

She blushed. "I hoped you wouldn't find out."

"I have found out, and it pleases me that you are. Tell me about dancing, about your dancing."

Ellen looked down at her hands. "It's not much. I had hoped to be a great ballet dancer. I had good teachers and I thought I was good. I was good. But Minneapolis is not New York. New York is full of good dancers. I saw that I would never be prima ballerina. Banking seems a far cry from dancing, I know. Please believe that I have forgotten my dream of dancing."

He smiled at her. "I won't forget, and I won't let you forget. We'll go dancing sometime if you can put up with a heavy-footed banker trampling on you."

She looked up at him with some sadness in her eyes. "I don't think we should do that."

"Of course, you're right. I'm sorry."

Again the silence came between them. The music was sad now, haunting, telling of sacrifice and death. The proprietor came with the *dolmadakia* and smiled at them. "You like the music? Is the *Kalamatianis*. Tells of Greek women who throw themselves over cliff to escape Turks." The music changed as he spoke. A flirtatious duet of clarinet and drum gradually became faster and more intense. "This is better for you. *Ballos*, a love dance." He smiled at them again and left them with the *dolmadakia* and the wine.

Alan spoke quietly, "I'm sorry. He meant well."

She put her hand on his. "You've given me one of the best days I can remember. Don't be sorry."

He looked into her eyes. "I don't want to hurt you."

Her hand was warm and firm on his, and she left it there as she spoke. "I'll dance with you if you want me to. But we must do nothing to hurt your wife. Promise that, and you won't hurt me."

He took her hand. "I promise."

"You look so sad. Is it the music?"

He shook his head. "No, it isn't that. I was thinking of other things, of the future."

Her eyes showed her concern. "The future? Why does that make you sad?"

He smiled ruefully. "Sometimes things from the past come to haunt our future. Mistakes we have made that cannot be undone – things that affect other people as well as ourselves. People we don't want to hurt."

Her eyes were sad for him. He saw that she knew what his sadness was, and he went no further. He said, "I promised you a good meal, and now I have spoiled it. Let's talk of something else. Tell me how it feels for a girl who has lived in Minneapolis and New York City to be working in a one-horse bank, to be living in a little prairie town where they roll up the sidewalks at night. Tell me while we eat, or they will find two skeletons here when they come to sweep up."

She laughed then, the sadness leaving her eyes. "If you start me giggling in here, our host will be very disillusioned." She took a small bite of the *dolmadakia*. "Believe it or not, I am happy in Centerford, and you know I'm happy at the bank. New York City is glamorous and perhaps the center of the world, but I find the small-town life and pleasures to be a welcome change. Of course the time spent in college and business school was a change too, but now, for the first time, I feel that I'm working at something with a future, something worthwhile."

"You mean like helping the Dacias, feeling that in our way we may be able to do some good. Is that it?"

She nodded. "Exactly. Helping the Dacias and other deserving people who are really the salt of the earth, the people who come or have come here from other parts of the world to find a better life, just as our ancestors did. They may be farmers or factory workers or shopkeepers or scientists. They deserve the same chance that the earlier settlers had – the same opportunity without having to contend with discrimination."

"Ah, but don't forget, the earlier ones, our people, had other things to contend with: Indians, outlaws, grasshoppers, sickness, hunger, prairie fires, loneliness...."

"That's true, except for the Indians. If ever there was a mistreated people..." She stopped. "I'm sorry, I must be boring you, talking like a sophomore. You've probably heard these things a hundred times before, from every person you ever interviewed for a job who wanted to impress you."

Before he could answer, the proprietor came with the rest of their dinner, smiling as he placed the dishes on the table. "Music now is *Gerakina*. Tells story of beautiful young girl who goes to well, falls in. Handsome man rescues her with golden belt, makes her his wife. Is very beautiful."

When he had gone, Alan said, "In the story it is a handsome young man. Our host was kind enough not to mention that."

She smiled. "I like him. But tell me how it is you know the story of *Gerakina*. You don't look Greek."

"Oh, I bring a different girl here every week. The proprietor always tells the same story to each girl."

She raised an eyebrow. "Really!" She smiled at him. "I don't believe a word of it."

"You've found me out. What girl would go out with a broken-down college athlete who will never see thirty again?"

"You don't look very broken down to me, and plenty of girls would be thrilled to go out with you."

He wisely decided to leave that point where it was. "Thank you," he said. "To get back to our earlier discussion about the Dacias, let me tell you that I did not find your thoughts boring or sophomoric. It's good to hear someone talk with intelligence and compassion about our country and its problems. Not,

Wide open and unguarded stand our gates. And through them presses a wild motley throng...

"That awful poem! Thomas Aldrich should be ashamed to his dying day that he wrote it." She put down her fork. "The tragic thing is that so many people are influenced by that sort of bigotry. Can't intelligent Americans see the evil in such a philosophy? Think of the thousands of worthy human beings who are affected by such vicious attacks, the heartaches, the misery that results. It isn't right and it isn't fair."

He shook his head. "I couldn't agree with you more. And yet we must have some sort of a selection process. The sad and unfortunate thing is that our government has decided arbitrarily that certain races and nationalities are desirable while others are not. Such a policy is discrimination at its worst."

She looked at him in a new way. He could see it in her eyes. Not as the president of the bank, not as an athlete, but as a fellow human being with compassion for the downtrodden people of the world. "I can't tell you how much this day means to me," she said. "I think you'd better take me home now before I start to cry."

He put his hand on hers. "Is it something I've said? Something I've done? I wouldn't make you cry for the world."

"Yes, it is something you've said, something you've done. You have made me happy and glad that I know you. I wish..." She stopped, and he saw that there were tears in her eyes.

"What do you wish, Ellen?"

She wiped her eyes. "Please, I think we should go now."

He paid the proprietor and left a dollar tip on the table, then they went out to the car. He asked her, "Would you like another walk? The river and park aren't far away. We can still be home by 6:30," and she replied in a low voice, "That would be nice."

As they walked toward the river, she said, "I'm so ashamed of myself. Starting to cry in that poor man's restaurant when he was so nice to us. I should go back and apologize to him."

"He knew that you were happy. He told me so when I paid him. The Greeks understand these things."

"I'm not sure if I'm happy or sad." She looked up at him. "I don't think I should come up here with you again."

He said nothing, but he took her hand, and it was small and strong inside his. They came to a little park by the river, and they walked down across the dormant grass to the river-bank. There were rapids in the river, and the spring thaw had made the river high so that the water churned over the rocks and sent spray up into the March sunshine. He spoke softly to her, "There is an Indian legend about these rapids. Something to do with a beautiful maiden and a canoe."

She gazed out at the water. "Those legends are always so sad. As if they knew somehow that their future held only sorrow and sadness."

They walked slowly along the riverbank and then back through the park and along the street to the car. When they were out of the traffic and back on the highway, he said to her, "I want you to come with me again."

She was silent, staring ahead of them at the road. She spoke without looking at him. "I think I'm falling in love with you. I didn't want it to happen. It would be better if I left the bank before things go any further."

He passed a truck before he answered. He spoke slowly and truthfully. "I have been in love with you since the first day I saw you. It's my fault, not yours. I haven't been fair to you."

He heard her draw in her breath, making a little sound of sorrow or happiness; he couldn't tell which. She looked at him now as she spoke. "Did you hire me for that reason? Because you loved me?"

Again he was truthful. "Yes. I wanted you. I want you now. But I would've hired you if I hadn't loved you. You were the best candidate. You've done better in the job than anyone else could've. I want you to stay for that reason, but a thousand times more important, I want you to stay because I love you."

She did not speak for a long time. "What about your wife? You said that you wouldn't hurt her."

"It won't hurt her. We never really loved each other. She has other interests."

"I can't stay. We can't see each other every day and not have this get worse."

"I want to see you every day – I want you to stay. We love each other. That's what matters."

She looked up at him. "How can we live with ourselves? I love you, but 1 can't be your mistress. It isn't fair to your wife. I'll go back to Minneapolis as soon as you find a replacement for me. Sooner, if you want me to."

"I don't want you to go at all." He slowed the car and pulled off the highway onto a side road. He drove down it to where a clump of trees stood by the side of the road and stopped the engine. "We have to talk this out."

"How can we talk it out? There's only one answer. I must leave."

"Do you want to leave?"

"No. But I must."

"You don't have to leave. These things can be worked out. I can't let you go away; I love you."

"I'll start crying if you say any more."

He touched her face, lightly, with the back of his fingers. "Will you do one thing? One thing for me? Please stay for one more month. We'll go on just as before, and I'll never speak of loving you. We can still come to meetings together and swim together and eat Greek food together, but it will be as friends, not lovers. If you go, all of that will be gone. If at the end of the month you are unhappy, I'll look for a replacement."

She put her hand over his, holding it against her face. "I love you so much..."

He put his arm around her and drew her close, and she came eagerly to him. They kissed, and there was wonder and discovery and passion in their kissing. She said, "I want you to make love to me, but I can't let you. If you do, it will be a thing we will always regret."

He kissed her again, and his hand found her breasts. He touched them gently through the softness of her dress, feeling them respond. She pressed her face against his throat. "Please, Alan..."

He said, "I want to love you now, but not if it will bring you sorrow." He stroked her hair, her temples. "Will you stay? We can work it out somehow. At least we can be together part of the time..."

Her voice was muffled and faint against his throat, and he knew that she was crying softly. "I want to stay. I would stay forever if I could..."

He held her for a long time, held her while the sun slipped down toward the horizon and shadows crept across the fields, held her while the nighthawks swooped and plunged in the twilight sky, calling their strange cry that was lonely and sad and beautiful.

Chapter Seventeen
Clarence Sizes Things Up

On Tuesday many visitors came to see Alexander. All eight of the Wample sisters and the two Dordoine boys stopped in on their way home from school, and a little later the Bowmans and Mrs. Horsefall arrived in the Bowmans' car with schoolbooks and presents of fresh store fruit for Alexander. After supper the Wagner brothers appeared with their lantern. Fritz carried a large, covered plate.

"It's a cake Grandma sent over. She was so mad when she heard about Julius kickin' Alexander that she baked it."

August added, "She said she wished it was Julius in the oven."

Izabella put the plate on the table and lifted the cover. The cake was chocolate, two layers, dark and rich-looking. "It is beautiful. How can we thank your grandmother? Will you tell her?"

Fritz turned his cap in his big hands. "Well, you better taste it first. She was so mad she mighta forgot to put somethin' in it."

Josif smiled at the boys, "You want to see Alexander? He be real happy that you come."

"Well, sure, if it ain't too much trouble." The brothers took off their coats and hung them up, and Josif noticed that they wore clean overalls and shirts.

Izabella picked up the cake. "We will show him the cake. He will be so happy to see you." She went back through the living room and the girls' room, carrying the cake, and the

Wagners and the whole family followed, making a long procession through the house. Alexander looked up from the bed at Fritz and August. His voice was weak, but he tried to smile. "I heard you come."

Fritz stared at him. "Holy cow, that weasel of a Julius sure messed you up!"

August scowled, "He ain't at school. Mrs. Horsefall expelled him. If he ever comes back I'm gonna beat the sh–" He stopped. "I'm gonna pound that bast–." He tried once more. "I'm gonna fix him good."

Izabella held the cake so that Alexander could see it. "Look, Alexander, what Fritz and August have brought. Their grandmother made it for you!" She brought it near him. "Smell how good it is."

"Let's eat it now, Mama, so Alexander can have some," Michael-Joseph said eagerly.

"Can I, Mama?" Alexander tried to slide up on his pillow.

"Of course! We will all have some!" Izabella put the cake on the bed. "We will bring chairs here and to the girls' room and have a party with Fritz and August and Alexander."

They brought plates and chairs, and Izabella cut the cake and gave pieces to everyone."We have such good friends who bring such a nice cake to us, to Alexander."

Josif beamed. "We thank good neighbors Fritz and August and their grandma and grandpa." He held out his hand to the Wagners. "We not forget."

Fritz and August shook his hand awkwardly and stiffly, looking at the floor. "It ain't nothin'," Fritz said. "Like I told ya, you better taste this here cake first. Grandma mighta left the flour or somethin' out of it. She was mad as all get out."

They ate, and the cake was dark and thick with chocolate and delicious. Izabella fed Alexander a small forkful. He seemed to swallow with difficulty, but he said, "It's real good." Izabella offered him another bite, but he said, "Maybe I'll wait just a little while."

Izabella put the plate down and placed her hand on his forehead. "He is not hot...." She looked up at Josif, her eyes questioning and concerned.

Aunt Magda felt his forehead. "Izabella is right. He is not hot."

Izabella asked gently, "How do you feel, Alexander? Can you breathe all right?"

He looked up at her. "I just don't feel hungry, Mama. I'm all right."

"Nobody would feel like eatin' too much when they had their ribs kicked in," Fritz said. "I remember one time I tangled with that bull of ours. Grandma had pork chops and sauerkraut that night an' I didn't feel like havin' more'n about two helpings. I was really off my feed."

"How about the bull?" August said. "He wouldn't eat for two days." He turned to Uncle Jon, "Grandpa said he didn't know which one got banged up the most, but he hoped it wasn't the bull."

"You can't hurt a bull," Fritz said with authority. "Old Bent Nelson was shootin' at a coyote one time that was hangin' around his calves. Them dumb Swedes couldn't hit the barn wall if they was inside it, and he put a slug right through that old red bull a his. Well that bull never even felt it, and it didn't slow him up one bit when it came to bein' ornery or wantin' to jump the cows."

"Speakin' of bein' ornery," August said, "we was up at Sioux Falls yesterday with a load a hogs, and Fritz just about tangled with old Henry Gustavson, the commission man. That ol' dummy claimed there was gonna be hard times ahead and he wasn't gonna give us top price."

"You got it all wrong as usual, August," Fritz said with irritation. "I wasn't gonna tangle with him. I was just tryin' to point out to him that them 'experts' that think they can figure out what's gonna happen in farmin' ain't got no more idea about it than a billy goat. There wasn't no tanglin' involved. I was just explainin' things to him."

The brothers had rolled and lit cigarettes, and the air in the little room was thick with smoke. Josif turned toward the door, "Maybe Alexander should sleep. We talk more in kitchen."

Izabella looked gratefully at him through the smoke. She rose and began to collect the plates. "We will make coffee. It is time for Michael-Joseph and girls to go to bed, women will do mending."

As Fritz picked up his chair, he said to Alexander, "Well take it easy. Don't do nothin' I wouldn't do."

"Yeah," added August. "Don't let the bed bugs bite." He doubled up his fist and showed it to Alexander. "I'm gonna ram this right down Julius's throat next time I see 'im."

Alexander looked up at them. "I'm glad you came. Tell your grandma the cake was real good."

When the Wagners had finally gone home after spending an hour in the kitchen, Josif and Uncle Jon went with Izabella and Aunt Magda to Alexander's room, tiptoeing so as not to wake him. They felt of his forehead again and it seemed warmer than before, but not hot. Izabella knelt on the floor by the bed, looking at Alexander's face as he slept. When she stood up her eyes were dark with concern.

"The doctor will come tomorrow. He would not like it if we went to the Bowmans and called him now. But Alexander does not look right. What should we do?"

It was 11:00. They looked helplessly at one another, wanting to call the doctor, afraid that they would be a bother and a nuisance to the Bowmans and Dr. Sinclair. Finally they agreed that the two women would take turns sitting up with Alexander through the night. In the morning, if Alexander was not better, Josif would go to the Bowmans and ask them to call the doctor.

* * *

That same day Clarence Lamb was busy. He drove into Centerford early in the morning in his 1929 Model A Ford sedan, looking like an elderly country minister who was going into town to spend the day doing good works. There were differences, however, between Clarence and a minister.

The Model A had been modified with a special engine and transmission so that it was as fast or faster than any car on the road: its windows were made of bulletproof glass and its body was armored. Clarence wore his usual black suit, white shirt, and black bow-tie, and on his carefully parted, white hair he wore a flat-brimmed *ice cream* straw hat. But in the shoulder holster under his coat was the flat black pistol.

He went first to the office of Frank Ariosto in the courthouse. A small, sharp-faced deputy wearing a khaki uniform, badge, and a revolver sat with his feet on a desk in an outer room, drinking a cup of coffee. Clarence spoke politely to him, asking for the sheriff.

"He ain't in. There was a smashup up north on 77. He's up there tryin' to sort out the arms an' legs. Somethin' I can do for you?" The deputy took his feet off the desk in deference to Clarence's pastoral appearance.

Clarence smiled benignly at the deputy. "You must be Earl Snipes. My, but it's been a long time since I've seen you. You probably don't even remember me. I'm Clarence Lamb, Vincent's uncle."

"Clarence Lamb! Well I'll be." Earl got out of his chair and shook hands with Clarence. "You been back east there somewhere, ain't ya?"

Clarence nodded, smiling. "Chicago. I was in the meat-packing business. I have finally retired and come back here to the family farm. I'll just putter around, probably get in Vernon's way."

"Where the hell's Vince now? I ain't seen him for a hell of a long time."

"Vincent has come back, too. He's become very knowledgeable in the cattle business. He and Vernon are going to work together, expand the operation there at the farm. Apparently there's good money in feeding steers now."

"Well I'll be! So old Vince is back. Tell him to come in and look me up." Earl hitched his gun up. "We sure had some good times, ol' Vince and me."

"I'll do that. I'll be happy to do that." Clarence turned toward the door. "I think I'll go over and have a chat with young Alan Johnson at the bank. I haven't seen him for a number of years, either."

"I hope he's got time to see ya. He's head man at the bank now. Got himself a fancy wife and a big car. Doesn't have much to do with us peons, what with belongin' to the country club and such, plus grabbin' up any land that ain't tied down."

Clarence raised his eyebrows. "I am surprised. Young Alan? I always thought he was well liked."

"Oh, sure, by the rich bastards here in town. They all stick together, them lawyers and bankers. He thinks we don't know what's goin' on."

"You mean Alan is not honest?"

"Oh, hell. Is any of them bankers honest? On top a that, he's runnin' 'round with that blonde he hired. I asked her to go out dancin' once and she turned me down. It ain't hard to tell where she's gettin' it."

Clarence looked distressed. "Dear me. Surely Alan's wife can't approve of that?"

Earl smirked. "Who the hell knows? She's runnin' 'round with one a them lawyers. We hear some real choice stories about what goes on with that country club gang."

"I am sorry to hear that. I still think I'll go over and have a chat with young Alan." Clarence smiled at Earl. "It's been good talking with you, Earl, after all these years. Please tell Frank that I stopped in. I'll try to get back to see him around noon if I can."

Earl shook his hand again. "It sure was nice seein' you again. Tell Vince to stop in. He knows where to find me."

Clarence went out and walked down the street toward the bank. The town had changed since he had last been there. The main street was now paved; high, concrete side-walks with curbing fronted the stores; and several new build-ings rose along main street, brick structures with arty designs in molded concrete along their corners and roof lines.

He went up the steps into the bank, noting the look and feeling of prosperity about it. Several customers stood at the cashiers' windows where two severe-faced, older women waited on them. He walked hesitantly with a bewildered look on his face toward the offices beyond the cashiers.

A golden-haired girl working at a desk in the first office looked up at him. She smiled and said, "May I help you?" and Clarence understood why Alan Johnson would be at-tracted to her and why she had not gone dancing with Earl Snipes.

He took off his hat and gave her his kindly but help-less grandfather smile. "I was looking for young Alan. I was a good friend of his father. Just wanted to stop in and say *hello*." He fumbled with his glasses. "I seem to have gotten lost."

She stood up, easily and gracefully, and came out to him. "Mr. Johnson has a visitor right now, but I'm sure he'll want to see you. Why don't you come into my office while you wait? I have an extra chair there that's more comfort-able than those hard benches."

Clarence looked around at the benches, then smiled gratefully at her. "That's awfully nice of you." He turned his hat in his hands. "But I'm afraid I'd be a nuisance, interfere with your work."

"Not at all." She smiled at him. "Come in and sit down. My name is Ellen Olson. If you'll tell me your name, I'll let Mr. Johnson know that you're here."

He let her lead him to the chair. "My name is Clarence, Clarence Lamb." He saw the tiny change in her eyes. "Not the bad Lambs. I come from the other side of the family." He looked at the floor, then up at her. "It's something I've had to bear all my life."

He knew he was close to overdoing it. He could feel her intelligence, sense it in the way she moved and talked. He got up. "I'd better go...."

"No, please wait. Mr. Johnson would be sorry to have you go." She smiled at him again. "So would I."

He fumbled with his hat, then sat down. "Thank you. You're very kind."

"I'll tell Mr. Johnson you're here. Please excuse me." As she went out of the office, Clarence watched her retreating figure with appreciation. He remembered lookers he had known in Chicago, and this girl looked as good as any of them, if not better. He wondered why she was in Centerford.

Ellen came back in a few minutes. "Mr. Johnson will see you just as soon as his other visitor leaves. Can I get you anything while you wait? A magazine?" She smiled. "A history of the bank?"

He shook his head. "Thank you, no. I'll just wait. Please, don't stop your work on my account."

"It's all right. I'd just finished."

He smiled gratefully again. "You make an old man feel welcome. I appreciate it."

A farmer in clean overalls went by the door, and Ellen smiled at Clarence. "Mr. Johnson is free now," she said. "Please come with me." She led Clarence to a mahogany door and tapped on it lightly, then opened the door and ushered him into the room. Clarence looked at Alan Johnson's face as she entered, and he smiled to himself. He now understood why Ellen was in Centerford, and knew that if the banker turned stubborn there was a way to change his mind.

Ellen spoke to Alan while smiling at Clarence. "Mr. Lamb didn't want to bother you. I had a hard time convincing him that he should stay."

"Of course he should've stayed!" Alan got up from his chair and extended his hand to Clarence. "Welcome back, Clarence. It must be ten years since I've seen you." He smiled at Clarence and Ellen. "I'm glad you two had a chance to talk. Clarence was one of Dad's best friends."

"I'm afraid that was quite awhile ago." Clarence made a little bow to Ellen. "Miss Olson was very kind to me. She almost made me forget my age."

She smiled at him and went out, closing the door quietly, leaving the scent of fresh flowers in the room.

Alan pushed a chair forward. "Sit down, Clarence. Tell me what you've been up to in Chicago, and how it happens that you're back in Centerford."

Clarence let himself down into the chair. He fumbled with his hat, and Alan apologized and hung it on a hook for him.

"Thank you, Alan. You always were a polite young fellow." Clarence adjusted his glasses. "After thirty years in the meat-packing business, Alan, I've decided to give this old mind and body a rest. I've come back to Centerford, back to my real home, back to real people. I have retired."

"Good for you, Clarence. Centerford will be better off for it, having a man of your integrity back in the community. I hope you'll find a good house here in town, or do you plan to stay on the farm?"

Clarence wiped his glasses with his clean, white, pocket handkerchief, polishing them, looking up at the light through them. "I'm trying to decide that, Alan. I had hoped to stay with Vernon and Belle on the farm, but with poor Belle being as sick as she is, it hardly seems right for me to bother them."

He put the glasses back on. "What I'm wondering now is if it would be possible to buy a place somewhere near them that I could fix up a bit, maybe get a housekeeper, and pretend that I'm a farmer again. I'd have to get someone to do the actual farming, of course, but at least it would make an old man feel as if he were back on the soil."

Alan nodded. "I think I know how you feel. 'You can take the boy away from the farm....'"

"That's it, Alan. That's the feeling exactly." Clarence reached in his outside coat pocket. "I have a little cash here that I didn't get a chance to deposit in my Chicago bank. I was wondering if I could open an account here, now that I'm back home, make me feel a little more settled."

"You know we're always happy to deposit your money, Clarence. I can handle it right here if you'd like."

"Oh, no, I wouldn't think of bothering you with it, Alan."

"No problem, Clarence." Alan pulled a form from his desk drawer. "We'll just fill this out, and I'll have one of the cashiers deposit it for you."

Clarence filled out the form and handed a roll of bills to Alan. "It isn't very much, just $15,000 to get started, but there'll be more." As Alan gave him a receipt, Clarence looked bewildered. "Now what were we talking about?"

"A place for you to live. A farm."

"Oh, yes, a farm." Clarence looked up toward his hat. "I've taken enough of your time, Alan. I'd better be on my way." He started to rise, then said, "You know, it just occurred to me. The old Ariosto place, Belle's folks' place. It would be just about what I'm looking for. I don't suppose it's for sale, though."

Alan tapped on the desktop with a pencil. "Clarence, the bank owns that place now. I offered it to Verne, but he's apparently very upset about Belle's folks losing it. Believe me, we had no part in that. The farm was put up for sale for back taxes, and the bank simply was there with the money."

"I understand, although, as you say, I'm afraid Vernon isn't very happy about it," Clarence looked down at his shoes. "I don't have the bad feeling about it that Vernon has. Matter of fact, I would be interested in buying it. I don't think the price would be too much of an issue."

Alan stopped tapping the pencil. "Do you really mean that, Clarence? You'd like to buy it?"

"I certainly do. Cash on the barrelhead or terms, which-ever the bank prefers."

Alan looked toward the door. "Clarence, I'd like to sell you that place. The trouble is, we gave the family that's on it now first refusal just a few days ago. If they don't buy it, we still have an oral agreement to let them rent it for a year. They're an immigrant family with five children and very little money. I can't just throw them off the place."

"Of course not, Alan. I am surprised, though, that the bank doesn't have a binding and legal rent agreement with them. As you know, an oral agreement really wouldn't stand up in a court of law." Clarence frowned, thinking. "Suppose I bought it now, let them rent it for the rest of the year?" he asked. "That would be fair enough, wouldn't it?"

Alan began tapping with the pencil again. "There is no written agreement, it's true...."

"The more I think about it, the more the idea appeals to me. I'm afraid I've gotten sentimental in my old age, and I really would like to have the old farm." Clarence fumbled with his glasses again. "What do you think a fair price for that property might be? Say about $10,000?"

Alan stopped tapping the pencil. "That sounds like a more than fair price, Clarence. I really couldn't let you pay that much."

"Tut tut, my boy. It happens that I've done quite well in the meat-packing business. I'm sure you and I could come to some mutually acceptable figure."

"Clarence, I'm sure we can. Why don't you just let me talk to the Dacias once more. I'm almost certain that I can convince them not to buy the place. If they decide to rent, they certainly could have no objection to having you as landlord."

Clarence beamed at him. "Excellent! I'll wait to hear from you then." He shook hands with Alan and took his hat from the hook. "It's been nice talking with you, Alan. Good to see you sitting in Norman's chair."

On his way out, Clarence stopped for a moment to speak with Ellen Olson in her office. "I just wanted to thank you again for making me feel at home." He smiled at her. "Pardon an old man's curiosity, but I have a feeling that you're not a local girl. Too pretty."

She blushed. "I was born in Minneapolis."

"I knew it! Those Minnesota Swedish girls are the prettiest in the world!" He dropped his hat and and bent slowly to pick it up. "I hope you've found a good place to stay here in Centerford. With a good Swedish family, that is."

"I was lucky enough to find a room at Mrs. Swanson's. It's a beautiful old house, and Amanda treats me as if I were her own daughter."

Clarence gave an approving smile. "Perfect! That's one of the nicest houses in this area, and Mrs. Swanson is a gem. A real gem." He looked at the floor. "Amanda probably doesn't even remember me, I've been away for so long, but you know, at one time when I was quite a lot younger than I am now, I had hopes that she might look favorably on me."

Ellen was delighted. "You should come and see her! I can't wait to tell her that you're here. Will you be here very long?"

"Ah, you don't know. Of course not." He shook his head. "The older I get, the more forgetful I am. I never told you. I have returned to Centerford to stay. It was my home once, and now it will be my home again."

"How wonderful!" Ellen almost hugged him. "That's so nice. I'm so happy for you, coming back to your old home."

"It seems good to me. Of course I keep telling myself not to expect too much, not to get my hopes too high. It's not as if I were a boy again. It can never be quite the same." He smiled at her. "But meeting you has made me think that maybe it can be." He touched his glasses and looked away for a moment, then said to her, "Thank you. You have made this day a bright one for an old man." He left then, walking slowly toward the cashier's window, a brave figure of an elderly gentleman who had not yet been beaten by the world.

* * *

Frank Ariosto was in his office when Clarence returned. Every time that Clarence saw Frank, he thought of Tom Mix, the cowboy movie star. Frank had the same strong face, the same look of fearlessness. But while Tom Mix was handsome, Frank was homely, his features too strong for beauty. Moreover, Frank did not dress like a cowboy, nor even like a sheriff; he dressed like a farmer. His explanation was always the same, except that no one who knew him ever asked for it, and those who didn't know him never asked him twice.

"I was born on a farm. My people have been farm people for two hundred years. I'm not ashamed of being a farmer. Just because some people wanted me to be sheriff doesn't mean I have to get dressed up like some city dude or put on some sort of monkey suit like I was a general in some place in South America. You got something against farmers, mister?"

Frank wore his gun up high around his overalls, not slung low the way Earl Snipes did, and in summer he wore a farmer's straw hat, while in winter he wore an old, motheaten fur cap that looked as if it might have been in the family for two or three generations.

Clarence knew that Frank couldn't be bribed or threatened. The only concession Frank would make to his in-law relatives, the Lambs, was that, because they were family, he might overlook things once in awhile. With other people Frank tended to be severe, and aside from Verne's small still, there was remarkably little real crime in the county.

Frank called from his office for Clarence to come in. He sent Earl Snipes out to get sandwiches and coffee at Al's Cafe, telling him to have his own lunch there first, then he shut the door to his office and pointed to a chair.

"How's Chicago getting along without you, Clarence? Must be three or four years since you've been back here."

"Four years. Four years this April. I'm back to stay this time, Frank."

"That's what Earl said."

Clarence knew there was no point in giving Frank anything but straight talk. "We want to expand Vernon's operation a little. Some things happened in Chicago that make it desirable. We want to clear it with you first."

"I thought you might have been in on that deal. Valentine's Day in a garage. Chicago too hot for you right now?"

"You might put it that way. We thought it wise to move out before things got out of hand."

Frank's eyes were cold. "I don't want any of that stuff out here. None of it. What makes you think you're clear?"

"They don't know where we are, for one thing. For another, they're so busy trying to consolidate that they can't worry too much about anything outside their area."

Frank raised an eyebrow. "If you want to expand your operation, you must have brought some big equipment with you. You don't move anything that size without somebody noticing it."

"True. But we headed east to Detroit. We changed route there and circled back through St. Louis. I can't guarantee it, but I don't believe they know or care where we are. I think they're glad to have us out."

"How about insiders? Who'd you bring with you, and how do you know they're clean?"

"Just Vincent, no one else."

"That's another thing – bringing that damned Vince back. He's nothing but trouble. I don't want him in this county."

"I will take personal responsibility for Vincent."

"That's not good enough. You know, don't you, that Julius beat up on the son of the family that's on Belle's place? Doc Sinclair told me the boy's in bad shape."

Clarence shook his head. "Vernon didn't tell me about that. I'm sorry about the boy. But that has little bearing on our discussion. All we want to do is expand Vernon's operation. It should cause no trouble to you or anyone else."

"You make it sound too good, Clarence. First thing I know, we're gonna have you Chicago hoods shooting at each other out here, and on top of that, Vince'll be up to his usual tricks of setting things on fire. I'm going to give you and Vince just three days to get out of the county. Do what you want to outside it, but not in my county."

"I'm sorry you take that attitude, Frank. I thought we were friends."

Frank got up from his chair, "Clarence, I want you out. Three days. That's all you have. I'll be out to see Belle on Sunday. I don't wanna see you or Vince when I come."

"Is that your final answer, Frank?"

"It is." Frank opened the door. "In three days I want you gone."

Clarence smiled at him."Good-bye, Frank."

Chapter Eighteen
Bad News

At first light Josif came into the room where Izabella sat by Alexander's bed, and he saw by the bearing of her body that the boy was worse. He put his hand on Alexander's forehead and felt the hotness and dryness of his skin. Alexander opened his eyes and they were dark with fever; his breathing was rapid and shallow. Josif bent over him, "I will go call the doctor now, Alexander. How do you feel?"

"All right, Papa." Alexander's voice was a husky whisper.

Izabella gently stroked Alexander's hair. "He has slept, but there has been some coughing and chills, no blood. The doctor will make the fever better."

Josif looked at her eyes and saw the fear in them. "I will go now," he said. "I will ride Paul; it will be faster."

He rode bareback, fast through the gray morning, along the country road. He passed the flooded field and the Wagner farm and the school, galloping on faithful Paul, who had pulled the wagon with Peter across Oklahoma, Kansas, Nebraska, and part of South Dakota. Paul, who with Peter had raced the tornado and won, who had plunged through the snow drifts and the blizzard to the Hutterite building.

The Bowmans and Mrs. Horsefall came to the door at his pounding, and they understood his fear. Mrs. Bowman cranked the telephone fiercely and forced it to do her will, so that it brought her voice to Dr. Sinclair in Centerford. She spoke clearly to him, telling him that Alexander needed him. When she was done, the Bowmans gave him coffee and offered him eggs and bacon, but he could not eat.

Mr. Bowman said, "We'll come down with the car right away. In case we can help."

He thanked them and rode Paul back behind the car, slower now, knowing that the doctor had eight miles to come from Centerford. He let Paul drink at the tank, then put him back in the barn and fed him.

He found that Marie had already milked the cow and fed Peter, and as he came out of the barn, Dr. Sinclair drove into the yard in his old Oakland. Josif hurried to meet him and they went into the house together, going straight back to the little bedroom.

Izabella and Aunt Magda were in the room with Alexander, while everyone else was crowded into the girls' room.

The doctor put a thermometer in Alexander's mouth and then listened to his chest with his stethoscope. When he took the thermometer out, he shook it down after he had looked at it. He turned to Josif and there was a hint of defeat in his gaze, "We had better get him to a hospital. I think he has pneumonia."

At Dr. Sinclair's words, a silence fell in the old house, an impenetrable silence that seemed to smother all hope.

Dr. Sinclair looked at Izabella, then gently put his hand on her arm. "Here now, little lady, there are things we can do for pneumonia. These aren't the Dark Ages. We'll get him into an oxygen tent at the hospital. He'll have the best treatment possible."

They breathed again. Josif asked, "Oxygen tent cure Alexander? What is, please?"

"Oxygen is a gas. It's in the air we breathe along with another gas, nitrogen. If we give Alexander pure oxygen under a little tent, his lungs can fight the pneumonia better."

The Dacias listened in wonder to the doctor. Josif felt a ray of hope returning to him; perhaps this science would prove stronger than the omens. "You tell us what we do, we get Alexander to hospital."

"Don't you folks worry about that. I'll use the Bowmans' telephone and have an ambulance sent out for him. We can send him either to Sioux Falls or Sioux City. I think Sioux Falls would be better. It's closer, and they have just as good facilities." Dr. Sinclair patted Izabella's arm. "You can go with Alexander if you like in the ambulance. You two can go together up to the big city," he said smiling and trying to take some of the fear out of the situation.

Izabella put her hand on Alexander's and smiled at him through the tears in her eyes. "We will go together. You and I will go together to Sioux Falls."

Doctor Sinclair made three telephone calls from the Bowman's house—one to the fire department in Centerford, asking for the ambulance, one to the hospital in Sioux Falls, and one to Frank Ariosto, the sheriff.

Frank arrived at the Dacias' before the ambulance, just as Dr. Sinclair returned from the Bowmans'. He talked quietly with the doctor, then came into the house to meet the Dacias.

Josif recognized him as the man who had brought him the razor and let him out of the jail. It was hard to believe that the sheriff was dressed as an ordinary farmer, that he was an ordinary farmer, that he was a kind man. Frank said nothing about Josif being in jail, and he shook hands with all the family members and with the Bowmans. After he had seen Alexander, he asked Josif if he would come out to the car with him. They walked beyond the car, toward the barn.

Frank spoke. "I understand that Verne Lamb met you folks when you came out here from town a week ago. Can you tell me what was said between you at that time?"

"Was our fault first. We been in wagon all day, stopped in trees. Verne Lamb came in buggy."

"Where was this?"

Josif pointed. "South along road, about mile, west side."

"I know the place. What did he say to you? Did he threaten you?"

"Was not good for women or kids to hear. I not speak language here good yet, but was not good to hear."

The sheriff nodded. "Verne could do that." He looked directly into Josif's eyes. "I know how you must feel now with your boy being taken off to the hospital, but I want you to understand one thing: I don't want you to go looking for Verne Lamb with a knife or a gun or even a club. Promise me that."

"I understand what you say. I want be good American. But if Alexander die, I don't promise you nothing."

"We don't do things that way here. I want you to keep away from Verne. He's in bad shape right now because of his wife bein' sick, and he's liable to get that shotgun of his out if you go lookin' for him; then we'll have real trouble. There are some other people there now too that I want you to keep away from, and they're a lot worse than Verne. Do you understand what I'm saying? Keep away from that farm. I don't want you or any more of that nice family of yours to get hurt. Let me handle Verne Lamb."

Josif listened silently to the sheriff, then said quietly, "I thank you what you say about family. But I have honor. In my country a man have honor, even if nothing else."

"Honor can get you killed."

"Honor more important."

"You were in the war?"

"Yes."

"You know what a gun will do."

"My father, my brothers killed. Fight beside me."

"These people have guns. Shotguns, pistols, machine guns."

"It not matter."

"If you set foot on that farm I'll arrest you for trespassing."

"I still not promise you anything."

The sheriff said quietly, "I tried to reason with you. Now it's gone beyond reason. I don't know what kind of papers you or your family have, but if I have to do it to keep you from getting killed, I'll have the immigration people send you back where you came from."

"Maybe we should go back to our country," Josif said. "In this country they tell us have opportunity. Have justice. I see opportunity only for rich people. Justice not for immigrants. Here not even have honor."

* * *

As Josif finished speaking, the ambulance from Centerford came in the driveway and pulled up in front of the porch. Two men got out and pulled a stretcher from the rear door, and as they saw Frank Ariosto and Josif approaching, they waited to speak to them, raising their hands in greeting to Frank Ariosto.

One of them said, "You broke up our card game, Frank. Where's the kid?"

"He's in the house. This is his father."

"You two seemed to be havin' a pretty serious discussion."

"You wouldn't know anything about it," the sheriff said, "we've been talking about honor."

Josif rode with Dr. Sinclair behind the ambulance that carried Alexander and Izabella. There had been hurried farewells with those left at home, and he could still see in his mind the sad faces of the girls and Michael-Joseph as they stood with Uncle Jon and Aunt Magda in the driveway, watching the ambulance leave. It seemed as though the family had been torn apart by the thing that was in Alexander's chest.

They spoke little on the way north to Sioux Falls. Josif watched the rear door of the ambulance, and it seemed he could see inside, see Izabella and Alexander in the cramped rear compartment where so many people, dead and dying, had been carried.

The surge of hope Josif had felt at Dr. Sinclair's description of the oxygen tent had faded, and he now felt a sense of foreboding and hopelessness. He had seen pneumonia in the war, in the winter campaigns, soldiers lying hollow-eyed in the mud and filth, coughing up rusty phlegm, breathing the rasp of death. Alexander's breathing was like the soldiers'.

And there had been the omens of impending death. God had sent signs that Alexander would die, that this was to be his fate. Josif felt that Dr. Sinclair's words of encouragement were only meant to delay the acceptance of that fact. He desperately didn't want to accept that truth, but knew he must prepare himself for the loss of Alexander, his eldest son. His heart sank.

They came to Sioux Falls, and Dr. Sinclair pointed ahead. "The hospital isn't far now. You can see it on the left, the high, brick building." He glanced quickly at Josif. "If you and your wife want to stay up here with Alexander, there's a hotel right over there, not far from the hospital."

"We have no money for hotel. Could we stay with Alexander in hospital?"

"I'm afraid not. There just isn't room for families to do that. Sometimes they will let a mother stay with a child if..." Dr. Sinclair hesitated, "if it seems necessary."

They followed the ambulance up the drive to the hospital and into an area marked, "Emergency Entrance Only." Josif waited by the door of the ambulance and helped Izabella come out; then they watched as the attendants lifted Alexander out on the stretcher. He seemed small and helpless as they carried him into the hospital. Then it was a confusion of white-coated men and women; of a tall, distinguished looking man whom everyone obeyed; of doorways and elevators, wheeled carts and hurrying people; of the smell of ether, alcohol, and death.

Josif sensed Death in the hospital. He felt it. Death was there as He was on the battlefield; He had not changed. They had brought Alexander into Death's kingdom.

They came to an empty room and a bed, a high bed with crisp sheets, and they placed Alexander in it. Gas hissed under a hood that covered Alexander, and the white-coated people smiled at Josif, smiled at Izabella, their confident, intelligent faces saying, "Now we have cheated Death. We have done all that we have been taught, all that we know. We have held Death back with our magic, with our knowledge, with our science. He cannot prevail against us." And Josif knew they were wrong.

Dr. Sinclair talked quietly to them in the hallway. "Pneumonia usually runs its course in about a week or two. There will be a crisis when the patient seems worse. Alexander is strong and healthy, but the broken ribs make it more difficult for him to breathe and fight the infection; that is why we've placed him in the oxygen tent." He touched Izabella's arm. "I think you both should go home now and get some rest.

Izabella said sadly, "Alexander will be alone."

"I'll try to come up as often as I can, maybe every two or three days. You both can ride with me then. I'm sure the Bowmans will come up."

Josif saw the darkness in Izabella's eyes, the sadness. He said, "If they let her stay, we both thank you. If is not possible, we go home."

303

"I'll talk with them about it. I'll ask Dr. Benson."

Dr. Sinclair left them and went to the tall man who was still in Alexander's room with the people in white coats. They talked, and the tall man glanced at the Dacias, then came toward them with Dr. Sinclair. He wore a beautiful dark suit with a white shirt and a dark blue necktie, and his face had the same look of authority as a king or a general.

Dr. Sinclair introduced him, "This is Dr. Benson. Alexander will be under his care. Dr. Benson feels that there is no need for either of you to stay at this time."

Dr. Benson smiled down at them. "Your son will have the best care possible. I recommend that you go home now and not worry. When you come again in a few days I think you'll find him much improved." He shook hands with Josif, a gesture of dismissal that was as absolute as a command. "Goodbye, Mr. Dacia. Take this little wife of yours home now, and don't worry."

* * *

News spreads rapidly in a small town, and Alan Johnson and Ellen Olson learned of the call for the ambulance and Alexander's illness when the bank opened that same Wednesday morning. Elmer Eggert, the barber, stopped in to make a deposit and told Hazel, the cashier.

"The sheriff went sailin' out there too, fast. Somethin' more's up than just a case of pneumonia. Same family that pulled in here a week and a half ago with the whole barnyard in tow–the ones with the trick horse that splattered the marshal's new boots. Fella ended up spendin' the night in jail."

Hazel spoke behind her hand, looking first toward the offices. "He came in here the next day when they let him out. Believe you me, I was shivering in my boots, wondering whether he was gonna rob the bank or not. He's one of those foreigners, I could tell. Those black eyes of his just gave me the willies."

When Elmer had finished his transaction, Hazel hurried to Alan Johnson's office and told him of the morning's happenings, leaving the door open so that Ellen could hear. Ellen came to the doorway and stood there pale-faced as Hazel went back to her window.

Alan looked up at Ellen. "As soon as Dr. Sinclair gets back ,I'll go talk with him, find out how serious this is. Strange how the boy could get pneumonia this time of year."

Ellen was almost in tears. She brushed at her eyes and bit her lip before she could answer. "Those poor people. They were so happy, and now to have this happen..."

"It may not be as bad as it sounds. Dr. Sinclair lost a couple of patients to flu and pneumonia last winter; maybe he's just taking no chances now." Alan smiled at her. Let's wait and see what he says before we fear for the worst."

"I hope you're right. But it must be terrifying for them to have a serious illness when they're so new here. And they have no car. How hard it will be for them to visit Alexander in Sioux Falls...."

"That will be a problem," Alan said. "Especially if the illness is a long one. But they do have the Aunt and Uncle there at home to take care of the smaller children and do the chores. Perhaps the parents will stay in Sioux Falls until the worst is over."

Ellen brightened at this. "Of course! That would be the best thing for them to do." Then she bit her lip again. "But with the doctor bills and the ambulance and the hospital, how can they ever afford to stay up there?"

Alan reassured her. "If they can't stay in Sioux Falls, I'll make sure they get a ride up there. And Dr. Sinclair has never let payments bother him. The other bills could be handled with a small loan. The bank will do everything it can to help them."

He saw the change in her eyes, in her face. She said softly, "Alan, I'm so happy that you said that."

He smiled at her. "Why don't we go out there as soon as

we finish up here today? We can see how they are and find out what the parents have decided to do. Meanwhile, I'll leave a call with Dr. Sinclair's office, then we'll know just how serious this is."

At the same time that Alan and Ellen were talking in the bank, Frank Ariosto drove into the barnyard at Verne Lamb's farm.

Verne and Julius came from the direction of the feedlot, and Frank drove his car past the cow barn to meet them, noticing that Clarence's Model A was parked near Verne's new truck, and that Verne carried a pitchfork. He stopped the car when it was out of sight of the house, and got out to meet Verne and Julius.

Verne scowled at him. "You ain't too damned welcome here, Frank. Clarence said you told him to clear out."

"That's right, but I didn't come about that. The Dacia boy just left for the hospital in Sioux Falls in the ambulance. He's got pneumonia."

"So, why come bother us about it?"

"You know why, Verne. Julius here kicked the boy when he was down. He broke the boy's ribs; that's why he has pneumonia. Doc Sinclair says it's serious; the boy may die."

Julius' eyes were innocent. "It was a fair fight, Uncle Frank. That kid went after me first with his dinner bucket. Junior Jensen saw it; he can tell you."

Frank stared at Julius. "Don't call me Uncle Frank, you little liar, or I'm liable to step on you. Sixteen kids and the teacher saw you kicking the boy when he was down and helpless. Junior Jensen's word isn't worth a pile of pig shit, and neither are you."

Verne stepped toward Frank. "Hold on there, Frank. You can't talk to Julius like that on my farm. Now get the hell off my property before I throw you off."

"Verne, I came here today to tell you about the Dacia boy. If he dies, I'm gonna bring charges against both you and this kid of yours. I'm tellin' you that now. I'm also tellin' you the same thing I told Clarence, plus a little more. I want Clarence and Vince and their still outta this county before Sunday.

"The thing I'm tellin' you extra is that your days of bootlegging are over. If you make or move as much as one bottle of whiskey I'll run you in so quick your teeth'll rattle." Frank turned away from the Lambs and walked toward his car.

"Goddamn you, I'll kill you!" Verne ran at Frank with the pitchfork. Frank turned and brushed the pitchfork up with one arm, and in the same motion his other arm and fist came forward in a short jab that caught Verne on the side of the jaw. There was a sound like an axe hitting a block of wood and Verne dropped as if he had run into a wall. He came to his hands and knees, shaking his head, his eyes glaring and wild. He reached for the pitchfork and came up fast. Frank hit him again, this time on the point of the chin, carefully and neatly as if he were driving a nail in with his fist, and Verne went down, his body suddenly limp. He fell loosely onto the barnyard dirt and lay still.

Frank kicked the pitchfork away. He turned to Julius, "If it weren't for Belle, I'd take him in for assault. When he wakes up, you'd better get him in the house for a while. Tell him I mean what I said."

Julius glared wildly at Frank. "I'll kill you someday!"

"You're goin' down the same road he is if you don't learn to handle your temper. I was goin' in to see Belle, but when Verne comes to, he might start something in the house. I'm coming out Sunday to see her. Tell her that." Frank turned his back on Julius and went to the car.

Julius spit after him. He shouted as Frank drove out of the barnyard, "Wait'll Pa gets his shotgun out. He's gonna blow your brains out!"

Clarence and Vince had watched the fight between Verne and Frank from the narrow slit of the slightly open door of the hay barn. When Frank had gone, they came to where Verne was trying groggily to sit up. Clarence looked down at him, "Attacking Frank with a pitchfork wasn't the best way to handle him, Vernon. I hope you realize that now."

Chapter Nineteen
A *Strigoi* in Lamb's Clothing

Dr. Sinclair brought Josif and Izabella home in the middle of the afternoon. There was a sense of despair and loss in the family that was only partially dispelled by the homecoming, and when the doctor had gone they all sat around the kitchen table together as though to draw strength from one another. Izabella held Michael-Joseph in her lap, while Caroline, Rose, and Marie stood next to Izabella and Aunt Magda to be hugged.

The parents told of the ride to Sioux Falls and of the hospital, and also of the words of hope given by the doctors, but over all of them, there hung a feeling of separation and dread.

While they sat there, a car pulled into the driveway and stopped in front of the house. A kindly-looking, white-haired elderly man wearing a neat black suit got out of the car and came slowly up to the porch. He carried his hat in his hand, and he seemed so bewildered and helpless that the family wondered if he might have lost his way. He tapped hesitantly at the kitchen door.

Josif went to the door and opened it.

The man smiled apologetically at him. "I am a neighbor. I heard of the illness of your son, and I just came to see if I could help in any way." He fumbled with his hat. "That is, if there's anything I can do to help make up for the terrible thing done to your son."

The man seemed so gentle and kind that it was as if

309

a favorite grandfather had come to the door. Josif said to him, "We thank you that you come about Alexander. You are good neighbor to care about him. We thank you."

The man looked down at the floor. "I'm afraid you will not think I'm a good neighbor. You would be right in driving me from your door. I have a shameful thing to tell you, and when I have told you, I will go." He looked up at Josif.

"My shame is that I am a distant relative of the family that has wronged you." He twisted his hat in his hands. "My name is Clarence Lamb. Now you know. I will go now. I just wanted to tell you how sorry I am." He turned slowly away toward the porch door.

Josif looked back at the family. He spoke in Romanian to them. "Did you understand him? He is related to Verne and Julius Lamb, and is sorry about Alexander."

Izabella said, "The poor man is so sad and ashamed. We cannot let him leave like this."

Aunt Magda agreed. "Ask him to come in, Josif."

Josif spoke kindly to Clarence, "Please. Come into our house. My family like to know good neighbor who cares about our son." He opened the door wide. "Please, come in."

The man said hesitantly, "You are kind to an old man... but I should not come in... how can your son's mother look at me without anger? I will go."

Izabella came to the door. "You are welcome in our house. Please come in."

He came in. He walked slowly over the threshold, under the bunch of garlic, past the cross of tar on the door, an old man who walked uncertainly as though he were bewildered and lost. He smiled sadly and apologetically at them and said, "You are kind to invite me into your house."

They seated Clarence at the table and brought him coffee and cake, and they introduced him to Uncle Jon and Aunt Magda, and to the girls and Michael-Joseph. He spoke to the children as a grandfather might – a grandfather who had come from a far country and did not yet know them as he would. He was so polite and shy with Aunt Magda that she smiled at him and offered him more coffee and cake in an effort to make him feel that he was truly welcome. To Izabella he was like a kind and understanding priest who knows the anguish and suffering of a mother whose first son is near death.

He looked around at the family. "I want to help you in any way that I can. Tell me what I can do that will help take the shame and guilt from me, that will let me sleep at night." He looked out at his car. "Would you let me take you to see your son in Sioux Falls? It's not much, but I would like to do it." He smiled at them. "I'm a good driver; don't let my age worry you. It would be something I could do to help you. We could go up together every day until he's well again. I would like to do that. I would not feel so guilty if you would let me do that."

"Is not right you do so much for us."

"It's not so much. I have to go to Sioux Falls at least once on business. The other times will not be too many; soon, I hope, your son will be home. It will be a favor to me if you let me take you to Sioux Falls to visit your son."

Izabella's eyes held tears as she spoke. "Alexander would not be alone then...."

Josif saw that some of the darkness had left her eyes. "Doctor say he take us when he goes. Maybe Mr. and Mrs. Bowman take us once. But other times, my wife be sad if she not see Alexander. We thank you. You good friend."

Clarence beamed at them. "Splendid! How about to-morrow? I could stop here and pick you up right after break-fast, say around 8:00. That would fit in with my business plans, and we could come back home in the late afternoon. That would give you almost all day with Alexander."

As he spoke, a car came up the driveway, and the Dacias recognized Alan Johnson's Chrysler. Ellen was with Alan, and they came up to the house together, carrying packages.

The whole family went to the door to meet them, and

there were hugging and tears and questions about Alexander. When Ellen and Alan came in and saw Clarence there, standing quietly with his hat in his hands, there were exclamations of surprise and pleasure. Clarence said that he should go, but everyone insisted that he stay to see the children open their packages.

The girls were ecstatic with their dolls. They stared unbelievingly at them at first, but when Ellen showed them how the dolls could move, close and open their eyes, and cry "Mama," they hugged them, and began to move their arms and legs, and sit them on their laps.

Michael-Joseph was the same with the stick horse, and he stared at his horse's painted face, running his fingers through its mane with a look of wonder and joy.

Ellen was almost crying when she gave the box with the model airplane to Josif. "Please, give this to Alexander." She bit her lip and looked down at the table. "Tell him... tell him we send our love...." She could not go on.

Josif felt tears in his own eyes, and he could not look at Izabella. He held the box tight in his hands. There was a picture of an airplane on the box, and also a picture of a young man in a flying helmet, a young man who looked very much like Alexander. The words on the box were The Spirit of St. Louis. Then he realized the picture was of Charles Lindbergh, the American flyer who had crossed the ocean alone in that airplane.

"We give to Alexander. He will like. He will like better than anything else anybody can...could... give him." Josif looked up at Ellen and Alan. "We thank you. You are good people."

There was a long silence when no one could speak. Finally Aunt Magda wiped her eyes with her apron. "I will bring more cups. You please excuse me, I forget to give you, our guests, coffee."

Alan turned to Josif and Izabella, "I talked with Dr. Sinclair this afternoon. He feels that Alexander is getting the very best care. He asked me to tell you that he will be going up to Sioux Falls again on Sunday. Of course he wants to take you with him, Mr. and Mrs. Dacia."

"He good man, good doctor," Josif replied. "You please tell him we thank him." He looked at Clarence. "Our good neighbor will take us to see Alexander tomorrow. We are lucky have such good friends."

"That is so nice of you, Mr. Lamb." Ellen smiled at Clarence. "I could just give you a big hug."

Clarence looked modestly down at the table. "Now don't embarrass an old man." He looked up at the Dacias. "I really have my own reasons for taking them. It's selfish on my part."

"Clarence, you're too modest. I've known you too long to believe that," Alan said. He turned to speak to the Dacias. "Clarence was one of my father's best friends, back in the 'gay nineties.' They sang in a barbershop quartet together. I have an old picture of them at home that I treasure." He asked Clarence, "Do you still sing? That tenor voice of yours and your red hair and blue eyes really had the girls going around in circles, if I can believe the stories my father told."

Clarence smiled sadly. "I am afraid the years have taken their toll. I do still enjoy singing, though. Now that I'm back home I thought I might see if one of the church choirs could find some use for me. I have always found great comfort in the good old hymns."

Ellen's eyes shone. "Our choir in the Centerford Lutheran Church would love to have you. We always need good tenors."

Clarence smiled at her. "Thank you, Miss Olson. Perhaps I'll drop in and talk to your director after services one of these Sundays. Of course, if I retire to a little piece of land in this neighborhood, then the Orkadallen Lutheran Church might have to put up with me."

Alan explained to the Dacias, "Clarence is looking for a small farm, something near the old family homestead."

Clarence waved his hand deprecatingly. "Tut tut, Alan, there is little hope of that. Just an old man's dream." He stood up. "I really have stayed too long, but it has been such a pleasure talking with all of you." He held out his hand to Josif. "You have a wonderful family, Mr. Dacia. You can be proud of them." He shook hands with all of them, patting the children's heads, smiling at them. "Don't forget, now, I'll be around bright and early tomorrow morning, about 8:00. The same holds for Friday and Saturday morning too."

"That's good of you, Clarence," Alan said, "but we can't let you have the Dacias all to yourself. I saw Mr. Bowman in town and he asked me to tell the Dacias that he would take them up on Friday. On Saturday, Miss Olson insists that she will take them in her car. I would take them, but unfortunately I have to go down to Omaha tonight and I'm not sure when I'll be back. Your kind offer to take them tomorrow works out just right, but you must remember, there are others who want to go up to see Alexander."

Clarence turned his hat in embarrassment. "I'm sorry. Of course there are many of Alexander's friends who will wish to visit him." He apologized to the Dacias. "Please forgive an old man who thinks only of himself. Will you still ride with me tomorrow? I feel so ashamed."

"We ride with you." Josif said. "You are good man. Not feel sorry."

Alan agreed. "I'm the one who should apologize, Clarence. I didn't mean any criticism of you for wanting to help out."

Clarence smiled gratefully at them. "You're too good to me. All of you." He moved toward the door. "My little Ford can hold about four of us, maybe five. You folks just pile in as many as you can in the morning and we'll be on our way." He waved to all of them. "Good-bye. Good-bye."

"Clarence, I'd like to come out and talk to you just a minute before you go," Alan said. He went out to the car with Clarence and spoke quietly to him through the front window as Clarence sat behind the steering wheel.

"Clarence, I can't sell this farm out from under the Dacias. I've been thinking about it, and it wouldn't be right. I offered them the farm, and I can't go back on my word."

Clarence raised an eyebrow. "Alan, I thought we had an agreement. Why have you changed your mind? You know I'm willing to pay far more than the farm is worth."

"This may sound foolish to you," Alan said, "but I've been taking a look at myself lately, and I don't like what I see. I'm going to try to change some things. It may be too late, but I'm going to try."

Clarence took off his glasses and polished them. "It wouldn't have anything to do with that Miss Olson, would it?"

"Clarence, I believe you must read minds. I think she is the reason I'm seeing myself in a different light. I'm just realizing that myself." He paused. "If she'll have me, I'm going to ask her to marry me. This is confidential, and I wouldn't tell anyone but you, but it could happen. Norma wants a divorce, so I could be free to marry Ellen."

Clarence was silent a moment. "You're going to be giving up a lot, Alan. I understand you want to open a branch of the bank in Haymarket. Charles Steadman's money won't be available for that if you divorce Norma."

"I know that. I'm willing to give that up. I hope this business over the farm isn't going to come between us, Clarence."

Clarence put his glasses back on. "Alan, I would think very carefully about the possible consequences of this. Believe me, I'm telling you this for your own good. I want this farm. You know I'm prepared to give you a good price for it. On top of that, I could loan you the money you need to open that branch."

"Clarence, I can't do it. I gave the Dacias my word."

Clarence's voice was cold. "Alan, falling in love with Ellen Olson is understandable. Losing your business sense is not. I want this farm. If you don't sell it to me, some things could happen that you may regret. I advise you to think about this carefully."

Alan pulled back from the window and puzzled over Clarence's last statement which sounded something like a threat. "I can't sell you the farm. I'm sorry."

Clarence smiled at Alan. "I'm sorry too, Alan. Say good-bye to Miss Olson for me."

* * *

The Dacias were ready by 7:30 the next morning, and when Clarence came at 8:00, they were in front of the house, worrying that he might have forgotten.

It had been decided that Aunt Magda and Michael-Joseph would go with Josif and Izabella. Uncle Jon would stay home to continue the plowing, while the three girls would go to school, making sure to walk with the Wample sisters.

Josif rode in front with Clarence, and the two women and Michael-Joseph sat in the back seat. Josif wore the stiff, blue suit he had brought from the old country, while Izabella and Aunt Magda wore their best white blouses, dark skirts, flowered aprons, headscarves and their new shoes. They had all bathed the night before so they would be clean when they saw Alexander in the hospital.

Clarence drove carefully and slowly with both hands firmly gripping the steering wheel. He seemed to sense the Dacias' depression, for he spoke quietly and soberly to them, pointing out things of interest as they drove along, but not trying to cheer them falsely with small talk or predictions of how well Alexander would be.

He explained how the early settlers had tended to group together according to what parish or village they had come from back in the Old Country, and how the Dacia farm was somehow in the middle of these communities with the Swedes living to the south of them, the Norwegians to the east, the Danes to the west, and the English to the north.

"Then, of course, there are people from other parts of Europe and the British Isles. Germans, Dutch, French, Russians, Finns, Scots, and Irish, all mixed together. Some came to America early, settling in the east, moving west as they felt crowded." Clarence smiled quickly at Josif. "I'm afraid there aren't many people from your particular part of the world here, at least not in this part of South Dakota."

"Romanians came to New York City," Josif said. "Many Romanians. We stay there a little, but we want land, want horses. We are only happy when have these things. We left, came to west."

Clarence nodded. "I understand how you feel. There is something about the land, about having your own land, that is important. Maybe it is because the land is permanent, because it is always there. Cities rise and fall, towns crumble into dust. The land stays. Generations of a family can live on the same farm, tilling the same soil that their fathers tilled, that their grandfathers tilled. It is there. It is theirs."

Josif felt a liking for Clarence. Few people seemed to understand his longing for land as Clarence did. He responded, "I not talk good in English, but what you say is how I feel. I am glad you our neighbor."

Clarence smiled at him. "I'm glad, too." He spoke over his shoulder to those in the back seat. "I was wondering about dinner. Can I take you folks out to dinner in Sioux Falls?"

Izabella said shyly, "We have brought bread and cheese. We thank you, but we will eat that. You do so much for us already."

Clarence shook his head. "You folks mustn't think that. I'm happy to do what little I can, and it makes me feel better, as I told you." He spoke without taking his eyes off the road. "We'll be there soon. Would you let me come in with you to see your son before I go to my business appointments? I promise not to stay long."

317

"We will be happy have you come," Josif replied. "Have Alexander meet good friend."

They came to Sioux Falls, and Clarence guided the car skillfully through the traffic to the hospital.

They entered the main lobby at 9:30AM, and Clarence led the family to the visitors' desk. The stern-faced woman behind the desk informed them that visiting hours were from 2:00 to 4:00PM, that only two persons at a time could see patients, and that in no case could children be allowed in the room.

Izabella said anxiously to her, "Is Alexander all right? Can tell us please? He is so sick."

The woman frowned. "I have no information on your son's condition. You'll have to talk with the doctor about that."

"Can we talk with doctor, please?"

The woman stared down at her. "Dr. Benson is at another hospital this morning. He does have other patients, you know."

Clarence came to stand beside Izabella. "Mrs. Dacia, let me talk to this lady for a moment, please. It seems that she does not understand the gravity of the situation. Indeed, not even the gravity of her own situation."

He studied the name tag on the woman's white coat. "Mrs. Axelrod. That is your name, is it?"

The woman looked uneasily at Clarence. "It is. What's that to you?"

"Just this: My name is Clarence Lamb. I happen to be an old friend of the director of this hospital. In thirty seconds I'm going to go have a little talk with him about a certain Mrs. Axelrod who refuses to give information to the parents of a critically ill patient. I would suggest that if you understand what I'm saying you act very quickly." He took a flat watch from his vest pocket. "It is now fifteen seconds after 9:37."

The woman's face became pale. "She didn't tell me it was a critical case! I can't read minds, you know!"

"You have twenty seconds."

The woman stared for a moment at Clarence, then picked up the telephone on the desk. "I'll have the intern come down." She spoke into the telephone, then put it down and said to Clarence, "I just try to do my best here. I can't help it if people don't tell me what they want."

Clarence smiled at her. "Of course not. But now you do understand, don't you, that Mrs. Dacia was telling you that her son's case is critical. I'm sure you will remember that in the future." He raised a finger. "I suggest that you make a notation on the boy's card that his parents are to be informed immediately of his condition when they ask. We know that you will inform them, but it will be best to let anyone else who may work at this desk also be informed, just so there will be no further misunderstanding, don't you agree?"

The woman's face was still pale. "No one told me it was a critical case. I just try to do my best." She wrote on the card, then she held it for Clarence to see. "I've marked it the way you asked."

Clarence beamed at her. "Excellent, Mrs. Axelrod, excellent. I'll not forget your kindness to Mr. and Mrs. Dacia and their family."

A young man in a white coat and stethoscope came from a doorway toward the visitors' desk. He walked briskly erect and his face had the same look of all-knowing power and authority as Dr. Benson's. He glanced quickly at the Dacias, then, ignoring them, he spoke to Mrs. Axelrod. "What's so urgent, Axelrod? You've interrupted morning rounds."

"I'm sorry, Doctor." Mrs. Axelrod looked meaningfully at Clarence and the Dacias. "This man insists that he see you or Dr. Benson. It's about these people's son." She showed him the card. "The pneumonia case in Twenty-three-B."

The young man flicked the card impatiently with his fingers. "Dr. Benson and I will confer on this case later this morning. What seems to be the problem?" He stared down at Clarence.

Clarence stared back at the doctor, a hint of menace in

his eyes. "The problem is this: Mr. and Mrs. Dacia have just traveled over thirty miles to see their son who is in this hospital. They would like to know his condition and prognosis. I would like to know his condition and prognosis. Before you give us any double-talk or start waving your new stethoscope around, I suggest that you have a quick word with your Mrs. Axelrod. It may be to your benefit."

The young man lifted one corner of his upper lip. "Really?" He turned to Mrs. Axelrod. "What is this quick word that I'm supposed to hear, Axelrod?"

Mrs. Axelrod whispered to him, looking once toward Clarence. When she had finished, the young man seemed to have shrunk in some strange manner, and when he slowly turned to face Clarence, the haughty look was gone.

"Mr. Lamb! Mr. Clarence Lamb! What a pleasure to meet you! Dr. Goldenstein just told us this morning at our staff meeting of your generous and timely contribution to the hospital. I'm Dr. Whipple. Dr. Richard Whipple."

Clarence smiled benignly at him. He held out his hand. "I'm pleased to meet you." He indicated the Dacias. "These are my good friends and neighbors, Mr. and Mrs. Josif Dacia; their aunt, Mrs. Jon Dacia; and their younger son, Michael-Joseph Dacia."

Dr. Whipple shook hands with all of them. "Why don't we go over to the couches where you can all be more comfortable and I can discuss your son's case with you."

They went to the couches, and Dr. Whipple sat down in a chair facing them. "I've been in to see Alexander this morning. He does have pneumonia in both lungs, and his temperature remains high. Dr. Benson and I both feel, however, that his chances for recovery are good. As soon as Dr. Benson returns from the other hospital, I'm sure that he'll want to talk with you."

Izabella's eyes were filled with tears. "Thank God, he is still alive!"

Dr. Whipple smiled confidently and reassuringly at her.

"Mrs. Dacia, we have the finest equipment here, the finest staff. The very latest technique is being used to treat Alexander." He looked appreciatively toward Clarence. "Thanks to the generosity of benefactors such as Mr. Lamb, this hospital can compare favorably with any in the state, with any in several states!"

"Can we see Alexander?" Josif asked. "Lady at desk said we could only visit in afternoon. We don't want to do wrong thing."

"The hospital does have rather strict rules about that. The mornings are for doctors' rounds, treatments, medications, baths, and so forth...." Dr. Whipple looked at Clarence. "In this case, however, I believe we can stretch the rules a little. Why don't I take Mr. and Mrs. Dacia up with me to see Alexander for a few minutes, then you can all see him during regular visiting hours?"

Clarence smiled. "That's just fine, Dr. Whipple. It's very good of you." He spoke to the Dacias. "I do have a business appointment in just a few minutes. I'm afraid I'll have to leave now, but perhaps I can see Alexander when I stop back to pick you up later this afternoon, say around 3:30 or 4:00?"

Josif shook his hand. "We want you to see Alexander. We thank you for help us so much. You are good friend."

Clarence smiled at all the Dacias. "It's my pleasure." He went toward the big main doors of the hospital, and he turned and waved at the family just before he went through the doors.

They went up in the elevator and into Alexander's room with Dr. Whipple.

Alexander was hardly visible under the white covers and the white tent, a shadowy, small figure who already seemed dim, as though he were at a great distance from them. They went to the bed and stood looking down at him through the tent, and Josif felt the sadness and fear in Izabella. Alexander's eyes looked up at them through the tent.

The only sounds were his rapid, labored breathing and the faint hiss of oxygen.

Izabella knelt down by the bed. She looked at Alexander, then up at Dr. Whipple. "It's all right," Dr. Whipple said. "You can talk to him through the tent."

Alexander's hand lay outside the covers and Izabella placed her hand gently on it. Alexander turned his head toward her. She said, "Alexander."

Alexander tried to speak. His voice was only a whisper. "I knew you would come."

"Aunt Magda and Michael-Joseph have come too, all that could come in the car."

He whispered, "Papa shouldn't leave the plowing."

Josif bent over the bed. "The plowing is all right. Uncle Jon is doing the plowing." He held the box with the model airplane so that Alexander could see it. "This is present for you. Mr. Johnson and Miss Olson get it for you. It is airplane. Airplane Charles Lindbergh flew across ocean in."

Alexander was silent, looking up at the box that held the airplane. Josif held it so that the picture of the airplane showed. "It is *The Spirit of Saint Louis*."

Alexander lifted his other hand and touched the box. Izabella's voice was choked. "They asked that we should... that we bring you... their love...."

Alexander's hand dropped back down on the covers of the bed, and Josif laid the box by his hand. Alexander's fingers moved so that they touched the box, so that they lay across the picture of the airplane as though he could feel it. Josif put his hand over Alexander's.

Alexander whispered, "Tell them I like it, Papa."

"I will. I will tell them that."

Alexander coughed under the tent. The cough was tight and it rasped deep in his chest, and Josif and Izabella felt his hands tighten with the pain. The cough was like there was something alive and tearing in Alexander's chest.

Dr. Whipple came to the bed and listened to Alexander's chest with his stethoscope. When he had listened a long time, he took the stethoscope away and removed the earpieces from his ears.

Josif felt Death standing in the room. He saw the darkness in Izabella's eyes, the sadness and the fear. He put one hand over hers, one over Alexander's – the small slender hand of his wife, the small square hand of his son.

Dr. Whipple looked at his wrist watch. "Dr. Benson should be back soon. I think it would be best now if we left Alexander to rest. As soon as Dr. Benson and I have consulted, I'm sure he'll want to talk with you."

They stood up, looking down at Alexander, then moved slowly away with Dr. Whipple guiding them out of the room where Alexander lay under the little white tent.

* * *

Clarence drove to a gasoline station in downtown Sioux Falls. He had the attendant fill the car with gas, then said to him, "I have to be at a meeting most of the day. If I could leave my car here with you, I wouldn't have to worry about a parking ticket." He held out a five-dollar bill. "Of course, I would want to make it worth your while." He smiled bewilderedly at the man.

"My name is Clarence Lamb. I'm from down near Centerford. Don't get up here to the city very often; I'd like to make sure I don't get any tickets."

After the man had taken his money and shown him where to park the car, Clarence walked slowly and hesitatingly toward the city center. Vince was waiting in Verne's truck by the post office. Clarence got in the truck and closed the door. "Is he there? You saw him?"

Vince blew smoke out the window. "He's there all right. I was watchin' him from the pool hall."

"You have the suitcase."

"In the back, under a tarp." Vince started the engine, and they drove back out of the city and south onto Route 77, going fast toward Centerford.

Three miles outside of Centerford, Vince pulled the truck off the road and up an old driveway through a grove of trees to an abandoned barn. Clarence hurried inside the barn with the suitcase, while Vince turned the truck around, and drove on toward Centerford.

Fifteen minutes later Clarence was dressed as a little old lady with a gray wig, a brown dress and coat, and black Cuban-heeled ladies' shoes. He wore a feathered bonnet on top of the wig, black cotton gloves, and had replaced his gold-rimmed glasses with a dark-rimmed pair. He also carried a large brown purse in which he had placed the flat pistol and the silencer.

An old Model T Ford stood inside the barn, and Clarence backed it out and closed the double doors of the barn. He drove the Model T toward Centerford, glancing periodically at the woman's gold watch which hung from his dress, sitting upright in the seat with the feathered bonnet perched on his head.

The noon whistle of the Centerford power plant blew just as Clarence entered town. He drove carefully down Main Street past Verne's truck parked outside Al's Cafe, and turned left at the courthouse corner. He parked the Model T on the cross street by the courthouse, headed east. Then he waited.

At 12:05PM, Earl Snipes came out of the courthouse and headed for Al's Cafe. When Earl had gone into the cafe, Clarence got out of the Model T and walked into the courthouse with his purse.

No one was in sight as he stopped outside the sheriff's office. He took the pistol and silencer from the purse, screwed the silencer on, and, holding the purse over the pistol, quietly opened the door to the outer office. It was empty. He stepped silently inside and softly closed the door.

He tapped on Frank Ariosto's door and opened it.

As Frank looked up, Clarence shot him in the chest and larynx, the flat, black pistol chuffing twice from behind the purse. Clarence watched as Frank fell forward on his desk, then shot him once more, this time in the back of the neck. He put the pistol and silencer in the purse and went out, carefully closing both doors.

He got back into the Model T and drove slowly out of town, east, toward the Iowa border. After two miles he turned north for three miles, then west for two, coming to the barn. He opened the doors, drove inside, and closed the doors. Then he changed his clothes and waited for Vince.

Vince came in the truck at 2:00PM. He stopped outside the barn and Clarence came out and slipped into the seat. "Jesus, Uncle Clarence," Vince said, "there's more damned commotion than a chivaree. When Earl came tearin' out of the courthouse and back to Al's, I thought the place was gonna explode."

"You and Verne both stayed in the cafe with Earl? You were both there all the time?"

"We sure were. We were both sittin' there at the front table when Earl came in for dinner. We had left the chair with its back to the window empty like you said, and he was so damned eager to tell me about his deputy job I don't think he ever seen anything up by the courthouse. When he went back to the courthouse after we ate, me and Verne stayed there at the table drinkin' coffee until Earl came runnin' back to Al's."

Vince eased the truck out onto the highway and headed north toward Sioux Falls. "We're as clean as a whistle." He spit out the window. "And Fat Fred Franklin is runnin' around like a chicken with his head cut off."

"Don't drive too fast, Vincent. We don't want to attract any attention."

"Hell, you could drive a herda elephants down the road now and nobody'd pay any attention. These shit-kickers act like they ain't never seen a hit before."

"There was no doubt about it then, Vincent? Frank was a big man. I put three rounds into him; it should have been enough."

"It was enough. Hell, everybody went crowdin' in there when Earl came bustin' out. Me and Verne was almost the first ones in. You took care of 'im all right. Even if he had lived a little while, that shot in the throat would've kept him quiet." He looked admiringly at Clarence. "You're the best. There ain't a button man anywhere can touch you."

"Tut tut, Vincent. It all comes with practice. Practice plus one more thing."

"What's that?"

"You can't feel sorry for them. If you do, there will be just the slightest hesitation. With someone like Frank, that could have made the difference."

"By god, he did have his hand on his gun. Had it partly out...."

"That's right, Vincent, he did. Frank was fast. If I had given him that extra split second, it might have been a different story."

Vince shook his head appreciatively. "Well, it sure was a professional job."

"That is the one thing that worries me a little."

"What thing? It looked professional as hell to me."

"That's just it, Vincent. Maybe too professional. If we had anybody other than Fred Franklin or Earl Snipes to deal with, it could be dangerous. Somebody like Frank would pick it up after they thought about it."

"Yeah, but Frank ain't gonna think about it anymore. I don't think you got a thing to worry about."

"You don't, Vincent?"

"Hell no. Not a thing."

Clarence looked speculatively at Vince. "I'm glad we had this little discussion, Vincent. You have helped me make my mind up about something."

They drove on toward Sioux Falls. Vince handled

Verne's truck expertly and they made good time, approaching the outskirts of the city by 3:00PM. Clarence, turned to Vince. "There are just a few more things I want you to do, Vincent."

"Sure, Uncle Clarence, just name 'em."

Clarence took the flat black pistol from his shoulder holster. "First, I want to trade guns with you. You take mine and give me yours. Then listen carefully to what I say."

* * *

Dr. Benson came at 11:30 that morning to talk with the Dacias. He repeated what Dr. Whipple had said about Alexander, assuring them that everything was being done that could be done. There was such an air of wisdom and authority about Dr. Benson that the Dacias felt guilty about taking his valuable time, and they were grateful that he went to the trouble to speak with them personally. They were silent and shy before him, listening humbly as he spoke.

They ate their cheese and bread self-consciously in a far corner of the waiting room, and afterward, when Michael-Joseph began to shift his feet silently and uneasily, it took all of their courage to ask the stern Mrs. Axelrod where they could find a toilet.

At 2:00, they went to the desk and got passes for two people to go to Alexander's room. Izabella and Aunt Magda went first leaving Michael-Joseph with Josif in the waiting room.

As they entered Alexander's room, Aunt Magda crossed herself, and as she looked silently down at Alexander through the partially transparent hood, she took Izabella's hand in hers, squeezing it gently.

They sat by the bed for an hour, speaking softly to Alexander, telling him of the farm and of the horses, and of Uncle Jon plowing in the far field. Izabella said softly, "Michael-Joseph is in the waiting room with Papa, but they will not let children come to visit. He wanted so much to see you. He wanted to tell you about his stick horse."

Aunt Magda added, "Marie, Rose and Caroline miss you too. They said that you should come home soon, Alexander, so you can see their dolls, and they want to watch you make the airplane of Charles Lindbergh."

Alexander held the airplane kit next to him on the bed. He whispered, "Tell them I miss them. I would like to see the dolls and Michael-Joseph's horse." He coughed, and the sound was deep and wracking in his chest. Aunt Magda and Izabella heard death in the cough, and they could not look at one another.

Josif came at 3:00 when Aunt Magda had said *good-bye* to Alexander, and he and Izabella sat by the bed with him until 4:00.

Just as the five-minute warning bell sounded for visitors to leave, Clarence Lamb came into the room. He came slowly, hesitatingly, and apologetically with his hat in his hands. "I'm sorry to intrude. I just wanted to meet Alexander, then I'll go so that you can have a few more minutes together."

Josif brought him to the bed. "Alexander, this is our good neighbor who has brought us here in his car."

Clarence smiled at Alexander. "I'm glad to meet you, Alexander."

A nurse came into the room. "You must go now. Visiting hours are over."

"It's my fault. I came late." Clarence took the nurse by the arm. "We'll just leave the Dacias alone with their son for another minute. Dr. Whipple won't object, I'm sure." He led the nurse into the hall and smiled back at the Dacias. "I'll talk with the nurse while you say good-bye to Alexander."

Josif and Izabella were filled with sadness as they bent over the bed. Alexander tried to smile at them, and they tried to smile at him, but it was impossible. Izabella had tears in her eyes, and Josif was struggling not to let his sadness and despair show.

They looked back at him as they left the room, and they waved from the door, saying, "Good-bye, Alexander. We will see you tomorrow." They went with Clarence into the elevator and down to the waiting room to Aunt Magda and Michael-Joseph, then out to Clarence's Model A and away from the hospital – away from the hospital and the room and the white tent where Alexander lay dying.

Chapter Twenty
Cries for Blood

Half an hour after Clarence had brought the Dacias home and left in his Model A, three cars came fast into the Dacias' driveway.

On the side of the first car was the word Sheriff, while on the second one were the words, Marshal, Centerford, South Dakota. A small, rat-faced man wearing his gun low around his hips was in the sheriff's car, while the fat Centerford marshal was in the second car. In the third car the Dacias saw Verne Lamb and an evil-looking younger man who looked like Verne.

The men all came to the door together, swaggering like bullies of the Iron Guard.

Josif and Uncle Jon met them in the porch, while the women and children huddled far back in the kitchen.

The fat man, the Centerford marshal, spoke first. "I've come to arrest you for the murder of Sheriff Frank Ariosto, and I've come to search these premises for the murder weapon." He glared at them, then spoke to the man with Verne.

"Which one a these damned Gypsies did you see go into the courthouse, Vince?"

Vince scowled at Uncle Jon. "The old one. The one in the overalls."

"You're sure about that? He's the one you saw?"

Vince showed his teeth. "That's the one. There ain't

any doubt about it. Got out of an old Model T. I didn't think anything about it at first. It kinda came back to me after Frank was killed, after I got to thinkin' about it."

The marshal turned to face Uncle Jon, "You're under arrest for murdering Frank Ariosto." He pulled a pair of handcuffs from his pocket. "Put out your hands."

Josif stepped in front of Uncle Jon. "My uncle didn't murder nobody. He been plowing in east field all day."

The marshal took his gun out of its holster and pointed it at Josif's stomach. "Mister, I had trouble with you before. Are you tryin' to interfere with the law? Now step back before I take you in as an accessory to the crime."

Josif didn't move. "Uncle Jon not got gun, not got car. How can he murder anybody? I told you, he been plowing all day."

The marshal put the muzzle of the revolver against Josif's stomach. "If you say one more word, and if you don't get outta my way, I'm gonna arrest you on the spot. You damned Gypsies think you can come in here and take over. Now move!"

Uncle Jon came out past Josif. He said in Romanian, "Josif, don't do anything. This man is crazy."

The marshal shouted at them, "Speak English, goddamn it. I don't want none of your Gypsy gibberish." He poked the gun in Uncle Jon's stomach. "Earl, hold your gun on this smart aleck here while I put the cuffs on the old man."

Earl Snipes already had his revolver out. He pointed it at Josif. "You make one move and you're dead."

Vince stuck out his chest authoritatively, "Any damned Gypsy that kills the sheriff oughta be shot on the spot. Blast the hell outta him if he even winks, Earl."

Uncle Jon held out his hands. "I not give any trouble." He looked at Josif. "Josif, is not for you to die for."

Josif stared at Verne Lamb as the marshal put the handcuffs on Uncle Jon. "You have kill Alexander. Now you do this." He smiled at Verne, the smile of death.

The marshal turned and slapped the barrel of his gun across Josif's face. "I told you to shut up." He pushed Uncle Jon toward his car. "Get in there. The sheriff's gonna search the premises right now. If you or that smart aleck nephew of yours even looks cross-eyed at me I'm gonna rap you across the head with this revolver. You understand?"

Uncle Jon got into the car. "I understand."

Earl Snipes went to his car and came back with a star and another revolver. He pinned the star on Vince's shirt and gave Verne the revolver. "I'm deputizing you right now, Vince. Verne, you hold the gun on this wise ass here while Vince and I take a look around."

Vince showed his teeth again. "Let me have the gun. I think maybe pluggin' a coupla these Gypsies might get me a promotion, hey, Earl? Save the county the cost of a trial."

"I wouldn't blame ya, Vince," Earl said. "You got every reason to do it, them shooting your Uncle Frank. But Verne's gonna need the gun to keep this bohunk in line while we search the house."

Earl and Vince pushed by Josif and went into the house.

Josif moved to go after them, and Verne said smugly, "If you take one more step, I'm gonna hafta shoot you. Don't move." Furniture crashed inside the house, doors slammed, dishes shattered. Then the house became silent. Josif stepped toward the porch, and Verne jammed the gun into his back. "Don't even think about it."

Izabella, Aunt Magda, and the children were in the house with Vince Lamb and Earl Snipes, and there was no sound. Josif felt such anger and frustration that he thought he would explode. These men needed killing, but to try that now would only result in his death and his family being left unprotected. He kept his rage under control, but knew he could not endure it for long.

Earl and Vince came out of the kitchen into the porch. Vince carried Josif's violin, and he held it up in front of Josif.

"Your women tried to hide this. I figure the gun might

be inside it." He laid the violin on the porch floor. "How about it, Gypsy? Want to tell me where the gun is?"

"If you touch our women, I kill you." Josif said matter-of-factly.

"Hell, I already touched 'em. Had to look for the gun, didn't I?" Vince smirked. "That wife of yours kinda enjoyed being searched."

The fury in Josif became cold. It sunk into his bones and became part of his being.

Vince raised his foot. "Watch this, Gypsy." He stamped his foot down on the violin, smashing it. He stamped again and again, slowly, deliberately, crushing the beautiful old instrument into splinters. He kicked at the pieces. "Ain't that funny. I thought sure as hell that gun would be in there."

"Well, hell, Vince," Earl said. "We all make mistakes."

Vince shrugged. "Why don't we go look in the granary? I got a feelin' that's about the kinda place these stupid bohunks would try to hide a gun. Prob'ly down in a sack of feed or somethin'."

Verne held the gun on Josif while Earl and Vince went out to the granary. "You shoulda got outta here the day you came, Gypsy," he said spitefully. "We found the Model T just down the road, outta gas. If they find the gun, there's gonna be a lotta people that'll want to hang the whole buncha ya."

A yell came from the granary, and Earl Snipes appeared with Vince behind him, waving something dark and metallic. "Here's the gun! Right in a sacka oats!"

They came up to the marshal's car and Earl held the gun out to him. "Looks like the murder weapon – a .38 with a silencer."

Fred Franklin took the gun and studied it, sniffing the silencer and the muzzle. "It's been fired – not long ago, either." He hitched up his gun-belt. "I'm takin' both these Gypsies in on suspicion of murder." He laid the gun on the seat of his car, then pointed his own gun at Josif.

"Hold out your hands while I cuff you, then get in beside

your uncle." He spoke to Earl. "Sheriff, you follow me in. If either one of these guys gets ornery, I might need backup."

"Hell," Vince said. "I'm a deputy now, Marshal. I'll just ride along with you and keep my gun on 'em. Verne can come along in his car behind Earl and bring me back home. It won't be no trouble at all." He prodded Josif with his re-volver. "Get the hell in the car. If either one of you sheriff-killing Gypsy bastards even blinks an eye I'll drop you so quick you'll hit the floor before your guts do." He prodded Josif again. "Move, you Gypsy son-of-a-bitch."

* * *

Ellen Olson arrived at the Dacias' farm shortly after Josif and Uncle Jon had been herded into the county jail in Centerford. She drove her own car, a 1927 Chevrolet Coupe; she had driven the eight miles from town in fifteen minutes.

When she saw the smashed violin and the interior of the house and the stricken faces of the family, she tried to put her arms around all of them, to hold them and com-fort them, to give them the knowledge that someone cared. There was such a feeling of shock and despair in the old house that it was a long time before any of them could speak.

"Who did this?" Ellen asked. "Who has done this to you? Did the marshal and the deputy do this?"

Izabella's eyes were dark. There was a look about her of such sadness – such sorrow, that it seemed she hardly heard Ellen.

Strigoi Aunt Magda whispered. "A *strigoi* came into the house and brought evil with him." Ellen shivered. For an instant it seemed that a cold wind blew through the house. Aunt Magda pointed to the southwest. "There." Her eyes were wild. "We did not know him. Three times we ask him to come into house, and he come. Even when we hear that he have red hair and blue eyes, we did not see him for what he was."

It seemed that she had gone mad. Ellen looked helplessly at Marie. "What does she mean? Who came into the house?"

Marie stood mutely. Her eyes were wide with the shock of what had happened, and she had her arms wrapped around herself in a protective gesture..

A car came fast from the north and turned into the driveway. It stopped in front of the house with a screech of brakes, and Mr. Bowman came hurrying up to the porch.

Ellen opened the kitchen door for him as he stared at the smashed violin on the porch floor. "Dr. Sinclair's nurse just telephoned from Centerford," he said. "The hospital in Sioux Falls called. Alexander is worse. They want his folks to come." He looked at the kitchen. "What happened here?"

"The deputy sheriff and the town marshal came," Ellen replied. "They did this. They arrested Mr. Dacia and his uncle and have taken them to jail."

"To jail? By gracious, what for?"

"Sheriff Ariosto was shot at noon today in his office. They've made a terrible mistake and arrested the Dacias." Ellen's eyes began to fill with tears. "It's so cruel, so unjust. And now Alexander...."

"Frank Ariosto was shot? At noon today? And they blame the Dacias?"

Ellen was almost crying. "Yes. They say they found the gun that killed him here."

Marie spoke for the first time. "Papa was at the hospital all day with Alexander. Uncle Jon plowed in the far field. The men lied."

Mr. Bowman looked down at her. "By gracious, that's right. They couldn't have done it."

"The men are bad men," Marie continued. "They broke Papa's violin, and they. . . did other things." Marie's voice trailed off and she began to sob.

Ellen put her arms around Marie. "You poor child, I'm so sorry you were exposed to such depravity, but try not to worry, we will find a way to make things right. Right now I'm going to take your mother to Sioux Falls to the hospital, to see Alexander. You will have to be strong and help Aunt Magda take care of the children while we're gone. Can you do that, dear?"

Marie nodded vaguely and looked at Ellen with eyes filled with sorrow and hopelessness.

"I'll go right into Centerford." Mr. Bowman started for the door. "We have to get Josif and his uncle out of jail. We have to get them up to the hospital. I'll bring them up there as soon as I can."

Ellen took Izabella's hand. "We'll go in my car. Soon you will see Alexander."

"Soon Alexander will be with God." Izabella said. "An owl called from the roof of the house the night he was hurt, an icon fell for no reason and broke, dogs howled all night. It is his fate. He will die." Her shoulders slumped and she slightly stumbled as she went to a drawer in the pantry and took a small, white candle and some matches which she put in her apron pocket. Then she let Ellen lead her out to the car. She did not look back.

Aunt Magda's eyes were bright as though there were a fire reflected in them. She watched the car disappear behind the trees, then said softly, "I saw it in a dream and did not know. But soon God will help us. He will destroy the evil ones. He will destroy the little man who has come into our house and deceived us... the little man who brings the evil of the devil with him."

* * *

Vince and Verne got back to the farm at 7:15PM with Verne's car and truck. Clarence and Julius were in the hay barn waiting for them. "It went just like you said it would, Uncle Clarence," Vince said proudly. "Both them Gypsies are in the county jail an' Earl an' the dumb marshal swallowed every bit of it. When Earl found your gun in that sacka oats, that cinched it."

"Excellent, Vincent. You did a good job today."

"Hell, it was fun. Why don't I go over there tonight an' burn the rest of 'em out. With them two guys in jail, torchin' the place will be easy as fallin' off a log."

Verne scowled at him. "Takin' care of the old man and the mouthy one is one thing. I don't hold with setting fire to a house with women and kids in it."

"Well, listen to the Boy Scout." Vince said sarcastically. "Since when did you start gettin' so chicken-hearted?"

Verne spat on the ground at Vince's feet. "You damned lunatic. You enjoyed pawing those women today, and now you wanna set fire to the place. You oughta be put away."

"Now, boys," Clarence remonstrated, "let's not fight between ourselves. We've gotten rid of Frank, and I think the Gypsy family will soon be gone, one way or another. Things seem quite tidy. It is time to start thinking of other things."

"I ain't so damned certain everything's as tidy as you think." Verne jerked a thumb in the direction of the Dacia farm. "What if that bastard of a banker decides not to sell to us? He could turn right around and rent it to somebody else."

Clarence frowned at him. "Let me worry about that, Vernon. I'm almost certain that he will sell to us. There's a way to convince him that he should."

"You mean that blonde in the bank?" Vince asked grinning. "Earl was tellin' me about her. Seems she wouldn't go out dancin' with him." He looked down at the star on his shirt. "She just might find herself in the 'hands of the law one of these nights. I wouldn't mind keepin' her in custody for a while. Course I might have to find a different jail; maybe kind of a special one out here in the country where I could give her special treatment."

"You crazy bastard," Verne said, "that sorta stuff might go in Chicago, but not out here."

Vince winked at Julius. "Your old man sure has got stuffy lately. Whaddaya say you an' me go down to the Pavilion tonight, kid? We could look over the girls and maybe have a little fun. That is, if your old man here ain't afraid to let you go out to a dance with your Uncle Vince."

"Hell," Julius said. "Pa don't worry about me none. I know how to handle myself."

Verne scowled at both of them. "I ain't too damned sure about that. I suppose you're gonna wanna take the car, too. The truck wouldn't be good enough for you."

"Jesus, Verne, take a truck to a dance? What in hell you think that would look like, me gettin' out of a truck and wearin' my Chicago suit?" Vince winked at Julius again. "And Julius here ain't gonna get any girl to dance with him if he shows up in a damned truck. Holy Christ, Julius an' me are goin' first class, not like a coupla' farm hands with cow shit on our shoes."

The pupils of Verne's eyes began to contract. "Shut up, Vince. There was another guy said that once. A wop if I remember right. He ain't talkin' too much right now about cow shit on us farmers' shoes."

Clarence's eyes were suddenly cold. "Let that drop, Vernon."

Julius looked from Clarence to Verne. "What're ya talkin' about, Pa? What's goin' on?"

"Nothin' that's any of your business. It doesn't have anything to do with you yet," Verne said angrily.

Vince looked quickly at Clarence. "Hell, Julius, we was just kiddin'. C'mon, let's go get somethin' to eat and get cleaned up for the dance. We're gonna meet Earl there and really get that place movin'. "He looked at Verne eagerly. "Say, Verne, how about diggin' out a bottle or two of your special stuff that you claim is so good. Me an' Earl are really gonna celebrate tonight."

Verne spat. "Why in hell should I give you any of my stuff? You didn't seem to think much of it a few days ago."

"Well, hell, it's the only hooch there is around here that's even half-ways fit to drink." Vince winked at Julius again. "I'm willin' to give it a try – how 'bout you, kid?"

Verne scowled. "He's too young to start drinkin'. If he goes along with you tonight, I don't want you bringin' him home drunk. You understand? Belle seems to be getting worse, and I don't want her to be upset by any of your stupid Chicago gangster stuff. We've had enough of that."

Clarence's voice was as cold as his eyes. "Vernon, I told you to drop it."

Verne turned to face Clarence, his jaw clenched and his fists coming up around his waist. "Clarence, this is my barn and my farm. You broke up my still, and you shot Frank, but you aren't gonna upset Belle." He glared at Clarence and Vince. "I'll kill you Chicago sons-a-bitches if you do that."

Clarence suddenly smiled. "Now Vernon, don't get yourself upset. These things have been a little disconcerting to you, I know, but I promise, you will have little cause to worry from now on. Everything will be taken care of."

"I've heard your smooth talk before, an' I'm tellin' you, if you upset Belle, I'll kill you."

Clarence turned to Vince, "You heard what Vernon said, Vincent. Now see that you don't do anything to upset him. You and Julius just have a good time at the dance, like you used to have in Detroit. Vernon and I will have a quiet evening here at home."

"Sure, Uncle Clarence. We'll both have a good time all right, like we had in Detroit."

Clarence smiled. "That's it, Vincent. Enjoy yourself."

"What the hell kinda talk is that?" Verne asked angrily. "What're you two gangsters tryin' to do, be funny?"

"You got it, Verne," Vince said. "We're just bein' funny. Ain't that right, Uncle Clarence?"

Clarence smiled, looking like a kindly little grandfather. "That's right, Vincent. Just trying to be funny. Just one of our little Chicago jokes."

* * *

Mr. Bowman parked the Overland in front of the courthouse and hurried up the steps to the entrance and down the flight of stairs to the county jail. Marshal Franklin sat in a revolving oak chair in the outer office with his cowboy boots up on his desk, lazily working at his teeth with a big, round toothpick. Mr. Bowman spoke with urgency, "Marshal, Josif Dacia's son is dying in the hospital in Sioux Falls. We've got to get him up there."

Fred Franklin sucked at his toothpick. "We do, do we? Right after I get a murderer behind bars, we have to let him out, do we?"

"By gracious, he's no murderer, Fred. He was up in Sioux Falls all day in the hospital with his son. Clarence Lamb took him and his wife up."

The marshal folded his arms. "We found the murder weapon in his granary. That makes him an accessory to the crime. We know the old man did it; we have an eyewitness. Vince Lamb saw him go into the courthouse just before he shot the sheriff. Just after the noon whistle."

"Vince Lamb! Is that firebug back? You aren't taking his word for anything, are you?"

The marshal yawned. "Vince is deputy sheriff now. You ain't tryin' to tell me I can't take the word of an officer of the law, are you?"

"Vince Lamb is deputy sheriff!?"

"That's right. Earl deputized him this afternoon when we were arrestin' the murderers."

Mr. Bowman's red nose began to glow as though there were a small fire within it. "You idiots! If you keep this stupidity up, the voters of Centerford will have you run out of town right after the next election!" He shook a big and bony fist in the marshal's face. "I'm going in to see the prisoners.

341

As soon as I've done that, I'm going to hire the best lawyer in town and have you sued for false arrest."

He marched past the marshal and went into the next room to the big, iron-barred cell. Josif and Uncle Jon were in the cell along with a prostrate figure that lay on one of the wooden benches that served as beds in the jail. They stared unbelievingly at Mr. Bowman and then came to the bars to meet him.

Mr. Bowman shook their hands through the bars. "By gracious, we have to get you out of here right away!"

Josif's hands were tight on the bars. "Is about Alexander?"

Mr. Bowman nodded sadly. "The hospital called. He's worse. Miss Olson is taking your wife up there right now."

"He will die."

Mr. Bowman shook his head. "We must have hope." He spoke to Uncle Jon. "They say you were seen going into the courthouse just at noon today. Were you in town? Were you in town at noon today?"

"I plow in far field all day with Peter and Paul. I was not in town. Why you say at noon?"

"Because it was at noon that someone shot the sheriff. Right here in the courthouse. Just after 12:00."

Uncle Jon pulled at his mustache. "They never tell us that."

"The marshal and deputy never told you what time? By gracious, I'm not surprised," said Mr. Bowman. "There're a couple of morons in office here."

"Today I have good dinner with good neighbors Fritz and August and their grandPapa and grandMama. Everyone else either in Sioux Falls or at school. Was very nice of Wagners to invite me to eat." Uncle Jon said.

Mr. Bowman stared at Uncle Jon. "You had dinner with the Wagners? In their house?"

Uncle Jon nodded. "We have pork with sauerkraut."

Mr. Bowman ran out of the cell room, back into the

outer office, almost colliding with Fred Franklin, who was listening just around the doorjamb.

"You heard that, Fred! He had dinner with the Wagners. He couldn't have been here at noon. He couldn't have killed the sheriff!"

"He's lying. We found the car and the gun." Fred Franklin folded his arms across his chest.

Mr. Bowman seemed to grow six inches taller. He loomed over the fat marshal like a great blue heron over a toad. "You ignoramus! Don't you have brains enough to know when you've made a mistake? A bad mistake! If you don't let both of these men out right now, I'm going to strike you down, by gracious I will!" He raised his big fist.

The marshal stepped back and hauled the revolver from his low-slung holster. "You threaten me again, Horace Bowman, and you're gonna end up behind bars too. These men are guilty of murder. None of their lies are gonna change my mind. We found the car and the gun, and that's evidence enough for me. They're guilty, and they're gonna stay locked up 'til they get hung." He pointed the revolver at Mr. Bowman's chest. "Now get outta my office or I'll arrest you for attemptin' a jail break."

Mr. Bowman's nose turned an even brighter red. He glared at the marshal, then he turned and spoke to Josif and Uncle Jon. "We have to get the Wagner boys. They don't have a telephone, so I'll drive out and get them. By gracious, don't give up!"

The marshal waved his gun. "I don't care if you bring the whole Wagner family, these men are guilty, and they're gonna stay locked up. If you come in here again, I'm gonna arrest you."

Josif spoke urgently, "Mr. Bowman, you are good friend, good neighbor. I ask you now to not try help us. You only get in jail. I do ask you, please, can you make telephone call as far as hospital in Sioux Falls? Tell Alexander he will be okay.

Tell him his Papa say the family will be okay. You do that, I thank you from my heart."

Uncle Jon's eyes were moist.

"I'll do that. I'll do it right away."

Josif held his hand out through the bars. "I thank you."

In his heart Josif said much more. He apologized to Alexander for being so hard on him and not understanding how brave he had been. He asked Alexander to forgive him, then he asked the same of God.

* * *

Izabella and Ellen were led into the hospital room by Dr. Whipple. Dr. Benson and a nurse were at Alexander's bedside, and they looked up as the two women came into the room. Dr. Benson put his hand on Izabella's arm and spoke to her in a low voice. "He's failing, Mrs. Dacia. You should know. It can't be too long now."

Izabella seemed not to see him. "Alexander will be with God. Soon his pain will be over." She went to the bed and knelt down beside it. She took Alexander's hand in hers and held it to her cheek. "We are here, Alexander," she said gently. "You will not be alone anymore."

Dr. Benson said softly to Ellen, "It can only be a matter of hours now. The priest will be here soon." He paused, "Are you a relative?"

"I am only a friend. Is there nothing more that can be done? No medicine, no drug?"

The doctor shook his head. "We have nothing more we can do. Everything possible has been done."

Ellen tiptoed to the bed and looked down at Alexander. His skin was pale although his cheeks were flushed. With each rough and tortured breath his chest slowly rose and fell and one could see that it hurt him to breathe. The oxygen hissed into the little tent, but it did no good for Alexander. Ellen placed her hand on Izabella's hand, on Alexander's, where they lay together.

"I'll be near. The nurse will bring me when you want me." She moved quietly away from the bed and spoke to the nurse. "Is there a chapel in the hospital? If I go there, will you come and get me when they need me?"

The nurse touched her arm. "I'll take you there. It's not far away." She looked at her wrist watch. "It's 8:30 now. I think I'll have to come get you soon. I'm afraid it will be before midnight.

* * *

Vince and Julius roared into the entrance of the Pavilion dance-hall grounds in Verne's '29 Whippet. Vince parked close to the building near the main doors and gave the engine full throttle a couple of times to let the locals know they had arrived. He pushed the button in the center of the steering wheel three times and the horn blasted, then killed the engine and turned the horn button to put out the car's lights. He reached under the seat and pulled out one of Verne's bottles of whiskey.

"Let's have a slug now, Julius. Get us kinda warmed up for the dancin'." Vince inspected the bottle, then uncorked it and tipped it up. The band inside the dance hall was working its way through the Varsity Drag.

"Jesus Christ," Vince said. "Verne must make this outta old corn cobs. It tastes like silage."

Julius licked his lips. "Hell, Uncle Vince, it tastes all right to me. I been samplin' it for a coupla years now."

Vince took another swallow. "I s'pose you could get kinda used to it after a while." He passed the bottle to Julius. "Listen, Julius, don't call me Uncle Vince no more. Them girls are gonna think I'm some old fart. You just call me Vince." He polished the star that was pinned to his Chicago suit. "Course, if you was to call me Sheriff it wouldn't be too damned bad, either. Just don't do that when Earl's around or he might get huffy."

345

Julius snickered. "Hell, Vince, I mean, Sheriff, Earl ain't got brains enough to get huffy."

Vince took the bottle back from Julius and tipped it up. He wiped the back of his hand across his lips. "This is just between you and me, Julius, but I kinda think there might be a new sheriff pretty soon. 'Course I ain't sayin' who, but let's just say it could be a guy from Chicago who knows his way around."

Julius took the bottle again and drank. "I sure am glad you an' Uncle Clarence came back. How about makin' me deputy when you get to be sheriff?"

"Soon as you get a little older, that ain't too damned bad an idea. We could have things just about the way we wanted 'em in this county."

"Except for Uncle Clarence and Pa. How come everybody jumps when Uncle Clarence says so?"

Vince scowled. "It ain't always gonna be that way. Someday he's gonna find out he ain't the only one that can handle a gun."

"That's another thing." Julius was starting to slur his words a little. "How come he took care of Frank? Clarence looks too goddamned old and feeble to fart. Why didn't you do it, Vince? I bet you coulda done it better."

"I coulda done it, all right, but don't ever think that ol' Clarence is old and feeble. That's just an act he puts on. He's prob'ly the best triggerman there is, and he can move fast as a cat when he wants to." Vince looked at Julius. "Don't ever cross him, or you'll end up pushin' up daisies. There's a lotta guys in Chicago made that mistake."

"What the hell were you and Pa talkin' about? About some wop. What was that all about?"

Vince brushed at his suit. "Maybe I'll tell you about that someday, kid. It just happens that I pulled the trigger a coupla times on that job. There's a big bastard that thought he was a fighter that ain't never gonna throw another punch." He fished in his coat pocket. "See them? Them's his brass knucks."

Julius put the brass knuckles on and hit into the palm of his hand. "Jesus, Vince, let me borrow 'em, will ya? If any of them town kids get feelin' porky tonight, I'll bust hell outta 'em."

Vince held out his hand. "Give 'em back, Julius, I might use 'em myself." He looked down at his star. "Course, with this, I don't think I'm gonna have much trouble with any of these hicks. Plus, I got my convincer here where it's real handy." He slipped the flat automatic out of his shoulder holster. "I usually carry two, but I lent my other one to Uncle Clarence today."

Julius whistled. "Jesus, that's some gun. Lemme take a look at it."

Vince shook his head. "That's the first thing you gotta learn. Never let somebody have your weapon. I wouldn't let President Herbert H. Hoover himself touch this, even if he got down and begged for it."

"Aw, hell, I knew that, Vince. How about me gettin' my own gun? If I'm gonna be deputy, I oughta start gettin' handy with it."

Vince took another pull at the bottle. "I'm gonna start your education tonight, kid. Me and you are gonna do two little jobs that'll be real fun. Clarence gave me the okay on both of 'em."

"What kinda jobs, Vince?" Julius took the bottle again.

"Just keep it quiet. We don't want nobody to get any ideas, 'specially Earl." Vince looked out the windows of the car then back at Julius. "After the dance," he said softly, "and after we do one other thing, we're gonna go over and burn that Gypsy family out. I got a can of gasoline in the back that we'll splash around on the house and barn. When we touch that off, it's bye-bye, Gypsies."

"Jesus!"

"The first thing is gonna be even more fun. We're gonna pick up that blonde from the bank. Sort of arrest her, like." Vince jiggled a pair of handcuffs. "Clarence is gonna

347

use her to put a little pressure on that bank bastard so he'll sell us that farm the Gypsies are on. When she doesn't show up for a week or so, he'll see it our way if he wants her back."

Julius stared at Vince. "You really gonna do that? How? How you gonna pick her up? Where you gonna keep her?" He squirmed on the car seat in excitement.

"It's gonna be easy. That's why I brought you along. You got an important part to do. But I gotta make sure you can do it right."

"Just tell me, Vince. I can handle it. You'll see."

Vince looked out the window to make sure no one was within earshot, then spoke quietly to Julius. "When me and Verne was in town, takin' them two Gypsies in, I saw her headin' out toward their farm in that Chevy of hers. I asked a few questions and found out she was plannin' to take that kid's old lady up to Sioux Falls to see him in the hospital." He looked at Julius. "Seems they don't think he's gonna make it through the night."

Julius shrugged. "Ain't that too damned bad. Now that damned Frank ain't around, it ain't gonna worry me none."

"Well, anyhow, I figure she'll be bringing the Gypsy woman back sometime in the middle of the night. We're gonna just wait at a nice quiet spot, and when she heads back to town, we're gonna get her to stop." Vince looked sideways at Julius. "I got a nice place picked out to keep her in. Slug her around a little and pour a little of this hooch down her every night and she'll be one hell of a lotta fun."

Julius squirmed again. "How you gonna get her to stop, Vince? What if she just sails on by?"

"That's what I got you along for, Julius. You're gonna be a poor hurt boy layin' out on the side of the road. I hear she's a sucker for helpin' people. I'll come along and arrest her for hittin' you with her car. You just do your job and I'll take care of the rest."

"Jesus Christ, I can't hardly wait."

"I can't either. But now we're goin' in and dance awhile.

The night is young, as they say, and we got a lotta dancin' an' drinkin' to do before we have our real fun. Vince got out of the car. "They're playin' *Hello My Baby*. Let's get the hell in there and find us a coupla girls."

* * *

Mr. Bowman pulled into the Wagner barnyard fast, the headlights of the Overland sweeping around over the barn, water tank, and granary as he circled and came back in front of the house.

The yard light and the porch light came on, and Fritz and August came out of the house and onto the porch; they stood watching Mr. Bowman as he hurried up the concrete walk toward them. "What in hell you doin' out this late, Horace?" Fritz asked. "You come for a game a pitch?"

Mr. Bowman came up onto the wide porch. "We have to go into town right away. That ignoramus of a marshal has got Josif and Jon Dacia in jail on some sort of a trumped-up charge of killing Frank Ariosto! Did Jon Dacia have dinner with you today?"

They stared open-mouthed at him. "Frank Ariosto?" Fritz dropped his cigarette. "Frank Ariosto? What the hell you talkin' about, Horace? Frank Ariosto would shoot the balls off anybody that even looked cross-eyed at him." He turned to speak to August. "Did you hear that? Sayin' somebody shot Frank Ariosto!" He bent and picked up his cigarette in disgust.

"Course I heard it. Waddaya think I am, deaf?"

"Well, how in hell could Horace here get the idea that anybody shot Frank Ariosto?" Fritz demanded.

"Well, Jesus Christ, don't ask me. How am I supposed to know. Waddaya think I am, some sorta fortune teller?" August fished for the makings of a cigarette.

"By gracious, you two are the absolute limit!" Mr. Bowman roared in a voice that shook the windows of the house. "Now listen! Somebody shot and killed Frank Ariosto at noon today in his office. That weasel of a deputy, Earl Snipes, and Fat Fred have arrested the Dacias for it. We know that Josif was in Sioux Falls all day. Jon Dacia told me he had dinner today with you. If he did, he couldn't have been in Centerford killing the sheriff, could he? Did he have dinner with you today? Just say yes or no!"

Grandma Wagner stepped out onto the porch with a small tablecloth full of crumbs to shake over the railing. "Why, Horace Bowman! My how you surprised me. Out here having a nice quiet chat with the boys are you?"

Mr. Bowman's nose began to glow in the shadows of the porch. He put his mouth next to Grandma Wagner's ear and bellowed, "Did Jon Dacia have dinner with you folks today?"

Grandma Wagner smiled at him. "We've had dinner, Horace. You're too late. You can come in for a cup of coffee, though."

Mr. Bowman clutched his head in despair. Just then Grandpa Wagner came stomping out on his crutch. His fierce eyes darted from face to face. "What in hell are you all yelling about? Woke me up from my nap!" He banged on the porch floor with his crutch and then swung it in a vicious arc toward August. "Goddamn it, August, get Horace a piece a' cake! Ain't you got no manners?"

August leapt nimbly backward out of the way of the crutch. "Jesus Christ, Grandpa, Horace don't want no cake. He wants to know if Jon Dacia had dinner here today."

Mr. Bowman said weakly, "That's it, August. Did he?"

Fritz scowled at August. "Will you quit buttin' in when Horace and me are tryin' to talk? We don't need your two-cents worth." He spoke to Mr. Bowman. "Now just take it quiet and easy, Horace, and we'll get this all straightened out. Just tell me what it is you're gettin' so upset about."

Mr. Bowman spoke almost in a whisper. "Did Jon Dacia have dinner with you folks today? Was he here between noon and 1:00?"

Fritz looked up at the ceiling of the porch. "Between noon and one? Let's see now. It was about twenty to when I went out to ask him. Now I figure that field he was plowin' must be about a good half-mile from the house here...."

"Jesus H. Christ, Fritz," August said. "It's more than a half-mile from where he was when you went out and asked him. I'd say closer to five-eighths of a mile."

Mr. Bowman clutched at the inside pocket of his coat. He turned and ran back to the shelter of the darkness behind his car. He shuddered, then pulled the bottle from his coat and took a long, soothing drink, then another. He put the bottle back in his pocket and returned to the porch where Fritz and August were still arguing about the distance Uncle Jon had been from their house.

He said calmly, "By gracious, I have enjoyed just about as much of this as I can stand. Now you two boys climb in that car. We're going in to Centerford right now to get the Dacias out of jail. If either one of you says one more word about how far Jon Dacia was from your house when you asked him to come in to dinner, I am going to stop the car. I am going to take you by the neck. I am going to throttle you. I am going to take your dead body and tie knots in it. I am going to hang you up on the nearest tree with a sign around your neck that says, 'He couldn't say yes or no.' Do you understand that?"

"Hell, Horace," Fritz said, "why didn't you just come out and say what you wanted? There ain't no need to get so damned upset about it."

Grandpa Wagner shouted, "Goddamn it, you ain't goin' without me!" He flailed at August with his crutch. "Damn you, August, help me git into that car! we're goin' to town and beat the crap outta them loafers!"

Grandma Wagner smiled at Mr. Bowman. "It's real nice of you to come around for a visit, Horace. Gerhard and the boys always enjoy chitchatting with you."

* * *

The man sleeping on the bench stirred and groaned. He lay face down, and tried to roll over onto his side, then he slowly sat up with his back against the cell wall and his legs dangling down over the side of the bench.

It was Crazy Conklin, the town drunk. His hair was matted, his eyes were red and bleary, and he looked sick. He said to Josif, "I know you. You're the one with the horse." He held his head. "I think I'm gonna die...."

Josif and Uncle Jon went to the bench where Crazy Conklin sat. Josif took a dipper of water from the pail that stood on a wooden table and held it out to him. "Drink. Is good for you."

Conklin took the dipper and sipped from it, his hand shaking. He stared at Josif's face. "Somebody hit you. Did your horse mess up Fat Fred's boots again?"

Josif shook his head. "Is worse. Marshal think we kill sheriff."

"I saw who killed the sheriff. It wasn't you."

Josif and Uncle Jon stared at Crazy Conklin. Josif spoke urgently. "You saw who kill sheriff? You sure?"

"Sure, I'm sure." Crazy Conklin held his head. "I'm gonna be sick." He leaned over the edge of the bench and began to retch, and Uncle Jon ran for the slop pail and held it while Conklin threw up. When he had finished, Josif gave him another dipper of water to rinse out his mouth. Crazy Conklin lay back on the bench. He said weakly, "You're good to me."

Josif leaned over him, "Who kill sheriff?"

"He wasn't a woman. I could tell. He didn't see me, but I saw him. I'm good at hidin'. I can hide so nobody can see me. Sometimes I hide all day, and nobody can see me. I'm a fox, hidin' in the woods where nobody can see me." Crazy Conklin smiled secretly to himself. "I hide in my fox den, and nobody can see me."

352

Josif put his hand on Crazy Conklin's arm. "Please, you tell us who kill sheriff. Is important."

"It was that little man. He had on women's hair and women's shoes, but I knew it was him."

"What little man? You know his name?"

"I saw him in town before. He went in the courthouse and in the bank and in the courthouse and in the store. He had a different car. Today he came in an old car. He went in the courthouse right after the noon whistle blew. He killed the sheriff."

Josif knelt in front of Crazy Conklin and held him by both shoulders. "What is little man's name? You tell us now."

"Why, it was Clarence Lamb," Conklin said.

* * *

Alan Johnson drove back to Centerford after his meeting in Omaha. He stopped at the bank to drop off some papers and noted the large number of people on the street.

As he was just getting out of his car, Dr. Sinclair called to him from the sidewalk. In a matter of minutes the doctor told him of the murder of the sheriff, of Josif's and Uncle Jon's arrest, and of the call from the Sioux Falls hospital about Alexander. He concluded, "I was delivering a baby out in the country. My nurse told me about it just now. The whole town is in an uproar about the killing. There's talk of lynching the Dacias. All it would take is some hothead to set it off."

"How could they accuse the Dacias? What evidence do they have?"

"Earl Snipes and the marshal claim they found the murder weapon in a sack of oats in the Dacias' granary. Vince Lamb is back in town, and he claims to have seen Jon Dacia going into the courthouse at noon, just before the murder." Dr. Sinclair grimaced. "Vince Lamb's word is about as good as a pan of pus."

"And Clarence Lamb was going to take Josif and Mrs.

Dacia up to the hospital today." Alan shook his head. "The whole thing sounds ridiculous."

"We have to do something," Dr. Sinclair said urgently. "My nurse told me that Mr. Bowman had called her to say that Ellen Olson was taking Mrs. Dacia up in her car. I should go up too, but this thing about lynching sounds serious. We may have to call in a federal marshal to control things — Fred Franklin and Earl Snipes will be about as effective in coping with this as a pair of cross-eyed pullets."

"Worse. I don't trust either of them." Alan added, "I'm glad that Miss Olson is able to help. She's very fond of that family. As soon as we get the men out of jail, I'll take them up too."

The sound of loud voices came from Main Street, and Alan and Dr. Sinclair ran out past the bank building into the street. A crowd of people milled in front of the courthouse, and men shouted, waved their arms, and shook their fists in the circle of light from the streetlamp.

"It's happening! We have to act fast." Alan took Dr. Sinclair's arm. "You call the federal marshal in Yankton; I'll go and try to calm the crowd down."

As Dr. Sinclair ran toward his office, Alan ran down the street to the courthouse. He pushed through the mob of people and forced his way up the steps to the courthouse doors where Fred Franklin and Earl Snipes stood with their backs to the doors, looking out at the crowd with their arms folded complacently. "Move this crowd back! Send them home or they're going to get ugly!"

Fred Franklin shrugged. "We can't help it if the people of this town wanna see justice done. These Gypsies murdered the sheriff. Now they're gonna pay for it."

Earl Snipes addressed Alan with a sarcastic tone, "What the hell you doin' up here, banker? How come you ain't out at your country club screwin' somebody's wife or that blonde?"

Alan turned to face the crowd. He raised his arms to

354

try to quiet the shouting men. "Go on home! The men you want are innocent! Let them at least have a fair trial!"

Shouts came from the crowd. "Go home yourself, banker!" "Hang the Gypsies!" "Hang the banker!" There was loud laughter at this. Men began to push forward. "Pull him down offa there! Break down the door!" A big man with a club waved it and shouted, "Haul the Gypsies out!"

Mr. Bowman's old Overland pulled up to the curb next to the crowd, and Fritz, August, and Mr. Bowman came out of the car like three charging bulls; behind them came Grandpa Wagner, flailing at the crowd with his crutch. "Get outta my way, you Goddamned loafers! Kill 'em, Fritz! Kill 'em, August!"

Fritz and August went through the crowd like reapers through ripe grain, and men scattered and ran before their big fists. Fritz picked the man with the club up by the collar and the seat of his pants and raised him high in the air, then threw him into the crowd, sending half a dozen of the angry mob hurtling backward onto the pavement, while August hurled men right and left.

The mob broke and ran, while Grandpa Wagner slashed at them with his crutch as they streamed by him, and Mr. Bowman's bony fists hammered stragglers down.

Fritz and August met Alan Johnson as he came down the steps with his own fists leveling anyone rash enough to stand in front of him, and together they went back up the steps to where Fred Franklin and Earl Snipes stood open-mouthed.

Fritz picked Fat Fred up by the throat and front of his cowboy shirt and held him dangling up against the door of the courthouse, while August put a choke hold on Earl Snipes with one arm and lifted him up by the back of his gun belt with the other hand so that he hung like a plucked chicken in a butcher shop. While Fat Fred and Earl Snipes hung suspended, Mr. Bowman judiciously lifted their revolvers from their fancy holsters and handed one to Alan Johnson, while he kept one for himself.

While this was happening, Grandpa Wagner swung with his crutch at fallen wretches trying to crawl away from his fury as he hobbled toward the steps. "Run, you lily-livered sons a' bitches! Goddamned cowards!" He struck the last one with a vicious whack. "Goddamn it, August, run 'em by me again! go round 'em up and bring 'em back again!"

"Jesus Christ, Grandpa, there ain't no more." August jiggled Earl Snipes up and down by his gun-belt. "You feelin' comfortable, Earl?"

Fritz held Fat Fred up against the door with one hand and back-handed him across the mouth twice. "Jesus, Fred, I thought I saw a fly there." He lowered Fat Fred so that his cowboy boots just scraped the floor. "Let's go inside now, Fred. Me an' August an' Grandpa wanna have a little talk with you in private. It's about you not believin' Horace here when he told you we had company for dinner today. We ain't too damned happy about havin' people callin' us liars." He squinted at Fat Fred's face.

"Damned if I don't think I see another fly buzzin' around you. Whaddaya think, August?" He back-handed Fat Fred again.

"Hell, it looks like two or three of 'em to me," August said innocently. "I wouldn't be too surprised if they started hangin' around Earl here. He's beginnin' to smell kinda ripe." He jiggled Earl up and down.

Grandpa Wagner came hobbling up the steps. "Goddamn it, hold them bastards still, boys! I wanna get a good lick at 'em!"

Fat Fred whimpered, "If you got new evidence, I'm willing to listen to it."

Fritz lowered him another inch. "Now you're startin' to talk. How about your gopher-faced buddy here? Whaddaya say, Earl?"

August jiggled Earl again. "He don't seem to be too damned interested right now. Maybe I oughta let him breathe a little." He loosened the choke hold on Earl but still kept him hanging by his gun belt. "How about it, Earl?"

Earl gasped for breath and coughed. He said in a strangled voice, "Yeah, sure."

Grandpa Wagner swung his crutch at Earl and whacked him on his rear. "Goddamn it, August, hold him still, I said! This is just startin' to get fun!"

Dr. Sinclair came hurrying into the light of the streetlamp. He called up to them, "The marshal's coming from Yankton." He climbed the steps and stared at Fat Fred and Earl Snipes where they still dangled from the Wagner brothers' hands. "From the looks of things, we aren't gonna need him."

"By gracious," Mr. Bowman said, "I think we might. I believe we are going to have two people here who are going to turn in their badges. They're going to turn them in right after they release two prisoners. Then we have to get the Dacias up to Sioux Falls."

Dr. Sinclair was silent a moment. He said slowly, "There's no need for them to go up to Sioux Falls now. After I called the marshal, I called the hospital." He looked up at Mr. Bowman.

"The Dacia boy is dead. He died just fifteen minutes ago."

* * *

Alan Johnson brought Josif and Uncle Jon home at 10:45 that evening. He went in the house for only a few minutes, sensing that the family wished to be alone.

When Alan had gone, Josif brought his grandfather's knife from its hiding place under the mattress. He looked hard at Michael-Joseph, "If I do not come back, Uncle Jon is the man. When Uncle Jon dies, you will be the man. You will protect your mother and your sisters. You will keep our honor. Promise me that you will do that."

Michael-Joseph looked up at him. "I will, Papa."

357

Josif kissed him and the girls on their foreheads. "When your Mama comes back, take care of her." He went to Aunt Magda. "You are the strong one. Give your strength to these children."

"I will, Josif."

He took her hand. "Izabella will want to join Alexander."

She looked into his eyes. "God will decide that. Go with God, Josif."

He went to Uncle Jon. "My Uncle, there is no man I trust more than you. Take care of the family."

"I will, Josif," he said.

"I know that you must do this alone. If you do not kill all of them, I will go the next night. They will all die. I swear it."

Josif looked around the room at all of them, "Buy this land. Stay on it. It is ours now by our blood." He took the knife from the table and went out into the darkness.

Chapter Twenty-One
A Night of Reckoning

Just after Alexander had stopped breathing, the nurse turned off the oxygen and removed the tent. She left Izabella and Ellen alone with Alexander.

Izabella removed the white candle from her apron pocket and gave it to Ellen with a match. "Is our custom to have someone who is not in family hold candle so soul of one who died will see light and know where to go and will be known as Christian and at peace with God. Will you please light candle and hold where Alexander can see it."

Ellen did as she asked, and Izabella knelt by Alexander's body until the nurse came to them. She said gently, "It's almost 11:35. There are things that we must do. It would be best if you went back to your home now, Mrs. Dacia. Everything will be taken care of. Dr. Sinclair has made all of the arrangements."

Izabella seemed not to hear the nurse. Ellen blew out the candle and put her arm around her. "We will go back home now. Marie, Rose, Caroline, and Michael-Joseph all need you."

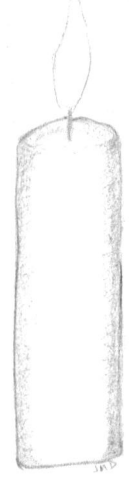

Alexander lay on the bed. His face was peaceful, and Ellen thought again how he looked like Charles Lindbergh. She said to Izabella, "Alan called from Centerford. Josif and your uncle have been released from jail. They will be home now, waiting for you."

"God waits for me. Alexander and God

wait for me." Izabella kissed Alexander. "You will not be alone, Alexander."

They went slowly out of the room where Alexander lay. They went down to the waiting room and out of the hospital where Death lived in spite of the gleaming instruments and the white tiles and the metal carts and the men and women in white coats and the doctors in their fine suits. Out into the night where the raw night wind moaned over the concrete steps and sidewalks and around the brick walls and away, over the black earth and into the empty night.

They drove out of the city where people with pale faces stood under the street lamps and where music blared from dingy dance halls and where no one knew or cared that Alexander Dacia had died. They went out onto the highway, and they drove down its cement surface in the darkness with the car lights making a tiny patch of light ahead of them, but all around them was darkness. Darkness stretching out forever over the bleak fields where the night wind moaned and there were no lights.

* * *

Julius and Vince danced with two town girls while the saxophones and the trumpets blared and the drums banged, and they felt Verne's whiskey in them and their eyes were wild in the colored lights that were strung over the ceiling and walls of the Pavilion dance hall. The girls laughed shrilly, their eyes bright with the drinks Vince had given them: Verne's whiskey in Bib-Label Lithiated Lemon-Lime Soda. The girls were excited and proud to be with the new deputy sheriff, and they let Vince and Julius dance close to them and fondle their thighs under the table where they sat between dances. Earl had not shown up, and Vince with his Chicago suit, his star, and his whiskey was clearly the king of the dance hall.

Two town boys had come to the table earlier in the evening, asking the girls they had brought to dance with them, looking with unfriendly eyes at Vince and Julius. Vince had invited the boys outside, and in the vomit-reeking darkness behind the dance hall he had smashed the brass knuckles into the nose of one of the boys, leaving him groaning in the dead grass and broken bottles on the urine-soaked ground. He slipped the brass knuckles to Julius, and Julius had beaten the other boy's face until it was bruised, swollen, and bloody. When they came swaggering back into the dance hall the girls had looked at them with wide eyes, and no more town boys came to challenge Vince and Julius.

At 1:00 they took the two girls out into the car. Vince let them drink Verne's whiskey straight out of the bottle, and when the girls were 'right,' Vince and Julius drove into the darkness of the cottonwood grove at the far end of the dance-hall grounds. There they stripped off the girls' panties and bras and fondled the girls roughly, while they moaned and protested drunkenly, then they raped them, taking turns in the back seat.

At 11:30 they dumped the girls off at the dance hall and headed north.

Vince drove fast down the concrete. He was feeling mean now after the girls and the whiskey, and he pushed the accelerator to the floor.

"Jesus, Vince, that sure as hell was fun." A second bottle of whiskey lay under the front seat, and Julius reached down and pulled it out, swaying unsteadily with the motion of the car. He uncorked the bottle and tilted it up, then handed it to Vince. "How about another slug, Sheriff?"

Vince took the bottle and drank, and the Whippet's tires screeched as the car veered toward the side of the road and then back.

"Goddamned car handles like a truck. That big President 8 Studebaker I had back in Chicago was a real car. This heap ain't got no speed."

"Hell, Vince, wait'll we get goin' on that new still. We'll get one of them Packards, or a Pierce-Arrow." Julius took the bottle back from Vince and drank again. "We gonna pick up that blonde now, Vince?"

"What in hell you think we're leavin' the dance for? We gotta make sure we're in the right spot when she heads back into town."

They came to Centerford, and Vince slowed the car as they went through town.

"That fuckin' Earl never did show up, and I ain't too damned unhappy about it. This way, we don't hafta have him gettin' nosy."

They went on to the north, and Vince accelerated the car when they were clear of the town. Julius said thickly, "You sure can handle this car, Sheriff."

Vince took the bottle back. "Hell, drivin' on a straight road like this ain't nothin'. You oughta see some of them roads over in Illinois and Indiana. All curvin' around, up and down hills. You ever see a bootleg turn, kid?"

"What's a bootleg turn?"

"Watch this."

Vince slammed on the brakes and pulled the car to the far left side of the road. Just as the car stopped its forward motion, he shifted into reverse and backed up at full throttle, making a tight backward turn to the right so that the car screeched around to the opposite side of the road, teetering on the edge of the ditch and facing the way they had come. He shifted into forward and, with the wheels spinning, accelerated the car back to the south. Julius whooped, "Jesus Christ, Vince, that's really somethin'!"

"Now I'm gonna do it again, 'cause we're headin' the wrong way. Hang onto that bottle, kid; we don't wanna spill it." Vince repeated the turn at even higher speed, and the car swayed on two wheels and the tires screeched on the pavement as they headed north again. "Now we gotta really pour it on. I sure as hell don't wanna have that blonde slip by us." Vince pressed the accelerator to full throttle and the car leapt forward, going north at top speed.

* * *

Josif crossed the creek at the stone bridge, and he stood there for a moment above the arterial gushing of the black water, then slipped into the shadows of the willows and cottonwoods on the south bank.

He followed the creek in the darkness, going to the southwest toward Verne Lamb's farm, sensing the silent flapping of bats, and hearing the scurrying of night creatures in the darkness of the trees. The creek passed under another bridge at the east-west road leading to the Wample and Dordoine farms, and bordered the Lamb property to the south.

He came up onto and across the road, trampling the stalks of old weeds in the ditches with a crackling like brittle bones snapping. He crawled through the barbed-wire fence that enclosed the Lamb place, the ancient wire and rusty staples groaning with his passing. Now he followed the creek southwest across the dank earth of the black fields that lay bleak and barren in the thin light of the gibbous moon.

Silent sheet-lightning flared to the west, and the circling stars glittered like cold eyes in the spiraling galaxy. He moved quietly and slowly, keeping hidden in the shelter of the trees and brush, moving ever closer to the lair of his enemies.

Josif left the creek bank and went south across the fields toward the dark bulks of Verne Lamb's silo and barns. The smell of cattle and the stench of manure and silage became stronger as he approached the buildings, and he heard the movement of the cattle in the night. He came to the feedlot and the cattle sheds, and circled out around them so that the cattle would not be alarmed. The silo towered over him, and he went beyond it toward the huge barn which loomed above him against the sky.

He came silently to the barn and followed its walls, going toward the cluster of smaller buildings and the lights of the house. The barn had no windows, but beyond a pile of planks he found a small, closed side door.

A sound came from inside the barn, a rustling of something moving in the darkness—something moving toward the place where Josif stood.

He drew the curved knife from his belt and moved quietly back from the door. Then he waited.

* * *

After Vince and Julius left for the dance, Verne had finished the chores and then gone up to Belle's room.

Belle had been sleeping, but now she looked up at him from the bed and smiled at him. She was so emaciated that the smile was grotesque, a smile of death. She whispered, "I knew you'd come to see me now."

Verne sat down on the chair next to the bed. He took her hand, and it was like taking the hand of a skeleton, but he held it, feeling the coldness of death in it. He said, "Is there anything you want? Do you want another pill? Are you feeling all right?"

She moved her hand within his. "Do you remember our honeymoon, Verne? That hotel we stayed in?"

"I remember."

"I can see it. I can see the light on top. Look out the window, Verne, way to the south. Can you see it? The light that they put up for the airplanes?"

"I can see it. Right on top of the hotel."

She smiled again. "I was pretty then, wasn't I, Verne? Didn't you think I was pretty?"

Verne put both his hands around hers. "You still are."

"Belle Ariosto. You always said my name was pretty."

"It is pretty." He smiled at her. "A pretty girl with a pretty name."

"Frank was coming to see me."

"Frank had to go away. He got called away on business."

Belle's hand moved again within his. "Frank's dead. I heard you talking in the barnyard."

"That was just a little argument. Frank's all right."

"I can hear things real well. I can hear voices in the barn, even." She looked up at him. "I know you didn't do it, Verne. Clarence killed Frank, not you."

Verne stared at her. "In the barn? You heard us in the barn?"

"I heard when Clarence shot those men. I heard Clarence talking about killing Frank. I heard Vince."

The pupils of Verne's eyes closed down to tiny points of blackness. When he spoke, each word was cold and deadly. "Belle, it isn't going to happen anymore. Vince and Clarence won't be around anymore. They'll never bother you again. I'll get rid of them. I promise that."

"I knew you would, Verne. You've always been good to me." She tried to squeeze his hand. "I think I'll sleep now."

Verne watched her as she slept. He sat by her bed while the hands of the little clock on the nightstand moved slowly around to11:30, its quiet ticking sounding harsh and ominous in the still room; then he gently took his hands away from hers. He whispered, "They won't bother you anymore, Belle. Not anymore."

His shotgun was in the still room, but the other one, the one he'd bought for Julius, was in the closet in Julius' room.

Verne went quietly into the room without turning on the light and opened the closet door. In the dim light from the hall, he felt in the corner where Julius kept the gun, then around the rest of the closet. The gun was gone.

Clarence spoke softly behind him. "The one in the barn's gone too, Vernon. Locked in one of the trucks with the machine guns."

Verne turned around slowly. Clarence held the flat pistol and the silencer pointed at Verne's stomach.

"I can shoot you right here, Vernon. If I do, Belle is going to know before I kill her. If you come out to the barn, I promise to just give her an overdose of her pills without letting her know I heard. She won't feel a thing."

"I can get to you with a coupla bullets in me."

Clarence smiled. He raised the pistol so that it pointed at Verne's face.

"Not if they're in the brain. Nobody keeps going that way. Are you coming with me?"

Verne looked toward Belle's room. "I'll go."

They went down the stairs and out of the house, Clarence walking behind Verne. The yard light was off, but Clarence held a flashlight with its beam on Verne as they walked through the darkness toward the barn.

Clarence spoke quietly and firmly, "The little door of the barn is open. I want you to walk back into the still room without touching anything. I'll turn the big lights on once we get in, and I'll lock the door, but I'll have the gun and the light on you all the time."

Verne entered the little door of the barn, and behind him Clarence closed the door and locked it, then turned on the overhead lights.

"That's good, Vernon. Now go back to the still room. I'll make the first shot count; you won't feel anything." Clarence kept well back from Verne as he spoke.

"Everything would have been fine if Belle hadn't heard us, but I can't have her talking to the doctor. Vincent is going to burn the Dacias out tonight, so they'll be gone. He's also going to pick up Miss Olson and hold her until Alan Johnson sells us the farm. I'm sorry, Vernon, but you won't be sharing our profits."

"I should've killed you when you first came on the farm," Verne said with disgust.

"Move along now, Vernon. I want you back in the still room."

Verne went past the trucks to the little door that led into the still room. He went in carefully, moving slowly.

The axe was still by the pile of wood. Just as Clarence stepped through the door, Verne threw himself sideways toward the woodpile. He came up with the axe as Clarence's pistol swung around toward him.

* * *

Alan Johnson and Mr. Bowman, along with the mayor of Centerford, had met the United States deputy marshal on the courthouse steps just after11:00.

The marshal, a slim, gray-haired man named Baxter, listened attentively as they told him of the night's happenings. He took Fat Fred Franklin and Earl Snipes one at a time into a closed room, and when the two emerged they were more cowed than when Fritz and August had inspected them for flies.

The marshal had a disgusted look on his face from the interviews and reported to the mayor, "It seems there isn't much more to do here, outside of electing a new sheriff and appointing a new town marshal. I wish you better luck with your next ones. I think the Dacias have a good case for suing somebody for false arrest and for breaking up their house without a search warrant."

"What about the murder of the sheriff?" Alan Johnson asked. "The death of Alexander Dacia? Vince Lamb must've planted the gun in the Dacias' granary. Julius Lamb's beating of Alexander at school undoubtedly led to the boy's death."

The marshal rubbed his chin. "Unless a federal law has been violated, I can make no arrests. It would be best for your own new marshal or sheriff to investigate those cases."

The Wagner brothers and Grandpa Wagner had been so saddened and angered by Alexander's death that they had been scouring the streets for stragglers from the lynch mob, and as the marshal finished speaking, they came rushing back into the courthouse. They had Crazy Conklin with them.

"Clarence Lamb's the one that shot Frank Ariosto!" Fritz maneuvered Crazy Conklin in front of the marshal. "We found him in the alley back of the pool hall. Tell 'em, Crazy."

Crazy Conklin shifted his feet uneasily. "I tried to tell Fat Fred. He threw me out of the jail. Are you gonna hurt me?"

The marshal studied Crazy Conklin's face. "No one's gonna hurt you. Tell us what you know."

"It was that little man with the white hair. Clarence Lamb, they also call him C.D. He went in the courthouse, then he came out. Right after the noon whistle. He didn't see me 'cuz I was hidin'. He was wearin' women's clothes, but he didn't fool me."

"Them damned Lambs," Fritz said, "ol' C.D. musta come back and Frank got in his way."

"Who's C.D.?" the marshal asked.

"Hell, everybody knows that," August said. "Clarence Lamb. He's been in Chicago about thirty years. He's hooked up with them gangsters."

"Will you shut up and quit buttin' in?" Fritz glared at August. "Me and this marshal here are tryin' to talk."

"Chicago gangsters?" the marshal asked. "And this Clarence is here now?"

"Clarence Lamb has been back here for several days," Alan Johnson said. "He came to see me at the bank. He told me he was coming back here to raise cattle."

"Oh, hell," Fritz said. "He's prob'ly runnin' hootch."

The marshal looked interested. "It sounds as though this case does come under federal jurisdiction. I think we'd better get out to wherever these Lambs live. I think we'd better get out there right away."

Grandpa Wagner flailed at August with his crutch. "Goddamn it, August, help me get into a car! We're goin' out and beat the crap outta them Lambs!"

* * *

The thing in the barn came to the door. Something scraped up the side of the door, then metal rasped against metal. Josif stepped beside the hinges of the door. He held his grandfather's knife low with the blade up.

The door opened outward a thin crack, and a hard bright light shone out through the crack. The door opened farther, and in the harsh light, Verne Lamb crawled out of the barn. He held one hand against his stomach as he crawled, and dark blood oozed over his hand. His eyes were fixed on the lights of the house, and he did not see Josif.

Josif let Verne crawl away from the door, then he silently closed the door and braced one of the planks against it. He moved through the darkness to where Verne crawled like a wounded animal toward the house.

Josif stepped beside Verne and pressed the razor-sharp blade of his grandfather's ancient curved knife against Verne's throat. "Alexander is dead. Now you die!"

Verne coughed and looked up at Josif. Blood came out of his mouth, black in the faint light from the house. He fell on his side in the dirt. "Go ahead, Gypsy. I got a bullet in my gut already. You're too late."

Josif pressed his knife harder against Verne's throat. "I watch you die a little. Then I cut your throat."

Verne coughed again. "You better cut fast. Vince is gonna set fire to your house and barn tonight and then kidnap the Olson girl. That bastard Clarence told him to. He's the one that shot the sheriff."

"Where are they? You tell me quick."

"Clarence is back in the barn. I split his head with the axe. Vince is out at a dance with Julius. He could be comin' back at any time now. You better get home quick. They've got five gallons of gasoline." Verne coughed and more blood ran from his mouth. "Take the truck." He looked up at Josif. "I didn't want it to come to this. Not burnin' women and kids. Not kidnappin' women."

The knife was heavy as death in Josif's hand. He looked down at Verne. The wind moaned around the barn in the darkness, and black clouds scudded across the night sky. Josif

369

suddenly saw Verne in a new light; as a man with his own terrible struggles who, though being angry and hateful, still had compassion and limits to his vengeance. "You are not my enemy," he said. He took out his handkerchief and put it by Verne's hand. "Hold this tight against bullet place."

Verne coughed again. "Get movin'. Take the truck"

Josif ran through the darkness toward the other buildings and the light of the house. The truck stood by the granary, and he fumbled with the keys, switches and levers. As the motor came to life he worked frantically with the clutch and the gear-shift lever, then with the wheels spinning in the dirt of the barnyard, and without lights, he brought the truck in a wild, careening path out past the house and onto the road. He found the light switch, and with the motor racing, he drove Verne's truck north at full speed toward the intersection with the road that led east to the farm.

Just before he came to the intersection, a ball of flame exploded and expanded in the darkness to the east. It rose into the night sky like a red flower, pushing its way upward into the blackness of the night with the long tendrils of its blossoms shooting out gracefully over the dark land.

* * *

Vince had overshot the side road leading to the Dacias, and the car continued north, weaving from side to side on the road at top speed.

The lights of an approaching southbound car appeared ahead, and as the Whippet veered toward the car, the other driver, by some miracle, pulled onto the shoulder of the road just as the two cars swept by one another. For an instant the headlights of the Whippet flashed on the faces of the two women in the other car.

"Jesus Christ, it's them!" Vince pounded the steering wheel. "We got 'em! We got 'em! It's the blonde!"

Julius shouted, "Turn her around, Vince, we're goin' the wrong way!"

"Not yet!" Vince shouted back, "Let 'em get down the road where they won't see us turn. Use your head, kid!"

They went on north for another half-mile, then Vince made one more bootleg turn with the tires screeching. The Whippet rocked wildly, and while bottles clattered under the front seat, a dull thump came from the back of the car.

Julius shouted drunkenly, "Ride 'em, cowboy!" and Vince accelerated the car back to the south at full speed. He turned onto the side road with the back end of the Whippet sliding around the corner on the loose dirt, then slowed the car and turned off the lights.

"Now we just go down to that buncha trees and wait. She oughta be comin' back in about half an hour. That's when you go into your act, Julius."

Vince drove the car down the road in the near darkness and backed through the open gate that led into the trees. He stopped the car and pulled out his package of cigarettes.

"Reach down in the back there and haul out that coil a rope. We wanna make sure everything's ready when I make the arrest." Vince tapped a cigarette out and held it loosely between his lips.

Julius squirmed in expectation. "You gonna tie her up, Vince?"

"Yeah. Handcuffs and rope. I got an idea she may put up a fight." Vince took Angelo's cigarette lighter from the pocket of his Chicago suit. "I hope she does. It'll be more fun that way. I'll beat hell outta her before I screw her." Vince flipped the top of the lighter back.

Julius leaned unsteadily back over the front seat and groped in the darkness for the rope. "Jesus Christ, Vince, that goddamned can a gas musta tipped over..."

"Well, for Christ's sake," Vince said with irritation, "Set it up." Then he snapped the lighter.

Chapter Twenty-Two
Alexander Comes Home

Everyone came to the Dacias' that night.

Josif brought the truck into the driveway just minutes behind Izabella and Ellen; Mrs. Bowman and Mrs. Horsefall appeared in a horse-drawn buggy ten minutes after that; and while they all guarded the buildings and watched the dying flames to the east, the Wagners, Mr. Bowman, Alan Johnson, Dr. Sinclair, and the United States deputy marshal arrived in three cars.

Dr. Sinclair and Mr. Bowman went on to the Bowmans' house to telephone for ambulances and undertakers from Centerford and the nearby town of Haymarket, but they stayed long enough to help explain what they had found on the side road and at the Lamb farm. "Vince and Julius Lamb were burned so badly we couldn't identify them. You have no need to fear them anymore," Dr. Sinclair said to the family who stood sadly in a group and seemed numb to his news.

When everyone had finally gone home, the Dacias were left alone with their sorrow. None of them cried, and their grief was greater because of this. They sat around the kitchen table without speaking while the hands of the clock on the oven door slowly crept around and the wind sighed all around.

Izabella held Michael-Joseph in her lap, but it was as if she were barely aware of him, as if she were in some distant place. The girls pressed close to her, but she did not hug or kiss them or even look at them. When they went to their beds, she lay like stone beside Josif throughout the night, and when morning came she rose and washed and dressed as she always did, but she spoke to no one.

The black hearse came in the mid-afternoon, and the undertaker and his son brought the casket into the house on a metal cart.

The undertaker spoke gently and calmly to the Dacias, asking about their wishes for the funeral and the gravesite. He and his son wheeled the casket into the living room and left it on the cart so it would not be on the floor.

The undertaker laid his hand on the lid of the casket. "Your son looks very natural, as though he is sleeping. Would you like to have the casket opened?"

"Yes," Josif said. "You open casket, please."

Alexander wore a dark suit, white shirt ,and dark blue tie. His hair was parted and combed as though he had just slicked it down with water, and his face was white and pink as if he had been running. The lashes of his closed eyes were dark against the whiteness of his skin, and his lips were pink and curved almost as though he smiled. His small square hands were folded across the new shirt and necktie.

They looked down at Alexander, and Josif and Uncle Jon lifted Michael-Joseph, Rose, and Caroline up so that they could see him.

The undertaker said quietly, "He's a fine-looking boy." He shook hands with Josif. "We will come tomorrow at 1:30. Would you like to have us bring cars for you to ride in, or will you ride with friends?"

"We will sit vigil for two nights for Alexander. Then we will take him to cemetery on third day," Josif replied. "Cemetery is only two miles, we take Alexander there in wagon, with Peter and Paul, our horses."

The undertaker's eyes widened, just for a moment. "Of course. I understand. The wagon you came here from Oklahoma in." He shook Uncle Jon's hand and Aunt Magda's. Then he went to Izabella.

"Mrs. Dacia, would you like to have Father Monihan come out to see you tonight?"

Izabella seemed not to hear him. She stood at the head of the casket, looking down at Alexander's face, and there were no tears in her eyes.

Josif replied for her. "Please, you ask priest to come."

The undertaker nodded. "I will. He's ready to come. He wasn't sure...."

Josif touched the casket. The wood was smooth and polished – a dark wood like the professors' fine bookcases in Cluj.

"We ask him to come. Please, you tell him that."

"I will. I think it's good to have him come over."

As soon as the undertaker had left, Aunt Magda went to Josif and quietly asked him to fetch the wedding outfit Izabella had made for Alexander during the long winter they had spent with the Hutterites.

In exchange for hours of carding and spinning wool, the women had been given a large bolt of fine homespun wool fabric. Izabella had made Alexander's wedding outfit during the long evening hours, as mothers were expected to have a child's wedding clothes made long before he or she would need them.

Alexander's outfit was a white tunic tied at the waist with a colorful sash. He would wear long white pants underneath. Aunt Magda had finished some beautiful red embroidery around the neck and down the front during the periods when Izabella had been in Alexander's room at the hospital without her. She believed the omens of the owl's call, the icon falling from the wall and breaking, and the howling of the dogs, and knew that Alexander's time had come; it was his fate, and there was no stopping it. She had wanted Alexander to be buried properly and knew that Izabella had no heart for the task.

Josif returned with the wedding outfit, and Aunt Magda ushered everyone out of the room but Izabella. Then the two women gently removed the suit and tie which the undertaker had dressed Alexander in, gave him a brief bath and dressed him in his beautiful tunic, sash, and pants. They left a pan of the bath water at the foot of the coffin for Alexander's soul to bathe in as was their custom.

Izabella regarded Alexander for a long moment, then she forced her eyes away and brought the model airplane kit of Charles Lindbergh's plane from the bedroom where she had put it the night before. She placed it in the coffin with Alexander and placed his hand on the box just as he had placed it himself in the hospital. Her eyes filled with sadness, and finally she was able to cry for the loss of her beautiful first-born son who she would never see grow up, get married, and have children.

She wept for Alexander and she wept for her loss and she felt that her heart would always feel ripped asunder and that she would spend the rest of her life in sadness.

* * *

Father Monihan came at 5:00 in a black Chevrolet. He was a small, blond man with blue eyes and a nose that looked like he had been a street scrapper in his youth.

After Josif met him at the door, Father Monihan came quietly into the living room where all the family were gathered. He knelt down at the casket beside Izabella, who still stood looking at Alexander. When he had prayed, he crossed himself and stood up.

He spoke to Izabella. "I am a Roman Catholic, and I know that you and your family are members of the Eastern Orthodox Church. There are several differences in the basic beliefs of the two churches. I promise you that in the service the day after tomorrow for Alexander, I will not impose my way upon yours."

Izabella barely nodded.

"I would like to read Psalm Forty-six from the Holy Bible to you and your family now. If you don't want me to do this, I won't. You have only to shake your head."

Izabella did not move or reply.

He picked up the Bible and read the verse. The family listened solemnly.

Father Monhian closed the Bible and spoke gently. "Pastor Nordquist and I will conduct the service tomorrow since Alexander will be buried in the churchyard of the Lutheran Church. I believe the pastor will come to see you either tonight or tomorrow morning." He looked around at the family.

"There is a Greek Orthodox priest in Sioux City. If you would prefer to have him conduct the service, I will call him as soon as I get back to Centerford."

"Is not necessary," Josif said. "We like you to say words for Alexander."

Father Monihan shook hands with Josif, Uncle Jon and Aunt Magda. He put his hand on the heads of each child as he said goodbye to them, then went to Izabella. "Alexander is with God. He has gone from us to a place of joy. Do not mourn for him, but mourn for those who are left behind."

There were tears in Izabella's eyes. She spoke for the first time since she left the hospital in Sioux Falls. "Pray for me, Father, for I have sinned. I have hoped that I would die and be with Alexander. I have forgotten my family."

Father Monihan spoke gently to her, "Your grief is great, but know that Alexander is in the arms of One who loves him even as much as you do. Also know that you are in His arms. Now you must return to your family who need your love and care, and who will also love and care for you. I will pray for all of you."

Chapter Twenty-Three
Not Alone in Their Grief

All the people came in wagons to the Dacia farm for the funeral. There were no cars or trucks, not even buggies; each family arrived in a farm wagon drawn by sturdy plow horses. The mayor of Centerford rode with his wife in the Bowmans' wagon along with Mrs. Horsefall, Dr. Sinclair, and Crazy Conklin, while Alan Johnson and Ellen Olson rode in the Wagners' big wagon along with Grandpa and Grandma Wagner and Fritz and August. Mr. and Mrs. Wample came with their eight girls, and the Dordoines, Deerfields, Jensens, Flanahans, Gunns, Nurmis, Croats, and Longyearbys all arrived with the students from Mt. Faith School. The two Swedish families to the south, the Nelsons and the Andersons, came last, and they stood awkwardly outside the Dacias' house until Mr. Bowman brought them in.

Father Monihan and the undertaker had come earlier in a wagon driven by Pastor Nordquist, and when all of the people had slowly filed by Alexander's casket and then lined up against the walls, Pastor Nordquist came to the casket. He began,

I am the resurrection and the life…

The procession to the cemetery was led by Peter and Paul pulling the Dacias' wagon. Joseph and Uncle John had curried and brushed the horses so that their coats shone, and their harness bells jingled as they walked.

Alexander's casket lay on a soft layer of straw in the center of the wagon, and the family encircled it with their bodies so that Alexander was not alone. They held hands with one another around the casket; Aunt Magda keened, and other joined in.

The wagons formed a long line across the prairie, and when they assembled beneath the white steeple of the Orkadallen Lutheran Church, the older people in the procession said, "This feels right. This is how it used to be."

They gathered at the graveside, and Father Monihan spoke in Latin and Greek, conducting the rites for the burial of the dead.

When they had lowered the casket into the grave, Pastor Nordquist cast earth upon it and began,

Unto Almighty God we commend the soul of our brother departed..., and when he had finished, all of the people said the *Lord's Prayer* together:

Our Father, who art in heaven, hallowed be thy name....

* * *

When they came back to the house, the women put the food they had brought onto the tables that had appeared in the house. There were great pots of steaming coffee, cakes and pies, casseroles, sandwiches, hams, desserts, salads, pickles, rolls, fried chicken, scalloped potatoes, cookies. Every good thing, prepared by the Swedes and Norwegians, the Finns and Danes, the French and English and Scots and Irish and Germans who were the good neighbors of the Dacias, the Romanian family who were now Americans.

Epilogue

Forty days after the funeral, on a warm summer Sunday afternoon near the beginning of June, while the corn and other crops sprouted in their fields, the Dacias had a picnic for their friends in the grove in back of their house.

That morning the family had met Father Monihan at Alexander's grave where the Father had swung a censor with incense over the grave and also sprinkled it with Holy Water, marking the end of the funeral ritual.

Izabella had stood at the grave in her black scarf and shawl and wept silent tears. She wondered if the sharp pain of Alexander's death might ever soften and be replaced by fond memories and the happy presence of Alexander in her heart. She was still numb from his loss, and although she tried very hard to focus on the rest of her family, she remained distracted at times, and her smile lacked true joy.

She understood her importance in the family and that she mustn't lose her other children in the heaviness of her grief. Izabella thanked God that Alexander had been her son, and also for the rest of her family and all their friends and neighbors who were now part of their lives.

She looked forward to seeing everyone who was coming to honor Alexander's life and to show their support for her family. She knew that most families had experienced terrible losses themselves, and understood the pain and emptiness, the difficulty of carrying on without the missing loved one, and the sadness at not being able to watch that person travel through life.

The family arrived home and immediately began preparing for their neighbors' arrival. They set up tables and hauled out all their chairs. They spread blankets in the dappled shade, and began to bring out the food they had prepared. Izabella, Aunt Magda, and the girls brought eggplant salad, chicken tocana, Transylvanian pancakes, *mamaliga* with white cheese, stuffed grape leaves, many loaves of fresh bread with a shiny egg wash, and fruit from the orchard. There were several coliva cakes, made traditionally for funerals, from boiled sprouted wheat, sugar, and nuts, a huge pot of coffee with sugar and cream especially for Fritz and August, and several other cakes and pies for dessert.

The Wagners and the Bowmans came, and Alan and Ellen Johnson, now husband and wife, drove out from Centerford. Everyone who had come to the funeral showed up. They sat on the chairs and benches under the big cottonwoods and sipped the Hutterite rhubarb wine, ate the good food ,and reminisced about Alexander, all commenting about what a fine boy he was.

Most of the women found a quiet moment to sit with Izabella, to take her hands and gently stroke her hair and share their losses with her, assuring her that the safest place for a loved one is in one's heart where there is only love and no harm will ever come to them again.

The men acknowledged Josif's loss, being sure to keep their emotions in check, and everyone smiled at the children with love and compassion.

As Izabella sat with her friends and neighbors and thought about Alexander, she realized that she felt understood and supported by these people. She realized that she felt part of their lives and that truly, they had found the home of green grass, fertile fields, and good neighbors.

* * *

Biography

John R. Dann was raised on the family homestead in South Dakota during the *Dust Bowl* and the *Great Depression*. He served in World War II in the Navy. With a Ph.D., in organic chemistry and biochemistry, he did research for a world-renowned laboratory. He and his wife, Barbara, retired to an island off the coast of Washington, where he pursued his lifelong interests in science, creative writing, and international folk dancing.

* * *

Janet M. Dann is a daughter of John R. Dann. Janet was born in upstate New York, and spent many summer vacations with her family visiting their relatives back on the farm in southeastern South Dakota. She also spent a year in VISTA on the Standing Rock Sioux Reservation in north central South Dakota. She has a BA in Anthropology from NYU, and a BS in Nursing from Alaska Methodist University. She is currently retired and with her husband, Tsolo, traveled the country for nine years in an RV. They are now living in the San Juan Islands in Washington. Her current interests are writing, astrology, and drawing.

Be sure to check www.DannWorks.com
for links to music and articles related to
the *Good Neighbors Series*.

www.ingramcontent.com/pod-product-compliance
Lightning Source LLC
Chambersburg PA
CBHW022244020726
47496CB00004B/1051